HOME FOR CHRISTMAS

Debbie Macomber
Shannon Waverly
Anne McAllister

Harlequin Books

TORONTO • NEW YORK • LONDON
AMSTERDAM • PARIS • SYDNEY • HAMBURG
STOCKHOLM • ATHENS • TOKYO • MILAN
MADRID • WARSAW • BUDAPEST • AUCKLAND

HARLEQUIN BOOKS

by Request—HOME FOR CHRISTMAS

ISBN 0-373-20130-3

This edition published by arrangement with Harlequin Books S.A.

Printed in U.S.A.

There's no place like...

All Caitlin wanted for Christmas was a date with her handsome boss. Instead, Santa delivered rugged Joe Rockwell, the *husband* Caitlin forgot she had.

All Angela wanted was Jon. But Jon had left her and never looked back. Now, nine years later, he's come home. Little does he know that Angela's expecting a different man in her stocking this year.

All Jess wanted was his own spread. How could he guess that the ranch would come equipped with a gorgeous woman who aimed to rope herself a cowboy for Christmas?

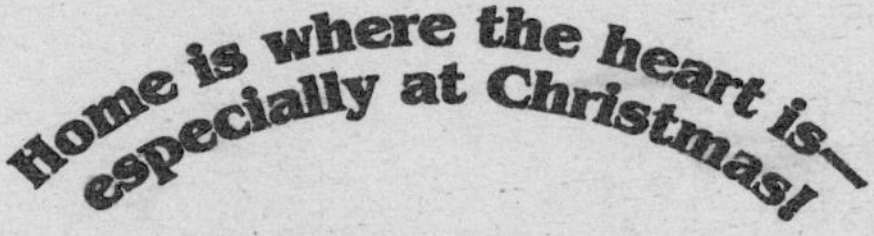

Relive the romance...

by Request™

Three complete novels by your favorite authors

DEBBIE MACOMBER
is one of today's most popular romance authors. She's written more than 70 romances for Harlequin and Silhouette, as well as several "mainstream" women's fiction novels. Be sure to watch for Debbie's upcoming six-book series, "The Heart of Texas," available from MIRA Books in early 1998.

SHANNON WAVERLY
An emerging star in women's romance fiction, Shannon Waverly is the author of more than 10 romance novels. Her evocative moving stories are often set in the New England area, where she lives with her husband of 27 years.

ANNE McALLISTER
Anne McAllister, author of more than 35 romance novels, has had a weakness for cowboys ever since she used to spend the summers at her grandparents' home in Colorado. She admits she's always been fixated by the dark, handsome lone-wolf type. And not only is Anne lucky enough to write about cowboys—she also married one!

CONTENTS

The last thing Caitlin wanted for Christmas was *her husband!*

THE FORGETFUL BRIDE

Debbie Macomber

PROLOGUE

"NOT UNLESS we're married."

Ten-year-old Martin Marshall slapped his hands against his thighs in disgust. "I told you she was going to be unreasonable about this."

Caitlin watched as her brother's best friend withdrew a second baseball card from his shirt pocket. If Joseph Rockwell wanted to kiss her, then he was going to have to do it the right way. She might be only eight, but Caitlin knew about these things. Glancing down at the doll held tightly in her arms, she realized instinctively that Barbie wouldn't approve of kissing a boy unless he married you first.

Martin approached her again. "Joe says he'll throw in his Don Drysdale baseball card."

"Not unless we're married," she repeated, smoothing the front of her sundress with a haughty air.

"All right, all right, I'll marry her," Joe muttered as he stalked across the backyard.

"How you gonna do that?" Martin demanded.

"Get your Bible."

For someone who wanted to kiss her so badly, Joseph didn't look very pleased. Caitlin decided to press her luck. "In the fort."

"The fort?" Joe exploded. "No girls are allowed in there and you know it."

"I refuse to get married to a boy who won't allow me into his fort."

"Call it off," Martin demanded. "She's asking too much."

"You don't have to give me the second baseball card," she said. The idea of being the first girl ever to view their precious fort had a certain appeal. For one thing, she'd probably get invited to Betsy McDonald's birthday party.

The boys exchanged glances and started whispering to each other, but Caitlin heard only snatches of their conversation. Martin clearly wasn't thrilled with Joseph's concessions, and he kept shaking his head as though he couldn't believe his friend might actually go through with this. For her part, Caitlin didn't know whether to trust Joseph. He liked playing practical jokes and everyone in the neighborhood knew it.

"It's time to feed my baby," she announced, preparing to leave.

"All right, all right," Joseph said with obvious reluctance. "I'll marry you in the fort. Martin'll say the words, only you can't tell anyone about going inside, understand?"

"If you do," Martin threatened, glaring at his sister, "you'll be sorry."

"I won't tell," Caitlin promised. It would have to be a secret, but that was fine because she liked keeping secrets.

"You ready?" Joseph demanded. Now that the terms were set, he seemed to be in a rush, which rather annoyed Caitlin. The frown on his face didn't please her, either. A bridegroom should at least *look* happy. She was about to say so, but decided not to.

"You'll have to change clothes, of course. The suit you wore on Easter Sunday will do nicely."

"What?" Joseph shrieked. "I'm not wearing any suit. Listen, Caitlin, you've gone about as far as you can with this. I get married exactly the way I am or we call it off."

She sighed, rolling her eyes expressively. "Oh, all right, but I'll need to get a few things first."

"Just hurry up, would you?"

Martin followed her into the house, letting the screen door slam behind him. He took his Bible off the hallway table and rushed back outside.

Caitlin hurried up to her room, where she grabbed a brush to run through her hair and straightened the two pink ribbons tied around her pigtails. She always insisted on pink ribbons because pink was a color for girls. Boys were supposed to wear blue and brown and boring colors like that. Boys were okay sometimes, but mostly they did disgusting things.

Her four dolls accompanied her across the backyard and into the wooded acre behind. She hated getting her Mary Janes dusty, but that couldn't be helped.

With a good deal of ceremony, she opened the rickety door and then slowly, the way she'd seen it done at her older cousin's wedding, Caitlin marched into the boys' packing-crate-and-cardboard fort.

Pausing inside the narrow entry, she glanced around. It wasn't anything to brag about. Martin had made it sound like a palace with marble floors and crystal chandeliers. She couldn't help feeling disillusioned. If she hadn't been so eager to see the fort, she would have insisted they do this properly, in church.

Her brother stood tall and proud on an upturned apple crate, the Bible clutched to his chest. His face was dutifully somber. Caitlin smiled approvingly. He, at least, was taking this seriously.

"You can't bring those dolls in here," Joseph said loudly.

"I most certainly can. Barbie and Ken and Paula and Jane are our children."

"Our children?"

"Naturally they haven't been born yet, so they're really just a glint in your eye." She'd heard her father say that once and it sounded special. "They're angels for now, but I thought they should be here so you could meet them." She was busily arranging her dolls in a tidy row behind Martin on another apple crate.

Joseph covered his face with his hands and it looked for a moment like he might actually change his mind.

"Are we going to get married or not?" she asked.

"All right, all right." Joseph sighed heavily and pulled her forward, a little more roughly than necessary, in Caitlin's opinion.

The two of them stood in front of Martin, who randomly opened his Bible. He gazed down at the leather-bound book and then at Caitlin and his best friend. He nodded solemnly. "Do you Joseph James Rockwell take Caitlin Rose Marshall for your wife?"

"Lawfully wedded," Caitlin corrected. She remembered this part from a television show.

"Lawfully wedded wife," Martin amended grudgingly.

"I do." Caitlin noticed that he didn't say it with any real enthusiasm. "I think there's supposed to be something about richer or poorer and sickness and health," Joseph said, smirking at Caitlin as if to say she wasn't the only one who knew the proper words.

Martin nodded and continued. "Do you, Caitlin Rose Marshall, hereby take Joseph James Rockwell in sickness and health and in riches and in poorness?"

"I'll only marry a man who's healthy and rich."

"You can't go putting conditions on this now," Joseph argued. "We already agreed."

"Just say 'I do,'" Martin urged, his voice tight with annoyance. Caitlin suspected that only the seriousness of the occasion prevented him from adding, "You pest."

She wasn't sure if she should go through with this or not. She was old enough to know she liked pretty things and that when she married, her husband would build her a castle at the edge of the forest. He would love her so much, he'd bring home silk ribbons for her hair, and bottles and bottles of expensive perfume. So many that there wouldn't be room for them all on her makeup table.

"Caitlin," Martin said through clenched teeth.

"I do," she answered solemnly.

"I hereby pronounce you married," Martin proclaimed, closing the Bible with a resounding thud. "You may kiss the bride."

Joseph turned to face Caitlin. He was several inches taller than she was. His eyes were a pretty shade of blue that reminded her of the way the sky looked the morning after a bad rainstorm. She liked Joseph's eyes.

"You ready?" he asked.

She nodded, closed her eyes and pressed her lips tightly together as she angled her head to the left. If the truth be known, she wasn't all that opposed to having Joseph kiss her, but she'd never let him know that because... well, because kissing wasn't something ladies talked about.

A long time passed before she felt his mouth touch hers. Actually his lips sort of bounced against hers. Gee, she thought. What a bunch of hullabaloo over nothing.

"Well?" Martin demanded of his friend.

Caitlin opened her eyes to discover Joseph frowning down at her. "It wasn't anything like Pete said it would be," he grumbled.

"Caitlin might be doing it wrong," Martin offered, glaring accusingly at his sister.

"If anyone did anything wrong, it's Joseph." They were making it sound like she'd purposely cheated them. If anyone was being cheated, it was Caitlin, because she couldn't tell Betsy McDonald about going inside their precious fort.

Joseph didn't say anything for a long moment. Then he slowly withdrew his prized baseball card from his shirt pocket. He gazed at it lovingly, then reluctantly held it out to her. "Here," he said, "this is yours now."

"You aren't going to *give* it to her, are you? Not when she flubbed up!" Martin cried. "Kissing a girl wasn't like Pete said, and that's got to be Caitlin's fault. I told you she's not really a girl, anyway. She's a pest."

"A deal's a deal," Joseph said sadly.

"You can keep your silly old baseball card." Head held high, Caitlin gathered up her dolls in a huff, prepared to make a proper exit.

"You won't tell anyone about us letting you into the fort, will you?" Martin shouted after her.

"No." She'd keep that promise.

But neither of them had said a word about telling everyone in school that she and Joseph Rockwell had gotten married.

CHAPTER ONE

FOR THE THIRD TIME that afternoon, Cait indignantly wiped sawdust from the top of her desk. If this remodeling mess got much worse, the particles were going to get into her computer, destroying her vital link with the New York Stock Exchange.

"We'll have to move her out," a gruff male voice said from behind her.

"I beg your pardon," Cait demanded, rising abruptly and whirling toward the doorway. She clapped the dust from her hands, preparing to do battle. So much for this being the season of peace and goodwill. All these men in hard hats strolling through the office, moving things about, was inconvenient enough. But at least she'd been able to close her door to reduce the noise. Now, it seemed, even that would be impossible.

"We're going to have to pull some electrical wires through there," the same brusque voice explained. She couldn't see the man's face, since he stood just outside her doorway, but she had an impression of broad-shouldered height. "We'll have everything back to normal within a week."

"A week!" She wouldn't be able to service her customers, let alone function, without her desk and phone. And just exactly where did they intend to put her? Certainly not in a hallway! She wouldn't stand for it.

The mess this simple remodeling project had created was one thing, but transplanting her entire office as if she were nothing more than a...a tulip bulb was something else again.

"I'm sorry about this, Cait," Paul Jamison said, slipping past the crew foreman to her side.

The wind went out of her argument at the merest hint of his devastating smile. "Don't worry about it," she said, the picture of meekness and tolerance. "Things like this happen when a company grows as quickly as ours."

She glanced across the hallway to her best friend's office, shrugging slightly as if to ask, *Is Paul ever going to notice me?* Lindy shot her a crooked grin and a quick nod that suggested Cait stop being so negative. Her friend's confidence didn't help. Paul was a wonderful district manager and she was fortunate to have the opportunity to work with him. He was both talented and resourceful. The brokerage firm of Webster, Rodale and Missen was an affiliate of the fastest-growing firm in the country. This branch had been open for less than two years and already they were breaking sales records all across the country. Due mainly, Cait believed, to Paul's administrative skills.

Paul was slender, dark-haired and handsome in an urbane, sophisticated way—every woman's dream man. Certainly Cait's. But as far as she could determine, he didn't see her in a similar romantic light. He thought of her as an important team member. One of the staff. At most, a friend.

Cait knew that friendship was often fertile ground for romance, and she hoped for an opportunity to cultivate it. Willingly surrendering her office to an irritating crew of carpenters and electricians was sure to gain her a few points with her boss.

"Where would you like me to set up my desk in the interval?" she asked, smiling warmly at Paul. From habit, she lifted her hand to push back a stray lock of hair, forgetting she'd recently had it cut. That had been another futile attempt to attract Paul's affections—or at least his attention.

Her shoulder-length chestnut-brown hair had been trimmed and permed into a pixie style with a halo of soft curls.

The difference from the tightly styled chignon she'd always worn to work was striking, or so everyone said. Everyone, except Paul. The hairdresser had claimed it changed Cait's cooly polished look into one of warmth and enthusiasm. It was exactly the image Cait wanted Paul to have of her.

Unfortunately he didn't seem to detect the slightest difference in her appearance. At least not until Lindy had pointedly commented on the change within earshot of their absentminded employer. Then, and only then, had Paul made a remark about noticing something different; he just hadn't been sure what it was, he'd said.

"I suppose we could move you..." Paul hesitated.

"Your office seems to be the best choice," the foreman said.

Cait resisted the urge to hug the man. He was tall, easily six three, and as solid as Mount Rainier, the majestic mountain she could see from her office window. She hadn't paid much attention to him until this moment and was surprised to note something vaguely familiar about him. She'd assumed he was the foreman, but she wasn't certain. He seemed to be around the office fairly often, although not on a predictable schedule. Every time he did show up, the level of activity rose dramatically.

"Ah...I suppose Cait could move in with me for the time being," Paul agreed. In her daydreams, Cait would play back this moment; her version had Paul looking at her with surprise and wonder, his mouth moving toward hers and—

"Miss?"

Cait broke out of her reverie and glanced toward the foreman—the man who'd suggested she share Paul's office. "Yes?"

"Would you show us exactly what you need moved?"

"Of course," she returned crisply. This romantic heart of hers was always getting her into trouble. She'd look at Paul and her head would start to spin with hopes and fantasies and she'd be lost....

Cait's arms were loaded with files as she followed the carpenters who hauled her desk into a corner of Paul's much larger office. Her computer and phone followed, and within fifteen minutes she was back in business.

She was on the phone, talking with one of her most important clients, when the same man walked back, unannounced, into the room. At first Caitlin assumed he was looking for Paul, who'd stepped out of the office. The foreman—or whatever he was—hesitated, then, scooping up her nameplate, he grinned at her as if he found something highly entertaining. Cait did her best to ignore him, flipping needlessly through the pages of the file.

Not taking the hint, he stepped forward and plunked the nameplate on the edge of her desk. As she glanced up in annoyance, he boldly winked at her.

Cait was not amused. How dare this...this...redneck flirt with her!

She glared at him, hoping he'd have the good manners and good sense to leave—which, of course, he didn't. In fact, he seemed downright stubborn about staying and making her as uncomfortable as possible. Her phone conversation ran its natural course and after making several notations, she replaced the receiver.

"You wanted something?" she demanded, her eyes finding his. Once more she noted his apparent amusement. It didn't make sense.

"No," he answered, grinning. "Sorry to have bothered you."

For the second time, Cait was struck by a twinge of something familiar. He strolled out of her makeshift office as if he owned the building.

Cait waited a few minutes, then approached Lindy. "Did you happen to catch his name?"

"Whose name?"

"The...man who insisted I vacate my office. I don't know who he is. I thought he was the foreman, but..." She crossed her arms and furrowed her brow, trying to remember if she'd heard anyone say his name.

"I have no idea." Lindy pushed back her chair and rolled a pencil between her palms. "He is kinda cute though, don't you think?"

A smile softened Cait's lips. "There's only one man for me and you know it."

"Then why are you asking questions about one of the construction crew?"

"I...don't know. He seems familiar for some reason, and he keeps grinning at me as if he knows something I don't. I hate it when men do that."

"Then ask one of the others what his name is. They'll tell you."

"I can't do that."

"Why not?"

"He might think I'm interested in him."

"And we both know how impossible that would be," Lindy said with mild sarcasm.

"Exactly." Lindy and probably everyone else in the office complex knew how Cait felt about Paul. The district manager himself, however, seemed to be completely oblivious. Other than throwing herself at him, which she'd seriously considered more than once, there was little she could do but be patient. One day when she was least expecting it, Cupid was going to let fly an arrow and hit her lovable boss directly between the eyes.

When it happened—and it would!—Cait planned to be ready.

"You want to go for lunch now?" Lindy asked.

Cait nodded. It was nearly two and she hadn't eaten since breakfast, which had consisted of a banana and a cup of coffee. A West Coast stockbroker's day started before dawn. Cait was generally in the office well before six and didn't stop work until the market closed at one-thirty, Seattle time. Only then did she break for something to eat.

Somewhere in the middle of her turkey on whole wheat, Cait convinced herself she was imagining things when it came to that construction worker. He'd probably been waiting around to ask her where Paul was and then changed his mind. He did say he was sorry for bothering her.

If only he hadn't winked.

HE WAS BACK the following day, a tool pouch riding on his hip like a six-shooter, hard hat in place. He was issuing orders like a drill sergeant, and Cait found herself gazing after him with reluctant fascination. She'd heard he owned the construction company, and she wasn't surprised.

As she studied him, she noted once again how striking he was. Not because he was extraordinarily handsome, but because he was somehow commanding. He possessed an authority, a presence, that attracted attention wherever he went. Cait was as drawn to it as those around her. She observed how the crew instinctively turned to him for directions and approval.

The more she analyzed him, the more she recognized that he was a man who had an appetite for life. Which meant excitement, adventure and probably women, and that confused her even more because she couldn't recall ever knowing anyone quite like him. Then why did she find him so...familiar?

Cait herself had a quiet nature. She rarely ventured out of the comfortable, compact world she'd built. She had her job, a nice apartment in Seattle's university district, and a few close friends. Excitement to her was growing herbs and participating in nature walks.

The following day while she was studying the construction worker, he'd unexpectedly turned and smiled at something one of his men had said. His smile, she decided, intrigued her most. It was slightly off center and seemed to tease the corners of his mouth. He looked her way more than once and each time she thought she detected a touch of humor, an amused knowledge that lurked just beneath the surface.

"It's driving me crazy," Cait confessed to Lindy over lunch.

"What is?"

"That I can't place him."

Lindy set her elbows on the table, holding her sandwich poised in front of her mouth. She nodded slowly, her eyes distant. "When you figure it out, introduce me, will you? I could go for a guy this sexy."

So Lindy had noticed that earthy sensuality about him, too. Well, of course she had—any woman would.

After lunch, Cait returned to the office to make a few calls. He was there again.

No matter how hard she tried, she couldn't place him. Work became a pretense as she continued to scrutinize him, racking her brain. Then, when she least expected it, he strolled past her and brazenly winked a second time.

As the color clawed up her neck, Cait flashed her attention back to her computer screen.

"His name is Joe," Lindy rushed in to tell her ten minutes later. "I heard one of the men call him that."

"Joe," Cait repeated slowly. She couldn't remember ever knowing anyone named Joe.

"Does that help?"

"No," Cait said, shaking her head regretfully. If she'd ever met this man, she wasn't likely to have overlooked the experience. He wasn't someone a woman easily forgot.

"Ask him," Lindy insisted. "It's ridiculous not to. It's driving you bananas. Then," she added with infuriating logic, "when you find out, you can nonchalantly introduce me."

"I can't just waltz up and start quizzing him," Cait argued. The idea was preposterous. "He'll think I'm trying to pick him up."

"You'll go crazy if you don't."

Cait sighed. "You're right. I'm not going to sleep tonight if I don't settle this."

With Lindy waiting expectantly in her office, Cait approached him. He was talking to another one of the crew and once he'd finished, he turned to her with one of his devastating lazy smiles.

"Hello," she said, and her voice shook slightly. "Do I know you?"

"You mean you've forgotten?" he asked, sounding shocked and insulted.

"Apparently. Though I'll admit you look somewhat familiar."

"I should certainly hope so. We shared something very special a few years back."

"We did?" Cait was more confused than ever.

"Hey, Joe, there's a problem over here," a male voice shouted. "Could you come look at this?"

"I'll be with you in a minute," he answered brusquely over his shoulder. "Sorry, we'll have to talk later."

"But—"

"Say hello to Martin for me, would you?" he asked as he stalked past her and into the room that had once been Cait's office.

Martin, her brother. Cait hadn't a clue what her brother could possibly have to do with this. Mentally she ran through a list of his teenage friends and came up blank.

Then it hit her. Bull's-eye. Her heart started to pound until it roared like a tropical storm in her ears. Mechanically Cait made her way back to Lindy's office. She sank into a chair beside the desk and stared into space.

"Well?" Lindy pressed. "Don't keep me in suspense."

"Um, it's not that easy to explain."

"You remember him, then?"

She nodded. Oh, Lord, did she ever.

"Good grief, what's wrong? You've gone so pale!"

Cait tried to come up with an explanation that wouldn't sound . . . ridiculous.

"Tell me," Lindy insisted. "Don't just sit there wearing a silly grin and looking like you're about to faint."

"Um, it goes back a few years."

"All right. Start there."

"Remember how kids sometimes do silly things? Like when you're young and foolish and don't know any better?"

"Me, yes, but not you," Lindy said calmly. "You're perfect. In all the time we've been friends, I haven't seen you do one impulsive thing. Not one. You analyze everything before you act. I can't imagine you ever doing anything silly."

"I did once," Cait corrected, "but I was only eight."

"What could you have possibly done at age eight?"

"I . . . I got married."

"Married?" Lindy half rose from her chair. "You've got to be kidding."

"I wish I was."

"I'll bet a week's commissions that your husband's name is Joe." Lindy was smiling now, smiling widely.

Cait nodded and tried to smile in return.

"What's there to worry about? Good grief, kids do that sort of thing all the time! It doesn't mean anything."

"But I was a real brat about it. Joe and my brother, Martin, were best friends. Joe wanted to know what it felt like to kiss a girl, and I insisted he marry me first. If that wasn't bad enough, I pressured them into performing the ceremony inside their boys-only fort."

"So, you were a bit of pain—most eight-year-old girls are when it comes to dealing with their brothers. He got what he wanted, didn't he?"

Cait took a deep breath and nodded again.

"What was kissing him like?" Lindy asked in a curiously throaty voice.

"Good heavens, I don't remember," Cait answered shortly, then reconsidered. "I take that back. As I recall, it wasn't so bad, though obviously neither one of us had a clue what we were doing."

"Lindy, you're still here," Paul said as he strolled into the office. He nodded briefly in Cait's direction, but she had the impression he barely saw her. He'd hardly been around in the past couple of days—almost as if he was purposely avoiding her, she mused, but that thought was too painful to consider.

"I was just finishing up," Lindy said, glancing guiltily toward Cait. "We both were."

"Fine, fine, I didn't mean to disturb you. I'll see you two in the morning." With that he was gone.

Cait gazed after him with thinly disguised emotion. She waited until Paul was out of earshot before she spoke. "He's so blind. What do I have to do, hit him over the head?"

"Quit being so negative," Lindy admonished. "You're going to be sharing an office with him for another five days. Do whatever you need to make darn sure he notices you."

"I've tried," Cait murmured, discouraged. And she had. She'd tried every trick known to woman, with little success.

Lindy left the office before her. Cait gathered up some stock reports to read that evening and stacked them neatly inside her leather briefcase. What Lindy had said about her being methodical and careful was true. It was also a source of pride; those traits had served her clients well.

To Cait's dismay, Joe followed her. "So," he said, smiling down at her, apparently oblivious to the other people clustering around the elevator. "Who have you been kissing these days?"

Hot color rose instantly to her face. Did he have to humiliate her in public?

"I could find myself jealous, you know."

"Would you kindly stop," she whispered furiously, glaring at him. Her hand tightened around the handle of her briefcase so hard her fingers ached.

"You figured it out?"

She nodded, her eyes darting to the lighted numbers above the elevator door, praying it would make its descent in record time instead of pausing on each floor.

"The years have been good to you."

"Thank you." *Please hurry,* she urged the elevator.

"I never would've believed Martin's little sister would turn out to be such a beauty."

If he was making fun of her, she didn't appreciate it. She was attractive, she knew that, but she certainly wasn't waiting for anyone to place a tiara on her head. "Thank you," she repeated grudgingly.

He gave an exaggerated sigh. "How are our children doing? What were their names again?" When she didn't answer right away, he added, "Don't tell me you've forgotten."

"Barbie and Ken," she muttered under her breath.

"That's right. I remember now."

If Joe hadn't drawn the attention of her co-workers before, he had now. Cait could have sworn every single person standing by the elevator turned to stare at her. The hope that no one was interested in their conversation was forever lost.

"Just how long do you intend to tease me about this?" she snapped.

"That depends," Joe responded with a chuckle Cait could only describe as sadistic. She gritted her teeth. He might have found the situation amusing, but she derived little enjoyment from being the office laughingstock.

Just then the elevator arrived, and not a moment too soon to suit Cait. The instant the doors slid open, she stepped toward it, determined to get as far away from this irritating man as possible.

He quickly caught up with her and she whirled around to face him, her back ramrod stiff. "Is this really necessary?" she hissed, painfully conscious of the other people crowding into the elevator ahead of her.

He grinned. "I suppose not. I just wanted to see if I could get a rise out of you. It never worked when we were kids, you know. You were always so prim and proper."

"Look, you didn't like me then and I see no reason for you to—"

"Not *like* you?" he countered loud enough for everyone in the building to hear. "I married you, didn't I?"

CHAPTER TWO

CAIT'S HEART seemed to stop. She realized that not only the people on the elevator but everyone left in the office was staring at her with unconcealed interest. The elevator was about to close and she quickly stepped forward, straightening her arms to hold the doors open. She felt like Samson balanced between two marble columns.

"It's not like it sounds," she felt obliged to explain in a loud voice, her gaze pleading.

No one made eye contact with her and, desperate, she turned to glare at Joe, issuing him a silent challenge to retract his words. His eyes were sparkling with mischief. If he did say anything, Cait thought in sudden horror, it was bound to make things even worse.

There didn't seem to be anything to do but tell the truth. "In case anyone has the wrong impression, this man and I are not married," she shouted. "Good grief, I was only eight!"

There was no reaction. It was as if she'd vanished into thin air. Defeated, she dropped her arms and stepped back, freeing the doors, which promptly closed.

Ignoring the other people on the elevator—who were carefully ignoring her—Cait clenched her hands into hard fists and glared up at Joe. Her face tightened with anger. "That was a rotten thing to do," she whispered hoarsely.

"What? It's true, isn't it?" he whispered back.

"You're being ridiculous to talk as though we're married!"

"We were once. It wounds me that you treat our marriage so lightly."

"I . . . it wasn't legal." The fact that they were even discussing this was preposterous. "You can't possibly hold me responsible for something that happened so long ago. To play this game now is . . . is infantile, and I refuse to be part of it."

The elevator finally came to a halt on the ground floor and, eager to make her escape, Cait rushed out. Straightening to keep her dignity intact, she headed through the crowded foyer toward the front doors. Although it was midafternoon, dusk was already settling, casting dark shadows between the towering office buildings.

Cait reached the first intersection and sighed in relief as she glanced around her. Good. No sign of Joseph Rockwell. The light was red and she paused, although others hurried across the street after checking for traffic; Cait always felt obliged to obey the signal.

"What do you think Paul's going to say when he hears about this?" Joe asked behind her.

Cait gave a start, then turned to look at her tormenter. She hadn't thought about Paul's reaction. Her throat seemed to constrict, rendering her speechless, otherwise she would have demanded Joe leave her alone. But he'd raised a question she dared not ignore. Paul might hear about her former relationship with Joe and might even think there was something between them.

"You're in love with him, aren't you?"

She nodded. At the very mention of Paul's name, her knees went weak. He was everything she wanted in a man and more. She'd been crazy about him for months and now it was all about to be ruined by this irritating, unreasonable ghost from her past.

"Who told you?" Cait snapped. She couldn't imagine Lindy betraying her confidence, but Cait hadn't told anyone else.

"No one had to tell me," Joe explained. "It's written all over you."

Shocked, Cait stared at Joe, her heart sinking. "Do...do you think Paul knows how I feel?"

Joe shrugged. "Maybe."

"But Lindy said..."

The light changed and, clasping her elbow, Joe urged her into the street. "What was it Lindy said?" he prompted when they'd crossed.

Cait glanced up, about to tell him, when she realized exactly what she was doing—conversing with her antagonist. This was the very man who'd gone out of his way to embarrass and humiliate her in front of the entire office staff. Not to mention assorted clients and carpenters.

She stiffened. "Never mind what Lindy said. Now if you'll kindly excuse me..." With her head held high, she marched down the sidewalk. She hadn't gone more than a few feet when the hearty sound of Joe's laughter caught up with her.

"You haven't changed in twenty years, Caitlin Marshall. Not a single bit."

Gritting her teeth, she marched on.

"DO YOU THINK Paul's heard?" Cait asked Lindy the instant she had a free moment the following afternoon. The New York Stock Exchange had closed for the day and Cait hadn't seen Paul since morning. It looked like he really *was* avoiding her.

"I wouldn't know," Lindy said as she typed some figures into her computer. "But the word about your childhood marriage has spread like wildfire everywhere else. It's the joke of the day. What did you and Joe do? Make a public announcement before you left the office yesterday afternoon?"

It was so nearly the truth that Cait guiltily looked away. "I didn't say a word," she defended herself. "Joe was the one."

"He told everyone you were married?" A suspicious tilt at the corner of her mouth betrayed Lindy's amusement.

"Not exactly. He started asking about our children in front of everyone."

"There were children?"

Cait resisted the urge to close her eyes and count to ten. "No. I brought my dolls to the wedding. Listen, I don't want to rehash a silly incident that happened years ago. I'm more afraid Paul's going to hear about it and put the wrong connotation on the whole thing. There's absolutely nothing between me and Joseph Rockwell. More than likely Paul won't give the matter a second thought, but I don't want there to be any...doubts between us, if you know what I mean."

"If you're so worried about it, talk to him," Lindy advised without lifting her eyes from the screen. "Honesty is the best policy, you know that."

"Yes, but it could prove to be a bit embarrassing, don't you think?"

"Paul will respect you for telling him the truth before he hears the rumors from someone else. Frankly, Cait, I think you're making a fuss over nothing. It isn't like you've committed a felony, you know."

"I realize that."

"Paul will probably be amused, like everyone else. He's not going to say anything." She looked up quickly, as though she expected Cait to try yet another argument.

Cait didn't. Instead she mulled over her friend's advice, gnawing on her lower lip. "I think you might be right. Paul will respect me for explaining the situation myself, instead of ignoring everything." Telling him the truth could be helpful in other respects, too, now that she thought about it.

If Paul had any feeling for her whatsoever, and oh, how she prayed he did, then he might become just a little jealous of her relationship with Joseph Rockwell. After all, Joe was an attractive man in a rugged outdoor sort of way. He was tall and muscular and, well, good-looking. The kind of good-looking that appealed to women—not Cait, of course, but other women. Hadn't Lindy commented almost immediately on how attractive he was?

"You're right," Cait said, walking resolutely toward the office she was temporarily sharing with Paul. Although she'd felt annoyed, at first, about being shuffled out of her own space, she'd come to think of this inconvenience as a blessing in disguise. However, she had to admit she'd been disappointed thus far. She had assumed she'd be spending a lot of time alone with him. That hadn't happened yet.

The more Cait considered the idea of a heart-to-heart talk with her boss, the more appealing it became. As was her habit, she mentally rehearsed what she wanted to say to him, then gave herself a small pep talk.

"I don't remember that you talked to yourself." The male voice booming behind her startled Cait. "But then there's a great deal I've missed over the years, isn't there, Caitlin?"

Cait was so rattled she nearly stumbled. "What are you doing here?" she demanded. "Why do you insist on following me around? Can't you see I'm busy?" He was the last person she wanted to confront just now.

"Sorry." He raised both hands in a gesture of apology contradicted by his twinkling blue eyes. "How about lunch later?"

He was teasing. He had to be. Besides, it would be insane for her to have anything to do with Joseph Rockwell. Heaven only knew what would happen if she gave him the least bit of encouragement. He'd probably hire a skywriter and announce to the entire city that they'd married as children.

"It shouldn't be that difficult to agree to a luncheon date," he informed her coolly.

"You're serious about this?"

"Of course I'm serious. We have a lot of years to catch up on." His hand rested on his leather pouch, giving him a rakish air of indifference.

"I've got an appointment this afternoon..." She offered the first plausible excuse she could think of; it might be uninspired but it also happened to be true. She'd made plans to eat lunch with Lindy.

"Dinner then. I'm anxious to hear what Martin's been up to."

"Martin," she repeated, stalling for time while she invented another excuse. This wasn't a situation she had much experience with. She did date, but infrequently.

"Listen, bright eyes, no need to look so concerned. This isn't an invitation to the senior prom. It's one friend to another. Strictly platonic."

"You won't mention...our wedding to the waiter. Or anyone else?"

"I promise." As if to offer proof of his intent, he licked the end of his index finger and crossed his heart. "That was Martin's and my secret pledge sign. If either of us broke our word, the other was entitled to come up with a punishment. We both understood it would be a fate worse than death."

"I don't need any broken pledge to torture you, Joseph Rockwell. In two days you've managed to turn my life into..." She paused midsentence as Paul Jamison casually strolled past. He glanced in Cait's direction and smiled benignly.

"Hello, Paul," she called out, weakly raising her right hand. He looked exceptionally handsome this morning in a three-piece dark blue suit. The contrast between him and Joe, who was wearing dust-covered jeans, heavy boots and a tool pouch, was so striking that Cait had to force herself not to stare at her boss. If only Paul had been the one to invite her to dinner...

"If you'll excuse me," she said politely, edging her way around Joe and toward Paul, who'd gone into his office. Their office. The need to talk to him burned within her. Words of explanation began to form themselves in her mind.

Joe caught her by the shoulders, bringing her up short. Cait gasped and raised shocked eyes to his.

"Dinner," he reminded her.

She blinked, hardly knowing what to say. "All right," she mumbled distractedly and recited her address, eager to have him gone.

"Good. I'll pick you up tonight at six." With that he released her and stalked away.

After taking a couple of moments to compose herself, Cait headed toward the office. "Hello, Paul," she said, standing just inside the doorway. "Do you have a moment to talk?"

He glanced up from a file on his desk and grinned warmly. "Of course, Cait. Sit down and make yourself comfortable."

She moved into the room and closed the door behind her. When she looked back to Paul, he'd cocked his eyebrows in surprise. "Problems?" he asked.

"Not exactly." She pulled out the chair opposite his desk and slowly sat down. Now that she had his full attention, she was at a loss. All her prepared explanations and witticisms had flown out of her head. "The rate on municipal bonds has been exceptionally high lately," she commented nervously.

Paul agreed with a quick nod. "They have been for several months now."

"Yes, I know. That's what makes them such excellent value." Cait had been selling bonds heavily in the past few weeks.

"You didn't close the door to talk to me about bonds," Paul said softly. "What's troubling you, Cait?"

She laughed uncomfortably, wondering how a man could be so astute in one area and blind in another. If only he would reveal some emotion toward her. Anything. All he did was sit across from her and wait. He was cordial enough, gracious even, but there was no hint of more. Nothing to give Cait any hope that he was starting to care for her.

"It's about Joseph Rockwell."

"The contractor who's handling the remodeling?"

Cait nodded. "I knew him years ago when we were just children." She glanced at Paul, whose face remained blank. "We were neighbors. In fact Joe and my brother, Martin, were best friends. Joe moved out to the suburbs when he and Martin were in the sixth grade and I hadn't heard anything from him since."

"It's a small world, isn't it?" Paul remarked affably enough.

"Joe and Martin were typical young boys," she said, rushing her words a little in her eagerness to have this out in the open. "Full of tomfoolery and pranks."

"Boys will be boys," Paul said without any real enthusiasm.

"Yes, I know. Once—" she forced a light laugh "—they actually involved me in one of their crazy schemes."

"What did they put you up to? Robbing a bank?"

She somehow managed a smile. "Not exactly. Joe—I always called him Joseph back then, because it irritated him. Anyway, Joe and Martin had this friend named Pete who was a year older and he'd spent part of his summer vacation visiting his aunt in Peoria, at least I think it was Peoria... Anyway he came back bragging about having kissed a girl. Naturally Martin and Joe were jealous and as you said, boys will be boys, so they decided that one of them should test it out and see if kissing a girl was everything Pete claimed it was."

"I take it they decided to make you their guinea pig."

"Exactly." Cait slid to the edge of the chair, delighted that Paul was following this rather convoluted explanation. "I was eight and considered something of a...pest." She paused, hoping Paul would make some comment about how impossible that was. When he didn't, she continued, a little disappointed at his restraint. "Apparently I was more of one than I remembered," she said, with another forced laugh. "At eight, I didn't think kissing was something nice girls did, at least not without a wedding band on their finger."

"So you kissed Joseph Rockwell," Paul said absently.

"Yes, but there was a tiny bit more than that. I made him marry me."

Paul's eyebrows shot to the ceiling.

"Now, almost twenty years later, he's getting his revenge by going around telling everyone within earshot that we're actually married. Which of course is ridiculous."

A couple of strained seconds followed her announcement.

"I'm not sure what to say," Paul murmured.

"Oh, I wasn't expecting you to say anything. I thought it was important to clear the air, that's all."

"I see."

"He's only doing it because...well, because that's Joe. Even when we were kids he enjoyed playing these little games. No one really minded, though, at least not the girls, because he was so cute." She certainly had Paul's attention now.

"I thought you should know," she added, "in case you happened to hear a rumor or something. I didn't want you thinking Joe and I were involved or even considering a relationship. I was fairly certain you wouldn't, but one never knows and I'm a firm believer in being forthright and honest."

Paul blinked. Wanting to fill the awkward silence, Cait chattered on. "Apparently Joe recognized my name when he and his men moved my office in here with yours. He was delighted when I didn't recognize him. In fact, he caused something of a commotion by asking me about our children in front of everyone."

"Children?"

"My dolls," Cait was quick to explain.

"Joe Rockwell's an excellent man. I couldn't fault your taste, Cait."

"The two of us aren't involved," she protested. "Good grief, I haven't seen him in nearly twenty years."

"I see," Paul said slowly. He sounded . . . disappointed, Cait thought. But she must have misread his tone because there wasn't a single, solitary reason for him to be disappointed. Cait felt foolish now for even trying to explain this fiasco. Paul was so blind when it came to her feelings that there was nothing she could say or do to make him understand.

"I just wanted you to know," she repeated, "in case you heard the rumors and were wondering if there was anything between me and Joseph Rockwell. I wanted to assure you there isn't."

"I see," he said again. "Don't worry about it, Cait. What happened between you and Rockwell isn't going to affect your job."

She stood up to leave, praying she would detect a suggestion of jealousy. A hint of rivalry. Anything to show he cared. There was nothing, so she tried again. "I agreed to have dinner with him, though."

Paul had returned his attention to the papers he'd been reading when she'd interrupted him.

"For old times' sake," she added in a reassuring voice—to fend off any violent display of resentment, she told herself. "I certainly don't have any intention of dating him on a regular basis."

Paul grinned. "Have a good time."

"Yes, I will, thanks." Her heart felt as heavy as a sinking battleship. Without thought of where she was headed or who she would talk to, Cait wandered out of Paul's office, forgetting for a second that she had no office of her own. The area where her desk once sat was cluttered with wire reels, ladders and men. Joe must have left, a fact for which Cait was grateful.

She walked into Lindy's small office across the aisle. Her friend glanced up. "So?" she murmured. "Did you talk to Paul?"

Cait nodded.

"How'd it go?"

"Fine, I guess." She perched on the corner of Lindy's desk, crossing her arms around her waist as her left leg swung rhythmically, keeping time with her discouraged heart. She should be accustomed to disappointment when it came to dealing with Paul, but somehow each rejection inflicted a fresh wound on her already battered ego. "I was hoping Paul might be jealous."

"And he wasn't?"

"Not that I could tell."

"It isn't as though you and Joe have anything to do with each other now," Lindy sensibly pointed out. "Marrying him was a childhood prank. It isn't likely to concern Paul."

"I even mentioned that I was going out to dinner with Joe," Cait said morosely.

"You are? When?" Lindy asked, her eyes lighting up. "Where?"

If only Paul had revealed half as much interest. "Tonight. And I don't know where."

"You are going, aren't you?"

"I guess. I can't see any way of avoiding it. No doubt he'll pester me until I give in. If I ever marry and have daughters, Lindy, I'm going to warn them about boys from the time they're old enough to understand."

"Don't you think you should follow your own advice?" Lindy asked, glancing pointedly in the direction of Paul's office.

"Not if I were to have Paul's children," Cait said, eager to defend her boss. "Our daughter would be so intelligent and perceptive she wouldn't need to be warned."

Lindy's returning smile was distracted. "Listen, I've got a few things to finish up here. Why don't you go over to the deli and grab us a table. I'll meet you there in fifteen minutes."

"Sure," Cait agreed. "Do you want me to order for you?"

"No. I don't know what I want yet."

"Okay, I'll see you in a few minutes."

They often ate at the deli across the street from their office complex. The food was good, the service fast, and generally by three in the afternoon, Cait was famished.

She was so wrapped up in her thoughts, which were muddled and gloomy following her talk with Paul, that she didn't notice how late Lindy was. Her friend rushed into the restaurant more than half an hour after Cait had arrived.

"I'm sorry," she said, sounding flustered and oddly shaken. "I had no idea those last odds and ends would take me so long. Oh, you must be starved. I hope you've ordered." Lindy removed her coat and stuffed it into the booth before sliding onto the red upholstered seat herself.

"Actually, no, I didn't." Cait sighed. "Just tea." Her spirits were at an all-time low. It was becoming painfully clear that Paul didn't harbor a single romantic feeling toward her. She was wasting her time and her emotional energy on him. If only she'd had more experience with the opposite sex. It seemed her whole love life had gone into neutral the moment she'd graduated from college. At the rate matters were developing, she'd still be single by the time she turned thirty—a possibility too dismal to contemplate. She hadn't given much thought to marriage and children, always assuming they'd become part of her life; now she wasn't so sure. Even as a child, she'd pictured her grown-up self with a career *and* a family. Behind the business exterior was a woman traditional enough to hunger for that most special of relationships.

She had to face the fact that marriage would never happen if she continued to love a man who didn't return her feelings. She gave a low groan, then noticed that Lindy was gazing at her in concern.

"Let's order something," Lindy said quickly, reaching for the menu tucked behind the napkin holder. "I'm starved."

"I was thinking I'd skip lunch today," Cait mumbled. She sipped her lukewarm tea and frowned. "Joe will be taking me out to dinner soon. And frankly, I don't have much of an appetite."

"This is all my fault, isn't it?" Lindy asked, looking guilty.

"Of course not. I'm just being practical." If Cait was anything, it was practical—except about Paul. "Go ahead and order."

"You're sure you don't mind?"

Cait gestured nonchalantly. "Heavens, no."

"If you're sure, then I'll have the turkey on whole wheat," Lindy said after a moment. "You know how I like turkey, though you'd think I'd have gotten enough over Thanksgiving."

"I'll just have a refill on my tea," Cait said.

"You're still flying to Minnesota for the holidays, aren't you?" Lindy asked, fidgeting with the menu.

"Mmm-hmm." Cait had purchased her ticket several months earlier. Martin and his family lived near Minneapolis. When their father had died several years earlier, Cait's mother moved to Minnesota, settling down in a new subdivision not far from Martin, his wife and their four children. Cait tried to visit at least once a year. However, she'd been there in August, stopping off on her way home from a business trip. Usually she made a point of visiting her brother and his family over the Christmas holidays. It was generally a slow week on the stock market, anyway. And if she was going to travel halfway across the country, she wanted to make it worth her while.

"When will you be leaving?" Lindy asked, although Cait was sure she'd already told her friend more than once.

"The twenty-third." For the past few years, Cait had used one week of her vacation at Christmas time, usually starting the weekend before.

But this year Paul was having a Christmas party and Cait didn't want to miss that, so she'd booked her flight closer to the holiday.

The waitress came to take Lindy's order and replenish the hot water for Cait's tea. The instant she moved away from their booth, Lindy launched into a lengthy tirade about how she hated Christmas shopping and how busy the malls were this time of year. Cait stared at her, bewildered. It wasn't like her friend to chat nonstop.

"Lindy," she interrupted, "is something wrong?"

"Wrong? What could possibly be wrong?"

"I don't know. You haven't stopped talking for the last ten minutes."

"I haven't?" There was an abrupt, uncomfortable silence.

Cait decided it was her turn to say something. "I think I'll wear my red velvet dress," she mused.

"To dinner with Joe?"

"No," she said, shaking her head. "To Paul's Christmas party."

Lindy sighed. "But what are you wearing tonight?"

The question took Cait by surprise. She didn't consider this dinner with Joe a real date. He just wanted to talk over old times, which was fine with Cait as long as he behaved himself. Suddenly she glanced up and frowned, then closed her eyes. "Martin's a Methodist minister," she said softly.

"Yes, I know," Lindy reminded her. "I've known that since I first met you, which was what? Three years ago now."

"Four last month."

"So what does Martin's occupation have to do with anything?" Lindy wanted to know.

"Joe Rockwell can't find out," Cait whispered.

"I didn't plan on telling him," Lindy whispered back.

"I've got to make up some other occupation like..."

"Counselor," Lindy suggested. "I'm curious, though. Why can't you tell Joe about Martin?"

"Think about it!"

"I am thinking. I really doubt Joe would care one way or the other."

"He might put some connotation on it. You don't know Joe the way I do. He'd razz me about it all evening, claiming the marriage was valid. You know, because Martin really *is* a minister, and since Martin performed the ceremony, we must really be married—that kind of nonsense."

"I didn't think of that."

But then, Lindy didn't seem to be thinking much about anything of late. It was as if she was walking about in a perpetual daydream. Cait couldn't remember Lindy's ever being so scatterbrained. If she didn't know better she'd think there was a man involved.

CHAPTER THREE

AT TEN TO SIX, Cait was blow-drying her hair in a haphazard fashion, regretting that she'd ever had it cut. She was looking forward to this dinner date about as much as a trip to the dentist. All she wanted was to get it over with, come home and bury her head under a pillow while she sorted out how she was going to get Paul to notice her.

Restyling her hair hadn't done the trick. Putting in extra hours at the office hadn't impressed him, either. Cait was beginning to think she could stand on top of his desk naked and not attract his attention.

She walked into her compact living room and smoothed the bulky-knit sweater over her slim hips. She hadn't dressed for the occasion, although the sweater was new and expensive. Gray wool slacks and a powder-blue turtleneck with a silver heart-shaped necklace dangling from her neck were about as dressy as she cared to get with someone like Joe. He'd probably be wearing cowboy boots and jeans, if not his hard hat and tool pouch.

Oh, yes, Cait had recognized his type when she'd first seen him. Joe Rockwell was a man's man. He walked and talked macho. No doubt he drove a truck with tires so high off the ground she'd need a stepladder to climb inside. He was tough and gruff and liked his women meek and submissive. In that case, of course, she had nothing to worry about.

He arrived right on time, which surprised Cait. Being prompt didn't fit the image she had of Joe Rockwell, redneck contractor. She sighed and painted on a smile, then walked slowly to the door.

The smile faded. Joe stood before her, tall and debonair, dressed in a dark gray pin-striped suit. His gray silk tie had *pink* stripes. He was the picture of smooth sophistication. She knew that Joe was the same man she'd seen earlier in dusty work clothes—yet he was different. He was nothing like Paul, of course. But Joseph Rockwell was a devastatingly handsome man. With a devastating charm. Rarely had she seen a man smile the way he did. His eyes twinkled with warmth and life and mischief. It wasn't difficult to imagine Joe with a little boy whose eyes mirrored his. Cait didn't know where that thought came from, but she pushed it aside before it could linger and take root.

"Hello," he said, flashing her that smile.

"Hi." She couldn't stop looking at him.

"May I come in?"

"Oh . . . of course. I'm sorry," she faltered, stumbling in her haste to step aside. He'd caught her completely off guard. "I was about to change clothes," she said quickly.

"You look fine."

"These old things?" She feigned a laugh. "If you'll excuse me, I'll only be a minute." She poured him a cup of coffee, then dashed into her bedroom, ripping the sweater over her head and closing the door with one foot. Her shoes went flying as she ran to her closet. Jerking aside the orderly row of business jackets and skirts, she pulled clothes off their hangers, considered them, then tossed them on the bed. Nearly everything she owned was more suitable for the office than a dinner date.

The only really special dress she owned was the red velvet one she'd purchased for Paul's Christmas party. The temptation to slip into that was strong but she resisted, wanting to save it for her boss, though heaven knew he probably wouldn't notice.

Deciding on a skirt and blazer, she hopped frantically around her bedroom as she pulled on her panty hose. Next she threw on a rose-colored silk blouse and managed to button it while stepping into her skirt. She tucked the blouse into the waistband and her feet into a pair of medium-heeled pumps. Finally, her velvet blazer and she was ready. Taking a deep breath, she returned to the living room in three minutes flat.

"That was fast," Joe commented, standing by the fireplace, hands clasped behind his back. He was examining a framed photograph that sat on the mantel. "Is this Martin's family?"

"Martin...why, yes, that's Martin, his wife and their children." She hoped he didn't detect the breathless catch in her voice.

"Four children."

"Yes, he and Rebecca decided they wanted a large family." Her heartbeat was slowly returning to normal though Cait still felt light-headed. She had a sneaking suspicion that she was suffering from the effects of unleashed male charm.

She realized with surprise that Joe hadn't once said or done anything to embarrass or fluster her. She'd expected him to arrive with a whole series of remarks designed to disconcert her.

"Timmy's ten, Kurt's eight, Jenny's six and Clay's four." She introduced the freckle-faced youngsters, pointing each one out.

"They're handsome children."

"They are, aren't they?"

Cait experienced a twinge of pride. The main reason she went to Minneapolis every year was Martin's children. They adored her and she was crazy about them. Christmas wouldn't be Christmas without Jenny and Clay snuggling on her lap while their father read them the Nativity story. Christmas was singing carols in front of a crackling wood fire, accompanied by Martin's guitar. It meant stringing popcorn and cranberries for the seven-foot-tall tree that always adorned the living room. It was having the children take turns licking fudge from the sides of the copper kettle, and supervising the decorating of sugar cookies with all four crowded around the kitchen table. Caitlin Marshall might be a dedicated stockbroker with an impressive clientele, but when it came to Martin's children, she was Auntie Cait.

"It's difficult to think of Martin with kids," Joe said, carefully placing the family photo back on the mantel.

"He met Rebecca his first year of college and the rest, as they say, is history."

"What about you?" Joe asked, turning unexpectedly to face her.

"What about me?"

"Why haven't you married?"

"Uh..." Cait wasn't sure how to answer him. She had a glib reply she usually gave when anyone asked, but somehow she knew Joe wouldn't accept that. "I...I've never really fallen in love."

"What about Paul?"

"Until Paul," she corrected, stunned that she'd forgotten the strong feelings she held for her employer. She'd been so concerned with being honest that she'd overlooked the obvious. "I am deeply in love with Paul," she said defiantly, wanting there to be no misunderstanding.

"There's no need to convince me, Caitlin."

"I'm not trying to convince you of anything. I've been in love with Paul for nearly a year. Once he realizes he loves me too, we'll be married."

Joe's mouth slanted in a wry line and he seemed about to argue with her. Cait waylaid any attempt by glancing pointedly at her watch. "Shouldn't we be leaving?"

After a long moment, Joe said, "Yes, I suppose we should," in a mild, neutral voice.

Cait went to the hall closet for her coat, aware with every step she took that Joe was watching her. She turned back to smile at him, but somehow the smile didn't materialize. His blue eyes met hers, and she found his look disturbing—caressing, somehow, and intimate.

Joe helped her on with her coat and led her to the parking lot, where he'd left his car. Another surprise awaited her. It wasn't a four-wheel-drive truck, but a late sixties black convertible in mint condition.

The restaurant was one of the most respected in Seattle, with a noted chef and a reputation for excellent seafood. Cait chose grilled salmon and Joe ordered Cajun shrimp.

"Do you remember the time Martin and I decided to open our own business?" Joe asked, as they sipped a predinner glass of wine.

Cait did indeed recall that summer. "You might have been a bit more ingenious. A lemonade stand wasn't the world's most creative enterprise."

"Perhaps not, but we were doing a brisk business until an annoying eight-year-old girl ruined everything."

Cait wasn't about to let that comment pass. "You were using moldy lemons and covering the taste with too much sugar. Besides, it's unhealthy to share paper cups."

Joe chuckled, the sound deep and rich. "I should have known then you were nothing but trouble."

"It seems to me that the whole mess was your own fault. You boys wouldn't listen to me. I had to do something before someone got sick on those lemons."

"Carrying a picket sign that read 'Talk to me before you buy this lemonade' was a bit drastic even for you, don't you think?"

"If anything, it brought you more business." Cait said dryly, recalling how her plan had backfired. "All the boys in the neighborhood wanted to see what contaminated lemonade tasted like."

"You were a damn nuisance, Cait. Own up to it." He smiled and Cait sincerely doubted that any woman could argue with him when he smiled full-force.

"I most certainly was not! If anything you two were—"

"Disgusting, I believe, was your favorite word for Martin and me."

"And you did your level best to live up to it," she said, struggling to hold back a smile. She reached for a breadstick and bit into it to disguise her amusement. She'd always enjoyed rankling Martin and Joe, though she'd never have admitted it, especially at the age of eight.

"Picketing our lemonade stand wasn't the worst trick you ever pulled, either," Joe said mischievously.

Cait had trouble swallowing. She should have been prepared for this. If he remembered her complaints about the lemonade stand, he was sure to remember what had happened once Betsy McDonald found out about the kissing incident.

"It wasn't a trick," Cait protested.

"But you told everyone at school that I'd kissed you—even though you'd promised not to."

"Not exactly." There was a small discrepancy that needed clarification. "If you think back you'll remember you said I couldn't tell anyone I'd been inside the fort. You didn't say anything about the kiss."

Joe frowned darkly as if attempting to jog his memory. "How can you remember details like that? All this happened years ago."

"I remember everything," Cait said grandly—a gross exaggeration. She hadn't recognized Joe, after all. But on this one point she was absolutely clear. "You and Martin were far more concerned that I not tell anyone about going inside the fort. You didn't say a word about keeping the kiss a secret."

"But did you have to tell Betsy McDonald? That girl had been making eyes at me for weeks. As soon as she learned I'd kissed you instead of her, she was furious."

"Betsy was the most popular girl in school. I wanted her for my friend, so I told."

"And sold me down the river."

"Would an apology help?" Confident he was teasing her once again, Cait gave him her most charming smile.

"An apology just might do it." Joe grinned back, a grin that brightened his eyes to a deeper, more tantalizing shade of blue. It was with some difficulty that Cait pulled her gaze away from his.

"If Betsy liked you," she asked, smoothing the linen napkin across her lap, "then why didn't you kiss her? She'd probably have let you. You wouldn't have had to bribe her with your precious baseball cards, either."

"You're kidding. If I kissed Betsy McDonald I might as well have signed over my soul," Joe said, continuing the joke.

"Even as mere children, men are afraid of commitment," Cait said solemnly.

Joe ignored her comment.

"Your memory's not as sharp as you think," Cait felt obliged to tell him, enjoying herself more than she'd thought possible.

Once again, Joe overlooked her comment. "I can remember Martin complaining about how you'd line up your dolls in a row and teach them school. Once you even got him to come in as a guest lecturer. Heaven knew what you had to do to get him to play professor to a bunch of dolls."

"I found a pair of dirty jeans stuffed under the sofa with something dead in the pocket. Mom would have tanned his hide if she'd found them, so Martin owed me a favor. Then he got all bent out of shape when I collected it. He didn't seem the least bit appreciative that I'd saved him."

"Good old Martin," Joe said, shaking his head. "I swear he was as big on ceremony as you were. Marrying us was a turning point in his life. From that point on, he started carting a Bible around with him the way some kids do a slingshot. Right in his hip pocket. If he wasn't burying something, he was holding revival meetings. Remember how he got in a pack of trouble at school for writing 'God loves you, ask Martin' on the back wall of the school?"

"I remember."

"I half expected him to become a missionary."

"Martin?" She gave an abrupt laugh. "Never. He likes his conveniences. He doesn't even go camping. Martin's idea of roughing it is doing without valet service."

She expected Joe to chuckle. He did smile at her attempted joke, but that was all. He seemed to be studying her the same way she'd been studying him.

"You surprise me," Joe announced suddenly.

"I do? Am I a disappointment to you?"

"Not in the least. I always thought you'd grow up and have a passel of children yourself. You used to haul those dolls of yours around with you everywhere. If Martin and I were too noisy, you'd shush us, saying the babies were asleep. If we wanted to play in the backyard, we couldn't because you were having a tea party with your dolls. It was enough to drive a ten-year-old boy crazy. But if we ever dared complain, you'd look at us serenely and with the sweetest smile tell us we had to be patient because it was for the children."

"I did get carried away with all that motherhood business, didn't I?" Joe's words stirred up uncomfortable memories, the same ones she'd entertained earlier that afternoon. She really did love children. Yet, somehow, without her quite knowing how it had happened, the years had passed and she'd buried the dream. Nowadays she didn't like to think too much about a husband and family—the life that hadn't happened. It haunted her at odd moments.

"I should have known you'd end up in construction," she said, switching the subject away from herself.

"How's that?" Joe asked.

"Wasn't it you who built the fort?"

"Martin helped."

"Sure, by staying out of the way." She grinned. "I know my brother. He's a marvel with people, but please don't ever give him a hammer."

Their dinner arrived, and it was as delicious as Cait had expected, although by then she was enjoying herself so much that even a plateful of dry toast would have tasted good. They drank two cups of cappuccino after their meal, and talked and laughed as the hours melted away. Cait couldn't remember the last time she'd laughed so much.

When at last she happened to glance at her watch, she was shocked to realize it was well past ten. "I had no idea it was so late!" she said. "I should probably get home." She had to be up by five.

Joe took care of the bill and collected her coat. When they walked outside, the December night was clear and chilly, with a multitude of stars twinkling brightly above.

"Are you cold?" he asked as they waited for the valet to deliver the car.

"Not at all." Nevertheless, he placed his arm around her shoulders, drawing her close.

Cait didn't protest. It felt natural for this man to hold her close.

His car arrived and they drove back to her apartment building in silence. When he pulled into the parking lot, she considered inviting him inside for coffee, then decided against it. They'd already drunk enough coffee, and besides, they both had to work the following morning. But more important, Joe might read something else into the invitation. He was an old friend. Nothing more. And she wanted to keep it that way.

She turned to him and smiled softly. "I had a lovely time. Thank you so much."

"You're welcome, Cait. We'll do it again."

Cait was astonished to realize how appealing another evening with Joseph Rockwell was. She'd underestimated him.

Or had she?

"There's something else I'd like to try again," he was saying, his eyes filled with devilry.

"Try again?"

He slid his arm behind her and for a breathless moment they looked at each other. "I don't know if I've got a chance without trading a few baseball cards, though."

Cait swallowed. "You want to kiss me?"

He nodded. His eyes seemed to grow darker, more intense. "For old times' sake." His hand caressed the curve of her neck, his thumb moving slowly toward the scented hollow of her throat.

"Well, sure. For old times' sake." She was amazed at the way her heart was reacting to the thought of Joe holding her...kissing her.

His mouth began a slow descent toward hers, his warm breath nuzzling her skin.

"Just remember," she whispered when his mouth was about to settle over hers. Her hands gripped his lapels. "Old times'..."

"I'll remember," he said as his lips came down on hers.

She sighed and slid her hands up his solid chest to link her fingers at the base of his neck. The kiss was slow and thorough. When it was over, Cait's hands were clenching his collar.

Joe's fingers were in her hair, tangled in the short, soft curls, cradling the back of her head.

A sweet rush of joy coursed through her veins. Cait felt a bubbling excitement, a burst of warmth, unlike anything she'd ever known before.

Then he kissed her a second time...

"Just remember..." she repeated when he pulled his mouth from hers and buried it in the delicate curve of her neck.

He drew in several ragged breaths before asking, "What is it I'm supposed to remember?"

"Yes, oh, please, remember."

He lifted his head and rested his hands lightly on her shoulders, his face only inches from hers. "What's so important you don't want me to forget?" he whispered.

It wasn't Joe who was supposed to remember; it was Cait. She didn't realize she'd spoken out loud. She blinked, uncertain, then tilted her head to gaze down at her hands, anywhere but at him. "Oh... that I'm in love with Paul."

There was a moment of silence. An awkward moment. "Right," he answered shortly. "You're in love with Paul." His arms fell away and he released her.

Cait hesitated, uneasy. "Thanks again for a wonderful dinner." Her hand closed around the door handle. She was eager now to make her escape.

"Any time," he said flippantly. His own hands gripped the steering wheel.

"I'll see you soon."

"Soon," he repeated. She climbed out of the car, not giving Joe a chance to come around and open the door for her. She was aware of him sitting in the car, waiting until she'd unlocked the lobby door and stepped inside. She hurried down the first-floor hall and into her apartment, turning on the lights so he'd know she'd made it safely home.

Then she slowly removed her coat and carefully hung it in the closet. When she peeked out the window, she noticed that Joe had already left.

LINDY WAS AT HER DESK working when Cait arrived the next morning. Cait smiled at her as she hurried past, but didn't stop to indulge in conversation.

Cait could feel Lindy's gaze trailing after her and she knew her friend was disappointed that she hadn't told her about the dinner date with Joe Rockwell.

Cait didn't want to talk about it. She was afraid that if she said anything to Lindy, she wouldn't be able to avoid mentioning the kiss, which was a subject she wanted to avoid at all costs. She wouldn't be able to delay her friend's questions forever, but Cait wanted to put them off until at least the end of the day. Longer, if possible.

What a fool she'd been to let Joe kiss her. It had seemed so right at the time, a natural conclusion to a delightful evening.

The fact that she'd let him do it without even making a token protest still confused her. If Paul was to hear of it, he might think she really *was* interested in Joe. Which, of course, she wasn't.

Her boss was a man of principle and integrity—and altogether a frustrating person to fall in love with. Judging by his reaction to her dinner with Joe, he seemed immune to jealousy. Now if only she could discover a way of letting him know how she felt . . . and spark his interest in the process!

The morning was hectic. Out of the corner of her eye, Cait saw Joe arrive. Although she was speaking to an important client on the phone, she stared after him as he approached the burly foreman. She watched Joe remove a blueprint from a long, narrow tube and roll it open so two other men could study it. There seemed to be some discussion, then the foreman nodded and Joe left, without so much as glancing in Cait's direction.

That stung.

At least he could have waved hello. But if he wanted to ignore her, well, fine. She'd do the same.

The market closed on the up side, the Dow Jones industrial average at 2600 points after brisk trading. The day's work was over.

As Cait had predicted, Lindy sought her out almost immediately.

"So how'd your dinner date go?"

"It was fun."

"Where'd he take you? Sam's Bar and Grill the way you thought?"

"Actually, no," she said, clearing her throat, feeling more than a little foolish for having suggested such a thing. "He took me to Henry's." She announced it louder than necessary, since Paul was strolling into the office just then. But for all the notice he gave her, she might as well have been fresh paint drying on the company wall.

"Henry's," Lindy echoed. "He took you to Henry's? Why, that's one of the best restaurants in town. It must have cost him a small fortune."

"I wouldn't know. My menu didn't list any prices."

"You're joking. No one's ever taken me anyplace so fancy. What did you order?"

"Grilled salmon." She continued to study Paul for some clue that he was listening in on her and Lindy's conversation. He was seated at his desk, reading a report on short-term partnerships as a tax advantage. Cait had read it earlier in the week and had recommended it to him.

"Was it wonderful?" Lindy pressed.

It took Cait a moment to realize her friend was quizzing her about the dinner. "Excellent. The best fish I've had in years."

"What did you do afterward?"

Cait looked back at her friend. "What makes you think we did anything? We had dinner, talked, and then he drove me home. Nothing more happened. Understand? Nothing."

"If you say so," Lindy said, eyeing her suspiciously. "But you're certainly defensive about it."

"I just want you to know that nothing happened. Joseph Rockwell is an old friend. That's all."

Paul glanced up from the report, but his gaze connected with Lindy's before slowly progressing to Cait.

"Hello, Paul," Cait greeted him cheerfully. "Are Lindy and I disturbing you? We'd be happy to go into the hallway if you'd like."

"No, no, you're fine. Don't worry about it." He glanced past them to the doorway and got to his feet. "Hello, Rockwell."

"Am I interrupting a meeting?" Joe asked, stepping into the office as if it didn't really matter whether he was or not. His hard hat was back in place, along with the dusty jeans and the tool pouch. And yet Cait had no difficulty remembering last night's sophisticated dinner companion when she looked at him.

"No, no," Paul answered, "we were just chatting. Come on in. Problems?"

"Not really. But there's something I'd like you to take a look at in the other room."

"I'll be right there."

Joe threw Cait a cool smile as he strolled past. "Hello, Cait."

"Joe." Her heart was pounding hard, and that was ridiculous. It must have been due to embarrassment, she told herself. Joe was a friend, a boy from the old neighborhood; just because she'd allowed him to kiss her, it didn't mean there was—or ever would be—anything romantic between them. The sooner she made him understand this, the better.

"Joe and Cait went out to dinner last night," Lindy said pointedly to Paul. "He took her to Henry's."

"How nice," Paul commented, clearly more interested in troubleshooting with Joe than discussing Cait's dating history.

"We had a good time, didn't we?" Joe asked Cait.

"Yes, very nice," she responded stiffly.

Joe waited until Paul was out of the room before he stepped back and dropped a kiss on her cheek. Then he announced loudly enough for everyone in the vicinity to hear, "You were incredible last night."

CHAPTER FOUR

"I THOUGHT YOU SAID nothing happened," Lindy said, looking intently at a red-faced Cait.

"Nothing did happen." Cait was furious enough to kick Joe Rockwell in the shins the way he deserved. How dared he say something so...so embarrassing in front of Lindy! And probably within earshot of Paul!

"But why would he say something like that?"

"How should I know?" Cait snapped. "One little kiss and he makes it sound like—"

"He kissed you?" Lindy asked sharply, her eyes narrowing. "You just got done telling me there's nothing between the two of you."

"Good grief, the kiss didn't mean anything. It was for old times' sake. Just a platonic little kiss." All right, she was exaggerating a bit, but it couldn't be helped.

While Cait was speaking, she gathered her things and shoved them in her briefcase. Then she slammed the lid closed and reached for her coat, thrusting her arms into the sleeves, her movements abrupt and ungraceful.

"Have a nice weekend," she said tightly, not completely understanding why she felt so annoyed with Lindy. "I'll see you Monday." She marched through the office, but paused in front of Joe.

"You wanted something, sweetheart?' he asked in a cajoling voice.

"You're despicable!"

Joe looked downright disappointed. "Not low and disgusting?"

"That, too."

He grinned ear to ear just the way she knew he would. "I'm glad to hear it."

Cait bit back an angry retort. It wouldn't do any good to engage in a verbal battle with Joe Rockwell. He'd have a comeback for any insult she could hurl. Seething, Cait marched to the elevator and jabbed the button impatiently.

"I'll be by later tonight, darling," Joe called to her just as the doors were closing, effectively cutting off any protest from her.

He was joking. He had to be joking. No man in his right mind could possibly expect her to invite him into her home after this latest stunt. Not even the impertinent Joe Rockwell.

Once home, Cait took a long, soothing shower, dried her hair and changed into jeans and a sweater. Friday nights were generally quiet ones for her. She was munching on pretzels and surveying the bleak contents of her refrigerator when there was a knock on the door.

It couldn't possibly be Joe, she told herself.

It was Joe, balancing a large pizza on the palm of one hand and clutching a bottle of red wine in the other.

Cait stared at him, too dumbfounded at his audacity to speak.

"I come bearing gifts," he said, presenting the pizza to her with more than a little ceremony.

"Listen here, you...you fool, it's going to take a whole lot more than pizza to make up for that stunt you pulled this afternoon."

"Come on, Cait, lighten up a little."

"Lighten up! You...you..."

"I believe the word you're looking for is fool."

"You have your nerve." She dug her fists into her hips, knowing she should slam the door in his face. She would have, too, but the pizza smelled *so* good it was difficult to maintain her indignation.

"Okay, I'll admit it," Joe said, his deep blue eyes revealing genuine contrition. "I got carried away. You're right, I am an idiot. All I can do is ask your forgiveness." He lifted the lid of the pizza box and Cait was confronted by the thickest, most mouth-watering masterpiece she'd ever seen. The top was crowded with no less than ten tempting toppings, all covered with a thick layer of hot melted cheese.

"Do you accept my humble apology?" Joe pressed, waving the pizza under her nose.

"Are there any anchovies on that thing?"

"Only on half."

"You're forgiven." She took him by the elbow and dragged him inside her apartment.

Cait led the way into the kitchen. She got two plates from the cupboard and collected knives, forks and napkins as she mentally reviewed his crimes. "I couldn't believe you actually said that," she mumbled, shaking her head. She set the kitchen table, neatly positioning the napkins after shoving the day's mail to one side. "The least you could do is tell me why you found it necessary to say that in front of Paul. Lindy had already started grilling me. Can you imagine what she and Paul must think now?" She retrieved two wineglasses from the cupboard and set them by the plates. "I've never been more embarrassed in my life."

"Never?" he prompted, opening and closing her kitchen drawers until he located a corkscrew.

"Never," she repeated. "And don't think a pizza's going to ensure lasting peace."

"I wouldn't dream of it."

"It's a start, but you're going to owe me a good long time for this prank, Joseph Rockwell."

"I'll be good," he promised, his eyes twinkling. He agilely removed the cork, tested the wine and then filled both glasses.

Cait jerked out a wicker-back chair and threw herself down. "Did Paul say anything after I left?"

"About what?" Joe slid out a chair and joined her.

Cait had already dished up a thick slice for each of them, fastidiously using a knife to disconnect the strings of melted cheese that stretched from the box to their plates.

"About me, of course," she growled.

Joe handed her a glass of wine. "Not really."

Cait paused and lifted her eyes to his. "Not really? What does that mean?"

"Only that he didn't say much about you."

Joe was taunting her, dangling bits and pieces of information, waiting for her reaction. She should have known better than to trust him, but she was so anxious to find out what Paul had said that she ignored her pride. "Tell me everything he said," she demanded, "word for word."

Joe had a mouthful of pizza and Cait was left to wait several moments until he swallowed. "I seem to recall he said something about your explaining that the two of us go back a long way."

Cait straightened, too curious to hide her interest. "Did he look concerned? Jealous?"

"Paul? No, if anything, he looked bored."

"Bored," Cait repeated. Her shoulders sagged with defeat. "I swear that man wouldn't notice me if I pranced around his office naked."

"That's a clever idea, and one that just might work. Maybe you should practice around the house first, get the hang of it. I'd be willing to help you out if you're really serious about this." He sounded utterly nonchalant, as though she'd suggested subscribing to cable television. "This is what friends are for. Do you need help undressing?"

Cait took a sip from her wine to hide a smile. Joe hadn't changed in twenty years. He was still witty and fun-loving and a terrible tease. "Very funny."

"Hey, I wasn't kidding. I'll pretend I'm Paul and—"

"You promised you were going to be good."

He wiggled his eyebrows suggestively. "I will be. Just you wait."

Cait could feel the tide of color flow into her cheeks. She quickly lowered her eyes to her plate. "Joe, cut it out. You're making me blush and I hate to blush. My face looks like a ripe tomato." She lifted her slice of pizza and bit into it, chewing thoughtfully. "I don't understand you. Every time I think I have you figured out you do something to surprise me."

"Like what?"

"Like yesterday. You invited me to dinner, but I never dreamed you'd take me someplace as elegant as Henry's. You were the perfect gentleman all evening and then today, you were so..."

"Low and disgusting."

"Exactly." She nodded righteously. "One minute you're the picture of charm and culture and the next you're badgering me with your wisecracks."

"I'm a tease, remember?"

"The problem is that I can't deal with you when I don't know what to expect."

"That's my charm." He reached for a second piece of pizza. "Women are said to adore the unexpected in a man."

"Not this woman," she informed him promptly. "I need to know where I stand with you."

"A little to the left."

"Joe, please, I'm not joking. I can't have you pulling stunts like you did today. I've lived a good, clean life for the past twenty-eight years. Two days with you has ruined my reputation with the company. I can't walk into the office and hold my head up any longer. I hear people whispering and I know they're talking about me."

"Us," he corrected. "They're talking about us."

"That's even worse. If they want to talk about me and a man, I'd rather it was Paul. Just how much longer is this remodeling project going to take, anyway?" As far as Cait was concerned, the sooner Joe and his renegade crew were out of her office, the sooner her life would settle back to normal.

"Not too much longer."

"At the rate you're progressing, Webster, Rodale and Missen will have offices on the moon."

"Before the end of the year, I promise."

"Yes, but just how reliable are your promises?"

"I'm being good, aren't I?"

"I suppose," she conceded ungraciously, jerking a stack of mail away from Joe as he started to sort through it.

"What's this?" Joe asked, rescuing a single piece of paper before it fluttered to the floor.

"A Christmas list. I'm going shopping tomorrow."

"I should have known you'd be organized about that, too." He sounded vaguely insulting.

"I've been organized all my life. It isn't likely to change now."

"That's why I want you to lighten up a little." He continued studying her list. "What time are you going?"

"The stores open at eight and I plan to be there then."

"I suppose you've written down everything you need to buy so you won't forget anything."

"Of course."

"Sounds sensible." His remark surprised her. He scanned her list, then yelped, "Hey, I'm not on here!" He withdrew a pen from his shirt pocket and added his own name. "Do you want me to give you a few suggestions on what I'd like?"

"I already know what I'm getting you."

Joe arched his brows. "You do? And please don't say 'nothing.'"

"No, but it'll be something appropriate—like a muzzle."

"Oh, Caitlin, darling, you injure me." He gave her one of his devilishly handsome smiles, and Cait could feel herself weakening. Just what she didn't want! She had every right to be angry with Joe. If he hadn't brought that pizza, she'd have slammed the door in his face. Wouldn't she? Sure, she would! But she'd always been susceptible to Italian food. Her only other fault was Paul. She did love him. No one seemed to believe that, but she'd known almost from the moment they'd met that she was destined to spend the rest of her life loving Paul Jamison. Only she'd rather do it as his wife than his employee!

"Have you finished your shopping?" she asked idly, making small talk with Joe since he seemed determined to hang around.

"I haven't started. I have good intentions every year, you know, like I'll get a head start on finding the perfect gifts for my nieces and nephews, but they never work out. Usually panic sets in Christmas Eve and I tear around the stores like mad and buy everything in sight. Last year I forgot wrapping paper. My mother saved the day."

"I doubt it'd do any good to suggest you get organized."

"I haven't got the time."

"What are you doing right now? Write out your list, stick to it and make the time to go shopping."

"My darling Cait, is this an invitation for me to join you tomorrow?"

"Uh..." Cait hadn't intended it to be, but she supposed she couldn't object as long as he behaved himself. "You're welcome on one condition."

"Name it."

"No jokes, no stunts like you pulled today and absolutely no teasing. If you announce to a single person that we're married, I'm walking away from you and that's a promise."

"You've got it." He raised his hand, then ceremoniously crossed his heart.

"Lick your fingertips first," Cait demanded. The instant the words were out of her mouth, she realized how ridiculous she sounded, as if they were eight and ten all over again. "Forget I said that."

His eyes were twinkling as he stood to deliver his plate to the sink. "I swear it's a shame you're so in love with Paul," he told her. "If I'm not careful, I could fall for you myself." With that, he kissed her on the cheek and let himself out the door.

Pressing her fingers to her cheek, Cait drew in a deep, shuddering breath and held it until she heard the door close. Then and only then did it seep out in ragged bursts, as if she'd forgotten how to breathe normally.

"Oh, Joe," she whispered. The last thing she wanted was for Joe to fall in love with her. Not that he wasn't handsome and sweet and wonderful. He was. He always had been. He just wasn't for her. Their personalities were poles apart. Joe was unpredictable, always doing the unexpected, whereas Cait's life ran like clockwork.

She liked Joe. She almost wished she didn't, but she couldn't help herself. However, a steady diet of his pranks would soon drive her into the nearest asylum.

Standing, Cait closed the pizza box and tucked the uneaten portion into the top shelf of her refrigerator. She was putting the dirty plates in her dishwasher when the phone rang. She quickly washed her hands and reached for it.

"Hello."

"Cait, it's Paul."

Cait was so startled that the receiver slipped out of her hand. Grabbing for it, she nearly stumbled over the open dishwasher door, knocking her shin against the sharp edge. She yelped and swallowed a cry as she jerked the dangling phone cord toward her.

"Sorry, sorry," she cried, once she'd rescued the telephone receiver. "Paul? Are you still there?"

"Yes, I'm here. Is this a bad time? I could call back later if this is inconvenient. You don't have company, do you? I wouldn't want to interrupt a party or anything."

"Oh, no, now is perfect. I didn't realize you had my home number...but obviously you do. After all, we've been working together for nearly a year now." Eleven months and four days, not that she was counting or anything. "Naturally my number would be in the personnel file."

He hesitated and Cait bent over to rub her shin where it had collided with the dishwasher door. She was sure to have an ugly bruise, but a bruised leg was a small price to pay. Paul had phoned her!

"The reason I'm calling..."

"Yes, Paul," she prompted when he didn't immediately continue.

The silence lengthened before he blurted out, "I just wanted to thank you for passing on that article on the tax advantages of limited partnerships. It was thoughtful of you and I appreciate it."

"Any time. I read quite a lot in that area, you know. There are several recent articles on the same subject. If you'd like, I could bring them in next week."

"Sure. That would be fine. Thanks again, Cait. Goodbye."

The line was disconnected before Cait could say anything else and she was left holding the receiver. A smile came, slow and confident, and with a small cry of triumph, she tossed the telephone receiver into the air, caught it behind her back and replaced it with a flourish.

CAIT WAS DRESSED and waiting for Joe early the next morning. "Joe," she cried, throwing open her apartment door, "I could just kiss you."

He was dressed in faded jeans and a hip-length bronze-colored leather jacket. "Hey, I'm not stopping you," he said, opening his arms.

Cait ignored the invitation. "Paul phoned me last night." She didn't even try to contain her excitement; she felt like leaping and skipping and singing out loud.

"Paul did?" Joe sounded surprised.

"Yes. It was shortly after you left. He thanked me for giving him an interesting article I found in one of the business journals and—this is the good part—he asked if I was alone...as if it really mattered to him."

"If you were alone?" Joe repeated, and frowned. "What's that got to do with anything?"

"Don't you understand?" For all his intelligence Joe could be pretty obtuse, sometimes. "He wanted to know if *you* were here with me. I makes sense, doesn't it? Paul's jealous, only he doesn't realize it yet. Oh, Joe, I can't remember ever being this happy. Not in years and years and years."

"Because Paul Jamison phoned?"

"Don't sound so skeptical. It's exactly the break I've been looking for all these months. Paul's finally noticed me and it's all thanks to you."

"At least you're willing to give credit where credit is due." But he still didn't seem particularly thrilled.

"It's just so incredible," she continued. "I don't think I slept a wink last night. There was something in his voice that I've never heard before. Something...deep and personal. I don't know how to explain it. For the first time in a whole year, Paul knows I'm alive!"

"Are we going Christmas shopping or not?" Joe demanded brusquely. "Damn it all, Cait, I never expected you to go soft over a stupid phone call."

"But this wasn't just any call," she reminded him. She reached for her purse and her coat in one sweeping motion. "This call was from *Paul.*"

"You sound like a silly schoolgirl." Joe frowned, but Cait wasn't about to let his short temper destroy her mood. Paul had phoned her at home and she was sure that this was the beginning of a *real* relationship. Next he'd ask her out for lunch, and then...

They left her apartment and walked down the hall, Cait grinning all the way. Standing just outside the front doors was a huge truck with gigantic wheels. Just the type of vehicle she'd expected him to drive the night he'd taken her to Henry's.

"This is your truck?" she asked when they were outside. She was unable to keep the laughter out of her voice.

"Is there something wrong with it?"

"Not a single thing, but Joe, honestly, you are so predictable."

"That's not what you said yesterday."

She grinned as he opened the truck door, set down a stool for her and helped her climb into the cab. The seat was cluttered, but so wide she was able to shove everything to one side. When she'd made room for herself, she fastened the seat belt, snapping it jauntily in place. She was so happy, the whole world seemed delightful this morning.

"Will you quit smiling before someone suggests you've been overdosing on vitamins?" Joe grumbled.

"My, aren't we testy this morning."

"Where to?" he asked, starting the engine.

"Any of the big shopping malls will do. You decide. Do you have your list all made out?"

Joe patted his heart. "It's in my shirt pocket."

"Good."

"Have you decided what you're going to buy for whom?"

His smile was slightly off kilter. "Not exactly. I thought I'd follow you around and buy whatever you did. Do you know what you're getting your mother? Mine's damn difficult to buy for. Last year I ended up getting her cat food. She's got five cats of her own and God only knows how many strays she's feeding."

"At least your idea was practical."

"Well, there's that, and the fact that by the time I started my Christmas shopping the only store open was a supermarket."

Cait laughed. "Honestly, Joe!"

"Hey, I was desperate and before you get all righteous on me, Mom thought the cat food and the two rib roasts were great gifts."

"I'm sure she did," Cait returned, grinning. She found herself doing a lot of that when she was with Joe. Imagine buying his mother rib roasts for Christmas!

"Give me some ideas, would you? Mom's a hard case."

"To be honest, I'm not all that imaginative myself. I buy my mother the same thing every year."

"What is it?"

"Long-distance phone coupons. That way she can phone her sister in Dubuque and her high-school friend in Olathe, Kansas. Of course she calls me every now and again, too."

"Okay, that takes care of Mom. What about Martin? What are you buying him?"

"A bronze eagle." She'd decided on that gift last summer when she'd attended Sunday services at Martin's church. In the opening part of his sermon, Martin had used eagles to illustrate a point of faith.

"An eagle," Joe repeated. "Any special reason?"

"Y-yes," she said, not wanting to explain. "It's a long story, but I happen to be partial to eagles myself."

"Any other hints you'd care to pass on?"

"Buy wrapping paper in the after-Christmas sales. It's about half the price and it stores easily under the bed."

"Great idea. I'll have to remember that for next year."

Joe chose Northgate, the shopping mall closest to Cait's apartment. The parking lot was already beginning to fill up and it was only a few minutes after eight.

Joe managed to park fairly close to the entrance and came around to help Cait out of the truck. This time he didn't bother with the step stool, but gripped her around the waist to lift her down. "What did you mean when you said I was so predictable?" he asked, giving her a reproachful look.

With her hands resting on his shoulders and her feet dangling in midair, she felt vulnerable and small. "Nothing. It was just that I assumed you drove one of those Sherman-tank trucks, and I was right. I just hadn't seen it before."

"The kind of truck I drive bothers you?" His brow furrowed in a scowl.

"Not at all. What's the matter with you today, Joe? You're so touchy."

"I am not touchy," he snapped.

"Fine. Would you mind putting me down then?" His large hands were squeezing her waist almost painfully, though she doubted he was aware of it. She couldn't imagine what had angered him. Unless it was the fact that Paul had called her—which didn't make sense. Maybe, like most men, he just hated shopping.

He lowered her slowly to the asphalt and released her with seeming reluctance. "I need a coffee break," he announced grimly.

"But we just arrived."

Joe forcefully expelled his breath. "It doesn't matter. I need something to calm my nerves."

If he needed a caffeine fix so early in the day, Cait wondered how he'd manage during the next few hours. The stores became quickly crowded this time of year, especially on a Saturday. By ten it would be nearly impossible to get from one aisle to the next.

By twelve, she knew: Joe disliked Christmas shopping every bit as much as she'd expected.

"I've had it," Joe complained after making three separate trips back to the truck to deposit their spoils.

"Me, too," Cait agreed laughingly. "This place is turning into a madhouse."

"How about some lunch?" Joe suggested. "Some place far away from here. Like Tibet."

Cait laughed again and tucked her arm in his. "That sounds like a great idea."

Outside, they noticed several cars circling the lot looking for a parking space and three of them rushed to fill the one Joe vacated. Two cars nearly collided in their eagerness. One man leapt out of his and shook an angry fist at the other driver.

"So much for peace and goodwill," Joe commented. "I swear Christmas brings out the worst in everyone."

"And the best," Cait reminded him.

"To be honest, I don't know what crammed shopping malls and fighting the crowds and all this commercialism have to do with Christmas in the first place," he grumbled. A car cut in front of him, and Joe blared his horn.

"Quite a lot when you think about it," Cait said softly. "Imagine the streets of Bethlehem, the crowds and the noise..." The Christmas before, fresh from a shopping expedition, Cait had asked herself the same question. Christmas seemed so commercial. The crowds had been unbearable. First at Northgate, where she did most of her shopping and then at the airport. Sea-Tac had been filled with activity and noise, everyone in a hurry to get someplace or another. There seemed to be little peace or good cheer and a whole lot of selfish concern and rudeness. Then, in the tranquility of church on Christmas Eve, everything had come into perspective for Cait. There had been crowds and rudeness that first Christmas, too, she reasoned. Yet in the midst of that confusion had come joy and peace and love. For most people, it was still the same. Christmas gifts and decorations and dinners were, after all, expressions of the love you felt for your family and friends. And if the preparations sometimes got a bit chaotic, well, that no longer bothered Cait.

"Where should we go to eat?" Joe asked, breaking into her thoughts. They were barely moving, stuck in heavy traffic.

She looked over at him and smiled serenely. "Any place will do. There're several excellent restaurants close by. You choose, only let it be my treat this time."

"We'll talk about who pays later. Right now, I'm more concerned with getting out of this traffic sometime within my life span."

Still smiling, Cait said, "I don't think it'll take much longer."

He returned her smile. "I don't, either." His eyes held hers for what seemed an eternity—until someone behind them honked irritably. Joe glanced up and saw that traffic ahead of them had started to move. He immediately stepped on the gas.

Cait didn't know what Joe had found so fascinating about her unless it was her unruly hair. She hadn't combed it since leaving the house; it was probably a mass of tight, disorderly curls. She'd been so concerned with finding the right gift for her nephews and niece that she hadn't given it a thought.

"What's wrong?" she asked, feeling self-conscious.

"What makes you think anything's wrong?"

"The way you were looking at me a few minutes ago."

"Oh, that," he said easing, into a restaurant parking lot. "I don't think I've ever fully appreciated how lovely you are," he answered in a calm, matter-of-fact voice.

Cait blushed and looked away. "I'm sure you're mistaken. I'm really not all that pretty. I sometimes wondered if Paul would have noticed me sooner if I was a little more attractive."

"Trust me, Bright Eyes," he said, turning off the engine. "You're pretty enough."

"For what?"

"For this." And he leaned across the seat and captured her mouth with his.

CHAPTER FIVE

"I...WISH YOU HADN'T done that," Cait whispered, slowly opening her eyes in an effort to pull herself back to reality.

As far as kisses went, Joe's were good. Very good. He kissed better than just about anyone she'd ever kissed before—but that didn't alter the fact that she was in love with Paul.

"You're right," he muttered, opening the door and climbing out of the cab. "I shouldn't have done that." He walked around to her side and yanked the door open with more force than necessary.

Cait frowned, wondering at his strange mood. One minute he was holding her in his arms, kissing her tenderly; the next he was short-tempered and irritable.

"I'm hungry," he barked, lifting her abruptly down onto the pavement. "I sometimes do irrational things when I haven't eaten."

"I see." The next time she went anywhere with Joseph Rockwell, she'd have to be certain he ate a good meal first.

The restaurant was crowded and Joe gave the receptionist their names to add to the growing waiting list. Sitting on the last empty chair in the foyer, Cait set her large black leather purse on her lap and started rooting through it.

"What are you looking for? Uranium?" Joe teased, watching her.

"Crackers," she answered, shifting the bulky bag and handing him several items to hold while she continued digging.

"You're looking for crackers? Whatever for?"

She glanced up long enough to give him a look that questioned his intelligence. "For obvious reasons. If you're irrational when you're hungry, you might do something stupid while we're here. Frankly, I don't want you to embarrass me." She returned to the task with renewed vigor. "I can just see you standing on top of the table tap-dancing."

"That's one way to gain the waiter's attention. Thanks for suggesting it."

"Aha!" Triumphantly Cait pulled two miniature bread sticks wrapped in cellophane from the bottom of her purse. "Eat," she instructed. "Before you're overcome by some other craziness."

"You mean before I kiss you again," he said in a low voice, bending his head toward hers.

She leaned back quickly, not giving him any chance of following through on that. "Exactly. Or waltz with the waitress or any of the other loony things you do."

"You have to admit I've been good all morning."

"With one minor slip," she reminded him, pressing the bread sticks into his hand. "Now eat."

Before Joe had a chance to open the package, the hostess approached then with two menus tucked under her arm. "Mr. and Mrs. Rockwell. Your table is ready."

"Mr. and Mrs. Rockwell," Cait muttered under her breath, glaring at Joe. She should have known she couldn't trust him.

"Excuse me, miss," Cait said, standing abruptly and raising her index finger. "His name is Rockwell, mine is Marshall," she explained patiently. She was not about to let Joe continue his silly games. "We're just friends here for lunch." Her narrowed eyes caught Joe's, which looked as innocent as freshly fallen snow. He shrugged as though to say any misunderstanding hadn't been *his* fault.

"I see," the hostess replied. "I'm sorry for the confusion."

"No problem." Cait hadn't wanted to make a big issue of this, but on the other hand she didn't want Joe to think he was going to get away with it, either.

The woman led them to a linen-covered table in the middle of the room. Joe held out Cait's chair for her and then whispered something to the hostess who immediately cast Cait a sympathetic glance. Joe's own gaze rested momentarily on Cait before he pulled out his chair and sat across from her.

"All right, what did you say to her?" she hissed.

The menu seemed to command his complete interest for a couple of minutes. "What makes you think I said anything?"

"I heard you whispering and then she gave me this pathetic look like she wanted to hug me and tell me everything was going to be all right."

"Then you know."

"Joe, don't play games with me," Cait warned.

"All right, if you must know, I explained that you'd suffered a head injury and developed amnesia."

"Amnesia," she repeated loudly enough to attract the attention of the diners at the next table. Gritting her teeth, Cait snatched up her menu, gripping it tightly enough to curl the edges. It didn't do any good to argue with Joe. The man was impossible. Every time she tried to reason with him, he did something to make her regret it.

"How else was I supposed to explain the fact you'd forgotten our marriage?" he asked reasonably.

"I did not forget our marriage," she informed him from between clenched teeth, reviewing the menu and quickly making her selection. "Good grief, it wasn't even legal."

She realized that the waitress was standing by their table, pen and pad in hand. The woman's ready smile faded as she looked from Cait to Joe and back again. Her mouth tightened as if she strongly suspected they really were involved in something illegal.

"Uh . . ." Cait hedged, feeling like even more of an idiot. The urge to explain was overwhelming, but every time she tried, she only made matters worse. "I'll have the club sandwich," she said, glaring across the table at Joe.

"That sounds good. I'll have the same," he said, closing his menu.

The woman scribbled down their order, then hurried away, pausing to glance over her shoulder as if she wanted to be able to identify them later in a police lineup.

"Now look what you've done," Cait whispered heatedly once the waitress was far enough away from their table not to overhear.

"Me?"

Maybe she was being unreasonable, but Joe was the one who'd started this nonsense in the first place. No one had ever gotten a rise out of her the way Joe did. No one could rattle her so effectively. And worse, she let him.

This shopping trip was a good example, and so was the pizza that led up to it. No woman in her right mind should have allowed Joe into her apartment after what he'd said to her in front of Lindy. Not only had she invited him inside her home, she'd agreed to let him accompany her Christmas shopping. She ought to have her head examined!

"What's wrong?" Joe asked, tearing open the package of bread sticks. Rather pointless in Cait's opinion, since their lunch would be served any minute.

"What's wrong?" she cried, dumbfounded that he had to ask. "You mean other than the hostess believing I've suffered a head injury and the waitress thinking that we're drug dealers or something equally disgusting?"

"Here." He handed her one of the miniature breadsticks. "Eat this and you'll feel better."

Cait sincerely doubted that, but she took it, anyway, muttering under her breath.

"Relax," he urged.

"Relax," she mocked. "How can I possibly relax when you're doing and saying things I find excruciatingly embarrassing?"

"I'm sorry, Cait. Really, I am." To his credit, he did look contrite. "But you're so easy to fluster and I can't seem to stop myself."

Their sandwiches arrived, thick with slices of turkey, ham and a variety of cheeses. Cait was reluctant to admit how much better she felt after she'd eaten. Joe's spirits had apparently improved, as well.

"So," he said, his hands resting on his abdomen. "What do you have planned for the rest of the afternoon?"

Cait hadn't given it much thought. "I suppose I should wrap the gifts I bought this morning." But the thought didn't particularly excite her. Good grief, after the adventures she'd had with Joe, it wasn't any wonder.

"You mean you actually wrap gifts before Christmas Eve?" Joe asked. "Doesn't that take all the fun out of it? I mean, for me it's a game just to see if I can get the presents bought."

She grinned, trying to imagine herself in such a disorganized race to the deadline. Definitely not her style.

"How about a movie?" he suggested out of the blue. "I have the feeling you don't get out enough."

"A movie?" Cait ignored the comment about her social life, mainly because he was right. She rarely took the time to go to a show.

"We're both exhausted from fighting the crowds," Joe added. "There's a six-cinema theater next to the restaurant. I'll even let you choose."

"I suppose you'd object to a love story?"

"We can see one if you insist, only..."

"Only what?"

"Only promise me you won't ever expect a man to say the things those guys on the screen do."

"I beg your pardon?"

"You heard me. Women hear actors say this incredible drivel and then they're disappointed when real men don't."

"Real men like you, I suppose?"

"Right." He looked smug, then suddenly he frowned. "Does Paul like romances?"

Cait hadn't a clue, since she'd never gone on a date with Paul and the subject wasn't one they'd ever discussed at the office. "I imagine he does," she said, dabbing her mouth with her napkin. "He isn't the type of man to be intimidated by such things."

Joe's deep blue eyes widened with surprise and a touch of respect. "Ouch. So Martin's little sister reveals her claws."

"I don't have claws. I just happen to have strong opinions on certain subjects." She reached for her purse while she was speaking and removed her wallet.

"What are you doing now?" Joe demanded.

"Paying for lunch." She sorted through the bills and withdrew a twenty. "It's my turn and I insist on paying..." She hesitated when she saw Joe's deepening frown. "Or don't real men allow women friends to buy their lunch?"

"Sure, go ahead," he returned flippantly.

It was all Cait could do to hide a smile. She guessed that her gesture in paying for their sandwiches would somehow be seen as compromising his male pride.

Apparently she was right. As they were walking toward the cashier, Joe stepped up his pace, grabbed the check from her hand and slapped some money on the counter. He glared at her as if he expected a drawn-out public argument. After the fuss they'd already caused in the restaurant, Cait was darned if she was going to let that happen.

"Joe," she argued, the minute they were out the door. "What was that all about?"

"All right, you win. Tell me my views are outdated, but when a woman goes out with me I pick up the tab, no matter how liberated she is."

"But this isn't a real date. We're only friends, and even that's—"

"I don't give a damn. Consider it an apology for the embarrassment I caused you earlier."

"You're a chauvinist, aren't you?"

"I'm not! I just have certain . . . standards."

"So I see." His attitude shouldn't have come as any big surprise. Just as Cait had told him earlier, he was shockingly predictable.

Hand at her elbow, Joe led the way across the car-filled lot toward the sprawling theater complex. The movies appealed to a wide audience. There was a Disney classic showing, along with a horror flick and a couple of adventure movies and last, but not least, a well-publicized love story.

As they stood in line, Cait caught Joe's gaze lingering on the poster for one of the adventure films, yet another story about a law-and-order cop with renegade ideas.

"I suppose you're more interested in seeing that than the romance."

"I already promised you could choose the show, and I'm a man of my word. If, however, you were to pick another movie—" he buried his hands in his pockets as he grinned at her appealingly "—I wouldn't complain."

"I'm willing to pick another movie, but on one condition."

"Name it." His eyes lit up.

"I pay."

"Those claws of yours are out again."

She raised her hands and flexed her fingers in a catlike motion. "It's your decision."

"What about popcorn?"

"You can buy that if you insist."

"All right," he said, "you've got yourself a deal."

When it was Cait's turn at the ticket window, she purchased two for the Disney classic.

"Disney?" Joe repeated, shocked when Cait handed him his ticket.

"It seemed like a good compromise," she answered.

For a moment it looked as if he was going to argue with her, then a slow grin spread across his face. "Disney," he said again. "You're right, it does sound like fun. Only I hope we're not the only ones there over the age of ten."

They sat toward the back of the theater, sharing a large bucket of buttered popcorn. The theater was crowded and several kids seemed to be taking turns running up and down the aisles. Joe needn't have worried; there were plenty of adults in attendance, but of course most of them were accompanying children.

The lights dimmed and Cait reached for a handful of popcorn, relaxing in her seat. "I love this movie."

"How many times have you seen it?"

"Five or six. But it's been several years now."

"Me, too." Joe relaxed beside her, crossing his long legs and leaning back.

The credits started to roll, but the noise level hadn't decreased much. "Will the kids bother you?" Joe wanted to know.

"Heavens, no. I love kids."

"You do?" The fact that he was so surprised seemed vaguely insulting and Cait stiffened.

"We've already had this discussion," she responded, licking the salt from her fingertips.

"We did? When?"

"The other day. You commented on how much I used to enjoy playing with my dolls and how you'd expected me to be married with a house full of children." His words had troubled her then, because "a house full of children" was exactly what Cait would have liked, and she seemed a long way from realizing her dream.

"Ah, yes, I remember our conversation about that now." He scooped up a large handful of popcorn. "You'd be a very good mother, you know."

That Joe would say this was enough to bring an unexpected rush of tears to her eyes. She blinked them back, surprised that she'd get weepy over something so silly.

The previews were over and the audience settled down as the movie started. Cait focused her attention on the screen, munching popcorn every now and then, reaching blindly for the bucket. Their hands collided more than once and almost before she was aware of it, their fingers were entwined. It was a peaceful sort of feeling, being linked to Joe this way. There was a *rightness* about it that she didn't want to explore just yet. He hadn't really changed; he was still lovable and funny and fun. For that matter, she hadn't changed very much, either....

The movie was as good as Cait remembered, better, even—perhaps because Joe was there to share it with her. She half expected him to make the occasional wisecrack, but he seemed to respect the artistic value of the classic animation and, judging by his wholehearted laughter, he enjoyed the story.

When the show was over, he released Cait's hand. Hurriedly she gathered her purse and coat. As they walked out of the noisy, crowded theater, it seemed only natural to hold hands again.

Joe opened the truck, lifted down the step stool and helped her inside. Dusk came early these days, and bright, cheery lights were ablaze on every street. A vacant lot across the street was now filled with Christmas trees. A row of red lights was strung between two posts, sagging in the middle, and a portable tape player sent forth saccharine versions of better-known Christmas carols.

"Have you bought your tree yet?" Joe asked, nodding in the direction of the lot after he'd climbed into the driver's seat and started the engine.

"No. I don't usually put one up since I spend the holidays with Martin and his family."

"Ah."

"What about you? Or is that something else you save for Christmas Eve?" she joked. It warmed her a little to imagine Joe staying up past midnight to decorate a Christmas tree for his nieces and nephews.

"Finding time to do the shopping is bad enough."

"Your construction projects keep you that busy?" She hadn't given much thought to Joe's business. She knew from little remarks Paul had made that Joe was very successful. It wasn't logical that she should feel pride in his accomplishments, but she did.

"Owning a business isn't like being in a nine-to-five job. I'm on call twenty-four hours a day, but I wouldn't have it any other way. I love what I do."

"I'm happy for you, Joe. I really am."

"Happy enough to decorate my Christmas tree with me?"

"When?"

"Next weekend."

"I'd like to," she told him, touched by the invitation, "but I'll have left for Minnesota by then."

"That's all right," Joe said, grinning at her. "Maybe next time."

She turned, frowning, to hide her blush.

They remained silent as he concentrated on easing the truck into the heavy late-afternoon traffic.

"I enjoyed the movie," she said some time later, resisting the urge to rest her head on his shoulder. The impulse to do that arose from her exhaustion, she told herself. Nothing else!

"So did I," he said softly. "Only next time, I'll be the one to pay. Understand?"

Next time. There it was again. She suspected Joe was beginning to take their relationship, such as it was, far too seriously. Already he was suggesting they'd be seeing each other soon, matter-of-factly discussing dates as if they were long-time companions. Almost as if they were married...

She was mulling over this realization when Joe pulled into the parking area in front of her building. He climbed out and began to gather her packages, bundling them in his arms. She managed to scramble down by herself, not giving him a chance to help her, then she led the way into the building and unlocked her door.

Cait stood just inside the doorway and turned slightly to take a couple of the larger packages from Joe's arms.

"I had a great time," she told him briskly.

"Me, too." He nudged her, forcing her to enter the living room. He followed close behind and unloaded her remaining things onto the sofa. His presence seemed to reach out and fill every corner of the room.

Neither of them spoke for several minutes, but Cait sensed Joe wanted her to invite him to stay for coffee. The idea was tempting but dangerous. She mustn't let him think there might ever be anything romantic between them. Not when she was in love with Paul. For the first time in nearly a year, Paul was actually beginning to notice her. She refused to ruin everything now by becoming involved with Joe.

"Thank you for...today," she said, returning to the door, intending to open it for him. Instead, Joe caught her by the wrist and pulled her against him. She was in his arms before she could voice a protest.

"I'm going to kiss you," he told her, his voice rough yet oddly tender.

"You are?" She'd never been more aware of a man, of his hard, muscular body against hers, his clean, masculine scent. Her own body reacted in a chaotic scramble of mixed sensations. Above all, though, it felt *good* to be in his arms. She wasn't sure why and dared not examine the feeling.

Slowly, leisurely, he lowered his head. She made a soft weak sound as his mouth touched hers.

Cait sighed, forgetting for a moment that she meant to free herself before his kiss deepened. Before things went any further...

Joe must have sensed her resolve because his hands slid down her spine in a gentle caress, drawing her even closer. His mouth began a sensuous journey along her jaw, and down her throat—

"Joe!" She moaned his name, uncertain of what she wanted to say.

"Hmm?"

"Are you hungry again?" She wondered desperately if there were any more bread sticks in the bottom of her purse. Maybe that would convince him to stop.

"Very hungry," he told her, his voice low and solemn. "I've never been hungrier."

"But you had lunch and then you ate nearly all the popcorn."

He hesitated, then slowly raised his head. "Cait, are we talking about the same things here? Oh, hell, what does it matter? The only thing that matters is this." He covered her parted lips with his.

Cait felt her knees go weak and sagged against him, her fingers gripping his jacket as though she expected to collapse any moment. Which was becoming a distinct possibility as he continued to kiss her....

"Joe, no more, please." But she was the one clinging to him. She had to do something, and fast, before her ability to reason was lost entirely.

He drew an unsteady breath and muttered something she couldn't decipher as his lips grazed the delicate line of her jaw.

"We...need to talk," she announced, keeping her eyes tightly closed. If she didn't look at Joe, then she could concentrate on what she had to do.

"All right," he agreed.

"I'll make a pot of coffee."

With a heavy sigh, Joe abruptly released her. Cait half fell against the sofa arm, requiring its support while she collected herself enough to walk into the kitchen. She unconsciously reached up and brushed her lips, as if she wasn't completely sure even now that he'd taken her in his arms and kissed her.

He hadn't been joking this time, or teasing. The kisses they'd shared were serious kisses. The type a man gives a woman he's strongly attracted to. A woman he's interested in developing a relationship with. Cait found herself shaking, unable to move.

"You want me to make that coffee?" he suggested.

She nodded and sank down on the couch. She could scarcely stand, let alone prepare a pot of coffee.

Joe returned a few minutes later, carrying two steaming mugs. Carefully he handed her one, then sat across from her on the blue velvet ottoman.

"You wanted to talk?"

Cait nodded. "Yes." Her throat felt thick, clogged with confused emotion, and forming coherent words suddenly seemed beyond her means. She tried gesturing with her free hand, but that only served to frustrate Joe.

"Cait," he asked, "what's wrong?"

"Paul." The name came out in an eerie squeak.

"What about him?"

"He phoned me."

"Yes, I know. You already told me that."

"Don't you understand?" she cried, her throat unexpectedly clearing. "Paul is finally showing some interest in me and now you're kissing me and telling anyone who'll listen that the two of us are married and you're doing ridiculous things like..." She paused to draw in a deep breath. "Joe, oh please, Joe, don't fall in love with me."

"Fall in love with you?" he echoed incredulously. "Caitlin, you can't be serious. It won't happen. No chance."

CHAPTER SIX

"NO CHANCE?" Cait repeated, convinced she'd misunderstood him. She blinked a couple of times as if that would correct her hearing. Either Joe was underestimating her intelligence, or he was more of a . . . a cad than she'd realized.

"You have nothing to worry about." He sipped coffee, his gaze steady, and emotionless. "I'm not falling in love with you."

"In other words you make a habit of kissing unsuspecting women."

"It isn't a habit," he answered thoughtfully. "It's more of a pastime."

"You certainly seem to be making a habit of it with me." Her anger was quickly gaining momentum and she was at odds to understand why she found his casual attitude so offensive. He was telling her exactly what she wanted to hear. But she hadn't expected her ego to take such a beating in the process. The fact that he wasn't the least bit tempted to fall in love with her should have pleased her.

It didn't.

It was as if their brief kisses were little more than a pleasant interlude for him. Something to occupy his time and keep him from growing bored with her company.

"This may come as something of a shock to you," Joe continued indifferently, "but a man doesn't have to be in love with a woman to kiss her."

"I know that," Cait snapped, fighting to hold back her temper, which was threatening to break free at any moment. "But you don't have to be so...so casual about it, either. If I wasn't involved with Paul, I might have taken you seriously."

"I didn't know you were involved with Paul," he returned with mild sarcasm. He leaned forward and rested his elbows on his knees, his pose infuriatingly relaxed. "If that was true I'd never have taken you out. The way I see it, the involvement is all on your part. Am I wrong?"

"No," she admitted reluctantly. How like a man to talk about semantics in the middle of an argument!

"So," he said, leaning back again and crossing his legs. "Are you enjoying the kisses? I take it I've improved from the first go-around."

"You honestly want me to rate you?" she sputtered.

"Obviously I'm much better than I was as a kid, otherwise you wouldn't be so worried." He took another drink of his coffee, smiling pleasantly all the while.

"Believe me, I'm not worried."

He arched his brows. "Really?"

"No doubt you expect me to fall at your feet, overcome by your masculine charm. Well, if that's what you're waiting for, you have one hell of a long wait!"

His grin was slightly off center, as if he was picturing her arrayed at his feet—and enjoying the sight. "I think the problem here is that *you* might be falling in love with *me* and just don't know it."

"Falling in love with you and not know it?" she repeated with a loud disbelieving snort. "You've gone completely out of your mind. There's no chance of that."

"Why not? Plenty of women have told me I'm a handsome son of a gun. Plus, I'm said to possess a certain amount of charm. Heaven knows, I'm generous enough and rather—"

"Who told you that? Your mother?" She made it sound like the most ludicrous thing she'd heard in years.

"You might be surprised to learn that I do have admirers."

Why this news should add fuel to the fire of her temper was beyond Cait, but she was so furious with him she could barely sit still. "I don't doubt it, but if I fall in love with a man you can believe it won't be just because he's 'a handsome son of a gun,'" she quoted sarcastically. "Look at Paul— He's the type of man I'm attracted to. What's on the inside matters more than outward appearances."

"Then why are you so worried about falling in love with me?"

"I'm not worried! You've got it the wrong way around. The only reason I mentioned anything was because I thought *you* were beginning to take our times together much too seriously."

"I already explained that wasn't a problem."

"So I heard." Cait set her coffee aside. Joe was upsetting her so much that her hand was shaking hard enough to spill it.

"Well," Joe murmured, glancing at her. "You never did answer my question."

"Which one?" she asked irritably.

"About how I rated as a kisser."

"You weren't serious!"

"On the contrary." He set his own coffee down and raised himself off the ottoman far enough to clasp her by the waist and pull her into his lap.

Caught off balance, Cait fell onto his thighs, too astonished to struggle.

"Let's try it again," he whispered in a rough undertone.

"Ah..." A frightening excitement took hold of Cait. Her mind commanded her to leap away from this man, but some emotion, far stronger than common sense or prudence, urged the opposite.

Before she could form a protest, Joe bent toward her and covered her mouth with his. She'd hold herself stiff in his arms, that was what she'd do, teach him the lesson he deserved. How dared he assume she'd automatically fall in love with him. How dared he insinuate he was some...some Greek god women adored. But the instant his lips met hers, Cait trembled with a mixture of shock and profound pleasure.

Everything within her longed to cry out at the unfairness of it all. It shouldn't be this good with Joe. They were friends, nothing more. This was the kind of response she expected when Paul kissed her. If he ever did.

She meant to pull away, but instead, Cait moaned softly. It felt so incredibly wonderful. So incredibly right. At that moment, there didn't seem to be anything to worry about—except the likelihood of dissolving in his arms then and there.

Suddenly Joe broke the contact. Her instinctive disappointment, even more than the unexpectedness of the action, sent her eyes flying open. Her own dark eyes met his blue ones, which now seemed almost aquamarine.

"So, how do I rate?" he murmured thickly, as though he was having trouble speaking himself.

"Good." A one-word reply was all she could manage, although she was furious with him for asking.

"Just good?"

She nodded forcefully.

"I thought we were better than that."

"We?"

"Naturally I'm only as good as my partner."

"Th-then how do you rate me?" She had to ask. Like a fool she handed him the ax and laid her neck on the chopping board. Joe was sure to use the opportunity to trample all over her ego, to turn the whole bewildering experience into a joke. She couldn't take that right now. She dropped her gaze, waiting for him to devastate her.

"Much improved."

She cocked one brow in surprise. She had no idea what to say next.

They were both silent. Then he said softly, "You know, Cait, we're getting better at this. Much, much better." He pressed his forehead to hers. "If we're not careful, you just might fall in love with me, after all."

"WHERE WERE YOU all day Saturday?" Lindy asked early Monday morning, walking into Cait's office. The renovations to it had just been completed late Friday and Cait had moved everything back into her office first thing this morning. "I must have tried calling you ten times."

"I told you I was going Christmas shopping. In fact, I bought some decorations for my office."

Lindy nodded. "But all day?" Her eyes narrowed suspiciously as she set down her briefcase and leaned against Cait's desk, crossing her arms. "You didn't happen to be with Joe Rockwell, did you?"

Cait could feel a telltale shade of pink creep up her neck. She lowered her gaze to the list of current Dow Jones stock prices and took a moment to compose herself. She couldn't admit the truth. "I said I was shopping," she said somewhat defensively. Then, in an effort to change the topic, she reached for a thick folder with Paul's name inked across the top and said, "You wouldn't happen to know what Paul's schedule is for the day, would you?"

"N-no, I haven't seen him yet. Why do you ask?"

Cait flashed her friend a bright smile. "He phoned me Friday night. Oh, Lindy, I was so excited I nearly fell all over myself." She dropped her voice as she glanced around to make sure none of the others could hear her. "I honestly think he intends to ask me out."

"Did he say so?"

"Not exactly." Cait frowned. Lindy wasn't revealing any of the enthusiasm she expected.

"Then why did he phone?"

Cait rolled her chair away from the desk and glanced around once again. "I think he might be jealous," she whispered.

"Really?" Lindy's eyes widened.

"Don't look so surprised." Cait, however, was much too excited recounting Paul's phone call to be offended by Lindy's attitude.

"What makes you think Paul would be jealous?" Lindy asked next.

"Maybe I'm magnifying everything in my own mind because it's what I so badly want to believe. But he did phone..."

"What did he say?" Lindy pressed, sounding more curious now. "It seems to me he must have had a reason."

"Oh, he did. He mentioned something about appreciating an article I'd given him, but we both know that was just an excuse. What clued me in to his jealousy was the way he kept asking if I was alone."

"But that could have several connotations, don't you think?" Lindy suggested.

"Yes, I know, but it made sense that he'd want to know if Joe was at the apartment or not."

"And was he?"

"Of course not," Cait said righteously. She didn't feel guilty about hiding the fact that he'd been there earlier, or that they'd spent nearly all of Saturday together. "I'm sure Joe's ridiculous remark when I left the office Friday is what convinced Paul to phone me. If I wasn't so furious with Joe, I might even be grateful."

"What's that?" Lindy asked abruptly, pointing to the thick folder in front of Cait. Her lips had thinned slightly as if she was confused or annoyed—about what, Cait couldn't figure out.

"This, my friend," she began, holding up the folder, "is the key to my future with our dedicated manager."

Lindy didn't immediately respond and looked more puzzled then before. "How do you mean?"

Cait couldn't get over the feeling that things weren't quite right with her best friend; she seemed to be holding something back. But Cait realized Lindy would tell her when she was ready. Lindy always hated being pushed or prodded.

"The folder?" Lindy prompted when Cait didn't answer.

Cait flipped it open. "I spent all day Sunday reading through old business journals looking for additional articles that might interest Paul. I must have gone back five years. I copied the articles I consider the most valuable and added a brief analysis of my own. I was hoping to give it to him sometime today. That's why I was asking if you knew his schedule."

"Unfortunately I don't," Lindy murmured. She straightened, reached for her briefcase and made a show of checking her watch. Then she looked up to smile reassuringly at Cait. "I'd better get to work. I'll come by later to help you put up your decorations, okay?"

"Thanks," Cait said, then added, "Wish me luck with Paul."

"You know I do," Lindy mumbled on her way out the door.

Mondays were generally slow for the stock market, slow, that is, unless there was a crisis. World events and financial reports had a significant impact on the market. However, as the day progressed, everything ran smoothly.

Cait glanced up every now and again, half expecting to see Joe lounging in her doorway. His men had started early that morning, but by noon, Joe hadn't arrived.

Not until much later did she realize it was Paul she should be anticipating, not Joe. Paul was the romantic interest of her life and it irritated her that Joe seemed to preoccupy her thoughts.

As it happened, Paul did stroll past her office shortly after the New York market closed. Grabbing the folder, Cait raced toward his office, not hesitating for an instant. This was her golden opportunity and she was taking hold of it with both hands.

"Good afternoon, Paul," she said cordially as she stood in his doorway, clutching the folder. "Do you have a moment or would you rather I came back later?"

He looked tired, as if the day had already been a grueling one. It was all Cait could do not to offer to massage away the stress and worry that complicated his life. Her heart swelled with a renewed wave of love. For a wild, impetuous moment, it was true, she'd suffered her doubts. Any woman would have when a man like Joe took her in his arms. He might be arrogant in the extreme and one of the worst pranksters she'd ever met, but despite all that, he had a certain charm. But now that she was with Paul, Cait remembered sharply who it was she really loved.

"I don't want to be a bother," she added softly.

He offered her a listless smile. "Come in, Cait. Now is fine." He gestured toward a chair.

She hurried into the office, trying to keep the bounce out of her step. Knowing she'd be spending a few extra minutes alone with Paul, Cait had taken special care with her appearance that morning.

He glanced up and smiled at her again, but this time Cait thought she could see a glimmer of appreciation in his eyes. "What can I do for you? I hope you're pleased with your office." He frowned slightly.

For a second, she forgot what she was doing in Paul's office and stared at him blankly until his own gaze fell to the folder. "The office looks great," she said quickly. "Um, the reason I'm here..." She faltered, then gulped in a quick breath and continued, "I went through some of the business journals I have at home and found several I felt would interest you." She extended the folder to him, like a ceremonial offering.

He took it from her and opened it gingerly. "Gracious," he said, flipping through the pages and scanning her written comments, "you must have spent hours on this."

"It was...nothing." She'd willingly have done a good deal more to gain his appreciation and eventually his love.

"I won't have a chance to look at this for a few days," he said.

"Oh, please, there's no rush. You happened to mention you got some useful insights from the previous article I gave you. So I thought I'd share a few others that seem relevant to what's happening with the market now."

"It's very thoughtful of you."

"I was happy to do it. More than happy," she amended with her most brilliant smile. When he didn't say anything more, Cait rose reluctantly to her feet. "You must be swamped after being in meetings most of the day, so I'll leave you for now."

She was almost at the door when he spoke. "Actually I only dropped into the office to collect a few things before heading out again. I've got an important date this evening."

Cait felt as if the floor had suddenly disappeared and she was plummeting through empty space. "Date?" she repeated before she could stop herself. It was a struggle to keep smiling.

Paul's grin was downright boyish. "Yes, I'm meeting her for dinner."

"In that case, have a good time."

"Thanks, I will," he returned confidently, his eyes alight with excitement. "Oh, and by the way," he added, indicating the folder she'd worked so hard on, "thanks for all the effort you put into this."

"You're... welcome."

By the time Cait returned to her office she felt numb. Paul had an important date. It wasn't as though she'd expected him to live the life of a hermit, but before today, he'd never mentioned going out with anyone. She might have suspected he'd thrown out the information hoping to make her jealous if it hadn't been for one thing. He seemed genuinely thrilled about this date. Besides, Paul wasn't the kind of man to resort to pretense.

"Cait, my goodness," Lindy said, strolling into her office a while later, "what's wrong? You look dreadful."

Cait swallowed against the lump in her throat and managed a shaky smile. "I talked to Paul and gave him the research I'd done."

"He didn't appreciate it?" Lindy picked up the wreath that lay on Cait's desk and pinned it to the door.

"I'm sure he did," she replied. "What he doesn't appreciate is me. I might as well be invisible to that man." She pushed the hair away from her forehead and braced both elbows on her desk, feeling totally disheartened. Unless she acted quickly, she was going to lose Paul to some faceless, nameless woman.

"You've been invisible to him before. What's different about this time?" She fastened a silver bell to the window as Cait abstractedly fingered her three ceramic Wise Men.

"Paul's got a date, and from the way he said it, this isn't with just any woman, either. Whoever she is must be important, otherwise he wouldn't have mentioned her. He looked like a little kid who's been given the keys to a candy store."

The information seemed to surprise Lindy as much as it had Cait. She was quiet for a few minutes before she asked quietly, "What are you going to do about it?"

"Heavens, I don't know," Cait cried, hiding her face in her hands. She'd once jokingly suggested to Joe that she parade around naked in an effort to gain Paul's attention.

Of course she'd been exaggerating, but some form of drastic action was obviously needed. If only she knew what.

Lindy mumbled an excuse and left. It wasn't until Cait looked up that she realized her friend was gone. She sighed wearily. She'd arrived at work this morning with such bright expectations, and now everything had gone wrong. She felt more depressed than she'd been in a long time. She knew the best remedy would be to force herself into some physical activity. Anything. The worst possible thing she could do was sit home alone and mope. Maybe she should plan to buy herself a Christmas tree and some ornaments. Her spirits couldn't help being at least a little improved by that; it would get her out of the house, if nothing else. And then she'd have something to entertain herself with, instead of brooding about this unexpected turn of events. Getting out of the house had an added advantage. If Joe phoned, she wouldn't be there to answer.

No sooner had that thought passed through her mind when a large form filled her doorway.

Joe.

A bright orange hard hat was pushed back on his head, the way movie cowboys wore their Stetsons. His boots were dusty and his tool pouch rode low on his hip, completing the gunslinger image. Even the way he stood with his thumbs tucked in his belt suggested he was expecting a showdown.

"Hi, beautiful," he drawled, giving her that lazy, intimate smile of his. The one designed, Cait swore, just to unnerve her. But it wasn't going to work, not in her present state of mind.

"Don't you have anyone else to pester?" she snapped.

"My, my," Joe said, shaking his head in mock chagrin. Disregarding her lack of welcome, he strode into the office and threw himself down in the chair beside her desk. "You're in a rare mood."

"You would be too after the day I've had. Listen, Joe, as you can see, I'm poor company. Go flirt with the receptionist if you're looking to make someone miserable."

"Those claws are certainly sharp this afternoon." He ran his hands down the front of his shirt, pretending to inspect the damage inflicted. "What's wrong?" Some of the teasing light faded from his eyes as he studied her.

She sent him a look meant to blister his ego, but as always Joe seemed invincible against her practiced glares.

"How do you know I'm not here to invest fifty thousand dollars?" he demanded, making himself at home by reaching across her desk for a pen. He rolled it casually between his palms.

Cait wasn't about to fall for this little game. "Are you here to invest money?"

"Not exactly. I wanted to ask you to—"

"Then come back when you are." She grabbed a stack of papers and slapped them down on her desk. But being rude, even to Joe, went against her nature. She was battling tears and the growing need to explain her behavior, apologize for it, when he slowly rose to his feet. He tossed the pen carelessly onto her desk.

"Have it your way. If asking you to join me to look for a Christmas tree is such a terrible crime, then—"

"You're going to buy a Christmas tree?"

"That's what I just said." He flung the words over his shoulder on his way out the door.

In that moment, Cait felt as though the whole world was tumbling down around her shoulders. She felt like such a shrew. He'd come here wanting to include her in his Christmas preparations and she'd driven him away with a spiteful tongue and a haughty attitude.

Cait wasn't a woman easily given to tears, but she struggled with them now. Her lower lip started to quiver. She might have been eight years old all over again—this was like the day she found out she wasn't invited to Betsy Mc-

Donald's birthday party. Only now it was Paul doing the excluding. He and this important woman of his were going out to have the time of their lives while she stayed home in her lonely apartment, suffering from a serious bout of self-pity.

Gathering up her things, Cait thrust the papers into her briefcase with uncharacteristic negligence. She put on her coat, buttoned it quickly and wrapped the scarf around her neck as though it was a hangman's noose.

Joe was talking to the foreman of the crew who'd been unobtrusively working around the office all day. He hesitated when he saw her, halting the conversation. Cait's eyes briefly met his and although she tried to disguise how regretful she felt, she obviously did a poor job of it. He took a step toward her, but she raised her chin a notch, too proud to admit her feelings.

She had to walk directly past Joe on her way to the elevator and forced herself to look anywhere but at him.

The stocky foreman clearly wanted to resume the discussion, but Joe ignored him and stared at Cait instead, with narrowed, assessing eyes. She could feel his questioning concern as profoundly as if he'd touched her. When she could bear it no longer, she turned to face him, her lower lip quivering uncontrollably.

"Cait," he called out.

She raced for the elevator, fearing she'd burst into tears before she could make her grand exit. She didn't bother to respond, knowing that if she said anything she'd make an even greater fool of herself than usual. She wasn't even sure what had prompted her to say the atrocious things to Joe that she had. He wasn't the one who'd upset her, yet she'd unfairly taken her frustrations out on him.

She should have known it would be impossible to make a clean getaway. She almost ran through the office, past the reception desk, toward the elevator.

"Aren't you going to answer me?" Joe demanded, following on her heels like a Mississippi hound.

"No." She concentrated on the lighted numbers above the elevator, which moved with painstaking slowness. Three more floors and she could make good her escape.

"What's so insulting about inviting you to go Christmas-tree shopping?" he asked.

Close to weeping, she waved her free hand, hoping he'd understand that she was incapable of explaining just then. Her throat was clogged up and it hurt to breathe, let alone talk. Her eyes filled with tears, and everything started to blur.

"Tell me," he commanded a second time.

Cait gulped at the tightness in her throat. "Y-you wouldn't understand." Why, oh why, wouldn't that elevator hurry?

"Try me."

It was either give in and explain, or stand there and argue. The first choice was easier; frankly, Cait hadn't the energy to fight with him. Sighing deeply, she began, "It—it all started when I made up this folder of business articles for Paul..."

"I might have known Paul had something to do with this," Joe muttered under his breath.

"I spent hours putting it together for him, adding little comments, and...and... I don't know what I expected but it wasn't..."

"What happened? What did Paul do?"

Cait rubbed her eyes with the back of her hand. "If you're going to interrupt me, then I can't see any reason to explain."

"Boss?" the foreman called out, sounding impatient.

Just then the elevator arrived and the doors opened, revealing half a dozen men and women. They stared out at Cait and Joe while he blocked the entrance, gripping her by the elbow.

"Joseph," she hissed, "let me go!" Recognizing her advantage, she called out, "This man refuses to release my arm." If she expected a knight in shining armor to leap to her rescue, Cait was to be sorely disappointed. It was as if no one had heard her.

"Don't worry, folks, we're married." Joe charmed them with another of his lazy, lopsided grins.

"Boss?" the foreman pleaded again.

"Take the rest of the day off," Joe shouted. "Tell the crew to go out and buy Christmas gifts for their wives."

"You want me to do what?" the foreman shouted back.

Joe moved into the elevator with Cait.

"You heard me."

"Let me make sure I understand you right. You want the men to go Christmas shopping for their wives? I thought you just said we're on a tight schedule?"

"That's right," Joe said loudly as the elevator doors closed.

Cait had never felt more conspicuous in her life. Every eye was focused on her and Joe, and it was all she could do to keep her head held high.

When the tension became intolerable, Cait turned to face her fellow passengers. "We are not married," she announced.

"Yes, we are," Joe insisted. "She's simply forgotten."

"I did not forget our marriage and don't you dare tell them that cock-and-bull story about amnesia."

"But, darling—"

"Stop it right now, Joseph Rockwell! No one believes you. These people can take one look at us and determine that I'm the one who's telling the truth."

The elevator finally stopped on the ground floor, a fact for which Cait was deeply grateful. The doors glided open and two women stepped out first, but not before pausing to get a good appreciative look at Joe.

"Does she do this often?" one of the men asked, directing his question to Joe, his amusement obvious.

"Unfortunately, yes," he answered, chuckling as he tucked his hand under Cait's elbow and led her into the foyer. She tried to jerk her arm away, but he wouldn't allow it. "You see, I married a forgetful bride."

CHAPTER SEVEN

PACING THE CARPET in the living room, Cait nervously smoothed the front of her red satin dress, her heart pumping a mile a second while she waited impatiently for Joe to arrive. She'd spent hours preparing for this Christmas party, which was being held in Paul's home. Her stomach was in knots and had been for hours.

She, the mysterious woman Paul was dating, would surely be there. Cait would have her first opportunity to size up the competition. Cait had studied her reflection countless times, trying to be objective about her chances with Paul based on looks alone. The dress was gorgeous. Her hair flawless. Everything else was as perfect as she could make it.

The doorbell sounded and Cait hurried across the room, throwing open the door. "You know what you are, Joseph Rockwell?"

"Late?" he suggested.

Cait pretended not to hear him. "A bully," she furnished. "A badgering bully, no less. I'm sorry I ever agreed to let you take me to Paul's party. I don't know what I was thinking of."

"No doubt you were hoping to corner me under the mistletoe," he remarked, with a wink that implied he wouldn't be difficult to persuade.

"First you practically kidnap me into going Christmas-tree shopping with you," she raged on. "Then—"

"Come on, Cait, admit it, you had fun." He lounged indolently on her sofa while she got her coat and purse.

She hesitated, her mouth twitching with a smile. "Who'd ever believe that a man who bought his mother a rib roast and a case of cat food for Christmas last year would be so particular about a silly tree?" Joe had dragged her to no less than four lots, searching for the perfect tree.

"I took you to dinner afterward, didn't I?" he reminded her.

Cait nodded. She had to admit it: Joe had gone out of his way to help her forget her troubles. Although she'd made the tree-shopping expedition sound like a chore, he'd turned the evening into an enjoyable and, yes, a memorable one.

His good mood had been infectious and after a while she'd completely forgotten Paul was out with another woman—someone so special that his enthusiasm about her had overcome his normal restraint.

"I've changed my mind," Cait decided suddenly, clasping her hands over her stomach, which was in turmoil. "I don't want to go to this Christmas party, after all." The evening was already doomed. She couldn't possibly have a good time watching the man she loved entertain the woman *he* loved. Cait couldn't think of a single reason to expose herself to that kind of misery.

"Not go to the party?' Joe repeated. "But I thought you'd arranged your flight schedule just so you could."

"I did, but that was before." Cait stubbornly squared her shoulders and elevated her chin just enough to convince Joe she meant business. He might be able to bully her into going shopping with him for a Christmas tree, but this was something entirely different. "*She'll* be there," Cait added as an explanation.

"She?" Joe repeated slowly, burying his hands in his suit pockets. He was devilishly handsome in his dark blue suit and no doubt knew it. He was no less comfortable in tailored slacks than he was in dirty jeans.

A lock of thick hair slanted across his forehead; Cait managed—it was an effort—to resist brushing it back. An effort not because it disrupted his polished appearance, but because she had the strangest desire to run her fingers through his hair. Why she would think such a thing now was beyond her. She'd long since stopped trying to figure out her feelings for Joe. He was a friend and a confidant even if, at odd moments, he behaved like a lunatic. Just remembering some of the comments he'd made to embarrass her was enough to bring color to her cheeks.

"I'd think you'd want to meet her," Joe challenged. "That way you can size her up."

"I don't even want to know what she looks like," Cait countered sharply. She didn't need to. Cait already knew everything she cared to about Paul's hot date. "She's beautiful."

"So are you."

Cait gave a short, derisive laugh. She wasn't discounting her own homespun appeal. She was reasonably attractive, and never more so than this evening. Catching a glimpse of herself in the mirror, she was pleased to note how nice her hair looked, with the froth of curls circling her head. But she wasn't going to kid herself, either. Her allure wasn't extraordinary by any stretch of the imagination. Her eyes were a nice warm shade of brown, though, and her nose was kind of cute. Perky, Lindy had once called it. But none of that mattered. Measuring herself against Paul's sure-to-be-gorgeous, nameless date was like comparing bulky sweat socks with a silk stocking. She'd already spent hours picturing her as a classic beauty. . . tall. . . sophisticated.

"I've never taken you for a coward," Joe said in a flat tone as he headed toward the door.

Apparently he wasn't even going to argue with her. Cait almost wished he would, just so she could show him how strong her will was. Nothing he could say or do would convince her to attend this party. Besides, her feet hurt. She was wearing new heels and hadn't broken them in yet, and if she did go to the party, she'd probably be limping for days afterward.

"I'm not a coward," she insisted, schooling her face to remain as emotionless as possible. "All I'm doing is exercising a little common sense. Why depress myself over the holidays? This is the last time I'll see Paul before Christmas. I leave for Minnesota in the morning."

"Yes, I know." Joe frowned as he said it, hesitating before he opened her door. "You're sure about this?"

"Positive." She was mildly surprised Joe wasn't putting up more of a fuss. From past experience, she'd expected a full-scale verbal battle.

"The choice is yours of course," he granted, shrugging. "But if it was me, I know I'd spend the whole time I was away regretting it." He studied her when he'd finished, then smiled in a way Cait could only describe as crafty.

She groaned inwardly. If there was one thing that drove her crazy about Joe it was the way he made the most outrageous statements. Then every once in a while he'd say something so wise it caused her to doubt her own conclusions and beliefs. This was one of those times. He was right: if she didn't go to Paul's, she'd regret it. Since she was leaving the following day for Minnesota, she wouldn't be able to ask anyone about the party, either.

"Are you coming or not?" he demanded.

Grumbling under her breath, Cait let him help her on with her coat. "I'm coming, but I don't like it. Not one darn bit."

"You're going to do just fine."

"They probably said that to Joan of Arc."

CAIT CLUTCHED the punch glass in both hands, as though terrified someone might try to take it back. Standing next to the fireplace, with its garlanded mantel and cheerful blaze, she hadn't moved since they'd arrived a half hour earlier.

"Is *she* here yet?" she whispered to Lindy when her friend strolled past carrying in a tray of canapés.

"Who?"

"Paul's woman friend," Cait said pointedly. Both Joe and Lindy were beginning to exasperate her. "I've been standing here for the past thirty minutes hoping to catch a glimpse of her."

Lindy looked away. "I... I don't know if she's here or not."

"Stay with me, for heaven's sake," Cait requested, feeling shaky inside and out. Joe had deserted her almost as soon as they'd arrived. Oh, he'd stuck around long enough to bring her a cup of punch, but then he'd drifted away, leaving Cait to deal with the situation on her own. This was the very man who'd insisted she attend this Christmas party, claiming he'd be right by her side the entire evening in case she needed him.

"I'm helping Paul with the hors d'oeuvres," Lindy explained, "otherwise I'd be happy to stay and chat."

"See if you can find Joe for me, would you?" She'd do it herself, but her feet were killing her.

"Sure."

Once Lindy was gone, Cait scanned the crowded living room. Many of the guests were business associates and clients Paul had worked with over the years. Naturally everyone from the office was there, as well.

"You wanted to see me?" Joe asked, reaching her side.

"Thank you very much," she hissed, doing her best to sound sarcastic and keep a smile on her face at the same time.

"You're welcome." He leaned one elbow on the fireplace mantel and grinned boyishly at her. "Might I ask what you're thanking me for?"

"Don't play games with me, Joe. Not now, please." She shifted her weight from one foot to the other, drawing his attention to her shoes.

"Your feet hurt?" he asked, frowning.

"Walking across hot coals would be less painfúl than these stupid high heels."

"Then why did you wear them?"

"Because they go with the dress. Listen, would you mind very much if we got off the subject of my shoes and discussed the matter at hand?"

"Which is?"

Joe was being as obtuse as Lindy had been. Surely he was doing it deliberately, just to get a rise out of her. Well, it was working.

"Did you see her?" she asked with exaggerated patience.

"Not yet," he whispered back as though they were exchanging top-secret information. "She doesn't seem to have arrived."

"Have you talked to Paul?"

"No. Have you?"

"Not really." Paul had greeted them at the door, but other than that, Cait hadn't had a chance to do anything but watch him mingle with his guests. The day at the office hadn't been any help, either. Paul had breezed in and out without giving Cait more than a friendly wave. Since they hadn't exchanged a single word, it was impossible for her to determine how his date had gone.

It must have been a busy day for Lindy, as well, because Cait hadn't had a chance to talk to her, either. They'd met on their way out the door late in the afternoon and Lindy had hurried past, muttering that she'd see Cait at Paul's party.

"I think I'll go help Lindy with the hors d'oeuvres," Cait said now. "Do you want me to get you anything?"

"Nothing, thanks." He was grinning as he strolled away, leaving Cait to wonder what he found so amusing.

Cait limped into the kitchen, leaving the polished wooden door swinging in her wake. She stopped abruptly when she encountered Paul and Lindy in the middle of a heated discussion.

"Oh, sorry," Cait apologized automatically.

Paul's gaze darted to Cait's. "No problem," he said pointedly. "I was just leaving." He stalked past her, shoving the door open with the palm of his hand. Once again the door swung back and forth.

"What was that all about?" Cait wanted to know.

Lindy continued transferring the small cheese-dotted crackers from the cookie sheet onto the serving platter. "Nothing."

"It sounded as if you and Paul were arguing."

Lindy straightened and bit her lip. She avoided looking at Cait, concentrating on her task as if it was of vital importance to properly arrange the crackers on the plate.

"You were arguing, weren't you?" Cait pressed.

"Yes."

As far as she knew, Lindy and Paul had always gotten along. The fact that they were at odds with each other surprised her. "About what?"

"I—I gave Paul my two-week notice this afternoon."

Cait was so shocked, she pulled out a kitchen chair and sank down on it. "You did what?" Removing her high heels, she massaged her pinched toes.

"You heard me."

"But why? Good grief, Lindy, you never said a word to anyone. Not even me. The least you could have done was talk to me about it first." No wonder Paul was angry. If Lindy left, it would mean bringing in someone new when the office was short-staffed. With Cait and a number of other people away for the holidays, the place would be a madhouse.

"Did you receive an offer you couldn't refuse?" Cait hadn't had any idea her friend was unhappy at Webster, Rodale and Missen. That didn't shock her nearly as much as Lindy's remaining tight-lipped about it all.

"It wasn't exactly an offer—but it was something like that," Lindy replied vaguely. With that, she set aside the cookie sheet, smiled at Cait and then carried the platter into the living room.

For the past couple of weeks Cait had noticed that something was troubling her friend. It hadn't been anything she could readily name. Just that Lindy hadn't been her usual high-spirited self. Cait had meant to ask her about it, but she'd been so busy herself, so involved with her own problems, that she'd never brought it up.

She was still sitting there rubbing her feet when Joe sauntered into the kitchen, nibbling on a cheese cracker. "I thought I'd find you in here." He pulled out the chair across from her and sat down.

"Has she arrived yet?"

"Apparently so."

Cait dropped her foot and frantically worked the shoe back and forth until she'd managed to squeeze her toes inside. Then she forced her other foot into its shoe. "Well, for heaven's sake, why didn't you say something sooner?" she chastised. She straightened, ran her hands down the satin skirt and drew a shaky breath. "How do I look?"

"Like your feet hurt."

She sent him a scalding look. "Thank you very much," she muttered sarcastically. Hobbling to the door, she opened it a crack and peeked out, hoping to catch sight of the mystery woman. From what she could see, there weren't any new arrivals.

"What does she look like?" Cait demanded and whirled around to discover Joe standing directly behind her. She nearly collided with him and gave a small cry of surprise. Joe caught her by the shoulders to keep her from stumbling. Eager to question him about Paul's date, she didn't take the time to analyze why her heartrate soared when his hands made contact with her bare skin.

"What does she look like?" Cait demanded again.

"I don't know," Joe returned flippantly.

"What do you mean you don't know? You just said she'd arrived."

"Unfortunately she doesn't have a tattoo across her forehead announcing that she's the woman Paul's dating."

"Then how do you know she's here?" If Joe was playing games with her, she'd make damn sure he'd regret it. Her love for Paul was no joking matter.

"It's more a feeling I have."

"You had me stuff my feet back into these shoes for a stupid feeling?" It was all she could do not to slap him silly. "You are no friend of mine, Joseph Rockwell. No friend whatsoever." Having said that, she limped back into the living room.

Obviously unscathed by her remark, Joe strolled out of the kitchen behind her. He walked over to the tray of canapés and helped himself to three or four while Cait did her best to ignore him.

Since the punch bowl was close by, she poured herself a second glass. The taste was sweet and cold, but Cait noticed that she felt a bit light-headed afterward. Potent drinks didn't sit well on an empty stomach, so she scooped up a handful of mixed nuts.

"I remember a time when you used to line up all the Spanish peanuts and eat those first," Joe said from behind her. "Then it was the hazelnuts, followed by the—"

"Almonds." Leave it to him to bring up her foolish past. "I haven't done that since I was—"

"Twenty," he guessed.

"Twenty-five," she corrected.

Joe laughed, and despite her aching feet and the certainty that she should never have come to this party, Cait laughed, too.

Refilling her punch glass, she downed it all in a single drink. Once more, it tasted cool and refreshing.

"Cait," Joe warned, "how much punch have you had?"

"Not enough." She filled the crystal cup a third time—or was it the fourth?—squared her shoulders and gulped it down. When she'd finished, she wiped the back of her hand across her mouth and smiled bravely.

"Are you purposely trying to get drunk?" he demanded.

"No." She reached for another handful of nuts. "All I'm looking for is a little courage."

"Courage?"

"Yes," she said with a sigh. "The way I figure it..." She paused, smiling giddily, then twisted around in a full circle. "There *is* some mistletoe here, isn't there?"

"I think so," Joe said, frowning. "What makes you ask?"

"I'm going to kiss Paul," she announced proudly. "All I have to do is wait until he strolls past. Then I'll grab him by the hand, wish him a merry Christmas and give him a kiss he won't soon forget." If the fantasy fulfilled itself, Paul would then realize he'd met the woman of his dreams, and then and there propose marriage....

"What is kissing Paul supposed to prove?"

She returned to reality. "Well, this is where you come in. I want you to look around and watch the faces of the other women. If any one of them shows signs of jealousy, then we'll know who it is."

"I'm not sure this plan of yours will work."

"It's better than trusting those feelings of yours," she countered.

She spied the mistletoe hanging from the archway between the formal dining room and the living room. Slouched against the wall, hands tucked behind her back, Cait waited patiently for Paul to stroll past.

Ten minutes passed or maybe it was fifteen—Cait couldn't tell. Yawning, she covered her mouth. "I think we should leave," Joe suggested as he casually walked by. "You're ready to drop on your feet."

"I haven't kissed Paul yet," she reminded him.

"He seems to be involved in a lengthy discussion. This could take a while."

"I'm in no hurry." Her throat felt unusually dry. She would have preferred something nonalcoholic, but the only drink nearby was the punch.

"Cait," Joe warned when he saw her helping herself to yet another glass.

"Don't worry, I know what I'm doing."

"So did the captain of the *Titanic.*"

"Don't get cute with me, Joseph Rockwell. I'm in no mood to deal with someone amusing." Finding herself hilariously funny, she smothered a round of giggles.

"Oh, no," Joe groaned. "I was afraid of this."

"Afraid of what?"

"You're drunk!"

She gave him a sour look. "That's ridiculous. All I had is four little, bitty glasses of punch." To prove she knew exactly what she was doing, she held up three fingers, recognized her mistake and promptly corrected herself. At least she tried to do it promptly, figuring out how many fingers equaled four seemed to take an inordinate amount of time. She finally held up two from each hand.

Expelling her breath, she leaned back against the wall and closed her eyes. That was her second mistake. The world took a sharp and unexpected nosedive. Snapping open her eyes, Cait looked to Joe as the anchor that would keep her afloat. He must have read the panic in her expression because he walked over to her and slowly shook his head.

"That does it, Miss Singapore Sling. I'm getting you out of here."

"But I haven't been under the mistletoe yet."

"If you want anyone to kiss you, it'll be me."

The offer sounded tempting, but it was her stubborn boss Cait wanted to kiss, not Joe. "I'd rather dance with you."

"Unfortunately there isn't any music at the moment."

"You need music to dance?" It sounded like the saddest thing she'd ever heard, and her bottom lip started to tremble at the tragedy of it all. "Oh, dear, Joe," she whispered, placing both hands on the sides of her head. "I think you might be right. The liquor seems to be affecting me...."

"It's that bad, is it?"

"Uh, yes... The whole room's just started to pitch and heave. We're not having an earthquake, are we?"

"No." His hand was on her forearm, guiding her toward the front door.

"Wait," she said dramatically, raising her index finger. "I have a coat."

"I know. Wait here and I'll get it for you." He seemed worried about leaving her. Cait smiled at him, trying to reassure him she'd be perfectly fine, but she seemed unable to keep her balance. He urged her against the wall, stepped back a couple of paces as though he expected her to slip sideways, then hurriedly located her coat.

"What's wrong?" he asked when he returned.

"What makes you think anything's wrong?"

"Other than the fact that you're crying?"

"My feet hurt."

Joe rolled his eyes. "Why did you wear those stupid shoes in the first place?"

"I already told you," she whimpered. "Don't be mad at me." She held out her arms to him, needing his comfort. "Would you carry me to the car?"

Joe hesitated. "You want me to carry you?" He sounded as though it was a task of Herculean proportions.

"I can't walk." She'd taken the shoes off, and it would take God's own army to get them back on. She couldn't very well traipse outside in her stocking feet.

"If I carry you, we'd better find another way out of the house."

"All right." She agreed just to prove what an amicable person she actually was. When she was a child, she'd been a pest, but she wasn't anymore and she wanted to be sure Joe understood that.

Grasping Cait's hand, he led her into the kitchen.

"Don't you think we should make our farewells?" she asked. It seemed the polite thing to do.

"No," he answered sharply. "With the mood you're in you're likely to throw yourself in Paul's arms and demand that he make mad passionate love to you there on the spot."

Cait's face went fire-engine red. "That's ridiculous."

Joe mumbled something she couldn't hear while he lifted her hand and slipped one arm, then the other, into the satin-lined sleeves of her full-length coat.

When he'd finished, Cait climbed on top of the kitchen chair, stretching out her arms to him. Joe stared at her as though she'd suddenly turned into a werewolf.

"What are you doing now?" he demanded in an exasperated voice.

"You're going to carry me, aren't you?"

"I was considering it."

"I want a piggyback ride. You gave Betsy McDonald a piggyback ride once and not me."

"Cait," Joe groaned. He jerked his fingers through his hair, and offered her his hand, wanting her to climb down from the chair. "Get down before you fall. Good Lord, I swear you'd try the patience of a saint."

"I want you to carry me piggyback," she insisted. "Oh, please, Joe. My toes hurt so bad."

Once again her hero grumbled under his breath. She couldn't make out everything he said, but what she did hear was enough to curl her hair. With obvious reluctance, he walked to the chair, and giving a sigh of pure bliss, Cait wrapped her arms around his neck and hugged his lean hips with her legs. She laid her head on his shoulder and sighed again.

Still grumbling, Joe moved toward the back door.

Just then the kitchen door opened and Paul and Lindy walked in. Lindy gasped. Paul just stared.

"It's all right," Cait was quick to assure them. "Really it is. I was waiting under the mistletoe and you—"

"She downed four glasses of punch nonstop," Joe inserted before Cait could admit she'd been waiting there for Paul.

"Do you need any help?" Paul asked.

"None, thanks," Joe returned. "There's nothing to worry about."

"But..." Lindy looked concerned.

"She ain't heavy," Joe teased. "She's my wife."

THE PHONE RANG, waking Cait from a sound sleep. Her head began throbbing in time to the painful noise and she groped for the telephone receiver.

"Hello," she barked, instantly regretting that she'd spoken loudly.

"How are you feeling?" Joe asked.

"About like you'd expect," she whispered, keeping her eyes closed and gently massaging one temple. It felt as though tiny men had taken up residence in her head and were pounding away, hoping to attract her attention.

"What time does your flight leave?" he asked.

"It's okay. I'm not scheduled to leave until afternoon."

"It is afternoon."

Her eyes flew open. "What?"

"Do you still need me to take you to the airport?"

"Yes...please." She tossed aside the covers and reached for her clock, stunned to realize Joe was right. "I'm already packed. I'll be dressed by the time you arrive. Oh, thank goodness you phoned."

Cait didn't have time to listen to the pounding of the tiny men in her head. She showered and dressed in record time, swallowed a cup of coffee and a couple of aspirin, and was just shrugging into her coat when Joe arrived at the door.

She let him in, despite the suspiciously wide grin he wore.

"What's so amusing?"

"What makes you think I'm amused?" He strolled into the room, hands behind his back, as if he owned the place.

"Joe, we don't have time for your little games. Come on, or I'm going to miss my plane. What's with you, anyway?"

"Nothing." He circled her living room, still wearing that silly grin. "I don't suppose you realize it, but liquor has a peculiar effect on you."

Cait stiffened. "It does?" She remembered most of the party with great clarity. Good thing Joe had taken her home when he had.

"Liquor loosens your tongue."

"So?" She picked up two shopping bags filled with wrapped packages, leaving the lone suitcase for him. "Did I say anything of interest?"

"Oh my, yes."

"Joe," she groaned, glancing quickly at her watch. They needed to get moving if she was to catch her flight. "Discount whatever I said—I'm sure I didn't mean it. If I insulted you, I apologize. If I told any family secrets, kindly forget I mentioned them."

He strolled to her side and tucked his finger under her chin. "This was a secret all right," he informed her in a lazy drawl.

"Are you sure it's true?"

"Relatively sure."

"What did I do? Declare undying love for you? Because if I did—"

"No, no, nothing like that."

"Just how long do you intend to torment me like this?" She was rapidly losing interest in his little game.

"Not much longer." He looked exceptionally pleased with himself. "So Martin's a minister now. Funny you never thought to mention that before."

"Ah..." Cait set aside the two bags and lowered herself to the sofa. So he'd found out. Worse, she'd been the one to tell him.

"That may well have some interesting ramifications, my dear. Have you ever stopped to think about them?"

CHAPTER EIGHT

"THIS IS EXACTLY why I didn't tell you about Martin," Cait informed Joe as he tossed her suitcase into the back seat of his car. She checked her watch again and groaned. They had barely an hour and a half before her flight was scheduled to leave. Cait was never late. Never—at least not when it was her own fault.

"It seems to me," Joe continued, his face deadpan, "there could very well be some legal grounds to our marriage."

Joe was saying that just to annoy her, and unfortunately it was working. "I've never heard anything more ridiculous in my life."

"Think about it, Cait," he said, ignoring her protest. "We could be celebrating our anniversary this spring. How many years is it now? Eighteen? My, how the years fly."

"Listen, Joe, I don't find this amusing." Again she glanced at her watch. If only she hadn't slept so late. Never again would she sample Christmas punch. Briefly she wondered what else she'd said to Joe, then decided it was better not to know.

"I heard a news report of a three-car pileup on the freeway, so we'd better take the side streets."

"Just hurry," Cait urged in an anxious voice.

"I'll do the best I can," Joe said, "but worrying about it isn't going to get us there any faster."

She glared at him. She couldn't help it. He wasn't the one who'd been planning this trip for months. If she missed this flight, her nephews and niece wouldn't have their Christmas presents from their Auntie Cait. Nor would she share in the family traditions that were so much a part of her Christmas. It was vital she get to the airport on time.

Everyone else had apparently heard about the accident on the freeway, too, and the downtown area was crowded with the overflow. Cait and Joe were delayed at every intersection and twice were forced to sit through two changes of the traffic signal.

Cait was growing more panicky by the moment. She just had to make this flight. But it almost seemed that she'd get to the airport faster if she simply jumped out of the car and ran there.

Joe stopped for another red light, but when the signal turned green, they still couldn't move—a delivery truck in front of them had stalled. Furious, Cait rolled down the window and stuck out her head. "Listen here, buster, get this show on the road," she shouted at the top of her lungs.

Her head was pounding and she prayed the aspirin would soon take affect.

"Quite the Christmas spirit," Joe muttered dryly under his breath.

"I can't help it. I have to catch this plane."

"You'll be there in plenty of time."

"At this rate we won't make it to Sea-Tac Airport before Easter!"

"Relax, will you?" Joe suggested gently. He turned on the radio and a medley of Christmas carols filled the air. Normally the music would have had a calming effect on Cait, but she was suffering from a hangover, depression and severe anxiety, all at the same time. Her fingernails found their way into her mouth.

Suddenly she straightened. "Darn! I forgot to give you your Christmas gift. I left it at home."

"Don't worry about it."

"I didn't get you a gag gift the way I said." Actually she was pleased with the book she'd managed to find—an attractive coffee-table volume about the history of baseball.

Cait waited for Joe to mention *her* gift. Surely he'd bought her one. At least she fervently hoped he had, otherwise she'd feel like a fool. Though, admittedly, that was a feeling she'd grown accustomed to in the past few weeks.

"I think we might be able to get back on the freeway here," Joe said, as he made a sharp lefthand turn. They crossed the overpass, and from their vantage point, Cait could see that the freeway was unclogged and running smoothly.

"Thank God," she whispered, relaxing against the back of the thickly cushioned seat as Joe drove quickly ahead.

Her chauffeur chuckled. "I seem to remember you lecturing me—"

"I never lecture," she said testily. "I may have a strong opinion on certain subjects, but let me assure you, I never lecture."

"You were right, though. The streets of Bethlehem must have been crowded and bustling with activity at the time of that first Christmas. I can see it all now, can't you? A rug dealer is held up by a shepherd driving his flock through the middle of town."

Cait smiled for the first time that morning, because she could easily picture the scene Joe was describing.

"Then some furious woman, impatient to make it to the local camel merchant on time, sticks her nose in the middle of everything and shouts at the rug dealer to get his show on the road." He paused to chuckle at his own wit. "I'm convinced she wouldn't have been so testy except that she was suffering from one whopper of a hangover."

"Very funny," Cait grumbled, smiling despite herself.

He took the exit for the airport and Cait was gratified to note that her flight wasn't scheduled to leave for another thirty minutes. She was cutting it close, closer than she ever had before, but she'd confirmed her ticket two days earlier and had already been assigned her seat.

Joe pulled up at the drop-off point for her airline and gave her suitcase to a skycap while Cait rummaged around in her purse for her ticket.

"I suppose this is goodbye for now," he said with an endearingly crooked grin that sent her pulses racing.

"I'll be back in less than two weeks," she reminded him, trying to keep her tone light and casual.

"You'll phone once you arrive?"

She nodded. For all her earlier panic, Cait now felt oddly unwilling to part company with Joe. She should be rushing through the airport to her gate assignment, but she lingered, her heart overflowing with emotions she couldn't name.

"Have a safe trip," he said quietly.

"I will. Thanks so much . . . for everything."

"You're welcome." His expression sobered and the ever-ready mirth drained from his eyes. Cait wasn't sure who moved first. All she knew was that she was in Joe's arms, his thumb caressing the softness of her cheek as they gazed hungrily into each other's eyes.

Slowly he leaned forward to kiss her. Cait's eyes drifted shut as his mouth met hers.

Joe's kiss was heart-stoppingly tender. The noise and activity around them seemed to fade into the distance. Cait could feel herself dissolving. She moaned and arched closer, not wanting to leave the protective haven of his arms. Joe shuddered and hugged her tight, as if he, too, found it difficult to part.

"Merry Christmas, love," he whispered, releasing her with a reluctance that made her heart sing.

"Merry Christmas," she echoed, but she didn't move.

Joe gave her the gentlest of nudges. "You'd better hurry, Cait."

"Oh, right," she said, momentarily forgetting why she was at the airport. Reaching for the bags filled with gaily wrapped Christmas packages, she took two steps backward. "I'll phone when I arrive."

"Do. I'll be waiting to hear from you." He thrust his hands into his pockets and Cait had the distinct impression he did it to stop himself from reaching out for her again. The thought was a romantic one, a certainty straight from her heart.

Her heart... Her heart was full of feeling for Joe. More than she'd ever realized. He'd dominated her life these past few weeks—taking her to dinner, bribing his way back into her good graces with a pizza, taking her on a Christmas shopping expedition, escorting her to Paul's party. Joe had become her whole world. Joe, not Paul. Joe.

Given no other choice, Cait abruptly turned and hurried into the airport, through the security check and down the concourse to the proper gate.

The flight had already been called and only a handful of passengers had yet to board. Several were making lingering farewells to loved ones.

Cait dashed to the ticket counter to check in. A young soldier stood just ahead of her. "But you don't understand," the tall marine was saying to the airline employee. "I booked this flight over a month ago. I've got to be on that plane!"

"I couldn't be more sorry," the woman apologized, her dark eyes filled with regret. "This sort of thing happens, especially during holidays, but your ticket's for standby. I wish I could do something for you, but there isn't a single seat available."

"But I haven't seen my family in over a year. My Uncle Harvey is driving from Duluth to visit. He was in the marines, too. My mom's been baking for three weeks. Don't you see? I can't disappoint them now!"

Cait watched as the ticket agent rechecked her computer. "If I could magically create a seat for you, I would," she said sympathetically. "But there just isn't one."

"But when I bought the ticket, the woman told me I wouldn't have a problem getting on the flight. She said there're always no-shows. She sounded so sure."

"I couldn't be more sorry," the agent repeated, looking past the young marine to Cait.

"All right," he said, forcefully expelling his breath. "When's the next flight with available space? Any flight within a hundred miles of Minneapolis. I'll walk the rest of the way if I have to."

Once again, the woman consulted her computer. "We have space available the evening of the twenty-sixth."

"The twenty-sixth!" the young man shouted. "But that's after Christmas and eats up nearly all my leave. I'd be home less than a week."

"May I help you?" the airline employee said to Cait. She looked almost as unhappy as the marine, but apparently there wasn't anything she could do to help him.

Cait stepped forward and handed the woman her ticket. The soldier gazed at it longingly, then moved dejectedly from the counter and lowered himself into one of the molded plastic chairs.

Cait hesitated, remembering how she'd stuck her head out the window of Joe's truck that morning and shouted impatiently at the truck driver who was holding up traffic. A conversation she'd had with Joe earlier returned to haunt her. She'd argued that Christmas was a time filled with love and good cheer, the one time of year that brought out the very best in everyone. And sometimes, Joe had insisted, the very worst.

"Since you already have your seat assignment, you may board the flight now."

Cait grabbed the ticket with both hands, the urge to hurry nearly overwhelming her. Yet she hesitated.

"Excuse me," Cait said, drawing a breath and making her decision. She approached the soldier. He seemed impossibly young now that she had a good look at him. No more than eighteen, maybe nineteen. He'd probably joined the service right out of high school. His hair was cropped close to his head and his combat boots were so shiny Cait could see her reflection in them.

The marine glanced up at her, his face heavy with defeat. "Yes?"

"Did I hear you say you needed a ticket for this plane?"

"I have a ticket, ma'am. But it's standby and there aren't any seats."

"Here," she said, giving him her ticket. "Take mine."

The way his face lit up was enough to blot out her own disappointment at missing Christmas with Martin and her sister-in-law. The kids. Her mother... "My family's in Minneapolis, too, but I was there this summer."

"Ma'am, I can't let you do this."

"Don't cheat me out of the pleasure."

The last call for their flight was announced. The marine stood, his eyes wide with disbelief. "I insist," Cait said, her throat growing thick. "Here," she handed him the two bags full of gifts for her nephews and nieces. "There'll be a man waiting on the other end. A tall minister—he'll have on a collar. Give him these. I'll phone so he'll know to look for you."

"But, ma'am—"

"We don't have time to argue. Just do it."

"Thank you...I can't believe you're doing this." He reached inside his jacket and gave her his ticket. "Here. At least you'll be able to get a refund."

Cait smiled and nodded. Impulsively the marine hugged her, then swinging his duffel bag over his shoulder, he picked up the two bags of gifts and jogged down the ramp.

Cait waited for a couple of minutes, then wiped the tears from her eyes. She wasn't completely sure why she was crying. She'd never felt better in her life.

IT WAS AROUND SIX when she awoke. The apartment was dark and silent. Sighing, she picked up the phone, dragged it onto the bed with her and punched out Joe's number.

He answered on the first ring, as if he'd been waiting for her call. "How was the flight?" he asked immediately.

"I wouldn't know. I wasn't on it."

"You missed the plane!" he shouted incredulously. "But you were there in plenty of time."

"I know. It's a long story, but basically, I gave my seat to someone who needed it more than I did." She smiled dreamily, remembering how the young marine's face had lit up. "I'll tell you about it sometime."

"Where are you now?"

"Home."

He exhaled sharply, then said, "I'll be over in fifteen minutes."

Actually it took him twelve. By then Cait had brewed a pot of coffee and made herself a peanut-butter-and-jelly sandwich. She hadn't eaten all day and was starved. She'd just finished the sandwich when Joe arrived.

"What about your luggage?" Joe asked, looking concerned. He didn't give her a chance to respond. "Exactly what do you mean, you gave your seat away?"

Cait explained as best she could. Even now she found herself surprised by her actions. Cait rarely behaved spontaneously. But something about that young soldier had reached deep within her heart and she'd reacted instinctively.

"The airline is sending my suitcase back to Seattle on the next available flight, so there's no need to worry," Cait explained. "I talked to Martin, who was quick to tell me the Lord would reward my generosity."

"Are you going to catch a later flight, then?" Joe asked. He helped himself to a cup of coffee and pulled out the chair across from hers.

"There aren't any seats," Cait said. She leaned back, yawning, and covered her mouth. Why she should be so tired after sleeping away most of the afternoon was beyond her. "Besides, the office is short-staffed. Lindy gave Paul her notice and a trainee is coming in, which makes everything even more difficult. They can use me."

Joe frowned. "Giving up your vacation is one way to impress Paul."

Words of explanation crowded on the end of her tongue. She realized Joe wasn't insulting her; he was only stating a fact. What he didn't understand was that Cait hadn't thought of Paul once the entire day. Her staying or leaving had absolutely nothing to do with him.

If she'd been thinking of anyone, it was Joe. She knew now that giving up her seat to the marine hadn't been entirely unselfish. When Joe kissed her goodbye, her heart had started telegraphing messages she had yet to fully decode. The plain and honest truth was that she hadn't wanted to leave him. It was as if she really did belong to him....

That perception had been with her from the moment they'd parted at the airport. It had followed her in the taxi on the ride back to the apartment. Joe was the last person she thought of when she'd fallen asleep, and the first person she remembered when she awoke.

It was the most amazing thing.

"What are you going to do for Christmas?" Joe asked, still frowning into his coffee cup. For someone who'd seemed downright regretful that she was flying halfway across the country, he didn't seem all that pleased to be sharing her company now.

"I...haven't decided yet. I suppose I'll spend a quiet day by myself." She'd wake up late, indulge in a lazy scented bath, find something sinful for breakfast. Ice cream, maybe.

Then she'd paint her toenails and settle down with a good book. The day would be lonely, true, but certainly not wasted.

"It'll be anything but quiet," Joe challenged.

"Oh?"

"You'll be spending it with me and my family."

"THIS IS THE FIRST TIME Joe has ever brought a girl to join us for Christmas," Virginia Rockwell said as she set a large tray of freshly baked cinnamon rolls in the center of the huge kitchen table. She wiped her hands clean on the apron that was secured around her thick waist.

Cait felt she should explain. She was a little uncomfortable arriving unannounced with Joe this way. "Joe and I are just friends."

Mrs. Rockwell shook her head, which set the white curls bobbing. "I saw my son's eyes when he brought you into the house." She grinned knowingly. "I remember you from the old neighborhood, with your starched dresses and the pigtails with those bright pink ribbons. You were a pretty girl then and you're even prettier now."

"The starched dresses were me all right," Cait confirmed. She'd been the only girl for blocks around who always wore dresses to school.

Joe's mother chuckled again. "I remember the sensation you caused in the neighborhood when you revealed that Joe had kissed you." She chuckled, her eyes shining. "His father and I got quite a kick out of that. I still remember how furious Joe was when he learned his secret was out."

"I only told one person," Cait protested. But Betsy had told plenty of others, and the news had spread with alarming speed. However, Cait figured she'd since paid for her sins tenfold. Joe had made sure of that in the past few weeks.

"It's so good to see you again, Caitlin. When we've got a minute I want you to sit down and tell me all about your mother. We lost contact years ago, but I always thought she was a darling."

"I think so, too," Cait agreed, carrying a platter of scrambled eggs to the table. She did miss being with her family, but Joe's mother made it almost as good as being home. "I know that's how Mom feels about you, too. She'll want to thank you for being kind enough to invite me into your home for Christmas."

"I wouldn't have it any other way."

"I know." She glanced into the other room where Joe was sitting with his brother and sister-in-law. Her heart throbbed at the sight of him with his family. But these newfound feelings for Joe left her at a complete loss. What she'd told Mrs. Rockwell was true. Joe was her friend. The very best friend she'd ever had. She was grateful for everything he'd done for her since they'd chanced upon each other, just weeks ago, really. But their friendship was developing into something much stronger. If only she didn't feel so...so ardent about Paul. If only she didn't feel so confused!

Joe laughed at something one of his nephews said and Cait couldn't help smiling. She loved the sound of his laughter. It was vigorous and robust and lively—just like his personality.

"Joe says you're working as a stockbroker right here in Seattle."

"Yes. I've been with Webster, Rodale and Missen for over a year now. My degree was in accounting but—"

"Accounting?" Mrs. Rockwell nodded approvingly. "My Joe has his own accountant now. Good thing, too. His books were in a terrible mess. He's a builder, not a pencil pusher, that boy."

"Are you telling tales on me, Mom?" Joe asked as he sauntered into the kitchen. He picked up a piece of bacon and bit off the end. "When are we going to open the gifts? The kids are getting restless."

"The kids, nothing. You're the one who's eager to tear into those packages," his mother admonished. "We'll open them after breakfast, the way we do every Christmas."

Joe winked at Cait and disappeared into the living room once more.

Mrs. Rockwell watched her son affectionately. "Last year he shows up on my doorstep bright and early Christmas morning needing gift wrap. Then, once he's got all his presents wrapped, he walks into my kitchen—" her face crinkled in a wide grin "—and he sticks all those presents in my refrigerator." She chuckled at the memory. "For his brother, he bought two canned hams and three gallons of ice cream. For me it was canned cat food and a couple of rib roasts."

Breakfast was a bustling affair, with Joe's younger brother, his wife and their children gathered around the table. Joe sat next to Cait and held her hand while his mother offered the blessing. Although she wasn't home with her own family, Cait felt she had a good deal for which to be thankful.

Conversation was pleasant and relaxed, but foremost on the children's minds was opening the gifts. The table was cleared and the dishes washed in record time.

Cait sat beside Joe, holding a cup of coffee, as the oldest grandchild gave out the presents. Christmas music played softly in the background as the children tore into their packages. The youngest, a two-year-old girl, was more interested in the box than in the gift itself.

When Joe came to the square package Cait had given him, he shook it enthusiastically.

"Be careful, it might break," she warned, knowing there was no chance of that happening.

Carefully he removed the bows, then slowly unwrapped his gift. Cait watched expectantly as he lifted the book from the layers of bright paper. "A book on baseball?"

Cait nodded, smiling. "As I recall, you used to collect baseball cards."

"I ended up trading away my two favorites."

"I'm sure it was for a very good reason."

"Of course."

Their eyes held until it became apparent that everyone in the room was watching them. Cait glanced self-consciously away.

Joe cleared his throat. "This is a great gift, Cait. Thank you, very much."

"You're welcome very much."

He leaned over and kissed her as if it was the most natural thing in the world. It felt right, their kiss. If anything Cait was sorry to stop at one.

"Surely you have something for Cait," Virginia Rockwell prompted her son.

"Of course I do."

"He's probably keeping it in the refrigerator," Cait suggested, to the delight of Joe's family.

"Oh, ye of little faith," he said, removing a box from his shirt pocket.

"I recognize that paper," Sally, Joe's sister-in-law, murmured to Cait. "It's from Stanley's."

Cait's eyes widened at the name of an expensive local jewelry store. "Joe?"

"Go ahead and open it," he urged.

Cait did as he suggested, hands fumbling in her eagerness. She slipped off the ribbon and peeled away the gold textured wrap to reveal a white jeweler's box. It contained a second box, a small black velvet one, which she opened very slowly, She gasped at the lovely cameo brooch inside.

"Oh, Joe," she whispered. It was a lovely piece carved in onyx and overlaid with ivory. She'd longed for a cameo, a really nice one, for years and wondered how Joe could possibly have known.

"You gonna kiss Uncle Joe?" his nephew asked, "'cause if you are, I'm hiding my eyes."

"Of course she's going to kiss me," Joe answered for her. "Only she can do it later when there aren't so many curious people watching her." He glanced swiftly at his mother. "Just the way Mom used to thank Dad for her Christmas gift. Isn't that right, Mom?"

"I'm sure Cait... will," Virginia answered, clearly flustered. She patted her hand against the side of her head as though she feared the pins had fallen from her hair, her gaze skirting around the room.

Cait didn't blame the older woman for being embarrassed, but one look at the cameo and she was willing to forgive him anything.

The day flew past. After the gifts were opened—with everyone exclaiming in surprised delight over the gifts Joe had bought, with Cait's help—the family gathered around the piano. Mrs. Rockwell played as they sang a variety of Christmas carols, their voices loud and cheerful. Joe's father had died several years earlier, but often throughout the day he was mentioned with affection and love. Cait hadn't known Joe's father well. She barely remembered his mother, but the family obviously felt Andrew Rockwell's presence far more than his absence on this festive day.

Joe drove Cait back to her apartment late that night. Mrs. Rockwell had insisted on sending a plate of cookies and candy home with her, and Cait swore it was enough goodies to last her a month of Sundays. Now she felt sleepy and warm; leaning her head against the seat, she closed her eyes.

"We're here," Joe whispered close to her ear.

Reluctantly Cait opened her eyes and sighed. "I had such a wonderful day. Thank you, Joe." She couldn't quite stifle a yawn as she reached for the door handle, thinking longingly of bed.

"That's it?" He sounded disappointed.

"What do you mean, that's it?"

"I seem to remember a certain promise you made this morning."

Cait frowned, not sure she understood what he meant. "When?"

"When we were opening the gifts," he reminded her.

"Oh," Cait said, straightening. "You mean when I opened your gift to me and saw the brooch."

Joe nodded with slow, exaggerated emphasis. "Right. Now do you remember?"

"Of course." The kiss. He planned to claim the kiss she'd promised him. She brushed her mouth quickly over his and grinned. "There."

"If that's the best you can do, you should have kissed me in front of Charlie."

"You're faulting my kissing ability?"

"Charlie's dog gives better kisses than that."

Cait felt more than a little insulted. "Is this a challenge, Joseph Rockwell?"

"Yes," he returned archly. "You're darn right it is."

"All right, then you're on." She set the plate of cookies aside, slid over on the wide seat and slipped her arms around Joe's neck. Next she wove her fingers into his thick hair.

"This is more like it," Joe murmured contentedly.

Cait paused. She wasn't entirely sure why. Perhaps it was because she'd suddenly lost all interest in making fun out of something that had always been so wonderful between them.

Joe's eyes met hers, and the laughter and fun seemed to empty out of them. Slowly he expelled his breath and brushed his lips along her jaw. The warmth of his breath was exciting as his mouth skimmed toward her temple. His arms closed around her waist and pulled her tight against him.

Impatiently he began to kiss her, introducing her to a world of warm, thrilling sensations. His moist mouth then explored the curve of her neck. It felt so good that Cait closed her eyes and experienced a curious weightlessness she'd never known—a heightened awareness of physical longing.

"Oh, Cait..." He broke away from her, his breathing labored and heavy. She knew instinctively that he wanted to say more, but he changed his mind and buried his face in her hair, exhaling sharply.

"How am I doing?" she whispered once she found her voice.

"Just fine."

"Are you ready to retract your statement?"

He hesitated. "I don't know. Convince me again." So she did, her kiss moist and gentle, her heart fluttering hard against her ribs.

"Is that good enough?" she asked when she'd recovered her breath.

Joe nodded, as though he didn't quite trust his own voice. "Excellent."

"I had a wonderful day," she whispered. "I can't thank you enough for including me."

Joe shook his head lightly as though there was so much more he wanted to say to her and couldn't. Cait slipped out of the car and walked into her building, turning on the lights when she reached her apartment. She slowly put away her things, wanting to wrap this feeling around her like a warm quilt. Minutes later, she glanced out her window to see Joe still sitting in his car, his hands gripping the steering wheel and his head bent over. It looked to Cait as though he was battling with himself to keep from following her inside. And she would have welcomed him if he had.

CHAPTER NINE

CAIT STARED at the computer screen for several minutes, blind to the information in front of her. Deep in thought, she released a long, slow breath.

Paul had seemed grateful to see her when she'd shown up at the office that morning. The week between Christmas and New Year's could be a harried one. Lindy had looked surprised, then quickly retreated into her own office after exchanging a brief good-morning and little else. Her friend's behavior continued to baffle Cait, but she couldn't concentrate on Lindy's problems just now, or even on her work.

No matter what she did, Cait couldn't stop thinking about Joe and the kisses they'd exchanged Christmas evening. Nor could she forget his tortured look as he'd sat in his car after she'd gone into her apartment. Even now she wasn't certain why she hadn't immediately run back outside. And by the time she'd decided to do that, he was gone.

Cait was so absorbed in her musings that she barely heard the knock at her office door. Guiltily she glanced up to find Paul standing just inside her doorway, his hands in his pockets, his eyes weary.

"Paul!" Cait waited for her heart to trip into double time the way it usually did whenever she was anywhere near him. It didn't, which was a relief but no longer much of a surprise.

"Hello, Cait." His smile was uneven, his face tight. He seemed ill at ease and struggling to disguise it. "Have you got a moment?"

"Sure. Come on in." She stood and motioned toward her client chair. "This is a pleasant surprise. What can I do for you?"

"Nothing much," he said vaguely, sitting down. "Uh, I just wanted you to know how pleased I am that you're here. I'm sorry you canceled your vacation, but I appreciate your coming in today. Especially in light of the fact that Lindy will be leaving." His mouth thinned briefly.

No one, other than Joe and Martin, was aware of the real reason Cait wasn't in Minnesota the way she'd planned. Nor had she suggested to Paul that she'd changed her plans to help him out because they'd be short-staffed; apparently he'd drawn his own conclusions.

"So Lindy's decided to follow through with her resignation?"

Paul nodded, then frowned anew. "Nothing I say will change her mind. That woman's got a stubborn streak as wide as a..." He shrugged, apparently unable to come up with an appropriate comparison.

"The construction project's nearly finished," Cait offered, making small talk rather than joining in his criticism of Lindy. Absently she stood up and wandered around her office, stopping to straighten the large Christmas wreath on her door, the one she and Lindy had put up earlier in the month. Lindy was her friend and she wasn't about to agree with Paul, or argue with him, for that matter. Actually she should have been pleased that Paul had sought her out this way, but she felt curiously indifferent. And she did have several things that needed to be done.

"Yes, I'm delighted with the way everything's turned out," Paul said, "Joe Rockwell's done a fine job. His reputation is excellent and I imagine he'll be one of the big-time contractors in the area within the next few years."

Cait nodded casually, hoping she'd concealed the thrill of excitement that had surged through her at the mention of Joe's name. She didn't need Paul to tell her Joe's future was bright; she could see that for herself. At Christmas, his mother had boasted freely about his success. Joe had recently received a contract for a large government project—his most important to date—and she was exceptionally proud of him. He might have trouble keeping his books straight, but he left his customers satisfied. If he worked as hard at satisfying them as he did at finding the right Christmas tree, Cait could well believe that he was gaining a reputation for excellence.

"Well, listen," Paul said, drawing in a deep breath, "I won't keep you." His eyes were clouded as he stood and headed toward the door. He hesitated, turning back to face her. "I don't suppose you'd be free for dinner tonight, would you?"

"Dinner," Cait repeated as though she'd never heard the word before. Paul was inviting her to dinner? After all these months? Now, when she least expected it? Now, when it no longer mattered? After all the times she'd ached to the bottom of her heart for some attention from him, he was finally asking her out on a date? Now?

"That is, if you're free."

"Uh . . . yes, sure . . . that would be nice."

"Great. How about if I pick you up around five-thirty? Unless that's too early for you?"

"Five-thirty will be fine."

"I'll see you then."

"Thanks, Paul." Cait felt numb. There wasn't any other way to describe it. It was as if her dreams were finally beginning to play themselves out—too late. Paul, whom she'd loved from afar for so long, wanted to take her to dinner. She should be dancing around the office with glee, or at least feeling something other than this peculiar dull sensation in the pit of her stomach. If this was such a significant, exciting, hoped-for event, why didn't she feel any of the exhilaration she'd expected?

After taking a moment to collect her thoughts, Cait walked down the hallway to Lindy's office and found her friend on the phone. Lindy glanced up, smiled feebly in Cait's direction, then abruptly dropped her gaze as if the call demanded her full attention.

Cait waited a couple of minutes, then decided to return later when Lindy wasn't so busy. She needed to talk to her friend, needed her counsel. Lindy had always encouraged Cait in her dreams of a relationship with Paul. When she was discouraged, it was Lindy who cheered her sagging spirits. Yes, it was definitely time for a talk. She'd try to get Lindy to confide in her, too. Cait valued Lindy's friendship; true, she couldn't help being hurt that the person she considered one of her best friends would give notice to leave the firm without so much as discussing it with her. But Lindy must have had her reasons. And maybe she, too, needed some support just about now.

Hearing her own phone ring, Cait hurried back to her office. She was busy for the remainder of the day. The New York Stock Exchange was due to close in a matter of minutes when Joe happened by.

"Hi," Cait greeted, her smile wide and welcoming. Her gaze connected with Joe's and he returned her smile. Her heart reacted automatically, leaping with sheer happiness.

"Hi, yourself." He sauntered into her office and threw himself down in the same chair Paul had taken earlier, stretching out his long legs in front of him and folding his hands over his stomach. "So how's the world of finance this fine day?"

"About as well as always."

"Then we're in deep trouble," he joked.

His smile was infectious. It always had been, but Cait had initially resisted him. Her defenses had weakened long before, though, and she responded readily with a smile of her own.

"You done for the day?"

"Just about." She checked the time. In another five minutes, New York would be closing down. There were several items she needed to clear from her desk, but nothing pressing. "Why?"

"Why?" It was little short of astonishing how far Joe's eyebrows could reach, Cait noted, all but disappearing into his hairline.

"Can't a man ask a simple question?" Joe asked.

"Of course." The banter between them was like a well-rehearsed play. Never had Cait been more at ease with a man—or had more fun with a man. Or with anyone, really. "What I want to know is whether 'simple' refers to the question or to the man asking it."

"Ouch," Joe said, grinning broadly. "Those claws are sharp this afternoon."

"Actually today's been good." Or at least it had since he'd arrived.

"I'm glad to hear it. How about dinner?" He jumped to his feet and pretended to waltz around her office, playing a violin. "You and me. Wine and moonlight and music. Romance and roses." He wiggled his eyebrows at her suggestively. "You work too hard. You always have. I want you to enjoy life a little more. It would be good for both of us."

Joe didn't need to give her an incentive to go out with him. Cait's heart soared at the mere idea. Joe made her laugh, made her feel good about herself and the world. Of course, he possessed a remarkable talent for driving her crazy, too. But she supposed a little craziness was good for the spirit.

"Only promise me you won't wear those high heels of yours," he chided, pressing his hand to the small of her back. "I've suffered excruciating back pains ever since Paul's Christmas party."

Paul's name seemed to leap out and grab Cait by the throat. "Paul," she repeated, sagging against the back of her chair. "Oh, dear."

"I know you consider him a dear," Joe teased. "What has your stalwart employer done this time?"

"He asked me out to dinner," Cait admitted, frowning. "Out of the blue this morning he popped into my office and invited me to dinner as if we'd been dating for months. I was so stunned, I didn't know what to think."

"What did you tell him?" Joe seemed to consider the whole thing a huge joke. "Wait—" he held up his hand "—you don't need to answer that. I already know. You sprang at the offer."

"I didn't exactly spring," she contended, somewhat offended by Joe's attitude. The least he could do was show a little concern. She'd spent Christmas with him, and according to his own mother this was the first time he'd ever brought a woman home for the holiday. Furthermore, despite his insisting to all and sundry that they were married, he certainly didn't seem to mind her seeing another man.

"I'll bet you nearly went into shock." A smile trembled at the edges of his mouth as if he was picturing her reaction to Paul's invitation and finding it all terribly amusing.

"I did not go into shock," she defended herself heatedly. She'd been taken by surprise, that was all.

"Listen," he said walking toward the door, "have a great time. I'll catch you later." With that he was gone.

Cait couldn't believe it. Her mouth dropped open and she paced frantically, clenching and unclenching her fists. It took her a full minute to recover enough to run after him.

Joe was talking to his foreman, the same stocky man he'd been with the day he followed Cait into the elevator.

"Excuse me," she said, interrupting their conversation, "but when you're finished I'd like a few words with you, Joe." Her back was ramrod stiff and she kept flexing her hands as though preparing for a fight.

Joe glanced at his watch. "It might be a while."

"Then might I have a few minutes of your time now?"

The foreman stepped away, his step cocky. "You want me to dismiss the crew again, boss? I can tell them to go out and buy a New Year's present for their wives, if you like."

The man was rewarded with a look that was hot enough to barbecue spareribs. "That won't be necessary, thanks, anyway, Harry."

"You're welcome, boss. We only serve to please."

"Then please me by kindly shutting up."

Harry chuckled and returned to another section of the office.

"You wanted something?" Joe demanded of Cait.

Boy, did she. "Is that all you're going to say?"

"About what?"

"About my going to dinner with Paul? I expected you to be... I don't know, upset or something."

"Why should I be upset? Is he going to have his way with you? I sincerely doubt it, but if you're worried, invite me along and I'll be more than happy to protect your honor."

"What's the matter with you?" she demanded, not bothering to disguise her fury and disappointment. She stared at Joe, waiting for him to mock her again, but once more he surprised her. His gaze sobered.

"You honestly expect me to be jealous?"

"Not jealous exactly," she corrected, although he wasn't far from the truth. "Concerned."

"I'm not. Paul's a good man."

"I know, but—"

"You've been in love with him for months—"

"I think it was more of an infatuation."

"True. But he's finally asked you out, and you've accepted."

"Yes, but—"

"We know each other well, Cait. We were married, remember?"

"I'm not likely to forget it." Especially when Joe took pains to point it out at every opportunity. "Shouldn't that mean . . . something?" Cait couldn't believe she'd said that. For weeks she'd suffered acute mortification every time Joe mentioned the childhood stunt. Now she was using it to suit her own purposes.

Joe reached out and took hold of her shoulders. "As a matter of fact, our marriage does mean a good deal."

Hearing Joe admit as much was gratifying.

"I want only the best for you," he continued. "It's what you deserve. All I can say is that I'd be more than pleased if everything works out between you and Paul. Now if you'll excuse me, I need to talk over some matters with Harry."

"Oh, right, sure, go ahead." She couldn't seem to get the words out fast enough. When she'd called Martin to explain why she wouldn't be in Minnesota for Christmas, he'd claimed that God would reward her sacrifice. If Paul's invitation to dinner was God's reward, she wanted her airline ticket back.

The numb feeling returned as Cait walked back to her office. She didn't know what to think. She'd believed . . . she'd hoped she and Joe shared something very special. Clearly their times together meant something entirely different to him than they had to her. Otherwise he wouldn't behave so casually about her going out with Paul. And he certainly wouldn't seem so pleased about it!

That was what hurt Cait the most, and yes, she was hurt. It had taken her several minutes to identify her feelings, but now she did.

More by accident than design, Cait walked into Lindy's office. Her friend had already put on her coat and was carrying her briefcase, ready to leave the office.

"Paul asked me out to dinner," Cait blurted out.

"He did?" Lindy's eyes widened with surprise. But she didn't turn it into a joke, the way Joe had.

Cait nodded. "He just strolled in as if it was something he did every day and asked me out."

"Are you happy about it?"

"I don't know," Cait answered honestly. "I suppose I should be pleased. It's what I'd prayed would happen for months."

"Then what's the problem?" Lindy asked.

"Joe doesn't seem to care. He said he hopes everything works out the way I want it to."

"Which is?" Lindy pressed.

Cait had to think about that a moment, her heart in her throat. "Honest to heaven, Lindy, I don't know anymore."

"I UNDERSTAND the salmon here is superb," Paul was saying, reading over the Boathouse menu. It was a well-known restaurant on Lake Union.

Cait scanned the list of entrées, which featured fresh seafood, then chose the grilled salmon—the same dish she'd ordered that night with Joe. Tonight, though, she wasn't sure why she was even bothering. She wasn't hungry, and Paul was going to be wasting good money while she made a pretense of enjoying her meal.

"I understand you've been seeing a lot of Joe Rockwell," he said conversationally.

That Paul should mention Joe's name right now was ironic. Cait hadn't stopped thinking about him from the moment he'd dropped into her office earlier that afternoon. Their conversation had left a bitter taste in her mouth. She'd sincerely believed their relationship was developing into something...special. Yet Joe had gone out of his way to give her the opposite impression.

"Cait?" Paul stared at her.

"I'm sorry, what were you saying?"

"Simply that you and Joe Rockwell have been seeing a lot of each other recently."

"Uh, yes. As you know, we were childhood friends," she murmured. "Actually Joe and my older brother were best friends. Then Joe's family moved to the suburbs and our families lost contact."

"Yes, I remember you mentioned that."

The waitress came for their order, and Paul requested a bottle of white wine. Then he chatted amicably for several minutes, mentioning subjects of shared interest from the office.

Cait listened attentively, nodding from time to time or adding the occasional comment. Now that she had his undivided attention, Cait wondered what it was about Paul that she'd found so extraordinary. He was attractive, but not nearly as dynamic or exciting as she found Joe. True, Paul possessed a certain charm, but compared to Joe, he was subdued and perhaps even a little dull. Cait couldn't imagine her stalwart boss carrying her piggyback out the back door because her high heels were too tight. Nor could she see Paul bantering with her the way Joe did.

The waitress delivered the wine bottle, opened it and poured them each a glass, after Paul had given his approval. Their dinners followed shortly afterward. After taking a bite or two of her delicious salmon, Cait noticed that Paul hadn't touched his meal. If anything, he seemed restless.

He rolled the stem of the wineglass between his fingers, watching the wine swirl inside. Then he suddenly blurted out, "What do you think of Lindy's leaving the firm?"

Cait was taken aback by the fervor in his voice when he mentioned Lindy's name. "Frankly I was shocked," Cait said. "Lindy and I have been good friends for a couple of years now." There'd been a time when the two had done nearly everything together. The summer before, they'd vacationed in Mexico and returned to Seattle with enough handwoven baskets and bulky blankets to set up shop themselves.

"Lindy's resigning came as a surprise to you, then?"

"Yes, this whole thing caught me completely unaware. Lindy didn't even mention the other job offer to me. I always thought we were good friends."

"Lindy *is* your friend," Paul said with enough conviction to persuade the patrons at the nearby tables. "You wouldn't believe what a good friend she is."

"I...know that." But friends sometimes had surprises up their sleeves. Lindy was a good example of that, and apparently so was Joe.

"I find Lindy an exceptional woman," Paul commented, watching Cait closely.

"She's probably one of the best stockbrokers in the business," Cait said, taking a sip of her wine.

"My...admiration for her goes beyond her keen business mind."

"Oh, mine, too," Cait was quick to agree. Lindy was the kind of friend who would traipse through the blazing sun of Mexico looking for a conch shell because she knew Cait really wanted to take one home with her. And Lindy had listened to countless hours of Cait's bemoaning her sorry fate of unrequited love for Paul.

"She's a wonderful woman."

Joe was wonderful, too, Cait thought. So wonderful her heart ached at his indifference when she'd announced she would be dining with Paul.

"Lindy's the kind of woman a man could treasure all his life," Paul went on.

"I couldn't agree with you more," Cait said. Now, if only Joe would realize what a treasure *she* was. He'd married her once—well, sort of—and surely the thought of spending their lives together had crossed his mind in the past few weeks.

Paul hesitated as though he were at a loss for words. "I don't suppose you've given any thought to the reason Lindy made this unexpected decision to resign?"

Frankly Cait hadn't. Her mind and her heart had been so full of Joe that deciphering her friend's actions had somehow escaped her. "She received a better offer, didn't she?"

Which was understandable. Lindy would be an asset to any firm.

It was then that Cait understood. Paul hadn't asked her to dinner out of any desire to develop a romantic relationship with her. He saw her as a means of discovering what had prompted Lindy to resign. This new awareness came as a relief, a burden lifted from her shoulders. Paul wasn't interested in her. He never had been and probably never would be. A few weeks ago, that realization would have been a crushing defeat, but all Cait experienced now was an overwhelming sense of gratitude.

"I'm sure if you talk to Lindy, she might reconsider," Cait suggested.

"I've tried, trust me. But there's a problem."

"Oh?" Now that Cait had sampled the salmon, she discovered it to be truly delicious. She hadn't realized how hungry she was.

"Cait, look at me," Paul said, raising his voice slightly. His face was pinched, his eyes intense. "Damn, but you've made this nearly impossible."

She looked up at him, her face puzzled. "What is it, Paul?"

"You have no idea, do you? I swear you've got to be the most obtuse woman in the world." He pushed aside his plate and briefly closed his eyes, shaking his head. "I'm in love with Lindy. I have been for weeks...months. But for the life of me I couldn't get her to notice me. I swear I did everything but turn cartwheels in her office. It finally dawned on me why she wasn't responding."

"Me?" Cait asked in a feeble, mouselike squeak.

"Exactly. She didn't want to betray your friendship. Then one afternoon—I think it was the day you first recognized Joe—we, Lindy and I, were in my office alone together and— Oh hell, I don't know how it happened, but Lindy was looking something up for me and she stumbled over one of the cords the construction crew was using. Fortunately I was able to catch her before she fell to the floor. I know it wasn't her fault, but I was so angry, afraid she might have been hurt. Lindy was just as angry with me for being angry with her, and it seemed the only way to shut her up was to kiss her. That was the beginning and I swear to you everything exploded in our faces at that moment."

Cait swallowed, fascinated by the story. "Go on."

"I tried for days to get her to agree to go out with me. But she kept refusing until I demanded to know why."

"She told you…how I felt about you?" The thought was mortifying.

"Of course not. Lindy's too good a friend to divulge your confidence. Besides, she didn't need to tell me. I've known all along. Good grief, Cait, what did I have to do to discourage you? Hire a skywriter?"

"I don't think anything that drastic was necessary," she muttered, humiliated to the very marrow of her bones.

"I repeatedly told Lindy I wasn't attracted to you, but she wouldn't listen. Finally she told me if I'd talk to you, explain everything myself, she'd agree to go out with me."

"The phone call," Cait said on a stroke of genius. "That was the reason you called me, wasn't it? You wanted to talk about Lindy, not that business article."

"Yes." He looked deeply grateful for her insight, late though it was.

"Well, for heaven's sake, why didn't you?"

"Believe me, I've kicked myself a dozen times since. I wish I knew. At the time, it seemed so heartless to have such a frank discussion over the phone. Again and again, I promised myself I'd say something. Lord knows I dropped enough hints, but you weren't exactly receptive."

She winced. "But why is Lindy resigning?"

"Isn't it obvious?" Paul demanded. "It was becoming increasingly difficult for us to work together. She didn't want to betray her best friend, but at the same time…"

"But at the same time you two were falling in love."

"Exactly. I can't lose her, Cait. I don't want to hurt your feelings, and believe me, it's nothing personal—you're a trustworthy employee and a decent person—but I'm simply not attracted to you."

Paul didn't seem to be the only one. Other than treating their relationship like one big joke, Joe hadn't ever claimed any romantic feelings for her, either.

"I had to do something before I lost Lindy."

"I couldn't agree more."

"You're not angry with her, are you?"

"Good heavens, no," Cait said, offering him a brave smile.

"We both thought something was developing between you and Joe Rockwell. You seemed to be seeing quite a bit of each other, and then at the Christmas party—"

"Don't remind me," Cait said with a low groan.

Paul's face creased in a spontaneous smile. "Joe certainly has a wit about him, doesn't he?"

Cait gave a resigned nod.

Now that Paul had cleared the air, he seemed to develop an appetite. He reached for his dinner and ate heartily. By contrast, Cait's salmon had lost its appeal. She stared down at her plate, wondering how she could possibly make it through the rest of the evening.

She did, though, quite nicely. Paul didn't even seem to notice that anything was amiss. It wasn't that Cait was distressed by his confession. If anything, she was relieved at this turn of events and delighted that Lindy had fallen in love. Paul was obviously crazy about her; she'd never seen him more animated than when he was discussing Lindy. It still amazed Cait that she'd been so unperceptive about Lindy's real feelings. Not to mention Paul's...

Paul dropped her off at her building and saw her to the front door. "I can't thank you enough," he said, his voice warm. Impulsively he hugged her, then hurried back to his sports car.

Although she was certainly guilty of being obtuse, Cait knew exactly where Paul was headed. No doubt Lindy would be waiting for him, eager to hear the details of their conversation. Cait planned to talk to her friend herself first thing in the morning.

Cait's apartment was dark and lonely. So lonely the silence seemed to echo off the walls. She hung up her coat before turning on the lights, her thoughts as dark as the room had been.

She made herself a cup of tea. Then she sat on the sofa, tucking her feet beneath her as she stared unseeingly at the walls, assessing her options. They seemed terribly limited.

Paul was in love with Lindy. And Joe...Cait had no idea where she stood with him. For all she knew— Her thoughts were interrupted by the phone. She answered on the second ring.

"Cait?" It was Joe and he seemed surprised to find her back so early. "When did you get in?"

"A few minutes ago."

"You don't sound right. Is something wrong?"

"My goodness," she said, breaking into sobs. "What could possibly be wrong?"

CHAPTER TEN

THE FLOW OF EMOTION took Cait by storm. She'd had no intention of crying; in fact, the thought hadn't even entered her mind. One moment she was sitting there, contemplating the evening's revelations, and the next she was sobbing hysterically into the phone.

"Cait?"

"Oh," she wailed. "This is all your fault in the first place." Cait didn't know what made her say that. The words had slipped out before she'd realized it.

"What happened?"

"Nothing. I...I can't talk to you now. I'm going to bed." With that, she gently replaced the receiver. Part of her hoped Joe would call back, but the telephone remained stubbornly silent. She stared at it for several minutes. Apparently Joe didn't care if he talked to her or not.

The tears continued to flow. They remained a mystery to Cait. She wasn't a woman given to bouts of crying, but now that she'd started she couldn't seem to stop.

She changed out of her dress and into a pair of sweats, pausing halfway through to wash her face.

Sniffling and hiccuping, she sat on the end of her bed and dragged a shuddering breath through her lungs. Crying like this made absolutely no sense whatsoever.

Paul was in love with Lindy. At one time, the news would have devastated her, but not now. Cait felt a tingling happiness that her best friend had found a man to love. And the infatuation she'd held for Paul couldn't compare with the strength of her love for Joe.

Love.

There, she'd admitted it. She was in love with Joe. The man who told restaurant employees that she was suffering from amnesia. The man who walked into elevators and announced to total strangers that they were married. Yet this was the same man who hadn't revealed a minute's concern about her dating Paul Jamison.

Joe was also the man who'd gently held her hand through a children's movie. The man who made a practice of kissing her senseless. The man who'd held her in his arms Christmas night as though he never intended to let her go.

Joseph Rockwell was a fun-loving jokester who took delight in teasing her. He was also tender and thoughtful and loving—the man who'd captured her heart only to drop it carelessly.

Her doorbell chimed and she didn't need to look in the peephole to know it was Joe. But she felt panicky all of a sudden, too confused and vulnerable to see him now.

She walked slowly to the door and opened it a crack.

"What the hell is going on?" Joe demanded, not waiting for an invitation to march inside.

Cait wiped her eyes on her sleeve and shut the door. "Nothing."

"Did Paul try anything?"

She rolled her eyes. "Of course not."

"Then why are you crying?" He stood in the middle of her living room, fists planted on his hips as if he'd welcome the opportunity to punch out her boss.

If Cait knew why it was necessary to cry nonstop like this, she would have answered him. She opened her mouth, hoping some intelligent reason would emerge, but the only thing that came out was a low-pitched squeak. Joe was gazing at her in complete confusion. "I... Paul's in love."

"With you?" His voice rose half an octave with disbelief.

"Don't make it sound like such an impossibility," she said crossly. "I'm reasonably attractive, you know." If she was expecting Joe to list her myriad charms, Cait was disappointed.

Instead, his frown darkened. "So what's Paul being in love got to do with anything?"

"Absolutely nothing. I wished him and Lindy the very best."

"So it is Lindy?" Joe murmured as though he'd known it all along.

"You didn't honestly think it was me, did you?"

"Hell, how was I supposed to know? I *thought* it was Lindy, but it was you he was taking to dinner. Frankly it didn't make a whole lot of sense to me."

"Which is something else," Cait grumbled, standing so close to him, their faces were only inches apart. Her hands were planted on her hips, her pose mirroring his. They resembled a pair of gunslingers ready for a shootout, Cait thought absently. "I want to know one thing. Every time I turn around, you're telling anyone and everyone who'll listen that we're married. But when it really matters you—"

"When did it really matter?"

Cait ignored the question, thinking the answer was obvious. "You casually turn me over to Paul as if you couldn't wait to be rid of me. Obviously you couldn't have cared less."

"I cared," he shouted.

"Oh, right," she shouted back, "but if that was the case, you certainly didn't bother to show it!"

"What was I supposed to do, challenge him to a duel?"

He was being ridiculous, Cait decided, and she refused to take the bait. The more they talked, the more unreasonable they were both becoming.

"I thought dating Paul was what you wanted," he complained. "You talked about it long enough. Paul this and Paul that. He'd walk past and you'd all but swoon."

"That's not the least bit true." Maybe it had been at one time, but not now and not for weeks. "If you'd taken the trouble to ask me, you might have learned the truth."

"You mean you don't love Paul?"

Cait rolled her eyes again. "Bingo."

"It isn't like you to be so sarcastic."

"It isn't like you to be so... awful."

He seemed to mull that over for a moment. "If we're going to be throwing out accusations," he said tightly, "then maybe you should take a look at yourself."

"What exactly do you mean by that?" As usual, no one could get a reaction out of Cait more effectively than Joe. "Never mind," she answered, walking to the door. "This discussion isn't getting us anywhere. All we seem capable of doing is hurling insults at each other."

"I disagree," Joe answered calmly. "I think it's time we cleared the air."

She took a deep breath, feeling physically and emotionally deflated.

"Joe, it'll have to wait. I'm in no condition to be rational right now and I don't want either of us saying things we'll regret." She held open her door for him. "Please?"

He seemed about to argue with her, then he sighed and dropped a quick kiss on her mouth. Wide-eyed, she watched him leave.

LINDY WAS WAITING in Cait's office early the following morning, holding two plastic cups of freshly brewed coffee. Her eyes were wide and expectant as Cait entered the office. They stared at each other for several moments.

"Are you angry with me?" Lindy whispered. She handed Cait one of the cups in an apparent peace offering.

"Of course not," Cait murmured. She put down her briefcase and accepted the cup, which she placed carefully on her desk. Then she gave Lindy a reassuring hug, and the two of them sat down for their much postponed talk.

"Why didn't you tell me?" Cait burst out.

"I wanted to," Lindy said earnestly. "I had to stop myself a hundred times. The worst part of it was the guilt—knowing you were in love with Paul, and loving him myself."

Cait wasn't sure how she would have reacted to the truth, but she preferred to think she would've understood, and wished Lindy well. It wasn't as though Lindy had stolen Paul away from her.

"I don't think I realized how I felt," Lindy continued, "until one afternoon when I tripped over a stupid cord and fell into Paul's arms. From there, everything sort of snowballed."

"Paul told me."

"He... told you about that afternoon?"

Cait grinned and nodded. "I found the story wildly romantic."

"You don't mind?" Lindy watched her closely as if half-afraid of Cait's reaction even now.

"I think it's wonderful."

Lindy's smile was filled with warmth and excitement. "I never knew being in love could be so delightful, but at the same time cause so much pain."

"Amen to that," Cait stated emphatically.

Her words shot like live bullets into the room. If Cait could have reached out and pulled them back, she would have.

"Is it Joe Rockwell?" Lindy asked quietly.

Cait nodded, then shook her head. "See how much he's confused me?" She made a sound that was half sob, half giggle. "That man infuriates me so much I want to scream. Or cry." Cait had always thought of herself as a sane and sensible person. She lived a quiet life, worked hard at her job, enjoyed traveling and crossword puzzles. Then she'd bumped into Joe. Suddenly she found herself demanding piggyback rides, talking to strangers in elevators and seeking out phantom women at Christmas parties while downing spiked punch like it was soda pop.

"But then at other times?" Lindy prompted.

"At other times I love him so much I hurt all the way through. I love everything about him. Even those loony stunts of his. In fact, I usually laugh as hard as everyone else does. Even if I don't always want him to know it."

"So what's going to happen with you two?" Lindy asked. She took a sip of coffee and as she did so, Cait caught a flash of diamond.

"Lindy?" Cait demanded, jumping out of her seat. "What's that on your finger?"

Lindy's face broke into a smile so wide Cait was nearly blinded. "You noticed."

"Of course I did."

"It's from Paul. After he had dinner with you, he stopped over at my apartment. We talked for the longest time and then after a while he asked me to marry him. At first I didn't know what to say. It seems so soon. We . . . we hardly know each other."

"Good grief, you've worked together for months."

"I know," Lindy said with a shy smile. "That was what Paul told me. It didn't take him long to convince me. He had the ring all picked out. Isn't it beautiful?"

"Oh, Lindy." The diamond was a lovely solitaire set in a wide band of gold. The style and shape were perfect for Lindy's long, elegant finger.

"I didn't know if I should wear it until you and I had talked, but I couldn't make myself take it off this morning."

"Of course you should wear it!" The fact that Paul had been carting it around when he'd had dinner with her didn't exactly flatter her ego, but she was so thrilled for Lindy that seemed a minor concern.

Lindy splayed her fingers out in front of her to better show off the ring. "When he slipped it on my finger, I swear it was the most romantic moment of my life. Before I knew it, tears were streaming down my face. I still don't understand why I felt like crying. I think Paul was as surprised as I was."

There must have been something in the air that reduced susceptible females to tears, Cait decided. Whatever it was had certainly affected her.

"Now you've sidetracked me," Lindy said, looking up from her diamond, her gaze dreamy and warm. "You were telling me about you and Joe."

"I was?"

"Yes, you were," Lindy insisted.

"There's nothing to tell. If there was you'd be the first person to hear. I know," she admitted before her friend could bring up the point, "we have seen a lot of each other recently, but I don't think it meant anything to him. When he found out Paul had invited me to dinner, he seemed downright delighted."

"I'm sure it was all an act."

Cait wished she could believe that. Oh, how she wished it.

"You're in love with him?" Lindy asked softly, hesitantly.

Cait nodded and lowered her eyes. It hurt to think about Joe. Everything was a game to him—one big joke. Lindy had been right about one thing, though. Love was the most wonderful experience of her life. And the most painful.

THE NEW YORK Stock Exchange had closed and Cait was punching some figures into her computer when Joe strode into her office and closed the door.

"Feel free to come in," she muttered, continuing her work. Her heart was pounding but she dared not let him know the effect he had on her.

"I will make myself at home, thank you," he answered cheerfully, ignoring her sarcasm. He pulled out a chair and sat down expansively, resting one ankle on the opposite knee and relaxing as if he was in a movie theater, waiting for the main feature to begin.

"If you're here to discuss business, might I suggest investing in blue-chip stocks? They're always a safe bet." Cait went on typing, doing her best to ignore Joe—which was nearly impossible, although she gave an Oscar-winning performance, if she did say so herself.

"I'm here to talk business all right," Joe said, "but it has nothing to do with the stock market."

"What business could the two of us possibly have?" she asked, her voice deliberately ironic.

"I want to continue the discussion we were having last night."

"Perhaps you do, but unfortunately that was last night and this is now." How confident she sounded, Cait thought, mildly pleased with herself. "I can do without hearing you list my no doubt numerous flaws."

"It's your being my wife I want to discuss."

"Your wife?" She wished he'd quit throwing the subject at her as if it meant something to him. Something other than a joke.

"Yes, my wife." He gave a short laugh. "Believe me, it isn't your flaws I'm here to discuss."

Despite everything, Cait's heart raced. She reached for a stack of papers and switched them from one basket to another. Her entire filing system was probably in jeopardy, but she had to do something with her hands before she stood up and reached out to Joe. She did stand then, but it was to remove a large silver bell strung from a red velvet ribbon hanging in her office window.

"Paul and Lindy are getting married," he supplied next.

"Yes, I know. Lindy and I had a long talk this morning." She took the wreath off her door next.

"I take it the two of you are friends again?"

"We were never not friends," Cait answered stiffly, stuffing the wreath, the bell and the three ceramic Wise Men into the bottom drawer of her filing cabinet. Hard as she tried not to, she could feel her defenses crumbling. "Lindy's asked me to be her maid of honor and I've agreed."

"Will you return the favor?"

It took a moment for the implication to sink in, and even then Cait wasn't sure she should follow the trail Joe seemed to be forging through this conversation. She leaned forward and rested her hands on the edge of the desk.

"I'm destined to be an old maid," she said flippantly, although she couldn't help feeling a sliver of real hope.

"You'll never be that."

Cait was hoping he'd say her beauty would make her irresistible, or that her warmth and wit and intelligence was sure to attract a dozen suitors. Instead he said the very thing she could have predicted. "We're already married, so you don't need to worry about being a spinster."

Cait released a sigh of impatience. "I wish you'd give up on that, Joe. It's growing increasingly old."

"As I recall, we celebrated our eighteenth wedding anniversary not long ago."

"Don't be ridiculous. All right," she said, straightening abruptly. If he wanted to play games, then she'd respond in kind. "Since we're married, I want a family."

"Hey, sweetheart," he cried, tossing his arms in the air, "that's music to my ears. I'm willing."

Cait prepared to leave the office, if not the building. "Somehow I knew you would be."

"Two or three," he interjected, then chuckled and added, "I suppose we should name the first two Barbie and Ken."

Cait sent him a scalding look that made him chuckle even louder.

"If you prefer, we'll leave the names open to negotiation," he said.

"Of all the colossal nerve..." Cait muttered, moving to the window and gazing out.

"If you want daughters, I've got no objection, but from what I understand that's not left up to us."

Cait turned around, folding her arms across her chest. "Correct me if I'm wrong," she said coldly, certain he'd delight in doing so. "But you did just ask me to marry you. Could you confirm that?"

"All I'm looking to do is make legal what's already been done."

Cait frowned. Was he serious, or wasn't he? He was talking about marriage, about joining their lives as if he were planning a bid on a construction project.

"When Paul asked Lindy to marry him, he had a diamond ring with him."

"I was going to buy you a ring," Joe said emphatically. "I still am. But I thought you'd want to pick it out yourself. If you wanted a diamond, why didn't you say so? I'll buy you the whole store if that'll make you happy."

"One ring will suffice, thank you."

"Pick out two or three. I understand diamonds are an excellent investment."

Cait frowned. "Not so fast," she said, holding out her arm. It was vital she maintain some distance between them. If Joe kissed her or started talking about having children again, they might never get the facts clear.

"Not so fast?" he repeated incredulously. "Honey, I've been waiting eighteen years to discuss this. You're not going to ruin everything now, are you?" He advanced a couple of steps toward her.

"I'm not agreeing to anything until you explain yourself." For every step he took toward her, Cait retreated two.

"About what?" Joe was frowning, which wasn't a good sign.

"Paul."

His eyelids slammed shut, then slowly raised. "I don't understand why that man's name has to come into every conversation you and I have."

Cait decided it was better to ignore that comment. "You haven't even told me you love me."

"I love you." He actually sounded annoyed, as if she'd insisted on having the obvious reiterated.

"You might say it with a little more feeling," Cait suggested.

"If you want feeling, come here and let me kiss you."

"No."

"Why not?" By now they'd completely circled her desk. "We're talking serious things here. Trust me, sweetheart, a man doesn't bring up marriage and babies with just any woman. I love you. I've loved you for years, only I didn't know it."

"Then why did you let Paul take me out to dinner?"

"You mean I could have stopped you?"

"Of course. I didn't want to go out with him! I was sick about having to turn down your offer for dinner, and you didn't even seem to care that I was going out with another man. And as far as you were concerned, he was your main competition."

"I wasn't worried."

"That wasn't the impression I got later."

"All right, all right," Joe said, rifling his fingers through his hair. "I didn't think Paul was interested in you. I saw him and Lindy together one night at the office and the electricity between them was so thick it could have lit up Seattle."

"You knew about Lindy and Paul?"

Joe shrugged. "Let me put it this way. I had a sneaking suspicion. But when you started talking about Paul as though you were in love with him, I got worried."

"You should have been." Which was a bold-faced lie.

Somehow without her being quite sure how it happened, Joe maneuvered himself so only a few inches separated them.

"Are you ever going to kiss me?" he demanded.

Meekly Cait nodded and walked into his arms like a child opening the gate and skipping up the walkway to home. This was the place she belonged. With Joe. This was home and she need never doubt his love again.

With a sigh that seemed to come from the deepest part of him, Joe swept her close. For a breathless moment they looked into each other's eyes. He was about to kiss her when there was a knock at her door.

Harry, Joe's foreman, walked in without waiting for a response. "I don't suppose you've seen Joe—" He stopped abruptly. "Oh, sorry," he said, flustered and eager to make his escape.

"No problem," Cait assured him. "We're married. We have been for years and years."

Joe was chuckling as his mouth settled over hers, and in a single kiss he wiped out all the doubts and misgivings, replacing them with promises and thrills.

EPILOGUE

THE ROBUST SOUND of organ music filled the Seattle church as Cait slowly stepped down the center aisle, her feet moving in time to the traditional music. As the maid of honor, Lindy stood to one side of the altar while Joe and his brother, who was serving as the best man, waited on the other.

Cait's brother, Martin, stood directly ahead of her. He smiled at Cait as the assembly rose and she came down the aisle, her heart overflowing with happiness.

Cait and Joe had planned this day for months. If there'd been any lingering doubts that Joe really loved her, they were long gone. He wasn't the type of man who expressed his love with flowery words and gifts. But Cait had known that from the first. He'd insisted on building their home before the wedding and they'd spent countless hours going over the plans. Cait was helping him with his accounting and would be taking over the task full-time as soon as they started their family. Which would be soon, very soon. The way Cait figured it, she'd be pregnant by next Christmas.

But before they began their real life together, they'd enjoy a perfect honeymoon in New Zealand. He'd wanted to surprise her with the trip, but Cait had needed a passport. They'd only be gone two weeks, which was all the time Joe could afford to take, since he had several large projects coming up.

As the organ concluded the "Wedding March," Cait handed her bouquet to Lindy and placed her hands in Joe's.

He smiled down on her as if he'd never seen a more beautiful woman in his life. From the look on his face, Cait knew he could hardly keep from kissing her right then and there.

"Dearly beloved," Martin said, stepping forward, "we are gathered here today in the sight of God and man to celebrate the love of Joseph James Rockwell and Caitlin Rose Marshall."

Cait's eyes locked with Joe's. She did love him, so much her heart felt close to bursting. After all these months of waiting for this moment, Cait was sure she'd be so nervous her voice would falter. That didn't happen. She'd never felt more confident of anything than her feelings for Joe and his for her. Cait's voice rang out strong and clear, as did Joe's.

As they exchanged the rings, Cait could hear her mother and Joe's weeping softly in the background. But these were tears of shared happiness. The two women had renewed their friendship and were excited about the prospect of grandchildren.

Cait waited for the moment when Martin would tell Joe he could kiss his bride. Instead he closed his Bible, reverently set it aside, and said, "Joseph James Rockwell, do you have the baseball cards with you?"

"I do."

Cait looked at them as if they'd both lost their minds. Joe reached inside his tuxedo jacket and produced two flashy baseball cards.

"You may give them to your bride."

With a dramatic flourish, Joe did as Martin instructed. Cait stared down at the two cards and grinned broadly.

"You may now kiss the bride," Martin declared.

Joe was more than happy to comply.

Sometimes even an angel
can hold a grudge....

CHRISTMAS ANGEL

Shannon Waverly

CHAPTER ONE

ANGELA CAME TO with a start, realizing the music around her had subsided.

"Where were you, Miss Westgate?" Mr. Beech inquired.

Embarrassment climbed up her cheeks like mercury in a thermometer. Usually she didn't make mistakes, and *never* two weeks before a concert.

"All right, let's pick it up at the top of page seven, third bar." The white-maned conductor tapped his baton, and Angela raised her flute, determined to concentrate extra hard on her playing—which was what she should have been doing, not thinking about her argument with Ivan.

It was unlike her to let personal problems interfere with rehearsal. Just the opposite, rehearsal usually calmed whatever ailed her. But apparently today's argument had dug in deeper than she'd realized. It was the same one they'd been having on and off for a couple of weeks now. Why couldn't their relationship take a step forward? he wanted to know. Why couldn't he move into her place?

She'd repeated the answer she'd given him on the other occasions when the issue had arisen: she wasn't capable of making a decision of that magnitude at this particular juncture of her life. She couldn't think straight. She was too keyed up waiting to hear if she'd be named Mr. Beech's successor. Maybe in a month, after the appointment was made...

But Ivan had kept pressing until finally she'd agreed to

give the matter serious thought and get back to him with a definite decision by the weekend.

She'd eventually got him out the door, but hadn't been able to return to the Christmas cards she'd been writing before his arrival. Instead, she'd curled up in a wing chair by her empty fireplace, wrapped in an afghan her mother had finished crocheting just a month before she'd died, and for the rest of the afternoon wondered why she couldn't give the man she supposedly loved a simple affirmative answer.

Angela tensed as the orchestra approached the passage she'd missed a few minutes earlier. This time her playing was flawless.

On an objective level, she had no trouble understanding Ivan's impatience to move in. They *had* been seeing each other exclusively for nearly half a year. Sharing expenses *would* save them money. And it *would* be nice to spend the holiday season together.

Still, Angela couldn't help feeling rushed—and resentful—which only added to her sense of guilt. But, damn it all, it didn't seem fair, Ivan's putting such pressure on her right now. Directorship of the Winston Symphony Orchestra meant everything to her.

She fully realized that to an outsider the WSO was probably just one more unremarkable community orchestra, but to her it was home. Her center. Her source of energy and emotional healing. She didn't know why this was so. She had other jobs to satisfy her love of music, jobs, unlike this one, that paid more than a token salary. But she was never quite as happy at her other pursuits as she was here.

And Ivan knew it, too. He also knew how frightened she was that she wouldn't get the position. And who knew when it would open up again? Mr. Beech had been at the helm for thirty-five years. The new conductor might very well do the same.

Angela's résumé was good. She had the right training, a broad range of experience—including being Mr. Beech's assistant for the past three years—and she'd certainly paid her dues. She'd been with the orchestra for seven years, having joined while still in college, had never missed a rehearsal and served on more committees than she cared to remember. She wasn't just qualified; she *deserved* the position, yet she knew the board of directors might easily arrive at a different conclusion.

For one thing, she was a woman, and the idea of a female conductor was probably as foreign to the small town of Winston, New Hampshire, as a Martian running for tax assessor. The board might also dismiss her application simply because she was a local, perversely reasoning that no one from the area could possibly be good.

Angela's deepest fear, however, was that someone better qualified had also applied for the job. It was precisely this uncertainty, this not knowing who her competition was, that was turning her into a certifiable tangle of nerves, and Ivan had no right throwing yet another worry onto the heap!

The last triumphant notes of the Jupiter Symphony reverberated around the red velvet curtains and gilded cornices of the theater, then faded in a series of diminishing after-echoes. Angela smiled, ripples of pleasure running along her arms.

With long knob-knuckled hands, Mr. Beech smoothed back his thick hair. "That was good. Very nice," he said, which was as profuse as he got with his compliments. "Let's proceed, then, to the sing-along carol medley."

Angela bent forward, searching for the folder of sheet music under her chair. While she was down there, a shiver raced down her back, causing her to wonder if someone had opened a door offstage, letting in a draft. But then the shiver changed, deepened, and Angela went very still. She swallowed, hardly breathing, as the sensation became a visceral awareness—of something. Something out in the dark center aisle. Without straightening, she lifted her gaze just as that something moved into the arc of light cast from the stage. First, she noticed brown leather boots, broken in and mellow, then long lean legs molded by faded denim jeans and, as her eyes continued to lift, a black French-horn case gripped in a leather-gloved hand. Her heart pounded, and her impatient gaze flew to the newcomer's face.

"Merciful Mozart!" Angela breathed. She sat up, moving as if the stage lights were suddenly pouring down thick warm molasses. Everything around her faded to nothing, leaving her with only one all-consuming awareness. Jon!

He paused at the first row of seats, carefully set his instrument case on the floor, unzipped his brown leather jacket and took the aisle seat.

"Oh, my!" the girl beside Angela sighed. She'd apparently been watching his entrance, too. "What do we have here?"

What indeed? Angela thought, gripping her arms tight in an attempt to control their trembling. Jonathan Stoddard couldn't be explained in a minute, nor in an hour. Maybe not at all. Jon was one of those rare individuals better defined as a force of nature, like spontaneous combustion or winter lightning.

For years, he'd also been her very best friend.

But that was all so long ago, before college separated them, before his family moved away. So many years had passed since they'd even seen each other that Angela had begun to believe they'd never meet again.

But there he was. And though she was absolutely overwhelmed and had no idea what a world-class performer was doing at a small-town orchestra rehearsal in southern New Hampshire on a cold December Wednesday, she also felt the oddest sensation of a thread unbroken. His appearance was both the most startling occurrence in her life and yet the most natural.

Someone in the cello section caught the elderly conductor's attention and pointed. He turned from his podium.

"Ah, Jonathan!" Mr. Beech hobbled across the stage and down the side steps, a smile crinkling unfamiliar lines into his face. They shook hands and spoke quietly while a hush of curiosity fell over the musicians on stage.

The girl beside Angela sighed again. "I think I'm in love."

Angela chuckled because that was the expected response, but the reality of the situation was just sinking home. Oh, Lord, oh, Lord! This couldn't be happening! Jon wasn't really here, was he? She closed her eyes and with all her might willed him to disappear. But when she peeked through her lashes a few seconds later he was still there, looking more forceful and vibrant than ever.

Growing up, Angela hadn't paid much attention to Jon's looks. He'd always been just Jon to her, the boy she'd known since before she could cross the street on her own. Just Jon, who'd played space cadets with her and grumbled over starched recital clothes and shared her case of chicken pox. But somewhere around the age of fifteen, she'd become aware of his entourage, those flocks of pea-brained girls panting after him down the corridors of Winston High or parading their wares in front of the stage whenever the band played an engagement. It was then that she'd taken an objective look and grudgingly admitted that, yes, her best friend was indeed a heartbreaker.

Now, unable to bridle her curiosity, Angela peered around the musician in front of her to get a better look. As usual, Jon needed a haircut, his coarse, nearly black curls springing about his handsome face with rakish abandon. And he still refused to dress professionally.

But time had changed him, too, she noticed. He was broader in the shoulders, thicker in the thighs, the coltish beauty of his youth transformed into something fiercely male and disturbingly adult. Angela wasn't prepared for seeing him like this, all her images of him, fixed in her mind nine years ago, jarred by the unsettling reality before her now. His face looked darker, leaner, too, carved by experiences she knew nothing about, a fact that inexplicably saddened her.

The girl beside Angela pointed with her flute and said, enunciating very distinctly, "That guy is absolutely gorgeous!"

Angela remained silent. Poor Lynn didn't know the half of it, for although Jon's looks were formidable, they weren't his most attractive feature. What really drew people to him was something even more intriguing and addictive. It was his attitude; his confidence that bordered on arrogance; the effortlessness with which he succeeded at everything he tried; his energy and humor; his mercurial spontaneity. Jon was a comet whose tail people had always wanted to ride, just to feel the exhilaration.

He tossed his jacket over a seat and followed Mr. Beech onto the stage. If Angela's heart had been hammering before, it now pounded close to panic. She wasn't ready for this. How was she supposed to act? What was she supposed to say?

She and Jon had parted badly, their lifelong friendship in shambles. They'd been eighteen at the time.

No, not shambles, she amended. Shambles was what was left after a fight, but they hadn't fought. On the contrary, when they'd arrived home after that ill-fated backpacking trip, Jon had actually apologized and even tried to joke about what had happened on Mount Adams, as if it was a trivial mistake that could easily be forgotten, and his cavalier attitude had hurt. Hurt? She'd been devastated.

Then, just to grind salt into her wounds, he'd spent the remainder of that summer ignoring her. He'd blithely apologized for that, too, saying he was busy packing for college. But Angela wasn't blind. She saw the long-legged beauties he sat with on his porch. She heard their laughter as they drove off in his car. He had time, plenty of time, but apparently not for her.

And when that summer ended, he didn't even take the trouble to say goodbye in person. He'd phoned, a conversation she remembered as painfully impersonal and far too brief. And then it was over. A lifetime of friendship, over.

Sure, they'd visited each other on Christmas break; their parents expected it of them. But by then their uneasiness had grown so palpable, their conversation so strained, that Angela felt exhausted afterward. And then, that spring his parents moved to Florida, and they hadn't seen each other since. For a while they wrote, sporadic letters that eventually dwindled to sporadic postcards, but she always had the feeling they were just going through the motions of communication for the sake of politeness. And then even the postcards had stopped....

Jon paused at the footlights a few feet behind Mr. Beech, his hands in the back pockets of his jeans, drawing taut his Aran-knit sweater across his broad chest. Angela held her breath as his coal-dark, fire-bright eyes scanned the interested gathering. His talent and ambition had taken him so many exciting places that for one fleeting moment she wondered if he would even recognize her now. Not that it mattered. In fact, she hoped he wouldn't. She no more wanted to resume an acquaintance with Jon Stoddard than she wanted to enter shock therapy.

His gaze moved over the orchestra, across the first violins, through the violas and steadily on to the flutes. Suddenly his head jerked back with a jolt of recognition.

Caught in his dark stare, Angela swallowed hard and waited through an electrified few seconds. And then he smiled, that slow sensuous grin that was unmistakably Jon's.

"Ladies and gentlemen—" the conductor tapped his mottled hand on the podium "—many of you have asked me if we're going to have a guest artist at this year's Christmas concert...."

Still staring at Jon, Angela's eyes widened. Guest artist? she thought, and Jon nodded almost imperceptibly.

"Until yesterday," Mr. Beech continued, "I wasn't sure myself, finances being what they are. But tonight I can finally announce that we will indeed have a soloist. His name is Jonathan Stoddard...."

A rustle of recognition moved through the orchestra.

Jon finally released her from his gaze, and she blew out a breath she hadn't been aware of holding.

"Some of you may already know Jonathan," the conductor intoned, straightening his curved spine and warming to his subject. "He grew up right here in Winston, where even as a youngster he distinguished himself as a gifted and versatile musician, winning the Young Concert Artist award at the age of..."

Angela sighed. Yes, she remembered: the breezy way Jon mastered instruments, one after another, while she continued to struggle with the flute; that sickening feeling whenever he won another competition—not envy, never envy—but of his pulling inexorably away.

"Therefore, it was no surprise to anyone who knew him when he won a full-tuition scholarship to Juilliard...."

Angela lowered her eyes, memories of that red-letter day assailing her without warning: the rumble of his vintage Mustang idling at his mailbox; the tinny squawk as she opened her own mailbox, only to find it empty; the fragrance of daffodils that inextricably mixed those days with painful anticipation; the toot of the horn, his grin as she'd turned, his minimal thumbs-up gesture—and then her heart exploding in joy for him.

With an effort Angela directed her thoughts away from the past and back to Mr. Beech. He was telling the others what she already knew: that Jon had spent a couple of summers studying at Tanglewood and Aspen; that he'd gone on to play with a small philharmonic in Spain and another in Brazil; that he'd recorded several albums, both classical and jazz; and that he'd recently returned from an unprecedented tour of China. Since moving to Florida, Jon's mother had kept old neighbors apprised of his accomplishments by sending press releases to the local paper.

Angela's gaze swept over him slowly, all six feet two inches of him. The distance between them had grown abysmal. But then, maybe there had been an abyss there all along. That thought caused eddies of resentment to stir deep inside her.

Why they'd been best friends was beyond her, except that fate had put their homes across the street from each other. Jon was everything she was not—extroverted, unconventional, intuitive and daring. Being so strong-willed, he had dominated the friendship and far too often coerced her into accepting his choices, adopting his interests and, alas, doing things she never would have done on her own. In retrospect, Angela sometimes wondered if he'd thought she had no mind of her own.

"Jonathan finally returned to the United States in August," Mr. Beech went on, "and soon afterward learned he'd won a coveted first-horn seat with the Boston Symphony Orchestra."

Angela's back pressed into the chair. Good Lord! Jon had landed a job with the BSO? How had that news gotten by her?

Still grappling with this impressive fact, Angela was suddenly struck by another. Jon was now working in *Boston?* He was that close to Winston?

She didn't realize she was staring at him openmouthed, until he winked back. A couple of heads turned in her direction. She covered her burning cheeks with damp palms and tried to concentrate on Mr. Beech's voice.

"When I found out Jonathan was in the area, I called to see if he could fit in a brief appearance with us. He was extremely gracious and accepted my request on the spot. And so, ladies and gentlemen, please welcome our guest soloist for this year's Christmas concert, Mr. Jonathan Stoddard."

Jon acknowledged the applause of the seated musicians with a lazy smile and a low sweeping gaze. Like a bored monarch, Angela thought resentfully.

Mr. Beech held up his hand. "Mr. Stoddard has also volunteered to sit in on the rest of the program, so if you'll add another chair..."

The remainder of the rehearsal passed in a blur. Angela was jumpy, conscious every second of Jon sitting just two rows behind her. She told herself to relax. Their friendship had ended nine years ago, and nothing was expected of her now. Still, she continued to worry. After rehearsal, they'd have to say hello—common courtesy demanded at least that much—and though the transaction wouldn't take but a minute, she dreaded it more than a root canal.

Inevitably, Mr. Beech clicked off the light on his podium. "Until next Wednesday. We have only two rehearsals left." He glared sternly. "So, be here." He stepped down and made his way to the back of the stage where Jon was packing up his horn.

They probably needed to discuss the selections Jon would be playing as guest artist, Angela thought. The next moment she felt giddy with relief. Quickly and as unobtrusively as possible, she put on her coat, gathered up her things and headed for the exit.

Outside snow was falling, muting the multicolored lights decorating Winston's main downtown street. Angela paused under the street lamp in front of the theater to dig out her keys from her purse, her legs still quivering.

The door behind her opened, and her already strung-out nerves pulled even tighter. Which was ridiculous, she told herself. It was probably just another musician eager to leave. Nevertheless, she took a hurried step off the curb.

"Hey, Westgate. Slow down."

Angela's heart stopped. No, it wasn't just another musician. Had she actually believed it would be? Suddenly she felt trapped, light-headed and almost sick to her stomach.

With cheeks ablaze, she turned and stepped back onto the sidewalk. "Hello, Jon."

He covered the distance between them in an instant, then set down his horn case and pulled her into a tight embrace. "I can't believe this!" He laughed, hugging her right off her feet. Angela was overwhelmed by a sudden onslaught of leather and wool, coarse beard and hard muscle.

"I can't believe this!" he repeated, and she wondered what was so strange about finding her playing with the WSO. Where else would she be? *She* wasn't the one who'd left town.

Finally he set her down but still held on to her shoulders. "How are you, Angel?"

Her breath caught. Angel. She'd forgotten. Jon was the only person who called her that. Angel. A name she'd always secretly loved, his own private endearment for her. But then, maybe she'd invested it with more than he'd ever intended.

She tried to remain impassive. "Very well. Yourself?"

"Great, great." He flashed her one of his ten-thousand-watt smiles, but with a flick of her long blond hair she looked away. Maybe nine years had done the trick for him, but if he thought *she* had forgotten any of his callous, self-centered and hurtful behavior, he had a big surprise coming.

At last he released her and stepped back. "Well, you're certainly looking good these days. All grown-up and polished."

"Thank you." She didn't smile. She'd always favored clothing with a polished classic look.

"Not just your clothes," he said uncannily. "It's your face, your hair. Are you doing something different with it?"

Angela thought about the three years it had taken her to grow it so long, the regular hot-oil treatments and expensive highlighting she had done at the salon. "Yes. I've taken to combing it."

Jon's smile reached his eyes. "Well, you're doing a good job."

Angela refused to be charmed. "So, Boston, huh?"

"Yeah." She heard the slow pleased grin in his voice.

"You must be very happy."

"I am."

Angela chewed on the inside of her cheek. Although the BSO was one of the most prestigious orchestras in the world, Jon probably saw it as just one more whistle-stop reference to add to his résumé.

"Where are you living?" she asked, resigned to the fact that the situation called for at least a modicum of conversation. As soon as they'd talked enough to fill the courtesy quota, she'd get in her car and drive off, forgetting that Jon Stoddard had ever been here.

"Cambridge. I'm subletting an apartment from a Harvard professor who's teaching abroad this semester." His gaze traveled the gaily lit street, over the plate-glass-and-brick facades of the small stores that looked the very same as when he and Angela had been children. His eyes narrowed with an emotion she couldn't quite peg.

"Say, is there someplace we can go for coffee?" he asked abruptly.

"C-coffee?" This wasn't supposed to happen. What was wrong with the man? Didn't he feel any of the awkwardness she was suffering? "Gosh, I'm sorry, Jon. I...I can't."

A tiny frown etched itself between his brows. "Sure. Maybe next week."

"Next week?"

"Mmm. Rehearsal?"

With a hand that shook visibly, Angela brushed snow from her eyelashes. "Jon, if there's anyone who doesn't need to come to rehearsal, it's you. I could hear you over those seventy other people."

He shrugged. "It's a good excuse to visit you again."

Angela's discomfort deepened. She didn't want Jon visiting. She knew what he was like. One day a visit, and the next your life turned into an amusement-park ride. Well, she wouldn't allow it. She liked her life exactly as it was—quiet, ordered, purposeful.

"Angel, are you sure you can't squeeze a cup of coffee into your evening?"

She fidgeted with the strap of her shoulder bag. "I have things to do."

"Half a cup?" He brought himself down to her eye level, smiling his most winsome smile.

She sighed, feeling transparent. "Well, maybe half a cup. There's a diner up the road."

She noted the disappointment in his eyes even as he said, "Sounds good."

She felt thoroughly ungracious. "Or," she added, "you could come to my place..."

"Sounds even better." Jon's smile returned in full.

Snow swirled against her scalding cheek. Now she'd done it.

"Let's go then." Jon picked up his horn case. "Where are you parked?"

"Across the street."

"Great. I'll follow you." He walked briskly to a low-slung sportscar glinting a deep blue in the streetlight.

Angela's guard fell for a moment and she gave an incredulous gasp. "This isn't yours, is it?"

"My pride and joy."

She stepped into the street and stalked the car as if it were an alien craft. "It's a Mercedes, Jon!"

"Is it really? Hot damn!"

She leaned over to admire the rich interior. "I thought we took a vow against owning Mercedes."

"That was then. Besides, why are you drooling?"

"W-why?" she stammered, realizing she had initiated this slide into familiarity. "Uh, because I have to toodle home in that thing." She pointed across the street to her sensible five-year-old Ford.

"How very like you, Westgate."

Angela bristled under his knowing tone, and she snapped, "See you in a few minutes."

As Angela drove the four miles to her condo, her foul mood deepened. "How very like you," she repeated mockingly, glaring at Jon's low headlights in her rearview mirror. Her eyes caught the reflected light and sparkled back at her, big and blue, belying the long trying day she'd put in.

Jon didn't know her any better than he knew the man in the moon. She'd changed, and the changes ran a lot deeper than outward polish. She drummed her gloved fingers on the steering wheel, then gave it a short sharp jab.

Jon had *never* known her, the big conceited jerk! One day when they were sixteen, he'd mentioned that he was writing a piano piece for her. She'd been intrigued, maybe even a little flattered—until she'd heard the stupid thing. It was a waltz. "The Angel Waltz," he'd called it.

She didn't say anything then, because at the time she didn't understand the reasons herself, but she'd hated it. With its steady one-two-three rhythm and sweet predictable melody, the piece had been a perfect emblem of their relationship. Jon had never seen her for the complex person she really was. The waltz had said it all: here was a person you didn't have to think too hard about or expect to be surprised by.

Well, Jon Stoddard would have his socks blown off if he got to know her now. But she wasn't about to give him the opportunity. Oh, no! This was going to be the fastest cup of coffee he'd ever had!

CHAPTER TWO

ANGELA FLIPPED ON her directional blinker and led Jon through the stone gate and up the lighted drive toward a hamlet of two-storied quasi-colonial row houses, one of which she now called home. Candles and Christmas trees glowed in almost every window, a sharp contrast to the darkness of her own place.

Jon parked beside her and got out of his car. Planting his hands low on his hips, he turned slowly, giving the development an assessing gaze. "Give me a break, Westgate! You really live here?"

She cocked her chin. "Lock, stock and barrel."

"But I thought we took a vow against condos."

"That was then." She marched up the path to her door, leaving him to whatever recollections he was trying to exhume. She would have none of it. What was the point?

Inside, she stamped the snow off her boots and switched on a living room lamp. "Here, let me take your jacket."

"Thanks." Jon's penetrating gaze was already roving, taking in the neat room and its traditional furnishings. "All sarcasm aside, how did you end up living here?"

"It was my mother's idea. She got tired of dealing with the old house, especially after my father died. It was unwieldy—so big, so many repairs."

"True, but it had character. All the houses in our neighborhood did."

Angela shrugged noncommittally. "Come on into the kitchen. We can talk while I put on the coffee."

"Do you miss it? The old house?"

Angela willed her face to remain blank. "This is so convenient and modern, how could I?" She opened the refrigerator and reached for the coffee.

"Well, I miss ours. My parents have a nice place now, but it's just not the same." He took the can from her, and while she filled the glass carafe with water, measured out the fragrant grind.

"I'm sorry I wasn't here for her funeral."

"I didn't expect you. You were...heaven knows where."

"I still feel bad. Your mother was a wonderful lady, and what I'm trying to say is, I'm sorry she's gone."

Angela gazed up into his dark velvet eyes and allowed a moment of honesty. "I know."

"It must be tough, with Christmas coming up."

She swallowed. "Sometimes. More than half a year has passed, but still..."

Jon tipped up her chin. "If there's anything I can do..."

Angela wished she could believe he was serious, but she couldn't. Even if he hadn't treated her so hurtfully, leaving her with a heart full of resentment, too much time had passed. They had drifted, grown apart. They weren't friends anymore, no matter what he tried to pretend.

"Let's go sit where it's more comfortable while the coffee's brewing," she suggested coolly.

He followed her into the living room. "So, what's going on in your life these days, besides playing flute for old man Beech and the Winston Symphony?"

Angela sat in one of the wing chairs and wondered how to respond to the sarcasm she thought she heard in Jon's voice. "Winston might not be the BSO, but it isn't chopped liver, either."

Jon looked slightly confused.

"I'm teaching mostly," she replied. "I split my time between the high school and Winston College."

Instead of sitting, Jon paced the room, taking in the details. "That right? College? You must have an advanced degree, then."

"Yes. In musicology."

"Ah." He brushed his long fingers across a shelf of books, then stepped back to take in the floor-to-ceiling array. "You were always such a good student." His voice was lightly mocking.

"Bet your life I was," she replied more vehemently than she'd intended. Jon didn't really know, did he? He hadn't been around to see her truly shine.

He crossed in front of the fireplace over to the entertainment center. "How did the University of New Hampshire turn out for you?" But he seemed more interested in her videotape collection than in her college career.

"It was great." Something deep inside her made her add, "It wasn't Juilliard, of course...."

Jon glanced over his shoulder, frowning again.

"Come sit," she said. "You're making me nervous."

"Oh, sorry." Before he did, though, he pressed a button on her stereo system and a soft-rock radio station came wafting through the speakers—an old Karen Carpenter song.

"I hear Beech is retiring after this concert." He sat on the camelback sofa opposite her and, resting his elbows on his knees, tapped his fingertips together, tense with nervous energy.

"Uh...yes. He suffered a mild heart attack last summer."

"That's too bad. He'll be hard to replace."

"Yes." Her pulse hammered. She considered telling Jon that she was hoping to be that replacement, but then remembered she wanted to keep him out of her life. Besides, he wouldn't understand either her drive or her ability.

"So, how do you like the place?" she asked.

"It's okay, even if it is a condo. It's solid, substantial. Has a strong sense of permanence. Or is that just because you have so much furniture from the old house?"

Angela tipped her head. "You remember?"

"Yes." For a moment she almost offered to take him on a tour, but she used her mother's room as an office now, and too much of herself was scattered about: the poster of Catherine Comet, her favorite female conductor; a score she'd already started to annotate in anticipation of the March concert. It wasn't so much that she was embarrassed over her presumption that she was going to get the directorship—the marked-up score was more a sign of her need to be prepared than of her ego—she just didn't want Jon to see it and start asking questions.

"Our coffee smells about ready." She almost launched herself from the chair, eager to escape the tension created by their thin conversation.

But even when she was alone preparing the tray, her uneasiness remained with her. She wished Jon hadn't come back, wished she'd skipped rehearsal tonight, wished she hadn't opened her big mouth and invited him over. She had the feeling she'd dragged in a lighted Roman candle and was just standing by waiting for it to go off.

"Here we are." She set the laden silver tray on the coffee table. In her absence, Jon had changed the radio station—Miles Davis replacing Karen Carpenter—and resumed wandering again.

"Do you still take one sugar?" she asked.

"Uh, no. No sugar. Who's this?"

Angela glanced up to find Jon holding a small framed photograph. The spoon slipped from her hand with a clatter. "His name's Ivan Dillane."

Jon scowled. "Yvonne?"

"Ivan. I-v-a-n," she spelled out. "But he prefers a more ethnic pronunciation. Ee-von. He teaches at the college, too."

"Ah. Is he your man of the hour?"

"And when have I ever had a man of the hour?" Loving-and-leaving had always been Jon's specialty, not hers.

"Of course. You started looking for Mr. Right when you were ten. I forgot. So, is he it? Mr. Right?"

"Could be. He's just about everything I've ever looked for in a man." She attempted a confident smile, but the afternoon's argument repeated on her.

"Hmm. I didn't realize you were into the tweedy professorial type."

"Why not?" Her mouth tightened. "We only have everything in common—our jobs, acquaintances, our sense of traditional family values, even our leisure activities. We both love to attend auctions and spend quiet nights at home."

"Hmm. How old's this guy, anyway?"

"Only thirty-two. It's the beard that makes him look older."

Jon placed the picture on the coffee table and sat on the sofa. "What does he teach?" His eyes moved from the photo to her and back again as if trying to see them as a couple.

"Russian language and literature."

"Really? Must be an interesting guy."

"Yes." She fixed her gaze on the coffee cup in her lap, searching for a way to steer Jon clear of her private life. "How about you, Jon? Are you seeing anyone these days?"

He broke into a smile. "Yes, as a matter of fact. Her name is Cynthia Gardner. We met in Bahia a year ago when she was doing a shoot for *Mademoiselle*."

"A model?"

"Yes."

Angela should have expected as much. What she didn't expect was the dull ache of disappointment she felt as the words "a year ago" sank in.

"Are you two serious?"

He took a while to answer. "We could be."

"Really?" Angela stared into the middle space between them. Jon had never been serious about anyone in his life. "How do you and Cynthia keep in touch? Being a model, she must have to live in New York."

He nodded. "When she's working she does. Then she comes home to her parents in Boston."

"Oh. How...convenient." Angela took another sip of coffee, choking on barely enough to wet her lips. Is that why he'd applied for the BSO slot? To be near Cynthia?

"W-would you like a piece of cranberry bread?" She held out the plate and noticed it was shaking. "My sister Peg made it."

"No, thanks. How is Peg these days?"

"Very well. Would you believe she's expecting her first grandchild?"

"That right?" He smiled. "Well, she did have a head start on you, being nineteen years older and all. Where's she living?"

"Vermont, up by Stowe."

Jon's eyes narrowed. "Oh, that's too bad."

"What do you mean?"

He shook his head regretfully. "I was hoping you wouldn't be alone here after your mother died."

"I'm hardly alone, Jon. Granted, Peg isn't exactly within drop-in distance, but we visit often enough. And I have Ivan and my students and the WSO. I have more companionship than I know what to do with." Feeling inexplicably uneasy, she picked up the picture of Ivan and returned it to the shelf.

She and Jon had touched on just about every topic people cover after not seeing each other for a while—family, jobs, love lives. It was time for him to leave. So, why didn't he? And why did he have that disturbing little frown between his eyes, even when he smiled?

"Well, I should be hitting the road."

Angela turned from the bookshelf, somewhat startled. There had once been a time when, young and foolish, they'd believed they could pick up each other's thoughts telepathically.

"But before I go..." He paused.

Angela felt her scalp prickle in apprehension. "What?"

"When I was looking over your shelves before, I couldn't help noticing you have the first eighteen years of our lives preserved on videotape." Jon had always been observant, but now Angela felt positively invaded.

She glanced over her shoulder at the row of neatly marked video boxes. "Yes. Even the old eight-millimeter home movies my father took. I had them transferred to tape a few years ago." Her eyes were suddenly pleading. "You can't possibly want to see them now. There must be eight hours—"

"Oh, no. Of course not." Jon sounded sincere, yet he avoided her eyes.

But Angela didn't care if he was disappointed. She didn't want to go tripping down any damn memory lane with him. Their friendship was over, gone with the warm breeze that had blown over them that summer morning when they'd awakened on Mount Adams nine years ago.

"Maybe you'll let me borrow them sometime."

"Sure." Angela remained standing, trying to give him the hint.

"Though in all honesty, I'd give my eyeteeth to see the lip-synch contest right now." He paused, flashing her one of his most convincing grins.

"You can't be serious."

"C'mon, Angel. Just our act. How long can it take? Three, maybe four minutes?"

She laughed but stood her ground. "Sorry. You'll just have to wait until you borrow it. And I have to warn you, Jon, you'll probably be disappointed. The past is always brighter in memory."

Jon frowned and stared at her. "Angel, what's the matter?"

The genuine concern in his voice unnerved her. She looked away, swallowed, then replied, "Nothing." She could feel his hot scrutiny in the silence that followed.

"Sorry," he finally said. "I guess I'm pushing too hard, aren't I?"

Angela froze, realizing they'd been on the same wavelength all along. "What do you want from me, Jon?"

"I... I don't know." He hauled himself off the sofa and paced the room restlessly, his hand pressed to the nape of his neck. Finally he turned to her, his casual smile back in place. "Hey... gotta go. I have a long drive ahead of me."

Without arguing, Angela retrieved his jacket from the closet and held it open for him.

"Thanks for the coffee." He flipped up his collar and turned to leave.

Impulsively, Angela gripped his arm. "Jon, wait. I'm sorry if this visit hasn't turned out as you expected. But, well..." She let his arm go and stared through the storm door at the sugary snow glistening on her front steps. "A lot of time has passed since we last saw each other. We've changed, developed individual interests, made new friends. And all that—" she wafted a hand toward the videotapes "—that was then. Not that I don't have fond memories, but, well, friends drift apart. It just happens, as naturally as childhood ends."

Jon gazed through the fogging glass. "Even best friends?"

Unexpectedly, Angela felt a clutching in her chest. "Those especially."

He only nodded, a tight gesture of resignation, before stepping out into the night.

She closed the door as soon as the engine of his Mercedes turned over, then distractedly gathered up their coffee things and put them in the kitchen. She was right. They probably didn't have a thing in common anymore, and even if they did, his insensitive treatment of her nine years ago precluded any possibility of their acting on those commonalities. Besides, she was far better off without him in her life, coercing her into foolish stunts like that lip-sync contest.

Yawning, she turned off the living room lamp, determined to put Jon from her mind and get a good night's sleep. But as she rounded the sofa, the small red eye of the VCR caught her attention. She glanced away, but it drew her back magnetically. After a moment's hesitation, she switched on the TV and in its flickering glow drew forward the hassock.

Not that she was really interested in watching this adolescent nonsense, she told herself as she slipped in a tape. Just mildly curious, that was all.

She fast-forwarded through most of the event, sponsored annually by the high school drama club, and then pressed the play button. The screen came alive at the very moment the crewnecked president of their class stood at the microphone introducing them as the Rolling Stones—Jon, herself and three of their friends.

She shook her head, still unable to believe he'd gotten her up there. The introduction was followed by applause, whistles and catcalls from the audience. Then the music started, and the student response grew thunderous.

Angela blinked, still amazed by Jon's totally uninhibited mimicking of Mick Jagger singing "Satisfaction." From the distance at which Peg had been holding the camcorder, it hardly mattered that Jon didn't look like Mick Jagger. At seventeen, he'd been tall and slim—too slim to play football, but a person never told Jon what he couldn't do—and that was enough to evoke a satisfactory resemblance. What really did the trick, though, was the sinuous way he'd gyrated across the stage. He'd been positively outrageous, and the place had gone wild.

Now the camera shifted, and Angela ducked her head. She had no interest in seeing herself pretending to be Keith

Richards, no interest in being reminded that once she'd been that young and foolish.

She looked back just as the number ended. Over the applause she heard her sister's cheer—"Way to go, kids!"—and for a moment fought back a smile. On the screen, Jon dropped his stage persona and scooped a laughing seventeen-year-old Angela off her feet in an exultant twirling hug.

Quickly she fast-forwarded, over the remaining performances, over the announcement of winners and Jon's returning to the stage to claim his trophy. Of course he'd won first prize. Didn't he always?

The screen then went to fizzing static, but Angela's eyes remained fixed. A moment later the picture cleared, as she'd known it would, and suddenly it was summer. Graduation, saved for posterity on another tape, was a month behind them, college yet a month away, and she and Jon were packing his Mustang for one of their frequent trips into the White Mountains.

"And here they are, those world-famous climbers..." It was Peg's voice again, commentating in documentary style.

Angela sat on the edge of the hassock, coiled into a knot of remembrance and pain, the corners of her mouth turning ever downward. She had forgotten summer could be that golden.

"To survive the rugged terrain of New Hampshire's high country," Peg went on, "a camper must be prepared with the right equipment." Here, the camera zoomed in on Angela's sturdy boots. Then, "Do something, Angie."

To comply, Angela tucked her walking stick under her arm and did a lighthearted soft-shoe shuffle across the driveway, ending with a poke to Jon's backside as he bent over his car's engine. Jerking upright, he bumped his head on the raised hood and swore.

Angela, sitting in the dark of her living room, bit her quivering lower lip, laughed aloud and then drew in a shuddering breath. The next moment, two hot tears spilled down her cheeks.

She watched Jon join her dance, then pull her into an exaggerated tango, his thick dark curls falling in sharp contrast against her pale straight bob. She studied their open faces, looked hard into their guileless eyes and wondered if either of them had suspected that when the sun rose the next morning, they'd no longer be friends but lovers.

CHAPTER THREE

BY THREE-THIRTY, the campus was already darkening. Angela crossed the quadrangle as quickly as her leather-soled boots would allow. The snow that had been tramped to an opaque mush during the busy day was beginning to freeze in treacherous patches. She huddled into her white wool coat, wishing her day was over. Wishing, too, she wasn't so tired.

A snappy wind gusted down the open hill, rocking the tall lighted fir tree in the center of the quad and causing Angela's eyes to water. For the hundredth time that day she cursed Jon Stoddard for keeping her awake half the night. Oh, she'd tried to sleep, but hours after he'd left, the very air around her had still vibrated with his presence. She'd continued to hear the deepened timbre of his voice, see the new lines of maturity in his face, smell his spicy scent, feel his roughened cheek. In one short visit, it seemed, Jon had saturated her senses.

Well, it didn't matter now, she thought. It was over. Of course, she'd still have to face him again at possibly two more rehearsals and then at the concert, but there would be no repetition of last night's folly, no friendly chitchat or going back to her place for coffee. In fact, after the blunt send-off she'd given him, she'd be surprised if he even said hello next time they met.

"Angela!"

She recognized Ivan's voice and turned on the steps of the faculty building. He caught up with her and, removing his pipe, kissed the side of her mouth. Reflexively, she backed off, uncomfortable with public shows of affection.

"Heading upstairs?"

She nodded, ducking eagerly into the warmth of the building. "I have to get some things out of my office for my four o'clock class."

"I'll keep you company, then."

They climbed the stairs to the second floor where Angela unlocked the door to a space that could justifiably be called a cubicle. Ivan closed the door behind her, and the room seemed to shrink even more. He wasn't a particularly tall man, but he was broad and solid.

He unbuttoned his coat, then removed his karakul hat, lifting carefully from the crown and setting it on Angela's desk. His fine sandy hair crackled with static electricity.

With a small shrug of apology, Angela transferred his hat to a chair and opened her briefcase. "What are you doing for dinner tonight?" She smiled warmly, hoping to ease any lingering tension from the previous day's argument.

He tapped his pipe into an ashtray, kept on a windowsill just for him. "Not a helluva lot. I have a department meeting at five. We're sending out for pizza."

"Oh, that's too bad. I was hoping we could get together. Ah, well. Maybe tomorrow night."

"Yes, of course."

"What? Oh, that's right." They always ate together on Fridays. Chinese takeout and a rented movie. Her place. The routine never varied.

"Excuse me, Ivan." She brushed past him to get to her record cabinet.

"Why didn't you call me last night? You always call after rehearsal."

Angela's stomach muscles bunched. She selected an album and fitted it into her briefcase. The plain truth was she'd forgotten to call. After Jon had left, she'd been so upset she'd simply forgotten.

"Sorry. I really am. But..." She contemplated telling Ivan about Jon's visit, but instinct told her to keep the two men apart even though logic failed to come up with a reason. "I was so bushed I went straight to bed."

"Angela, Angela." Ivan sighed as if she were a child who constantly tried his patience. "You know how worried I get when you're out at night by yourself. Call me next time, all right?"

Angela nodded, opened a drawer and frisked the files within for the handouts she needed to copy.

"All right?" he asked more forcefully.

Her fingers stilled. Ivan's protectiveness toward her was one of his most endearing qualities, but the undertone in his voice now unsettled her. "Yes, I'll call." She shut her briefcase, glanced at her watch and headed for the door.

But on the way Ivan gripped her arm. "About yesterday..." The bunched muscles in her stomach knotted. "I was wondering, have you been thinking about what I said?"

"Yes. I told you I would." She tried to pull away, but he tightened his hold.

"I'm serious this time. We've been together too long, we're both adults, and these are the nineties. No one would condemn us or be surprised if we...loosened the reins on our relationship a bit. As it exists now, it *is* sort of Victorian, don't you agree? In fact, most people would be surprised if they knew just how chaste it's been."

Angela rubbed a spot between her brows where a headache was starting. "I said I'd think about it. And you agreed to give me until Sunday."

He let her go, nodding. "It just seems a thing one shouldn't have to think about. It's a romantic relationship, for heaven's sake, not a military strategy. If you really cared about me, you wouldn't have to think at all. We'd just be sleeping together, and I can't help wondering if something else isn't wrong, something you haven't told me."

Angela reared back, her cheeks warming. "Like what?"

"Well, like sexual dysfunction."

Her eyes snapped wide open.

"It's nothing to be embarrassed about. We could go to therapy together."

"Thank you. That's just what I needed to hear. Dysfunction." She took a determined step toward the door, only to have her path blocked.

"Well, how do you explain it? There isn't a couple we know who isn't... intimate."

"Really? And how have you verified such a fact, Ivan?"

"Now don't get testy. I'm only trying to help."

Angela took a deep breath. Then another. "I know, I know. And maybe we... I do have a problem. I'll give the possibility my undivided attention as soon as I can, honestly, but right now I have a class to prepare for."

She started for the door again, but suddenly Ivan pulled her against him and kissed her, hard. Angela went stiff with instinctive resistance—which he probably took as proof of dysfunction, she thought miserably. With a concerted effort, she willed herself to relax. She didn't want to hurt or upset him any more than she already had. He was too nice a person, and although relations between them were somewhat strained at present, they'd been good in the past and, no doubt, would be good again in the future.

After what seemed an eternity, he lifted his head and smiled. "Now we're making progress." When he bent to kiss her again, however, she pushed away.

"Really, I have work to do."

He moved in, anyway, encircling her in an embrace that felt more like a death lock.

"Ivan! Stop it!" Her unease became anger.

A sudden hard rap on the door made them both jump. Off guard for the moment, Ivan relaxed his hold and she was able to pull free. With a hasty pass at her hair, she swung open the door. She expected to find another teacher or a student on the other side. The last person she expected to see was Jon.

"Hello, Angel," he said evenly, but his eyes narrowed and fixed directly on Ivan.

She finally found her voice. "W-what are you doing here?"

Immediately Ivan's hand curled into her shoulder. "Who's he?" he demanded.

"Who are you?" Jon volleyed back.

Angela gulped. "Seems introductions are in order. Jon, this is my friend, Ivan Dillane. Ivan, this is Jon Stoddard, the guest soloist for this year's WSO Christmas concert."

She wondered if she could leave explanations at that, but from the scowling puzzlement in Ivan's gray eyes, she knew she couldn't. Why would the guest soloist be meeting her here? "Jon also happens to be—" she gulped again "—an old friend. He's just recently returned to the States after several years abroad."

The men sized each other up before shaking hands.

"I hope I'm not interrupting anything," Jon said.

Angela got the distinct impression he knew exactly what he was interrupting.

"I just thought I'd drive up for a visit."

She wanted to remind him he'd visited only last night, but then realized that would catch her out in her fib about going to bed early. "Well, how nice. We barely had a chance to talk last evening."

Jon glanced from her to Ivan. "Yes." He took her briefcase from her and, gripping her arm, made to escort her out of her office. "You were heading somewhere, right?"

"Uh . . . yes. The photocopy machine downstairs." From the corner of her eye she saw Ivan puff up with anger.

"A pity you came at such an inconvenient time, Mr. Stoddard. Angela has a class at four."

"Oh, does she?" Jon's expression brightened. "And what about you, Ivan? Do you have a class, too?"

Gripping Angela's other arm, Ivan replied, "No, I'm done for the day."

She eyed him curiously. "Except for your four o'clock tutorial, and it appears he's eager to get an early start. Hello, Kevin."

A rangy young man, sitting halfway up the stairs to the third floor, smiled at Angela and blushed.

"Ah, then this is where we say goodbye. It was a pleasure meeting you, Ivan," Jon said, dismissing him with infuriating congeniality.

"Ee-von."

"What?"

"You called me Eye-vin just now."

"I did? Oh, I'm so sorry."

Ivan hitched his shoulders, once, twice. "I'll call you later, Angela," he said. "Better yet, I'll stop by. My meeting should be done by seven, and you'll already be home. Right?" He glanced at Jon, his eyes sharp with challenge.

"Yes, of course."

"So long," Jon called amiably, as Ivan stamped up the stairs to his office. When he got no reply, he chuckled. "Cheerful fellow, your Yvette."

For a moment, Angela's guard fell and she grinned. Immediately she was sorry. They weren't fifteen anymore. The days when they could poke fun at each other's love interests were long gone.

"You shouldn't have done that," she snapped, tromping down the stairs.

"Done what?" Jon grinned rakishly.

"Made fun of him. Ivan isn't just some guy I'm hoping'll ask me to the prom. I happen to care about him. A lot." She received a careless shrug in response.

They entered the brightly lit workroom, and Angela headed straight for the photocopy machine in a flurry of busyness. She positioned a handout on the machine, closed the cover, pressed thirty copies and then the print button.

"So—" She faced Jon squarely "—what are you doing here?"

He leaned against the worktable, arms folded across his supple leather jacket, one booted ankle crossed over the other. Angela noticed a secretary on the far side of the room peeking at him with badly concealed interest. As upset as Angela was, she couldn't blame the woman. Jon was big and bad and beautiful, and she could barely keep from staring at him herself.

"I don't suppose you'd believe I missed you?" he drawled.

"Not a chance."

"Okay, how's this? I've picked up with a jazz band in Cambridge, and I was wondering if you'd like to come hear us play Sunday night."

Angela fixed her gaze on the bright seam of light oozing from the covered machine. "A *jazz* band?" she echoed.

"Yeah. I've always played jazz on the side. You know that."

She snatched up the fresh copies from the tray and tapped them into order as if trying to knock some sense into them.

"It's a great group of guys, and I like the place. It's small, intimate."

She opened her briefcase and tossed in the handouts, wondering why she was getting so riled. Jon wasn't her concern. She had her own affairs to tend to. "What do you play with this jazz band?"

"Piano. Just like the old days."

Angela shook back her long blond hair as if shaking off the phrase "old days." She said cooly, "I don't play that sort of stuff anymore myself. My schedule's too busy, and one would think yours is even busier."

Jon chuckled dryly. "You don't know the half of it."

"So, what are you trying to do to your career, Jon?" She slapped another sheet into the machine and lowered the cover.

"What's that supposed to mean?"

"It means you've just landed one of the best jobs on the planet, and instead of concentrating on it, you're diffusing your energy, losing focus."

"Huh?"

"Oh, I know, you never could sit still. But, Jon, this is it. Real life. Isn't it time you got serious?"

Jon's jaw hardened. "There was a time when a thought like that wouldn't have even crossed your mind, let alone your lips. What's happened to you, kid?"

Angela placed the stack of still-warm copies into her briefcase and snapped it shut. "Maybe I've just grown up."

His face dropped. "Thanks a million, pal."

Angela glanced aside, realizing she was vastly overreacting, and the worst part was she didn't even understand why. Perhaps it was merely a response to his showing up so unexpectedly.

"Jon, if all you wanted to do was invite me to Cambridge, you could've done that by phone. Why are you really here?"

With a glance toward the eavesdropping secretary, Jon picked up Angela's briefcase and ushered her out to the corridor.

"As briefly as I can put it, I've missed our friendship, Angel, and now that I've returned to the area, I want it back."

Angela shrugged out of his grip. "Just like that. You want it back."

"Yes."

"Just like..." She snapped her fingers.

"Yes. It isn't a complicated concept, sweetheart. I don't know why you're having such trouble with it."

"Don't be cute."

"I can't help it."

Angela pressed her fingers over her eyes and groaned. "I thought I made it clear to you last night—"

"The only thing that's clear, my friend, is that unlike you, I don't know how to turn off eighteen years of memories. You're woven too close into the fabric of my life. How do you do it, Angel? I'd really like to know."

Angela squirmed under the intensity of his stare. "If that's so, why didn't you contact me sooner? It's December, Jon. You returned in August."

"As I said, I've been busy. Do you have any idea what it's like being thrust into the full working schedule of the BSO, five, sometimes six performances a week, the program changing constantly?"

"But you still had time for Cynthia and a jazz band." Angela hated herself immediately. She sounded so peevish.

"If you really want to know, I was afraid to call you."

Angela laughed derisively. "You? Afraid?"

"Yes. I had a feeling this would be the reception I'd get."

She didn't know how to respond. Should she say she was sorry? She couldn't, not after what she'd suffered. Finally she just answered, "I have a class."

"May I sit in?"

"No!" What was wrong with the man?

"Why not?"

"Oh, I don't know. I'd just rather you didn't."

"Come on. I won't throw spitballs or pass notes."

Angela was beginning to feel trapped, and from that feeling sprang honesty. "But I won't be able to think with you there. I'll be awful."

Jon laughed, wrapped his arm around her shoulder and tugged her to his side. "No, you won't. You'll be great." And that, because he said so, was the end of the argument.

He sat in the last row, as he always had. Murderers' row, she remembered one harried teacher calling it. Students trickling in eyed him with interest, but Jon remained cool, his long legs stretched into the aisle, arms crossed over his chest and a hellish glint sparkling in his midnight eyes. Standing at the podium, Angela felt those eyes running an amused survey of her. She must look very staid to him, she thought, in her neat boiled-wool jacket and matching beige skirt, with simple gold studs adorning her ears and oh-so-sensible low-heeled boots protecting her feet.

The hands of the clock reached the hour, and her heart lodged in her throat. Damn him! she swore silently. This was her life, not a joke. She scanned the class, gathered up her dignity and began.

As usual, she was well prepared and somehow muddled through. But when her lecture came up fifteen minutes short, she decided to make Jon pay for causing her to talk so fast. She apologized to the class for hurrying—as if she'd planned it that way all along—but, she said, she wanted to introduce them to a special guest.

In the back row, Jon sat up as if he'd been poked.

When she explained what Jon did for a living, interest ignited immediately. "If you have any questions, I'm sure Mr. Stoddard will be happy to answer them."

A dozen hands went up. They asked about his background, who his favorite composers were, how often he practiced, even what he earned. They were still asking questions when the period ended.

Jon ambled up the aisle once the last of the students was gone. "Good save, Teach."

Angela turned her back to him to erase the board. If anyone had saved the day, it was Jon. He'd fielded the unexpected questions with such easy grace and humor.

"So, where's a good place to eat around here?" he asked.

She eyed him over her shoulder. "What?"

"Do you have a favorite restaurant?" He slapped his forehead. "Oh. That's the other reason I drove up here—to take you to dinner."

She wasn't amused. "Jon, all I want to do is get home, climb into my fuzzy bathrobe and..."

"That's okay, too. We can pick up a couple of hamburgers on the way."

With a soulful sigh, she slipped on her coat. "You aren't going to quit, are you?"

He shook his head fractionally, his firm sensuous mouth curled at one corner.

She huffed. "All right. We'll have dinner, but here, on campus."

"Here?"

"Yes." She didn't want to go off to any restaurant where conversation might grow too personal, and she certainly didn't want him back at her place. "It's . . . faster."

"Oh, yeah. I forgot. Yvette will be at your place by seven." He zipped his jacket and flipped up the collar. "Bundle up, Teach. It's cold out there."

"I know how to dress, and you'd better stop calling Ivan . . ." Jon looped her scarf around her neck and mouth twice, so that the rest of her words came out woolly.

"I've always wanted to do that."

"Wha?"

"Gag a teacher."

All Angela could do was glare.

Outside, evening had nearly fallen, a quarter moon gleaming silver in an indigo sky.

"This is a nice little school," Jon commented.

"Hmm." Angela scanned the neoclassic buildings, their white pediments pale in the moonlight. Christmas candles glowed from every multipaned window. "It's what you expect of a New England college. Brick and ivy and maple-lined paths."

"Are you happy here, Angel?"

"Sure, I'm happy," she answered automatically.

"Then . . . everything is good with you?"

She looked at him askance. "Yes. My life is very full, very rewarding."

He nodded, that disturbing little frown between his eyes again. "So, what do you teach, besides music appreciation?"

"Here? That's it. But I also direct the chorus. And over at the high school I have two classes in theory and, of course, my string orchestra."

Jon's steps slowed significantly. "You conduct?"

She turned on the icy path to face him. "Yeah, I conduct."

A slow smile lit his face. "Well, I'll be damned."

"You probably will be."

He laughed, scratching his head. "When the hell did you decide—"

"Junior year of college." They resumed walking. "And you don't have to look so astonished."

"Sorry. It just takes a little getting used to. You were always so quiet."

"Quiet doesn't mean timid, Jon."

"I'm surprised you're not interested in Mr. Beech's job."

"Who says I'm not interested?" Too late she realized the admission was out. She waited, feeling her cheeks grow warmer by the second.

When Jon failed to respond, she glanced over. He was staring straight ahead, his expression unreadable. *He doesn't believe I'm qualified,* she thought. *He's thinking I've become an overreaching fool.*

She wanted desperately to change the subject. "Let's take this path," she suggested. "It's quicker."

"To what? Are we still on our way to dinner?"

"Oh, yes."

They walked on, their breath billowing in white clouds over their heads.

"This is so strange," Jon said after a while.

"What is?"

"Being here like this, walking with you to dinner."

"I don't follow."

"Well . . . I can't help thinking that this is what college might've been like if we'd gone to the same school." His voice was thick and wistful.

"Oh."

"That was when the thread got broken, wasn't it, Angel? When we went off to school."

She tensed. "It couldn't be helped. It's where we applied, where we got scholarships..."

"I know. But I still feel I missed out on something. We stopped sharing things. There's a gap..."

"Well, you needn't beat me up with the fact. It wasn't *my* fault." Immediately she wished she'd kept the thought to herself. The air between them crackled with remembrance and recrimination.

"Where exactly are you taking us to dine?" Jon's question was an obvious digression, one she gladly embraced.

"The cafeteria."

"Oh, joy."

"I don't exactly relish the idea myself, but as I said, it's fast." And safe, she added to herself.

They entered the dining hall and were immediately hit with a wall of music pulsing from the jukebox. Silver and gold garlands hung in haphazard loops from the ceiling, while cardboard Santas and snowmen smiled from support columns. Angela gazed over the noisy sea of young people, took a moment to question her sanity, then plunged forward to the food line.

"Mm-mm. Tonight's special smells like greasy french fries and burnt coffee. Can't wait!" Jon's words caught in her hair, puffs of warm breath that sent shivers down her back. She pressed forward, needing to put more distance between them.

They finally purchased their meals and found space at a table. Four guys who looked like basketball players sat on either side of them. As she'd anticipated, it was difficult to talk, and so they ate, Jon looking increasingly frustrated.

"Tell me more about your Yvette," he said, leaning in. "How long've you two been together?" Apparently he was going to make a stab at conversation, anyway.

"Half a year, and stop calling him Yvette."

Jon's smirk told her he'd do whatever he wanted. "He surprises me. I thought he'd be proper and reserved."

"He is," Angela said.

"Yes, but he's rather a jealous sort, too, isn't he?"

Angela's lips tightened. "Don't be ridiculous." She glanced away uneasily. "And what if he is? I find jealousy flattering."

"I find it suffocating, a sure sign of insecurity."

"Insecurity? Ivan is the strongest person I know."

"I'm not talking biceps."

In an unguarded moment, Angela wondered what would happen if she flung a forkful of fries into Jon's know-it-all face. "Ivan is solid, mature, serious—"

"Hmm. He *is* serious, isn't he?" Jon rolled his eyes.

"Yes, he is," she returned proudly. "And he's ready to settle down. Eager to settle down. I like that in a guy."

"And you don't see his eagerness as a facet of his insecurity?"

"No! I see it as a strength. He knows what he wants. A home. A family. And I find that refreshing. I've had it up to here with guys who can't commit."

Jon pushed aside his half-eaten meal. "Are you done?"

For a moment she wasn't sure what he was referring to—her tirade against footloose egoists like himself or her meal. Her ears grew hot.

"Do you want any more of that?" he said.

"Oh. No, I'm done."

"Then let's get out of here." He scraped back his chair and stood. Angela's gaze traveled up the length of him. The differences between Jon and the boys who shared their table were remarkable, and again she was reminded of their lost years, the years that had wrought those differences.

She refused to get misty about them, though. Jon seemed to want her to, but she simply wouldn't. Those years had also been a time of confusion and pain, and she wasn't about to forget that he had been the cause. In fact, she'd had about all she could stand of Jon Stoddard for one night. He'd gotten around her attempts to send him packing two hours ago, but she wouldn't allow him to dictate any more of the evening.

Out on the sidewalk she set down her briefcase to tug on her gloves. "Well, Jon," she said in an unmistakably dismissive tone, "this has been nice." Dismissive, insincere and condescending. And she wanted him to hear it.

He didn't, or if he did, he chose to ignore it. "Let me walk you to wherever you're going."

"That's not necessary."

"I know. I'll walk you, anyway," he replied.

Frustrated and feeling somewhat disoriented, Angela headed toward the faculty building. She hadn't a thing to do there, but she'd concoct some excuse once they arrived.

They walked on, the crunch of their boots in the snow amplified by the silence of the night.

"Angel, I have to be honest..."

She tensed. She knew that tone, that presage to something too personal to bear.

"The real reason I drove up here today... I simply felt I had to. I felt compelled to finally apologize and try to explain."

Angela's heart raced. She felt it thumping against the weight of her coat. "I don't know what you're talking about."

"I think you do. This tension between us—I'd hoped time would cure it and we could just sweep the whole matter under the rug, but I guess it's bigger than I thought."

Angela spun on him. "Oh, you finally figured that out, huh? How insightful! How intelligent!" Immediately, she regretted her outburst. It was an obvious admission of her vulnerability. "What do you want from me?"

He resumed a slow pace up the walk. "As I said, I feel the need to apologize. I want us to be friends again, but I can see that's not going to happen until we get over the hurdle of that... that incident."

"I don't want to talk about it."

"Angel, it's been nine years, and it's still eating away at you. Me, too. We have no choice but to talk."

Angela gazed at the faculty building across campus, wishing she was there, safely cloistered from this nightmare. "Maybe you're overestimating its importance and the effect it had on me." She hoped she sounded more cavalier than she felt.

Jon turned her to face him. "Look at me, Angel, and if you can repeat what you just said, maybe I'll believe you." Framed by the upturned collar of his leather jacket, his face was intent, very male and far too handsome. In his dark eyes shimmered the heat of that fateful July day, every nuance of sensuality she'd learned in his arms. And though the temperature now was somewhere in the bracing twenties, Angela felt a flame curl through the pit of her stomach.

Slowly, the corner of his mouth lifted in a small sad smile. "Aw, Angel, I wish I could make you understand how truly sorry I am for what happened."

She ducked her head, her eyes stinging. "Do you know what hurt most, Jon? Not talking afterward. All those days, those weeks, when you ignored me."

Jon thrust a gloved hand through his hair. "And do you realize how scared I was, Angel?"

"Scared?"

"That's right. I kept thinking, 'What've I done to our friendship? What the hell have I done?' I mean, you and I had shared all kinds of experiences, but that one..." He glanced away, eyes narrowed as if in remembered pain. "That one was a bit too complicated for most people to handle, let alone a teenage boy. If I shunned you, it wasn't because I meant to hurt you. I just didn't know what else to do."

The moisture pooling in her eyes threatened to spill. She'd always known he hadn't wanted *it* to happen and didn't understand why his saying so now should hurt this much.

"Is that the only reason?"

"Yes." He raised his right hand. "Scout's honor."

"You were never a Scout, Jon." She pulled a shredded tissue from her pocket and dabbed her nose.

"Hey, what did *you* think was going on?"

Angela looked aside. How could she even begin to tell him? "Nothing. Nothing, honestly."

They walked on in uneasy silence.

Jon finally muttered, "To this day I still don't know why we did it."

"No mystery there. Too much was happening in our lives at the time, too much change. Everything familiar and secure was coming to an end, so we turned to each other, as if clinging could hold the future at bay."

Jon nodded circumspectly. "I suppose you're right. Damn, but you always could analyze the hell out of everything and come up with some theory. Me, I seem to recall the incident growing directly out of a conversation we were having about your virginity and how embarrassed you were going off to college without any sexual experience."

"Jon, please!" Her voice leapt in panic. "I'd rather drop this discussion if you don't mind."

"But if we don't talk, I don't see how we can get back to being friends."

"Who says I *want* to get back?" Angela stopped and squinched her eyes tight. "I didn't mean for that to come out quite as coldly as it did. It's just that you and I . . . we're different now, we're adults, and it's hard for a woman who's practically engaged to one man to carry on a friendship with another. Not only hard, it's not right. It compromises the relationship she has with her fiancé."

A frown worked its way over Jon's brow. "Oh. I guess I never thought of it in that light."

"Well, do. It's important."

"You're engaged?"

"Well . . . practically."

"Hmm." He walked on pensively. "About that incident, though . . ."

"Enough about the incident."

"But we haven't solved a damn thing!"

"So what?" Angela was startled when she actually stamped her foot. They'd reached the faculty building, and in the light thrown from the door, she clearly saw amusement in Jon's face.

"That a new dance step?"

"Yes. Want to see another?" She contemplated kicking him in the shins, but took a deep calming breath, instead. "Listen, Jon, I appreciate your intentions, and it was nice having dinner with you, but, well, this just isn't going to work. Nobody's fault. I'm simply not interested in complicating my life right now, and if nothing else, you're definitely a complication." She peeked up, wondering if he was finally getting the message.

Jon's gaze swept over her so slowly her stomach fluttered. "I understand."

"You do?"

"Sure. You're still in shock, my appearing out of the blue and all. I'll give you a few days, then we'll talk again." He grinned.

"Will you never give up?" she wailed, but it was becoming increasingly difficult to restrain her amusement. They were both laughing when the door of the faculty building opened and Ivan stepped out.

"Ivan. Hi," she said awkwardly. "Done with your meeting?"

He descended the steps with slow deliberation, his gaze sliding from her to Jon and then back to her again. "I thought you were going home."

"Yes, well . . ."

"I'm afraid I shanghaied her into going to dinner with me, Ivan." Jon pronounced Ivan's name correctly this time. "My fault entirely."

Angela wished Ivan would say something to ease the tension he was creating. She was sure it was inadvertent and he wasn't really as upset as he appeared.

"I'm glad we've run into each other again," Jon continued. "I mentioned to Angela that I'm playing with a jazz group in Cambridge on Sunday night, but of course she wouldn't commit you to a date without checking with you first."

Angela glanced at Jon quickly, wondering why he was bringing that up again. She'd already told him no. But even more perplexing, she wished she could divine the reason he'd just called her "Angela" and why it felt so much like protection.

"Sunday night is rather inconvenient," Ivan grumbled. "We both have work the next day."

"I realize that, but it's the only night I play. And we do start early, so you can leave early."

"It's a long drive."

"True. A little over an hour. But it would be a great opportunity for us to get to know each other. You and Angela, me and Cynthia." Jon paused, and Angela was sure he was waiting for the names to take hold.

They did. Ivan relaxed noticeably. "Are you married, Mr. Stoddard?"

"No. Not yet." But his tone left the possibility open. "About Sunday, the decision is yours, but personally I hope you'll come. We can have dinner—you'll be my guests, of course. We can sit and relax, get to know one another—kind of like a double date."

Angela finally realized what Jon was up to. If it was impossible for them to be friends as individuals, then he'd arrange for them to be friends as couples.

Ivan thought for a moment. "What do you say, Angela? It might be fun."

She shouldn't have been surprised. Ivan was scrupulously careful with his money, and she'd seen the glint enter his eyes as soon as Jon mentioned the prospect of a free meal. "The idea has possibilities." She tried to sound cheerfully polite yet noncommittal.

"What time should we meet you?" Apparently Ivan mistook her answer for a yes.

"Six would be good, and it'll be easier if you go directly to the club." Jon proceeded to give directions. When he was done, he held out his hand. "Looking forward to it, Ivan."

Ivan hesitated, then shook his hand.

Angela looked away, gnawing on the inside of her cheek. The more determined she was to keep Jon out of her life, the deeper he wormed his way in. And now she was locked into a whole social evening with him. Dinner, their dates, the works.

She glared as he walked off toward the parking lot. So, Jon wanted them to become friends as couples, did he? Well, fine! She'd give him a couple, the most perfectly united couple he'd ever met. Then he'd realize that friendship with her was out of the question and relinquish this impossible pursuit.

CHAPTER FOUR

ANGELA'S SLIP slid down her body with a silky sigh. She straightened the straps and, taking a seat at her vanity, rehearsed yet again what she planned to say to Ivan when he arrived to pick her up for their evening in Boston.

"Thank you for being so patient and understanding." She shook a bottle of translucent foundation. "I've given the matter of our living together careful thought, and the first thing I want to say is, all this reflection has made me realize how special you are to me and how much I enjoy your company."

Angela set down the bottle and groaned. She hated all this tap dancing. She wished she could be blunt and simply say, "Ivan, I don't want you to move in right now. Maybe sometime in the future, but not now." But she couldn't say that, because that was the same answer she'd been giving him for ages, when what he wanted was a definitive yes or no. No quibbling. No putting off decisions until later. Yes or no. And she suspected that unless she could find a few miracle phrases to plead her case, their relationship would suffer an early demise.

She finished applying her makeup and gave her reflection a hard objective look. She was taking special care with her appearance today, fussing with makeup and hot rollers. She was even planning to wear the dress Ivan liked best on her, the pearl gray knit with dolman sleeves. It was simple and classic, yet fell over her slender figure with soft sensuality. She hoped it helped.

But it probably wouldn't. A no didn't become a yes just because you wore a nice dress when you said it, and before the night was out, Ivan would undoubtedly be talking "dysfunction" again.

She combed unsteady fingers through her hair, fluffing out the waves. If only he had the patience to wait, she was sure everything would change in a few weeks. The holidays would be over, the WSO directorship would be settled, and her mind would be much more at ease.

A frown troubled the clear deep sapphire of her eyes. She'd had a lot on her mind that day on Mount Adams, too, and hadn't been bothered by dysfunction then.

Unexpectedly, a hot shudder raced through her, and her eyes drifted closed. How easy everything had been with Jon, how natural and joyous. Nothing she'd ever done, before or since, had ever been so spontaneous or, well, so easy....

They'd spent that hot July day hiking up some fairly rigorous new trails, had pitched camp, cooked their evening meal and cleaned their utensils. Angela was tired, yet she felt an unusually deep sense of well-being, the sort that comes from facing a hard challenge and meeting it. They were camped in an area with a particularly good view, and as the sun arced toward the horizon, she and Jon lay back to watch the fiery spectacle.

In that blissful state of well-being, their conversation ebbed and flowed with a comfortable languor, while before them, a dreamlike panorama of ridges and ravines swam in the gold of the westering sun. The air was fragrant with spruce and lay about them very still, as still as the peace that had settled in Angela's heart.

Inevitably, however, their conversation meandered into the subject that was on their minds almost constantly those days—college and leaving home and all the new experiences that awaited them. Jon, as usual, was eager to get started, but for Angela life seemed to be spinning increasingly out of control. Not only had her father passed away that year, but now Jon's parents were talking about moving, and the peace she'd been enjoying deteriorated into melancholy.

Angela didn't want anything to change. She wanted this golden time with Jon to go on forever. She didn't need new experiences. Everything she needed was right here....

In the nine years that had passed since, Angela had never quite figured out how they'd drifted onto the topic of sex. At the time, though, it seemed all one seamless conversation. Angela did know that at eighteen, not only was she filled with curiosity about the subject, she was also plagued by ignorance and self-doubt.

She'd never had the nerve to ask her mother the questions she asked Jon that evening. She suspected her prim, sixty-seven-year-old mother would have fainted dead away. She wasn't that close to her sister, either, also because of an unusual age gap.

But Jon was wonderful—patient, understanding, almost paternal in his concern. She became so caught up in his deep reassuring voice that when the sun finally set, she didn't even care that she'd missed it.

Yet doubts continued to plague her. Without experience, she found sexuality such a mystery, so remote, so easy to bungle. And that, she supposed, was what led to the startling moment when Jon's eyes lighted with a warmth she'd never noticed before and he murmured, "Come here, Angel." He braced himself up on one arm, lifted the other to her and whispered, "Come here...."

Angela snapped open her eyes and found her reflection in the mirror flushed to a hectic pink. She breathed out a shaky sigh and pressed a hand to her forehead. That night, high above the world, Jon had led her into paradise. In that vast wild Eden it had all been so easy, so spontaneous—like leaping off that mountainside and gliding, wings outstretched, through the pink-and-gold clouds.

They spent that entire night together in the close privacy of Jon's tent, lost in a glorious cycle of making love and drifting into sleep, only to awake a short time later to find the fires of their passion burning higher than before. Nothing had prepared Angela for the need Jon awakened in her that night or for the euphoria she felt afterward, lying in his arms. In retrospect, she recognized it as the single most important experience of her life, and even now, after nine long years, details were so vividly etched in her sense memory that all she had to do was close her eyes to be there again, to feel the soft flannel of Jon's sleeping bag against her legs, to hear the crickets and night birds, to taste the salt of Jon's skin—and remember how deeply in love she once had been.

Angela spun away from the vanity and snatched her dress off the bed. Yes, though it angered her to admit it, she'd been in love with Jon. For her, the emotion had been growing all their lives, and what happened that night had merely been the next natural step in its growth. And she'd thought Jon felt the same. She'd thought they were poised at the start of a romance that would last them the rest of their lives. From the way he'd held her, from the urgency in his voice as he'd murmured her name, what else was she supposed to think?

But apparently she'd interpreted Jon all wrong. The next morning he was uncharacteristically reticent, and after breakfast he suggested they break camp and return home, even though they'd originally planned to stay two more days. Angela's heart splintered. After what they'd shared, she'd thought he would want to stay in the mountains with her forever. But Jon didn't care to stay even one more day. He drove them home, barely speaking, a hard unreadable expression sealing off whatever was on his mind.

Only when they were unloading her gear from his car did he finally broach the subject, which now lay between them like a huge painful burr. "Well, we've done a lot of camping together, my friend." He laughed, somewhat incredulous. "But this trip's been something else." He barely looked at her. Are you okay?"

By then, Angela could taste the tears burning in her throat. "Yes, I'm fine."

"Good. I guess I really wasn't up for camping this time. I hope you don't mind." He already had one foot in the car.

"No, I don't mind."

"Okay, well, I'll call you later, okay? Maybe we can go out for a pizza or something."

"Sure." But even then, Angela knew he was going to break his promise. No sooner did she step inside the house than she felt the first clutches of nausea. She ran to the upstairs bathroom, dropped to her knees and was violently sick to her stomach.

"Angela dear, are you all right?" her mother called with typical alarm.

"Uh... I think I've picked up a stomach virus."

"Goodness. Is that why you came home early?"

"Yes." Angela leapt at the ready excuse and had never been sorry since. Her paleness, her keeping to her room for the next two days didn't raise a single suspicion.

When she finally did emerge, it was to find her deepest fears confirmed. Her lifelong friendship with Jon was over.

Angela's thoughts shifted to Jon's visit to Winston College three days ago, to his claiming that he'd been frightened and confused after they'd made love. He'd blamed his behavior on his youth, but Angela knew there was more to it than that. He didn't mind having her as a friend—but as a lover, a mate? No chance. Angela Westgate wasn't smart enough, wasn't pretty or talented or interesting enough. Jon was holding out for nothing short of perfection. And in the meantime, he had places to go, things to do, and nobody was going to weigh him down. How many times had he told her that himself?

Only trouble was, Angela had thought she might be special. His relationship with her had always been so different, so honest and deep, compared to his relationships with other girls. But apparently, once they'd made love, she'd fallen from that special place and become just one more boring conquest, and worse, another potential anchor, tying him to Winston and threatening to bog down his career. Their lovemaking had meant nothing. A kindness, a lesson, nothing more.

With a ragged sigh, Angela stepped into her gray pumps. More than a year had passed before she'd felt even remotely whole again. Stupid, ugly, insignificant—that was how she'd seen herself after Jon's rejection. Eventually, though, she'd healed, music being her salvation, and after she'd discovered her passion for conducting, she'd positively flowered.

Jon was now quite definitely a thing of the past, and tonight when they met at his jazz club, she wanted him to get that message. She didn't need to be his sidekick anymore in order to have a meaningful life. She was perfectly content all by herself. Moreover, she didn't *want* to be his sidekick. Their lives glided along on very different orbits, and hers, while slower and dimmer than his, suited her just fine.

He'd gone off to chase a dream, and she was happy he was living it. But he had to realize she had dreams of her own. She'd finally found herself, found her passion, her confidence, her niche in the world. Along the way she'd also found a man who treasured her. She wasn't about to give any of that up.

IVAN KNOCKED on her door wearing his best suit and an unusually bright smile. Angela felt terrible. He was in wonderful spirits undoubtedly because he assumed she was finally going to invite him to move in with her.

She hoped he'd put off the discussion until later, after they'd survived their night out with Jon and Cynthia. She so wanted to present a united happy front in their company. But no sooner did they swing onto the highway than

Ivan lowered the boom and asked if she had reached a decision. With a voice that wavered noticeably, Angela recited her practiced lines. Her heart was thumping.

"Fine," he said coldly. She glanced across the front seat to a profile set in stone. "Fine."

"You don't mind waiting, then?"

"Do I have a choice?" He was granting her a reprieve, which was what she wanted, but he wasn't going to be happy about it. She sank into her seat, wondering if he planned to sulk the rest of the night. Oh, Lord, oh, Lord, she worried. This wouldn't do.

The city of Boston came at them in a dazzle of lights, speed and heightened energy. Jon's world, Angela thought almost resentfully, a world where, as often as she'd visited, she still felt slightly lost.

"Do you know where you're going?" she asked, peering at the sleek towers of the financial district set against the pale evening sky. "Jon said the club is in Cambridge."

"Yes, but he told me this is the simplest route. Then we come back over the river at the Harvard Bridge."

"Ah. Storrow Drive. My favorite," she muttered through gritted teeth, while they raced along the narrow river-hugging roadway with the rest of the bumper-to-bumper seventy-mile-an-hour crazies.

Jon's world, she thought again, gripping the armrest with one hand, the upholstery with the other. On the radio, a jaunty Frank Sinatra was singing, "Come Fly With Me." She shut her eyes and didn't open them again until they'd crossed the Charles.

Jon's jazz club turned out to be a small street-level restaurant-cum-lounge in a nineteenth-century neighborhood that had undergone extensive gentrification. Brick sidewalks and old-fashioned laurel-wrapped street lamps lent the area a Dickensian atmosphere.

Upon entering, Ivan put their coats on a rack by the door, then ushered Angela farther into the dimly lit room. Elegant pinecone wreaths graced the walls, their red plaid bows matching the heavy linen covering the tables. Each of those tables glowed with the light of a fat red candle in a glass shade ringed with holly.

Jon was seated at the bar facing the entrance. Angela noticed him immediately. As he did her. His back straightened, while his dark eyes traveled from her hair to her toes with slow deliberation. Had she overdressed? she wondered, feeling her color heighten.

As they approached, he swiveled around to face them, his long legs spraddled negligently, his drink held loosely in two hands.

He was wearing a white T-shirt with a dark tweed sports jacket, a combination that alone should have jangled Angela's sense of fashion decorum. Paired with well-worn jeans and black basketball sneakers, the likes of which she hadn't seen since the sixth grade, her sensibilities should have been outraged. Instead, Angela could only smile, struck by how good Jon looked. How relaxed, how confident and, yes, how elementally male.

"Are we late?" she asked, angry with herself for thinking along such lines.

"Not at all. We just got here ourselves."

Angela glanced up and down the bar.

"She's in the powder room," he explained.

"Not anymore," came a sultry voice. Angela looked to its source just as a willowy beauty wrapped her arms around Jon's waist and fitted herself against him.

"Angela, Ivan, this is my friend, Cynthia Gardner."

Smiling as warmly as she knew how, Angela shook the young woman's hand, which immediately returned to Jon's waist as if attached there by a spring. She introduced Ivan, who, to her undying relief, offered up a brief smile, and then Jon led them all toward their reserved table in front of the stage.

Just as she'd anticipated, Cynthia was gorgeous. Using her own five foot four as a measure, Angela figured her to be close to six feet tall. Her skin was like flawless porcelain, her makeup warm and muted, her scent exotically spicy. But her hair, a red-gold cloud of thick ringlets cascading to midback . . . her hair rendered her practically ethereal. Only belatedly did Angela even notice her outfit, a long-sleeved ballet leotard that emphasized her surprisingly full bust, and a swingy jungle-patterned skirt. As she walked, khaki tigers and giraffes prowled to and fro about her long shapely legs. Angela glanced down at her own outfit and felt like somebody's maiden aunt. But at least Ivan matched her, and that was all that really mattered.

They sat, ordered drinks, opened menus, talked about the drive down from Winston and the pleasant upturn in the weather, and throughout, Angela noticed, Cynthia never once removed her hand from Jon's thigh. Nor did he exhibit anything but devoted attention toward Cynthia. If anyone was scoring points on the couple meter, it was Jon and his walking Barbie of the jungle.

As unobtrusively as possible, Angela scooted her chair closer to Ivan's, but she absolutely refused to do anything with her hands but keep them folded in her lap.

"Well, this is nice." Cynthia's smile was dazzling. "I'm glad we finally got together. Jon has talked so much about you."

"Is that so?" Ivan sipped his vodka, his eyes shifting narrowly from face to face.

"Mmm. You and Jon lived across the street from each other. Right, Angela?"

"Uh, yes," Angela replied hesitantly.

"And is it true that when you were little, you actually did one of those gross blood-brother things?"

"I'm afraid so." Angela's glance grazed Jon's. She didn't want to get into memory-dredging tonight, and she sensed neither did he. That would defeat the purpose of this double date.

"Oh, I have to tell you what Ivan and I did yesterday," she said hurriedly.

Cynthia blinked a few times, surprised by the sudden switch in gears.

"We always go flea-marketing on Saturdays—Ivan collects all sorts of wonderful things—and yesterday we found a mint-condition stereopticon."

Jon's head tilted. "Really?"

Ivan leaned in and, with a smile that was genuine now, proceeded to describe in detail his collection of turn-of-the-century viewers.

Angela was pleased she'd found a way to bring him into the conversation. But before long, she noticed that Jon and Cynthia were straining to look interested. Not that Ivan's hobby was *uninteresting,* but he tended to dwell on the technical side of it, how things worked, their history. The wonderful old pictures themselves left him cold, Angela realized.

Fortunately the waiter appeared to take their order, and when he left, Jon leapt right into the void. "Did I tell you how Cynthia and I met?" He draped his arm across Cynthia's shoulder, while she gazed at him adoringly.

Angela was dismayed by the tightness in her chest. "Uh, no."

"Well, I was strolling through an outdoor market in Bahia one day..."

While Jon told his story, Angela nervously picked at the holly that encircled their table's candle. Had Jon finally found his perfect woman? Physically, Cynthia certainly filled the bill. Professionally it seemed she was at the top of her field, too. Angela couldn't even fault her personality. The woman was warm, charming and guilelessly open.

Evidently this evening really had been planned for them to get to know each other as couples. Which was fine with

Angela. That was exactly what she'd set out to do herself, wasn't it? With a renewed sense of purpose, she buried her dismay and rejoined the conversation.

Cynthia had picked up a thread of Jon's story and was now spinning an elaborate complaint about the heat in Brazil and how hard it was to do a shoot there. Angela was a bit confused, not remembering how they'd arrived at that particular subject.

The waiter came with their food just then, and she thought she saw Jon's shoulders sag just a little in relief.

"Mmm. This food looks wonderful." Angela didn't have much of an appetite, but she tried to appear enthusiastic, anyway.

"It is," Jon added. "I try to eat here at least once a week."

"Do you eat out often?"

He nodded. "Especially the days I have double rehearsal."

Ivan looked from one to the other, a slight frown darkening his eyes. "Angela tells me you play with the Boston Symphony."

"Yes, I do."

"You know, Angela is applying for the position of conductor with the Winston Symphony..."

For some reason, her gaze was still locked with Jon's. At Ivan's words, they both froze—and then looked quickly away.

"It would be a tremendous favor if someone like you could write a letter of recommendation for her."

"Ivan!" She was mortified. "Jon's a very busy man."

"I'm sure he wouldn't mind, would you?"

Jon's lips parted, but he said nothing.

"Of course he wouldn't," Cynthia chimed in.

Angela moved her food around her plate. It was obvious that Jon did mind, and she knew precisely why. He didn't believe she was qualified.

"I'll see what I can do," Jon muttered. "So, have you seen any good movies lately?"

Hurt though she was, Angela still felt a weight lift. Finally a topic they could all safely sink their teeth into. As they talked about one favorite movie after another, she began to relax. She loved films, and soon her appetite returned. Luckily, she and Jon had seen almost all the same ones, a coincidence that fueled enough lively conversation to get them through to the end of the meal.

But finally Cynthia lay against Jon's shoulder and, in a jarring nonsequitor, inquired, "Why do you call her Angel?" The conversation came to a grinding halt.

"I've wondered about that myself," Ivan grumbled.

Angela met Jon's eloquent glance, and they both sighed in resignation. For several minutes now, Ivan and Cynthia had seemed to be growing bored with movies, anyway.

"I'm afraid I started calling her Angel as a taunt, then it just became habit. Her conscientiousness used to drive me crazy when we were kids. Homework always done. Clothing always tidy. She was punctual, kind, never swore or lied..."

"Ah, I see what you mean." Ivan smiled, obviously pleased with this explanation.

Cynthia draped an arm across Jon's chest and in a deep sardonic voice asked, "And what was my sweetie here like?"

Angela coughed behind her hand, smiling. "Your *sweetie* was an unadulterated devil."

"Was he?" Cynthia's green eyes widened expectantly. "Oh, do tell. I need some ammunition when he gets on my case. He says I whine, you know." With a roll of her expressive eyes, she clearly conveyed her opinion that the accusation was ridiculous.

Angela noticed Jon comb his fingers through his hair, several times, and for a moment wondered if the love of his life wasn't so ideal, after all.

"Ammunition, eh?" Maybe one story wouldn't hurt, and it just might give them a few more laughs. She really liked the easy mood they'd fallen into during dinner and hoped it would continue.

A moment later, Angela was deep into a story about an assembly that took place during her and Jon's junior year of high school.

"Our principal back then, Mr. Kelly, always gave a speech at assemblies. He was a sweet man, but unfortunately he could *not* tell a joke." Coffee arrived, and Angela was so animated by now, she was barely aware of spooning sugar and pouring cream.

"But during this one assembly, I realized the students were responding to him. I was sitting with the orchestra up front, below the stage, and I couldn't believe it. They were laughing at his dumb jokes. I mean, really keeling over. So, after about the fourth uproar, I turned around to find Jon, figuring he'd be just as lost as I was, and do you know what I saw?" She leaned toward Cynthia, the steam from her coffee warming her chin. "That monster was holding up a cardboard sign with the word 'Laugh' printed on it. He'd slipped it into his horn case, and everytime Mr. Kelly cracked a feeble joke, Jon, who, mind you, was sitting right under Mr. Kelly's nose, lifted his sign and the auditorium erupted."

Cynthia fell against Jon's arm, giggling helplessly.

Ivan, however, didn't seem to find the story one bit amusing. "Did the principal ever find out? Were you punished?"

"Afraid not." Jon smirked, sitting back comfortably. "To this day, Mr. Kelly probably dreams about that assembly with a big smile on his face."

Angela pointed with her dessert fork. "But some of the teachers saw."

"And?" Jon's smile broadened as his eyes locked with hers.

"And... nothing. That was the trouble with you, Jon. Everyone thought you were so charming you got away with murder."

Ivan was now tapping his spoon, rapidly, against his coffee cup. Was he angry about something? Angela blinked in confusion, and then, like a splash of cold water, it occurred to her: she and Jon had spent the better part of an hour talking either *to* each other or *about* each other.

That wasn't supposed to happen. She'd come here determined to prove he no longer fitted into her life. She'd planned to ignore him, avoid dredging up the past. Time had marched on, and she'd come here precisely to flaunt that fact. She'd wanted to knock away the nonsense he entertained about a renewed friendship and replace it with a crisp clear image of her and Ivan, instead.

She peeked up at Ivan. His expression had turned sullen again, his eyes shifting suspiciously from her to Jon. She reached over, squeezed his arm and smiled reassuringly, but his expression remained unchanged.

Angela was relieved when a young man carrying a saxophone interrupted.

"It's that time," he said, placing a hand on Jon's shoulder.

Jon pushed back his chair. "How long are you people staying?"

Angela glanced at Ivan. "One set."

"That's all?"

She nodded firmly.

Jon seemed disappointed but said nothing, simply rose and strode off to his waiting piano.

For the next forty minutes, Angela sat entranced. Each of the five musicians was excellent, but it was Jon who really held her attention. His improvisational solos took her into musical landscapes that were dazzling in their complexity and originality. Before long she was watching him exclusively, even when he wasn't in the spotlight.

In this setting, Jon was as loose and content as she'd ever seen him. And suddenly she also remembered how much he'd always needed jazz to unwind. Where ever had she gotten the idea it made him unfocused? If anything, he drew energy from playing this music.

She smiled, enjoying his joy vicariously. His thick black hair was mussed, his face relaxed. His whole body had shifted into another mode. Jon didn't just play; he caressed the piano keys, arousing a melody, awakening something in the rhythms that had been reluctant and elusive.

Angela slipped low in her chair, fingers pressed over her mouth, feeling an uncomfortable heat swirl through her. They'd played music together all their lives, but never had she associated sensuality with what he did. This was something new, and she wasn't sure she liked it. She was paying attention to details that had no relevance to the music, such as the sheen of his hair under the lights, the starlike intensity lent to his eyes by the thickness of his lashes, the firm curve of his lower lip, the cleft in his chin. Had his fingers always been so long? Had he always worn clothing with such negligent aplomb? And the energy that drove him, had it ever come so near the surface?

She glanced at Cynthia and for the first time that evening honestly admitted her envy. What was it like, she wondered, being close to Jon now that he was a man? How did it feel to be touched so intimately by his magic?

The number came to a stunning end, and Angela applauded along with the rest of the attentive audience. She was feeling rather fuzzy and warm from the wine she'd had with dinner and was taken totally off guard when Jon lifted the microphone from his piano, swept the audience with his hot dark gaze and smoothly announced, "Tonight I have the pleasure of being here with my oldest and dearest friend..."

She sat up like a shot, her nerves ringing with tension.

"It's been a long time since we've seen each other, but I distinctly remember that when we were kids, she used to play a mighty mean flute."

Angela gripped the seat of her chair, her breathing arrested. *Don't do this to me, Jon,* she pleaded silently.

"I know she'll probably slug me later, but..." Jon reached under his piano and came up with a flute case she hadn't noticed before now. "Angel? How about it?" He looked directly at her, one dark eyebrow arched, and the audience, knowing a cue when they heard one, applauded. She felt dizzy, confused. Blood pounded in her ears. A decade had passed since she'd played in Jon's jazz band. They'd been high school kids then, and she really hadn't been any good. She shook her head and laughed, trying to put him off in a gracefully amiable fashion.

But she should have known better. Jon never gave up until he got what he wanted. "She's really very good, ladies and gentleman. She just doesn't know it yet."

The clapping became more insistent. She looked at Ivan and whispered, "Help me out of this." But Ivan was scowling and continued to scowl until she realized she'd get no help from that quarter. She got to her feet, and on legs that threatened to give out, walked into the warm circle of stage light.

"I'm not just going to slug you, Jon," she said, butting him with her shoulder, "I'm going to kill you." She hoped he realized how truly furious she was.

He handed over the flute with a debonair wink. She considered beating him with it right then and there, but she raised the cold metal to her chin, instead, and ran a quick scale up the keys. She wished she could disappear. She was painfully aware of the audience, aware of the racing of her heart and the dangerous shallowness of her breathing.

She wasn't used to playing jazz. It upset her, always had. Especially improvisation. Just as she'd never been much good at speaking in front of a class unless her speech was memorized, she feared music she hadn't studied and thoroughly rehearsed. While Jon could wing his way through almost anything, her need to be prepared was nearly phobic.

Jon muttered instructions to the other members of the group, returned to his piano, and they started to play a number she was familiar with. They played it simply, straightforwardly. Nevertheless, Angela let the music flow over her for a long while, too terrified to join in.

Jon's gaze lifted to hers repeatedly, but never questioning, never doubting. With her eyes locked on his, she finally raised the flute—and then lost courage again. Instead of dismay, he shot her one of his killer grins. Everything was okay, he seemed to be telling her; she had time, all the time in the world.

She smiled back, and on a momentary wave of confidence, raised the flute and this time began to play. It was difficult at first, and she made a point to play softly. She wished the music could flow from her as it did from Jon, naturally, spontaneously, but that just wasn't the way she'd been born.

Sweat trickled down her sides, and again she contemplated murder. Yet, despite her anger, she clung to Jon's gaze, afraid to let go. More than anything, watching him helped her wherever the music was headed.

Her hair lay damp on her neck and her knees still trembled badly, yet she sensed that her playing was growing more secure, her fingers more nimble. Hanging on Jon's warm supportive gaze, she began to feel connected to him, his strength flowing into her, her insecurity draining away. And although anxiety still fluttered in her stomach like the wings of a thousand butterflies, her mind grew ever more peaceful, letting go of logic, flowing deep, and deeper still, into a river of instinct. Jon smiled, small lines fanning out at the corners of his eyes—and the butterflies invaded her giddy heart.

The saxophone player launched into a solo then, carrying the melody like a slim ribbon into a thicket of complex improvisation. Within seconds it was barely recognizable. Angela clutched the flute under her chin as he played, her mood swinging to terror again at the possibility that she'd be expected to solo, too.

He finished all too quickly, and although she shook her head, the sax player still made it clear that it was her turn to play.

Stage lights blurred, and Angela grew light-headed. Not knowing what else to do, she turned to Jon for grounding. *Please, don't leave me out on a limb,* she begged him with her eyes. And he replied, *Everything's okay. You're safe.*

They played together, flute and piano intermingling in a dance she'd never learned the steps to. Sounds weaving, ducking, leaping around each other in an unpracticed and utterly primal flow. And while she played, she was struck by a disturbing realization. Sometime during the night, she had entered Jon's world. Though she'd fought it, Jon had somehow pulled her into his sphere, into his magic circle. And even while she resented the seduction, she simultaneously experienced a moment of weightless floating joy in what she was doing.

Their duo ended, the audience applauded, and Angela was astonished to find herself laughing, the joy still jetting through her.

The drummer took up the spotlight next. When he was done, everyone returned to the straightforward melody, and before she even realized it, the number was over. Jon came around the piano and pulled her into a tight one-armed hug. She leaned against his side, feeling warm and expansive and so very, very clever.

"You were terrific." Jon's breath tickled her ear. "Now, say good-night to the folks, Gracie."

Still laughing, Angela nodded into the sea of faces, then floated back to her seat.

As the music resumed, Ivan leaned toward her and muttered something.

"What?" she asked distractedly.

"I said, I ought to take that jerk outside and give him what he's looking for."

Suddenly the magic drained out of the night. "Ivan, please."

"Please what? That was insensitive and totally uncalled-for. Making a spectacle of you like that..."

"Oh. Was I that bad?"

"No, no, of course not." But from the way his eyes avoided hers, she knew he didn't mean it.

Ivan was right, Angela thought, wrapping herself into a tight ball of self-examination. She'd hated being up there, hated being pushed to the limits of her abilities, and Jon hadn't had any right doing that to her.

By the time the band took a break, she was only too eager to leave. Jon and Cynthia walked with them to the door.

"Thanks for making the trip down." Jon patted Ivan on the back.

In the wake of Ivan's silence, Angela answered, "Thanks for suggesting the idea."

Jon's mouth tightened as he looked from her to Ivan.

As usual, Cynthia had draped herself around Jon's torso, like a lizard around a warm stone. Angela was surprised she didn't just lift her feet off the floor and wrap her legs around him, too.

Almost immediately she chided herself for harboring such negative feelings toward the young woman. She was a lovely person. Really.

As if to prove the point, Cynthia smiled magnificently. "We'll have to do this again some time."

Angela didn't look at anyone. All she could think was, *Not on your life!*

She crossed the street with her arm tucked under Ivan's—one last attempt to appear the happy couple, one last picture to leave with Jon. Ivan unlocked his car, but just before getting in, Angela looked back toward the restaurant. Jon was still standing at the door, and even though Cynthia remained glued to his side, for a moment, one terribly vivid and totally inappropriate moment, Angela again felt connected to him.

"Get in, Angela." Ivan stood holding her door impatiently. "I want to get home. All that damn noise has given me a headache."

AT TEN MINUTES TO TWO, Angela's telephone rang. "Yes?" she gasped into the receiver.

"Angel. Hi."

"Jon?" She lay very still. "Where are you?"

"Home. Just got in." His voice was dark, deep, tired.

She switched on her bedside lamp. "What's up?"

"Nothing. Just called. Well, not much." He breathed heavily. "Aw, hell, how am I supposed to say this?"

She sat up, uneasy with the serious undertone in his voice. "Say what?"

"Angel, tonight when we were having dinner... remember when Ivan asked if I'd write a letter of recommendation for you?"

"Oh, that." Her voice—and heart—stopped.

"Maybe I should've said something then, but I didn't want to spoil the evening."

"What? Spit it out."

"Angel, don't get all upset now, but I can't write you a letter of recommendation."

"That's okay. I understand." Her voice rasped with heartache.

"No, I don't think you do. I can't recommend you because... because I've applied for the job myself."

CHAPTER FIVE

"WHAT DID YOU SAY?" Angela swung her bare feet to the floor, instantly awake.

"I sent in an application, too. Last August, when the ad first went out. Is that a problem? If it is, I'll call the search committee and tell them to remove my application."

Angela wanted to cry in sudden frustration. What could she say? Yes? That she wanted him to withdraw? That she didn't trust her chances against someone like Jon who got everything he ever tried for?

"Why on earth did you apply for the conductorship of the WSO? Don't you have enough on your plate yet?" Her voice was shakier than she wanted it to be.

He hesitated. "Actually, I applied before I heard from the BSO. It was only one of a few ventures. No rhyme or reason for it."

Angela sensed he was lying. "Are you still interested?"

"Well . . . it might be fun."

Fun? She sprang to her feet and stomped as far as the phone cord would reach. "And what makes you think you're qualified to conduct a symphony orchestra?" Fun. As if the WSO was some easy backwater lark!

"Like you, I've been in the trenches a long time, I know what makes a conductor effective, and I understand music."

"For your information, my qualifications happen to extend a little beyond just being in the trenches."

He must have heard the fury in her voice. The line hummed with silence for too long an interval.

"I said I'd remove my application."

Angela's relief came and went in a flash. "Don't insult me, Jon. Remove your application, and I'll never speak to you again."

"What's that supposed to mean?"

"Isn't it obvious? You apparently believe that if you stay in the race, I can't possibly win." She waited for a denial, but it never came.

"Why are you so upset? I don't even want the job."

"You just said you did. You said it would be *fun.*" Her voice grated with sarcasm.

"Hey, listen, all I wanted to do was tell you I'd applied. I didn't want you hearing about it from somebody else and maybe thinking I'd pulled a fast one on you. The last thing I meant to do was start an argument. Honestly, Angel, you've got to be the most contrary person ever inflicted on the face of this earth."

"And you are undoubtedly the most arrogant. You're a musician, Jon, not a conductor."

"You're pacing. I can hear you pacing."

"So, arrest me!" With her free hand she bunched her hair into a fist and squeezed. She wanted to cry and hated herself for feeling that way. It was weak and irrational and everything she didn't want to be right now.

Jon sighed heavily. "It sounds like there's more to this than you're letting on, and I wish you'd tell me about it."

"It's nothing."

"Like hell. I picked up on this competition thing the other night at your place. Did somebody throw us into a ring when I wasn't looking? What's this all about, Angel?"

She groaned, sinking to the bed again. "You wouldn't understand if I gave you a blueprint."

"Oh. And what exactly is this mysterious thing I wouldn't understand?"

Angela dropped her head into her hand. "Me," she finally mumbled. "You don't know who I am, what's important to me or. . . or anything."

"Okay. I'll accept that as a possibility. I've been gone a while and people do change."

"But you've *never* known me. You've always ignored my needs, my strengths, my...my individuality. When we were kids, for instance, we always did what *you* wanted to do."

"That isn't true."

"It is. Think about it—the games we played, the people we hung around with. Granted, it wasn't entirely your fault. Everybody treated you special, and it went to your head. You got to believing that no one could possibly be as important as you."

"Wait. Could you slow down just a second? Talking to you is like running through a maze at sixty miles an hour. Are you trying to say you were miserable for eighteen years because I suppressed you?"

"'Bulldozed' is a better description."

"Well, thank you very much."

"You're welcome, and yes, you did."

"Like when?"

"Like all the time. That dumb lip-sync contest, for example. Do you think I actually enjoyed that?"

"Yes. Yes, I do."

"Think again, Stoddard. I hated it. I was so nervous I almost threw up before going onstage. I also hated hang gliding, pizza with the works, winter camping, half the movies we saw and all the creeps you fixed me up with. And I most definitely hated playing with your band tonight."

Jon laughed incredulously. "You had the time of your life, and you know it. If you hadn't had me around to keep you loose all those years, you would've atrophied, like you're doing now with that stiff you call a boyfriend. Eevon."

Angela punched her pillow. "You big conceited jerk! Atrophied? *Atrophied?* That's just the sort of blind egocentric attitude I'm talking about. I lead a wonderful life, one I'm perfectly happy with, but because it's not what you would choose, you say I've atrophied. Well, you can go to hell."

"Nice language, Angel."

"Want to hear more?" She paused, shaking. It was the middle of the night, all of New Hampshire was asleep, and here she was, bellowing like a demented fishwife. "Look, all I meant to say was, *you* left Winston, not me. I've made a life here, and I don't appreciate your barging in after all this time, thinking it's okay to do whatever you want and I won't care."

"And I don't appreciate your assumption that I'm some egomaniacal Neanderthal."

"Well, if the shoe fits... You already have a job most musicians would kill for, but for you that's not enough. You've always been that way, Jon. You always needed to win one more award, prove you were the best in one more competition. And it didn't matter that you hurt people along the way. Your ambition was like this huge insatiable—"

"Hey!" His shout made her jump. "I don't have to take any more of this swill. Call me when your brain comes back from the cleaners."

"Don't hold your breath." She slammed down the phone, but not fast enough to beat him to it.

BEFORE ANGELA HAD TIME to sort out all the perplexing emotions that had surfaced during her argument with Jon, it was Wednesday. She taught at the high school on Wednesdays—music theory fourth and fifth periods, string orchestra eighth.

As the last of her students filed out of the practice room, she decided that anyone involved with three different musical groups during the month of December had to be totally crazy. This Friday night was the high school concert, next Tuesday the college performed, on the following Sunday the WSO did its thing, and for each of those events Angela still had a thousand details to arrange. It was not a good week, she decided, leaning over the water fountain to swallow an aspirin.

Not that she didn't enjoy her work; she did. She just wished there wasn't so much of it. There was a side to her that longed to be more domestic, longed to have time to prepare for the holidays with the care her sister took, decorating sugar cookies and walking into the woods for greens, instead of slapping a homogenized, store-bought wreath on her door. And though she didn't often admit it, she also wished she had people in her life to do those things for—a husband, children.

She stepped away from the fountain and wiped her mouth with the back of her hand. Actually, her yearnings for family weren't as beyond reach as she made them out to be. Ivan had talked about marriage on several occasions, making it amply clear that their living together would only be a preliminary. She also knew he didn't expect her to work after they were married, at least not in the fragmented hectic manner she was accustomed to now. He wanted a gracious home, well-tended children, relaxed mealtimes—things she wanted herself. All she had to do was give him a yes.

What she decided to do at that moment, however, was take another aspirin. She couldn't think about a decision of that magnitide just yet. She had too many errands to run, and then she had to get braced for tonight's WSO rehearsal—and facing Jon again, if he still planned to attend. She was pretty sure he would. It all made sense to her now—his volunteering to be guest soloist, his sitting in on the rest of the concert and coming to rehearsal when he didn't have to. He was trying to make his presence felt, not only among the musicians whom he believed he'd soon be leading, but also with Mr. Beech, who held perhaps the most influential vote on the search committee.

Angela swallowed the second aspirin, then filled a long-spouted container and watered the six lushly blooming poinsettia plants on the window ledge. She told herself she shouldn't worry. She had the qualifications; Jon didn't. And she and Mr. Beech were pals. As crusty as the old guy was, he liked her, admired her, and she knew he'd go to bat for her no matter who her competition was.

But she worried nonetheless. Jon was flashy. Jon was a name. Handsome. Famous by local standards. He also possessed a charm the board would not be impervious to.

The board was made up of four middle-aged women whom Angela tried to see as indispensable philanthropists, giving generously of their time to keep the orchestra financially solvent. Yet she couldn't deny that their self-important posturing and lack of any real musical appreciation could sometimes try her patience, and she was sure they were going to roll over and die when they met Jon.

Unless he withdrew his application.

She picked up an empty gum wrapper from the floor and dropped it into the basket. She'd told him not to withdraw his application, but he'd said he would. A couple of times. Would he? Probably not. He didn't understand how important the job was to her, didn't understand it wasn't his natural right to take whatever he wanted. Besides, he never withdrew from a challenge.

As angry as she was with him, though, she still felt bad about the argument they'd had the other night. She wished she hadn't reacted so emotionally. It was totally unlike her to fly off the handle like that. But the WSO meant so much to her she hadn't been able to control herself. Words had simply poured out helter-skelter. Hurtful words.

She didn't resent Jon's success. She never had. So why had she stomped all over it, raving about his insatiable ambition? And what *was* this competition thing all about?

Angela had no answers. Nor did she know how she was going to get through tonight's rehearsal. She'd skip if that was possible, but unfortunately she was chairman of the Christmas party and still had money to collect from several people.

She sighed, unplugged the artificial Christmas tree, picked up her briefcase and turned to leave. A second later her heart was in her mouth.

Jon was standing in the doorway, arms crossed over his chest, the upturned collar of his leather jacket framing his handsome face. Under the jacket, he was wearing a thick gold-toned sweater over brown corduroy jeans. Everything about him was warm and earthy, she thought before remembering to scowl.

"What are *you* doing here?"

His dark starlike eyes traveled the length of her, making her conscious of the trim plum-colored suit she was wearing. His gaze lingered on her matching high-heeled shoes before returning slowly to her face. She wondered what he saw. All grown up and polished? Or atrophied?

He pushed away from the doorway and strolled toward her. "Rehearsal," he explained.

She glanced at her watched. "Bravo. You're five hours early."

"That right?" He looked good, rested, as if their argument hadn't cost him any sleep. Angela's anger heated to a healthy simmer.

"How'd you find me?"

"Easy. I went to the office and said I had a conference with you concerning my kid brother." Jon actually had the audacity to grin. "The secretary was most obliging. Found your schedule, gave me directions, even offered to walk me."

"I bet she did."

Jon stepped onto her podium and scanned the untidy arc of metal chairs and music stands before him.

"Didn't it occur to you," she said, "that I might not want to see you?"

"No," he returned readily. "You know, I could get used to this. What a sense of power."

The simmer rose to a boil. "Oh, really. Do you want this job, too?" She yanked on her coat and tried to hurry past him, but he reached out and caught her by the arm.

"Angel, wait. You know damn well the reason I'm here. Don't make it difficult."

Angela looked him up and down with as much scorn as she could muster. "I don't know what you're talking about."

"Knock it off. In all the years we've known each other, we've never fought the way we did the other night, never, and frankly I don't like it."

"Well, that's too bad. I can't take back what I said just because you don't like it."

"True, but maybe you'll accept an apology."

"I see no point."

"Angel, the point is, I don't want us to be angry with each other."

She slung her purse strap over her shoulder. "Fine. We're not angry."

He fell into step beside her. "Good. Then let's go for coffee."

Closing her eyes, she blew out a sigh. "I don't want any coffee."

He pushed open the heavy glass door, and the December afternoon hit her with a cold damp blast. She huddled into her coat, thinking a cup of coffee would be glorious right about now, and scanned the parking lot for her car. Jon's Mercedes was parked right next to it.

"Angel, stop a minute." He swung her around to face him. She watched the breeze lift his hair off his forehead and was again struck by how compellingly handsome he was.

"What!" she asked with sharp impatience.

"What's wrong with you? Can't you accept a simple apology? I'm sorry you led such a rotten repressed existence being my friend. I'm sorry I made you play music you didn't like, sorry I had the arrogance to apply for the same job you did, even though I didn't know you'd applied. I'm even sorry I like olives on my pizza."

Angela threw up her hands. "There. See? You can't even apologize right."

She turned and marched off toward her car, but not three steps later she stopped again, uncertain if she was seeing right. "What the...?" She inched closer. "Oh, my Lord!"

The entire back seat of her automobile was filled with red and green balloons, their big bright faces pressed gaily to the windows.

"Angel, what happened to your car?" Jon asked, a study in innocence.

She slowly walked a circle around the vehicle, trying to cling to her anger. She didn't want balloons. They were childish and didn't change a thing between them.

"You really ought to lock your car." Jon folded his arms and leaned against her fender. "Anybody could get in."

For one fleeting moment she considered the possibility that Ivan might have perpetrated this whimsical stunt, but the thought dissipated almost instantly. Ivan was too practical, a virtue she normally admired.

Jon opened the door, watching her with a twinkle of mischief in his eyes.

"Did you do this?" She tried to infuse her words with disgust. "What a waste of good money. These things are expensive." She thought of pulling the balloons out, letting them go and destroying his gesture. She didn't want to be cajoled.

But she couldn't. No one had ever given her a gift of balloons before, and they were delightful.

Jon reached around her, plucked a red balloon by its string and drew it out of the car. "Come on, lighten up, Angel," he admonished, bopping her over the head.

"Stop it!"

"Okay, that was childish." He composed his demeanor, the balloon now looking out of place in his long manly hand. "Obviously your anger runs deeper than I thought, and I'm diminishing its importance by thinking a few balloons are going to mollify you."

"Well, thank you, Einstein." She tossed her briefcase and purse onto the front seat, tucked up her coat and attempted to get in. Jon, however, was standing in her way.

"Since I'm here five hours early," he said, his fingers working at the lumpy knot on the neck of the balloon, "and since I have nowhere to go, how about letting me hang around with you?"

His closeness was beginning to disorient her. "Jon, I have a dozen errands to run between now and rehearsal. I can't stop everything just to socialize."

"Of course not. I don't expect you to." As serious as a judge, he lifted the untied balloon to his lips, released a spurt of helium and swallowed. "What I was hoping—" abruptly, his deep voice changed, leaping to a high squeaky register like a record shifting into a faster speed "—was that I could just stay at your place."

Angela's breathing came hard and heavy. She so wanted her reaction toward his juvenile behavior to be anger, but a moment later she was fighting not to smile, and a moment after that, fighting not to laugh.

"So how about it?" he squeaked. "I'll even spring for the beer and pizza."

Angela felt the last of her anger desert her. "What am I going to do with you, Stoddard?" she groaned.

For a few seconds, he fixed her with an enigmatic look, and then he grinned.

AT A RED LIGHT two blocks from the school, Jon beeped his horn and motioned for Angela to let him pull in front of her. When the light changed, she waited, perplexed, as he took the lead. At the next corner, instead of going straight, he turned left. This wasn't the way to her place. It wasn't even a shortcut.

What it was, she soon realized, was the route to their old neighborhood. She tapped her hand on the steering wheel, her resistance rising in a hot aching tide.

"What are you doing, Jonathan?" she complained while her car idled in the middle of Elm Street. He'd already pulled to the curb.

"Just decided to come take a look. I haven't seen the place since my parents moved." He unfolded himself from his sports car and gazed up at the large Victorian that had been his childhood home.

Reluctantly, Angela parked in front of him but kept her engine running. "This is stupid, Jon," she said, leaning out her window. "It's maudlin. Like visiting a cemetery."

He seemed not to hear her but went on walking the property frontage, peering into the backyard, then up to the turreted roof, then back down to the deep wraparound porch. Someone had covered the front door in gold foil and wide red ribbon to resemble a Christmas gift. "Hasn't changed much, has it?"

Her gaze moved across the street to the green-shuttered, white-clapboard colonial where she had been raised. She swallowed.

"This was a nice place to grow up, wasn't it?"

"Jon, let's go."

"I will. In a minute. Lord, will you look at the size of that tree." He turned slowly. Then, "Holy crow! Angel, look."

"What now?"

"The Thurgood house is for sale."

Angela peered through her fogging windshield as he jogged a long diagonal across the street. Groaning in resignation, she turned off her engine and followed.

The house that their sometime friends, Robby and Lisa Thurgood, had lived in would have been impressive in any setting. On this comfortably casual middle-class street, it approached castlehood. Angela was surprised to discover that time had not diminished her reaction to the sprawling English Tudor one bit.

Jon was standing in front of one of the street-facing, diamond-paned windows. The library windows, Angela recalled. He cupped his hand around his eyes and looked in.

"They're gone. The place is empty," he said.

She was more than slightly curious herself now. She crossed the frozen lawn, slipped between the shrubbery and peered through the parlor window. A huge stone fireplace, one of four in the house, faced her from the opposite wall. "Hmm. I wonder where they went."

"Frankly, I don't care. They were such tightwads. Remember the half-rotted apples they used to give out at Halloween?" Jon chuckled, a deep-throated sound that brought a grudging smile to Angela's lips.

"But they made up for it at Christmas. Three trees, remember? One in the parlor, another in the breakfast room, and then the fifteen-footer in the foyer. This was definitely a good Christmas house."

"I'll give them that." Jon walked back down the brick path, turning several times to give the place another speculative look. "Thanks for humoring me, Westgate. We can go run your errands now."

"Gee. Thanks a bunch."

They ate at the small round table in her balloon-festooned kitchen, watching a light snow sift down through the bright outdoor lights on her patio.

Angela remained rather quiet throughout, letting Jon take the reins of the conversation, because quite honestly she didn't understand what was happening between them. She'd been so angry with him just hours before, and if she thought about it objectively, she still had every reason to be angry. Nothing had changed. Unfortunately, what objective reason didn't understand was that it was nearly impossible to stay mad at someone who refused to be mad in return.

"By the way—" Jon closed the empty pizza box "—another reason I came up early... Can I interest you in spending the weekend in Boston?"

"Again? We were just there."

Jon rubbed his dark jaw, his day's growth of beard rasping under his hand. "No, not like last time. How about coming down on Friday night and staying over. That'll give us time to do the city on Saturday. Then at night, well, there's the symphony. You can return on Sunday."

"Oh, Jon, it sounds wonderful." Angela propped her chin on her hand. "But I don't foresee Ivan enjoying such an extended stay in the city."

Jon's face hardened. "Does that mean you wouldn't consider coming by yourself?"

"Jon!"

"No, I guess you wouldn't."

"Well, how do you think that'd go over? Not just with Ivan. What about Cynthia?"

He made a low growling sound of frustration. "You're right, you're right. Ask Ivan to come, anyway. You never know."

But she did know. Ivan disliked going away for weekends. Spending the weekend at Jon's—well, that was almost laughable.

Jon glanced at his watch. "Okay, kid. It's that time."

"Already?" Angela rose with a doleful sigh. They cleared the table quickly and headed for the door. But just before leaving the kitchen, she plucked a balloon down from the ceiling, found the scissors and snipped off the end.

"Okay, now I'm ready." Her sudden chipmunk voice stopped Jon in his tracks. "Will you get my coat out of..." She couldn't go on, succumbing to a fit of laughter.

Jon smiled at her, a deeply pleased smile, she thought. "Westgate, you're incorrigible."

"Thanks. And I owe it all to you." She let the balloon go and giggled again as it swooped about the room, taking a final nosedive into a lamp shade.

Rehearsal ran long, and even when it was over, Angela still had Christmas-party business to finish. She was yawning by the time Jon pulled up in front of her condo.

"Would you like to come in for something to drink? Coffee? Hot cocoa?" She didn't expect him to say yes. He looked pretty tired himself.

"Sure. Cocoa sounds good."

"Oh. Oh, well, sure, okay."

"Is that a problem? I can keep right on going..."

"No. Don't be silly." But she knew a problem did exist. She wanted him to come in. She didn't want their time together to end just yet, and that frightened her. She couldn't remember changing her mind about the status of their friendship. As far as she was concerned, it was still a dead issue. What was Jon doing to her resolve? For while her mind could tick off lots of reasons she was better off without him, her heart felt distinctly otherwise.

"Does this fireplace work, or is it just for show?" Jon called from the living room.

"It works. Why?" She poured milk into a pan and set it on the burner.

"It's chilly in here."

"So turn up the heat."

"Okay."

But when Angela walked into the living room, a log was blazing away. "Gee, make yourself at home, why don't you." She shook her head disparagingly, set down the tray and turned on the stereo. The soft-rock station she sometimes listened to came on, but the station's call letters, which she'd programmed into the machine, were not what she expected. She leaned in to get a better look, then let out an irrepressible laugh. Instead of "WXEB," it now read, "YECH." Would Jon leave no corner of her life untouched?

She composed her expression and turned to find him watching her. Her heart did an unexpected stutter. "It took me three weeks to learn how to program that machine," she complained. "How did you do it so fast?"

He only smiled.

She sat beside him on the sofa, tucking up her legs, and for a long while, they stared at the leaping flames in companionable silence.

"Jon, I'm sorry I blew up the other night." She looked aside, puzzled by her admission. "That's not to say I'm taking back what I said," she added quickly. "I meant it. Well . . . some of it."

Jon rested his hand on the back of her neck. It felt warm and comforting. "Shh. Let's drop it."

Angela nodded, trying not to pay attention to the shivers his gently stroking fingers were creating. "Before we do, though, I have one question."

"What's that?" He lay his head against the sofa back, his dark eyes half-closed.

"What do you intend to do with your application?"

He cast her a sleepy smile. "If you think I'm going to answer that, you're crazy."

"But why?"

"Because you'd damn me whether I withdrew or didn't withdraw. Either way you'd find some excuse to be angry."

"You mean I have to spend the next three weeks in suspense?"

"Uh-huh." He set his empty mug on the end table. "Hey, babe?"

"What?" She was tapping her foot in a sharp nervous rhythm.

"I think you should've made coffee, instead of hot milk."

Her tapping stopped. She turned and studied him in deepening alarm.

"What time do you get up, Angel?"

"Why?"

"Because I have to be at work by nine."

Angela swallowed convulsively. "But you can't stay here."

Jon pried off his boots and lay on his side, his legs slung heavily over her lap and a throw pillow tucked under his cheek. "Wake me by seven, will you, please?"

Angela lifted his legs and stood, folded her arms and huffed. His stubbled cheeks were flushed from sitting by the fire, and the thought crossed her mind that he'd probably catch cold if she turned him out now, to say nothing of the accident he might get into, given his state of alertness.

"Well, you might as well use the spare room." She sighed. "You'll wake up with a stiff back if you sleep here."

ANGELA WAS IN the upstairs bathroom brushing her teeth the next morning when the phone rang.

"Angel?" Jon called up the stairs.

Her heart lurched at the sound. It was so odd having him here, part of her everyday routine.

"Are you able to get that?" he asked.

"No. Will you? I'll be right down." She rinsed her brush, popped it into its holder and hurried down the stairs, carrying her shoes.

Standing at the bottom, Jon was frowning eloquently. Her steps slowed and before she could check herself, she muttered, "Oh, no." Jon's frown deepened.

She took the receiver from his hand and pulled in a shaky breath. "H-hello?"

"Angela, love. You forgot to call me last night."

"Good morning, Ivan. How are you?"

"Not too happy. Why didn't you call? I was worried." Ivan was speaking words of concern, but Angela only heard their steely undertone. Her mouth went dry.

She glanced toward the kitchen where Jon had thoughtfully retreated. What was Ivan thinking? Obviously she had to face the issue head-on.

"Jon stayed over last night. Rehearsal ran late, and he was so tired I was afraid he'd fall asleep at the wheel. I . . . I insisted he get some rest before heading back to Boston." She made a conscious effort to smile and speak in a confident manner.

"I know," Ivan returned. "I drove by your place around midnight and saw his car."

The floor seemed to dissolve from under Angela's feet. Ivan had taken to checking up on her now? "W-why didn't *you* call me?"

Ivan chuckled. "That's the question you have to answer, not I. You're the one with the, ahem, overnight guest."

Angela felt her cheeks warming. "I hope you're not thinking what I think you're thinking."

Again he laughed, a sound like dry leaves in a winter wind. "Yes, well, all I know is, within one short week that so-called friend of yours is sleeping over, something I haven't been able to do in six long months. So you'll have to excuse me if my nose is slightly out of joint."

She felt knotted with frustration. "There's no base of comparison between you two. Jon and I . . . we're just good friends." She pulled up short. What had she said? Did she mean those words? And if she didn't, why had they poured out so easily?

"Yeah, right. And I suppose you're about to tell me all the motels in the area were filled."

Angela pressed a hand to her forehead. "Listen, can we continue this later? I don't know what else to tell you."

"Fine, fine. I'm sorry I interrupted whatever you two were doing." His voice slithered with innuendo.

She was too hurt and angry to muster a defense. "See you on campus," she said quickly and hung up the phone.

Jon was at the kitchen sink rinsing their breakfast dishes.

"You don't have to do that. Leave them, Jon. Please. You've got a long drive ahead of you, commuter traffic..."

He turned from the sink and pinned her with his dark incisive stare. "What are you doing going out with that fool?"

Angela's back straightened. "That's inappropriate and totally uncalled for."

"Is it?"

"Yes." As angry as she was with Ivan, her pride still demanded that Jon see them as a happy couple. "I don't know how that phone conversation came across, but honestly, Ivan was just curious why you'd stayed over, that's all. Everything's fine." She moved to place her coffee mug in the sink but dropped it, instead. She stared at the broken pieces and felt an unexpected stinging in her eyes.

Jon let out a long tight breath. "Great. Everything's fine. Except that you're wound tighter than a top whenever he's around, and I can't help thinking you don't belong with him. I've known guys like Ivan, guys who are so possessive that eventually their girlfriends can't even sneeze without them demanding a written report. Is that what you want, Angel?"

Angela spun on him, resentment rising with unexpected force. "At least he cares." The silence between them throbbed with the unspoken accusation.

"It only looks like caring, babe."

"Jon, mind your own business, okay?"

"That's precisely what I'm doing," he said, his stare drilling into her until she couldn't hold it any longer. Then he turned and walked out to the living room where he shrugged on his jacket. "Thanks for letting me crash."

She tossed her hair back, not answering. Jon opened the front door and paused.

"Call if you need me."

"I won't."

He nodded, thoughtful. "I hope not."

As soon as he was gone, Angela pitched a chair pillow at the door and wailed a long frustrated "Aargh!" She didn't need Jon Stoddard, didn't need him telling her what was wrong with her love life, either. It was fine. Jon just didn't understand commitment—except to himself and his career. He didn't understand someone who cared as much as Ivan did, someone who was content with small-town life and unafraid of words like "roots" and "forever." It wasn't in his nature.

But as her anger ebbed, a pensive tension took its place. If nothing was wrong with her and Ivan's relationship, then why didn't she want him to move in with her? Why did she have this unshakable feeling that their romance had gone just about as far as she cared for it to go?

CHAPTER SIX

THE CHRISTMAS CONCERT at Winston High was in full swing. Angela's string orchestra had gone on first and was now scattering backstage while a noisy crew rearranged risers for the chorus. Directing them from the sidelines, Angela bit her lip trying not to laugh as the artificial snow, meant to fall during the singing of "Winter Wonderland," began to sift down on them.

"Angela?"

"Yes?" she replied, swinging around.

"Good job. Excellent." The young, newly hired director of the marching band was holding out his hand to congratulate her. With a laugh he decided to hug her, instead.

"Thanks, Bob."

"Now, if only I can get my bunch to do even half as well..."

"They will. Have faith."

He crossed his fingers, both hands. "Well, I'd better go check on them in the band room. See you later."

"Sure enough." She smiled happily, watching him hurry off. Angela was in exceptionally good spirits tonight. Being surrounded by dozens of exuberant teenagers was part of the reason, but improved relations with Ivan also helped.

After the words she'd had with him on the phone yesterday morning, she'd dreaded meeting up with him later. But when she'd walked into her office, a vase of carnations had been sitting on her desk, along with a note of apology. Ivan had apologized in person, too, and after her last class, had taken her to dinner. He couldn't have been more attentive.

After he'd dropped her off, Angela had sat for a long time examining their relationship. This was the Ivan she'd known for most of the time they'd been dating.

She'd started seeing him right after her mother died, a time when she'd been feeling rather lost and alone. But Ivan had been there for her, dependably phoning every night, stopping by to have supper, not only filling a void but making her forget it with the ardor of his pursuit. She didn't know what she would've done without him.

Remembering this, she realized the changes in his behavior had come about only recently, and perhaps *she* was the one who'd brought them on. Without realizing it, maybe she'd become inattentive, causing him to feel justifiably slighted. As for the argument they'd had because of Jon's sleeping over, upon reflection she decided that most men would've been just as upset as Ivan. She'd finally gone to bed firmly resolved to put more effort into their relationship.

Now she watched the chorus members, aglow in their festive red robes, file out onto the stage. When the last had taken her position on the risers, Angela gave their leader an encouraging thumbs-up and turned, bumping right into a solid chest.

"Oh. Ivan." She laughed. "What are you doing here?"

He didn't return her good humor. "I thought I'd come by and take you out for a drink. You are done here, aren't you?"

Angela opened her mouth, then closed it again. Her eyes wandered over the lively backstage crowd—musicians, baton twirlers dressed as elves, a portly senior in a Santa suit. She didn't have any specific duties left, but she'd wanted to stay. Being with these lively teenagers was doing wonders for her sagging spirits. It took her back vividly to her own high school days, spent right here in these corridors and classrooms, on this very stage. She was even beginning to catch some Christmas spirit, something she'd given up on this year.

Then again, she *had* made that resolution.

"I'll get my coat," she said with a sinking heart.

On the way out the back door, Ivan asked, "Who was that guy?"

Angela was trying to hear the chorus's first selection, a moving a cappella rendition of "The Christmas Song." "What guy?" she asked distractedly.

"The one who was so chummy."

"Bob?" She peered into Ivan's stern gray eyes and felt herself tense. "You can't be serious. That was just an innocent hug between colleagues. He was congratulating me on the kids' performance."

Ivan snorted contemptuously.

"For heaven's sake, he's married, Ivan. Blissfully so."

"Maybe you think it was innocent, but I'm a man and I know how so-called innocent hugs affect other men. It's flirting, Angela, out-and-out flirting, and I'll have none of it, do you hear?"

Angela stopped in her tracks, the apprehension she'd been feeling deepening to a chill. She'd thought she'd reasoned out Ivan's behavior last night, but this wasn't natural. She contemplated arguing against his irrational accusations, but because they *were* irrational, she doubted even the best defense would do any good.

Of course, she could apologize, reassure him it would never happen again. But giving in suddenly seemed terribly unappealing. She'd only be reinforcing an attitude that was totally invalid.

"Ivan, I hope you don't mind, but I'm not going for a drink, after all."

His brow lowered. "Going back in there, aren't you?"

That was precisely what she wanted to do, but she wouldn't. "No, I'm tired and I'm going home."

"Fine. I'll—"

"No. I'm going alone. I also think—" she swallowed "—I think we should give each other a rest this weekend."

"What?" His eyes chilled to steel.

"We need some space. Maybe the holidays are getting to us, I don't know, but we need to take a break from each other."

"Permanently?"

"That's not what I'm saying. Just...this weekend. It's for our own good. I'm sure we'll appreciate each other a whole lot more after a rest."

"But what'll you do?"

She shrugged. "Christmas shopping. Decorating. And of course, with the semester closing this week, I have a brief-case full of blue books to grade. Don't worry. I'll keep busy and so will you." She opened her car door.

"This is absurd!"

But she was done arguing. She got in quickly, shut her door and sped off.

Angela lit lights in all her downstairs rooms when she got home, poured herself a cinnamon schnapps and turned on the radio. She was still shaking. She hoped she'd done the right thing. It was so hard to tell anymore.

She took a fortifying sip from the glass in her hand, her gaze sweeping the room. What *would* she do this weekend? For while there was certainly plenty to do, she didn't feel like doing any of it.

She paced to the front window to stare at the lights shining from other town houses—white, green, red—their cheery glow only intensifying her growing sense of isolation.

Her mother had moved here because she'd been worried about Angela. She'd wanted to leave her in a place she could handle. Angela shook her head regretfully. It seemed her entire life had been overshadowed by an awareness of her parents' age and infirmity. With a waiting for their death.

She wished they'd stayed at the old house. Although her mother's intentions had been good, this cookie-cutter development had never felt like home. Tonight it felt like a burden, a weight crushing the air from her lungs.

When had everything closed in so tightly? And why was she suffering this sudden need to break free?

Angela closed the curtains with a hard yank, deciding she'd be far better off immersing herself in some task. She lifted her briefcase onto the coffee table and snapped open the locks, but a moment later she was sinking into the spot on the sofa that Jon seemed to favor.

Overhead, a few bright balloons still bobbed against the ceiling, swaying gently in the heat rising from the registers. How she wished he was here.

Angela covered her eyes and let the tears gather. "Oh, Jon," she whispered, her throat tight and achy. She shouldn't want to be his friend anymore. It was an impossible situation for so many, many reasons. Yet, at this moment there was no one on earth she wanted to talk to more than Jon.

Impulsively, she hauled herself off the couch and went to the phone. She was well aware that he might hang up on her, and her hands shook as she dialed. She'd practically thrown him out the last time he was here, telling him to keep his opinions of her and Ivan to himself, and when he'd offered his help, she'd tossed it right back.

"Jon? Hi!" She sounded like a cheerleader. A nasally sounding cheerleader.

"Hey, kid." A smile warmed his voice.

"Hi!" she repeated. "I didn't know if you'd be in."

"Been in for hours. We do a matinee on Fridays."

"Ah. Good concert?"

"Out of this world. Strauss's Alpine Symphony."

"Great, because you know what? I have the chance to attend tomorrow night's performance, after all." She waited for a response, but the line went silent. "That is, if the invitation is still open." *He knows something's wrong,* she thought. *Damn, he knows.*

"Of course. How many tickets will you need?"

"Uh, just one. Ivan...has something at the college. A b-banquet. But he insists I go and enjoy the weekend."

"He does?"

"Sure. You know how it is. There are just some times when people have too many commitments and have to go their own ways." She was almost choking on her words.

To her undying relief, Jon only replied, "Can I expect you tonight?"

"It's kind of late. How about tomorrow morning?"

"Sure. But you will be staying over on Saturday night, won't you?"

She hesitated, pulses thrumming. "I guess."

"Terrific. Got a pen? I'll give you directions."

When he finished, she stared at her handwriting and wondered if she'd ever be able to decipher the nervous scratches. Maybe it was a sign she shouldn't be doing this.

"Is Cynthia going to the concert, too?"

"Uh-uh. She's on a job out of town."

Angela wet her parched lips. "That's too bad. It would be nice to have someone to sit with."

"Angel, is everything okay with you?"

"Sure. Great," she answered, falsely bright. "Well, I'd better get some sleep. See you tomorrow." She hung up the phone and butted her head against the wall until it hurt.

THE APARTMENT Jon subletted was on the first floor of an elegant three-and-a-half-story brick house near Harvard Square. Angela rang the bell, and before she could even step back, the door opened with a vigorous *whoosh.*

"Hey! You made it." Jon was wearing gray cords and a heavy black sweater that looked hand-knit. He was clean-shaven; his thick curling hair, still damp from a recent shower, looked remarkably neat, and he smelled wonderful, a combination of soap and something cinnamon.

"Come in," he finally said, making her realize she was gaping.

The apartment was large and surprisingly bright, with a feeling of airiness created by the high ceilings, white walls and broad expanses of polished oak floor.

"Jon, this place is wonderful."

"Mmm. I'm enjoying it. Unfortunately, the couple who lives here'll be back after Christmas."

"What are you going to do then?"

"Not sure yet. Hey, let's take your stuff into the guest room and I'll show you around."

He led her toward one of two bedrooms, where she lay her garment bag over a bed.

"I hope I'm not interrupting anything. If you have to practice for tonight..."

"No, I'm done. Already put in my three hours."

Angela glanced at her watch, amazed by his industry.

He offered her coffee, which she declined, and took her on a hasty tour. On a windowsill over the kitchen sink, she spotted a row of photographs.

"Oh, your parents." She smiled, picking up one of the small framed pictures. "How are they?"

"Same as ever. Extremely busy. Still running their music shop. Oh, and now my mother's into scuba diving."

"They look wonderful." Angela peered intently at the photograph, at the handsome dark-eyed man Jon resembled, at the vibrantly smiling woman from whom he'd inherited his free spiritedness. "I miss them," she said without intending to.

"You'll just have to visit them sometime, then, won't you?"

"Mmm." She put the photo back and scanned the others. "Oh, gosh." Recognizing her senior-class picture, she grimaced, even though she was terribly pleased at having been included. "Who are these other people?"

"Friends I made in my travels, people I played with on the road. That was Vienna. That one there, Japan."

"You haven't talked much about those years. Do you miss it, being on the road, seeing all those exciting places?"

He was quiet a long while, eyes fixed but unfocused. "It was a wonderful experience. I learned a lot. But it catches up with you after a while. Living out of a suitcase, the tiredness..." He shook his head. "You may not believe this, but after a while I really got to missing New England. Missing Winston."

"You're right. I don't believe it." Angela was puzzled when he didn't return her humor, when his face continued to sober.

"One day I woke up and realized I didn't own a damn thing, Angel. Only my clothes, those pictures, a hot plate. Even worse, I didn't belong anywhere."

Angela would've liked to believe he was serious, and maybe right now he was, but she knew the mood wouldn't last. Jon didn't know the meaning of staying put. The only thing that was uncertain was how long it would be before he left. Two years? Six months? A frown tightened her brow. Already she knew his leaving was going to hurt.

"Ah, well," she sighed, "if you want to keep moving, you've got to travel light. Right?"

He blinked, emerging from his thoughts. "Oh... right." But he smiled only halfheartedly.

She followed him back to the living room, where he unhooked his leather jacket from a coat tree.

"Are you still up for doing the city?" he asked. The soft December light angling over his face unexpectedly caught her attention. Jon had always been handsome, but now his looks were overpowering. For a moment, she almost forgot to answer him.

"I—I'm looking forward to it."

"Good. I am, too."

Angela zipped up her pink ski jacket, a garment she didn't wear often, and pulled a pair of matching angora mittens from her pocket. From her other pocket, Jon pulled fuzzy pink earmuffs and, obviously quite amused by the things, slipped them on her head. "Cute, Westgate. Very cute." When he tucked and smoothed her hair, her breath grew alarmingly shallow.

"So, where would you like to go?" he asked.

She was sure her cheeks were as pink as her outfit by now, but she refused to make anything of it. Her reaction to Jon was perfectly understandable. He'd grown physically into a very compelling man, and she was simply having trouble reconciling the new with the old.

She reminded herself again of the reason she'd come here. A couple of days away from Winston would do her and Ivan a world of good. This weekend would relax her, recharge her batteries, and when she returned, their relationship would be better than before.

"Choose something." He opened the door. "The Museum of Fine Arts? Faneuil Hall? The aquarium?"

"So much to do, so little time." She felt his hand at the small of her back and shivered. "Faneuil Hall?"

"Okay."

"Are you sure? It's shopping, Jon."

He winked agreeably. "I know it's shopping. The question is, do you have the patience to help me with the list I've got tucked in my back pocket?"

She smiled. "Only if you have the patience to help me."

"What do you have to buy?" They stepped out onto the bright brick stoop.

"Everything, but I'll be content if I can just find some toys for my sister's youngest boy."

"Now, that's my kind of shopping."

The subway transit system was far more practical than driving a car into the congested city, and so they took the "T" from Cambridge across the river into Boston.

"We must be out of our minds," Angela complained, emerging from the subterranean dankness of the T-stop. Ahead of them the area seemed a near-solid mass of shoppers. "Ten days before Christmas, and we decide to do Faneuil Hall."

Jon gripped her mittened hand firmly in his. "Think of it as an adventure."

The Faneuil Hall marketplace, a collection of warehouselike buildings flanking the colonial assembly hall that lent the area its name, had been the center of Boston commerce for more than a century. Refurbished in the 1970s, it was now home to dozens of trendy shops and restaurants.

It was noon when they arrived, and the tantalizing aromas wafting from the main colonnade drew them in. They squeezed their way through the tight, slow-moving crowd, looking over the various temptations offered by the food vendors.

"Mmm. Everything looks and smells so good!" Angela felt as if her senses were being awakened after a long drugged sleep.

One vendor was grinding exotic coffee beans, another ladling eye-watering chili into paper cups. There were bright healthful fruit salads and irresistibly unhealthful pastries, long crusty breads, Indian curry and Italian gelato. On and on the stalls went, their delicious aromas mingling with the loud buzz of conversation and piped-in Christmas music.

"That." Angela pointed toward an olive-skinned chef spooning falafel into a large Syrian bread pocket. "That looks great."

They shouldered their way to the counter and ordered two. Then, finding only occupied tables in the dining area, they took their food outside. It was a mild day for December, and the sun was radiating warmth off the brick paving of the spacious mall. They found a bench in the middle of the cheerful holiday mayhem, then sat and unwrapped their food.

White fairy lights, twined in the bare trees, sparkled almost unnoticeably in the noonday sun. A block away, a magician was pulling doves from his sleeve to the delight of a large crowd, while from the opposite corner a prophet preached the end of the world. Angela was pleased to see he hadn't a single listener. This close to Christmas, she'd gladly choose magic over doom. She bit into her sandwich, stretched her legs and smiled contentedly. Yes, coming to Boston had definitely been a good idea.

"Jon, listen." Angela clutched his arm. They both sat still, ears perked, then swiveled around.

"Bell ringers!" She laughed in surprised delight.

Standing in the main square in front of Fanueil Hall were a group of professional bell ringers dressed in Victorian costume. They were playing "God Rest Ye Merry Gentlemen."

"It's so Christmasy." Angela laughed again. "Oh, Jon, this is too perfect!"

Jon propped his elbow on the back of the bench, braced his chin on his palm and studied her with amusement.

"What?" she asked warily.

His eyes glittered. "Nothing. It's just that you look happy, that's all. It's good to see you smiling again. I haven't seen you doing too much of that lately."

Angela couldn't hold his gaze. Her stomach was suddenly fluttering giddily. She rested her arm on the back of the bench, dropped her chin onto it and listened to the bell ringers.

Jon was right. She *was* happy today, happy in a pure carefree way she hadn't felt in years. And on a wave of honest insight, she realized she'd made this trip for no one but herself. Not for Ivan. Not to revitalize their relationship. She'd come here because *she* had wanted to. She'd missed having this deep and easy companionship in her life. And as infuriating as Jon could be, she had to admit she'd missed *him,* too.

She also realized that with this visit, the nature of their relationship had changed. She had come to him, not vice versa. Until now, he had made all the overtures. Did that mean she'd finally resigned herself to the fact of their friendship? She turned forward, pensive, and resumed eating.

But nothing was resolved. Nothing. They were ignoring all their recent arguments, as well as the problems that had caused those arguments. They were glossing over the fact that they were seriously involved with other people. But most of all, they were ignoring their painful venture into intimacy when they were eighteen. That incident alone should have made friendship impossible now.

Nevertheless, it felt good being here, and though Angela deplored giving in to feelings that had no sensible base, they were all that seemed to matter today.

Jon squeezed his sandwich wrapper into a ball and sent it in a graceful hook shot into a nearby trash barrel. "Ready?"

"Ready," she mumbled around a last mouthful of food. Wadding up her own wrapper, she pitched it toward the same container and let out a most unladylike crow when it actually went in.

That afternoon they shopped, toured the stately assembly hall above the market where the American Revolution had been engineered, played pinball, bought "Cheers" T-shirts and finally walked up over Beacon Hill to the Commons to watch the Christmas lights wink on in the deepening afternoon gray.

Throughout, Angela was aware of something odd happening to her—a sharpening of her senses, a feeling of awakening from a stupor. As she and Jon leaned toward each other, reading the price tag on a sweater for his mother, she became intensely aware of the clean spicy scent of him. As he took her hand in a crowded elevator, she registered the warmth of him, the hardness of his thigh when he pulled her to his side.

Now, walking through the Commons, Jon's vibrantly alive male presence lay so thick in the air she could hardly breathe.

He'd picked up on her reaction, too. She'd bet money on it. He'd become quiet, watchful, his eyes alert with questions whenever he glanced her way—which made her feel even more ridiculous. Bad enough she was having this problem with Jon's physical attractiveness, but to have him know about it . . . !

She was relieved when they finally returned to the elegant brick house off Harvard Square. Not only were Angela's legs ready to give out, but she'd had enough of walking through winter wonderlands with perhaps the most attractive man in Boston.

She helped him set the table and prepare their meal, fresh tortellini from the Italian north end of the city. They talked amiably enough, but she noticed they both ate quickly, avoiding each other's eyes, and as soon as the dishes were cleared, both dashed to their rooms to get ready for the evening.

Angela used the bathroom first, then relinquished it to Jon. While she stood before the dresser mirror applying her makeup, she heard the water running in the shower, and a vision of Jon in there suddenly flashed across her mind. She squeezed her eyes tight, stamping a raccoon ring of fresh mascara under her right eye.

"Drat!" she swore, though actually she was glad to have something to think about other than hot soapy water sluicing down a certain someone's hard muscled chest.

Half an hour later she emerged from her room, determined to ignore the oversensitized condition she'd worked herself into. She was simply having some sort of mixed-up reaction to how well she and Jon were getting along as friends. That was it. Sure. After all, they *had* made love at one time. It was understandable that her reactions now would be muddled and incapable of discerning what was real and current from what merely echoed from the past. She was certain that she'd be able to control the situation now that she understood its roots.

She found Jon in front of a music stand in the parlor, absorbed in a score. Angela paused in the doorway, making no sound to disturb his concentration. Her eyes traveled from his dark hair down to his polished black shoes. She'd heard of men born to wear tuxes, had even met a few, but Jon put all of them to shame.

He finally looked up, his thickly lashed eyes blinking as he emerged from the music before him. As he focused on her, her heart skipped a beat.

"Hi." Jon's slow warm-as-molasses smile made her fidget self-consciously.

She looked down at her simple black shift. It was fairly classic—straight, sleeveless, scoop-necked—but it was stylishly short, a feature that worried her. "Is this okay?"

Jon stood quite still, his eyes the only part of him that seemed capable of movement. They traveled from her hair, which she'd left loose and swinging about her shoulders, down her bare arms, over her black silk stockings to her ankle-strapped heels. He swallowed. "Yes."

"Yes?" That was it?

"Yes. You look very nice." He turned then and hurried to the coat closet.

Inside the lobby of Symphony Hall, Jon handed Angela her ticket—first balcony, front row, center. He drew a deep breath that lifted his shoulders, but it was several seconds before he expelled it. Small worry lines like quotation marks were etched between his brows.

"Well, I'll be seeing you in a couple of hours. I'm sorry you have to sit alone."

"I'm a big girl."

He coughed and shuffled his feet. "Okay, well..."

She couldn't help laughing as an improbable thought struck her. "Stoddard, are you nervous?"

He looked away, over the people mounting the broad marble steps, and tried to shake his head. It came out a tight confused jerk.

"Well, well! This is a first. I wish I had my camera."

Smiling sheepishly, Jon ducked his head. "It isn't funny."

"Of course it isn't." Still chuckling, Angela wrapped her arms around Jon's broad shoulders and hugged him to her. "You know you'll be brilliant. You always are. So, go have fun." Then she kissed his smooth-shaven cheek.

Almost immediately, she realized her mistake. She'd only meant the kiss as a gesture of comfort and support, but suddenly the nearness of him, the scent and heat and hardness of him, were making her knees weak. She gulped, glanced up into his eyes and noticed that the questions that had seemed to plague him earlier had returned. She tried to back off but discovered she couldn't. His hands, pressed against her shoulder blades, seemed frozen into place. For long moments they stared at each other, their lips just inches apart, hearts thudding like kettledrums.

Then, ever so reluctantly, Jon let her go. "Thanks, Angel." He cleared his throat, looking away. "Meet me down in the musicians' lounge when it's over, okay?"

"Will do," Angela called, hurrying off on legs that threatened to give out.

The first part of the program was a cello concerto featuring a guest artist. The performance was wonderful, but Angela was impatient to hear the second half. When the conductor returned to his podium after intermission, Angela was nearly beside herself with anticipation. She'd fully intended to keep her eyes on the maestro tonight, to feel the music through his perspective, but from the very first stroke of his baton, she realized her attention was elsewhere—there, in the horn section.

The symphony began, and unexpectedly Angela felt her eyes stinging, her stomach fluttering again. She usually didn't respond so emotionally at concerts, but tonight it seemed that all her objectivity was stripped away. She was forever poised on the edge of tears, her throat tight, her lips working for control.

It wasn't just the quality of the performance that was getting to her. It wasn't even the music itself. It was seeing Jon down there. Her pride in him was almost too much to bear.

All too soon the piece drew to an end. Angela caught her breath on a sob, and while everyone else got to their feet and applauded, she remained seated, tears streaming down her cheeks. She couldn't have explained her reaction if her life had depended on it.

Finally she gripped the rail before her and staggered to her feet. At the same time, Jon looked up from the stage. She couldn't fathom how he found her so fast, but he did. Given the poor lighting and the distance separating them, she *felt* his gaze more than anything—a direct steady burn that almost physically connected them. Her heart beat wildly. Dear God, she prayed, what was happening here?

She hurried to the nearest ladies' room as soon as possible. Her cheeks were afire and her eyes shone too brightly. She wet a paper towel with cold water and pressed it to her face. She had to get a grip on herself. She was letting her imagination run wild. *Nothing* was happening. She *wasn't* feeling what she thought she was feeling, and Jon definitely was not feeling it in return. They were just friends, and friends put things like physical attractiveness into proper perspective.

Nevertheless, when Angela was walking down the stairs to the musicians' lounge, she realized her stomach was still jumping. And when she spotted Jon walking toward her in his easy long-legged amble, undoing his bow tie, unbuttoning his collar and flashing her one of his knee-buckling grins, she realized that keeping perspective was going to be the hardest job she'd ever tackled.

CHAPTER SEVEN

ANGELA STEPPED OUT to the brick stoop and squinted against the sharp morning light. "Sorry I was such poor company last night. I was more tired than I realized." She didn't meet Jon's eyes. If anything, she'd been overstimulated after the concert, but fearing that her emotions were becoming far too transparent, she'd feigned exhaustion and retreated to her room as soon as they'd come in.

But she hadn't slept much. Perhaps it was the strange bed that had kept her awake, or the symphony that still played through her mind. But more than likely, it was Jon; Jon moving quietly just beyond her door, Jon turning book pages on the other side of the wall—and all the possibilities that lay within the night.

Which was ridiculous, she'd reminded herself with each tormented toss of her body. It couldn't be happening again, it couldn't. The physical attraction she'd felt for him had happened light-years ago. Surely nothing remained of those feelings now. She'd suffered too much as a consequence, learned too well how grievous a mistake it was to cross the line from friendship into intimacy.

Eventually she'd drifted into sleep, and when she'd awakened, she'd felt a renewed conviction that the only sparks flying between her and Jon were in her imagination. She'd joined him for breakfast, firmly resolved to normalize her behavior and return their friendship to firmer footing.

So far, she seemed to be succeeding. But she didn't want to press her luck, and while it was only nine-fifteen, she thought it best to be on her way.

"Are you sure you can't stay longer?" Jon carried her bag down the steps and set it on the walk beside her car.

"Positive. I have a horrid week ahead of me—exams to grade, the college concert Tuesday night, my interview with the WSO board on Thursday..."

Jon's expression sharpened. "That right? I had mine ages ago."

Angela's pulse abruptly leapt. "You...you went through with your interview?'

"Mmm. About a month ago. I'm surprised they scheduled you so late."

Angela said nothing, consumed as she was by the depressing realization that Jon had been interviewed—before he'd found out that she was interested in the directorship, too. That meant he'd given it his best shot. A small moan escaped her throat.

"Hey, no need to worry. They don't have any trick questions up their sleeves. I doubt they could think up any if they tried."

Angela peered up into his lean confident face. "Jon, are you sure you don't want to tell me if you're still in the race?"

He threw back his head and laughed. "Not on your life."

Angela felt a distinct urge to do him bodily harm. Instead, she just glowered.

"Relax, Westgate." He hung his hands over her shoulders, his onyx eyes moving from her hair, along the smooth curve of her cheek to her lips.

And suddenly it was happening again, Angela realized with mounting dread—that mutual awareness arcing between them like a high voltage line. Jon dropped his hands and stepped back awkwardly.

"It's a pity you can't stay longer." He pushed his hand through his hair. "I'm on vacation for the next two weeks, so you wouldn't be putting me out."

Angela moved to her car, quickly opened the door and slid in her bag. "Vacation? How come?" She knew she was blushing.

"The Pops take over, now through Christmas."

"Oh. That's good—I guess." She was feeling rather disoriented again and wished she was on her way.

"Yes, it is. I'm looking forward to the rest."

"Well, Jon, this was fun."

"Mmm. We'll have to do it again sometime."

"Yes. Maybe Cynthia and Ivan will be free to join us then." Angela stole a wary peek at his face. They were both mouthing polite but empty phrases, trying to cover that uncomfortable moment.

"Will you be at WSO rehearsal Wednesday?" she asked, slipping behind the wheel.

"I was planning on it. Would you care to meet up beforehand like we did last week?"

Angela didn't answer right away. Meeting up with him last rehearsal had landed her with a kitchen full of balloons, her determination to remain angry with him destroyed, him sleeping over and Ivan in a lather.

"On second thought," Jon said as if his mind had been running along a similar track, "let's play it by ear. As you say, it's a rough week for you, and frankly, I'm not sure where I'll be Wednesday."

They both knew it was a vague excuse, but it succeeded in getting them off the hook. They smiled, relieved.

"Drive carefully."

"Always do."

"Ha!"

"Ha, yourself. Only one of us got an A in driver education, and it wasn't you." Smiling warmly, she waved and pulled away from the curb.

But once she rounded the corner, her smile wilted. She couldn't be sure what Jon had been feeling back there, but as for herself—Angela groaned aloud—she was in one hell of a mess.

"DAMN!" ANGELA'S Christmas tree listed so far to the left it threatened to topple. This was her first attempt at setting up a tree by herself.

She brushed aside her momentary melancholy and made another stab at adjusting the stand. But when she stepped back, the tree was listing more than ever.

"I give up," she muttered, deciding she'd just have to wait until someone dropped by.

She picked up her half-eaten meat loaf sandwich and took a bite. A sudden thump on her front door nearly made her choke. "Ivan," she whispered. He never used the bell.

Before she could even swallow the bite of sandwich he banged again.

"Coming, coming." She hurried across the room, peered through the window and unlocked the door. "Hi, there."

Ivan walked in, jaw set hard. "So, you're finally home."

Angela clutched her arms against the cold that came in with him. "Yes. Did you go in to school today? I didn't see you."

"You couldn't have looked very hard. Yes, I was there."

Trying to set up her tree alone had deflated most of the Christmas spirit she'd brought home with her from college today. Ivan's attitude now finished off the job.

"What did you do this weekend, Angela?"

Her nerves pulled taut. " Oh, all sorts of things." She smiled forcibly. "I went Christmas shopping, bought a tree." Her smile drooped under his cold stare. "W-what did you do?"

"Does it matter? Do you actually care?"

Angela threaded her fingers together and wrung them like a dishcloth. "Of course I care."

Ivan took a step toward her, planting his fists on his hips. "Where were you Saturday night?"

Angela's brain felt fevered. Ivan's irrational jealousy was the reason they'd argued in the first place. How could she now say she'd spent half the weekend with another man?

"D-did you call me? I thought the plan was we weren't going to have any contact."

Ivan's complexion darkened. "Plan? Seems to me the only person making plans around here is you."

"But... it was only an attempt to improve our relationship. Sometimes people who are together too much need a little space."

He pinned her with a derisive stare. "Where were you, Angela?"

"I... I..."

Ivan's lips curled. "You were with Stoddard, weren't you?"

"I..."

"Weren't you?"

Suddenly, Angela had had enough of his bullying. "And what if I was?"

Ivan's fist came down against the sofa. "I knew it!"

Angela's head snapped back with the vehemence of his response.

"Angela, this has got to stop, right here, right now." His pounding fist accented each phrase.

Angela had seen Ivan in a variety of unattractive moods lately, but this anger was something new. Yet it all fit a pattern, a pattern that turned her blood to ice. On legs that threatened to give out, she marched to the door. "I think you'd better leave."

"Not until we settle this."

"We have." She jerked open the door. "I'm tired of your possessiveness, Ivan. I'm tired of a lot of things. Now get out of my house and don't bother coming back. Ever."

His eyes grew fiery. "You're breaking up with me?"

"That's right. Now go." Not knowing where she got the courage, she stepped around him and shoved with all her strength, then slammed the door and turned the lock.

For long minutes afterward, she barely breathed, leaning against the door, knowing he was still out there on the front step. Sweat trickled down her sides. But finally she heard footfalls crunching down the snowy walk and, moments later, his car starting.

She slid down the door, shaking with delayed reaction, and sat on the floor, clutching her head in her hands. Dear Lord, what had happened to her life? It used to be so calm and ordered.

She lifted her gaze to the ceiling, blinking against the stinging in her eyes. Jon was back, Mr. Chaos incarnate—that was what had happened. Unfortunately, at this particular moment, she wished with all her heart that he were here.

She took a deep breath and expelled it slowly. Should she call?

She squinched her eyes tight. No, she'd better not. After the physical awareness she'd felt crackling between them this weekend, the last thing she wanted was for Jon to know she and Ivan had broken up. He'd probably misconstrue her unhappiness as a desire to rekindle a nine-year-old ember. And even if Jon didn't misconstrue her motives, even if those moments of sensual awareness *had* been only figments of her imagination, she still felt disinclined to admit to Jon that her life wasn't perfect.

She didn't know why that bothered her so much. Pride? Was that it? She bobbed her head in a somber rhythm. Yeah, probably, considering how deeply Jon had hurt her nine years ago. The need to prove she'd survived him—and thrived—burned in her like a hard white flame.

Angela hauled herself off the floor, brushed the pine needles from her skirt and headed for the kitchen to put on water for tea. As she puttered, the reality began to sink in: she was free of Ivan.

"Eye-vin," she said aloud. "His name is Eye-vin, not Ee-von, the pretentious jerk!" And that was what she was going to call him from now on.

Angela leaned on the counter, dropping a tea bag into an empty cup, trying to figure out how she'd let herself get involved with such a bozo. But of course she hadn't always seen him in that light. When they'd first started dating, he seemed to possess all the traits she wanted in a man. He'd seemed so mature, so steady and solid, so content with domesticity. With a small wry smile, she realized Ivan had appeared to be everything Jon wasn't, and she wondered if she'd gravitated toward him for precisely that reason.

Hearing the water boil, she pushed herself away from the counter. She prepared her tea, then took the steaming cup over to the patio doors.

As time passed, however, Angela came to realize that Ivan wasn't just solid, didn't just enjoy domestic life. He was practically inert. He did nothing of interest, went nowhere, and he apparently wanted her to do the same. It was almost as if he felt threatened by her activities and the people she came in contact with. Funny—in the beginning, she'd been flattered by how fervently he'd wanted and pursued her. Now she felt suffocated.

How could I have been so stupid? she asked her dim reflection. Jon figured him out, first time they met.

The glass pane was cold against her forehead. Outside the sky had lowered, heavy and gunmetal gray. Such short dark days this time of year. She shivered.

To give herself some credit, she'd started seeing Ivan at one of the lowest ebbs in her life. He'd been there offering her security and companionship for the rest of her days. She supposed it was only natural for her to lean on him.

But he wasn't strong and secure. Ivan was a bully, a weak scared bully, and she was relieved she was finally free of him.

But that was going to be something she kept to herself, at least for a while, she decided. She still needed a protective wedge between her and a certain someone down in Boston.

A smile tugged at the corners of her mouth. Lord, how she wished Jon was here. If anyone knew how to pull her out of the doldrums, it was Jon. She turned and stared at the phone. Maybe it wouldn't do any harm to call. After all, they hadn't really settled the matter of next Wednesday's rehearsal yet....

With her spirits already lifting, Angela set down her cup, flicked on the light switch, chasing the winter gloom, and reached for the phone.

ON WEDNESDAY, Angela opened her front door to find Jon standing there, holding a large ornamental brass horn decorated with holly and a red bow.

"It's very nice, Jon, but I don't think Mr. Beech will allow it."

He smirked. "Very funny."

"It isn't for me, is it? I've already got a wreath."

"No. This is for my door. Come help me hang it."

"I will not. We've got rehearsal in three hours. Come inside. You're letting out all the heat."

Jon strode in, charging the air as he always did with his presence. "Nice tree, Westgate. Going for the natural look this year, I see."

"Oh, that." She cast the still-tipsy tree a pitying look. "I just haven't had time to decorate it yet."

Angela was beginning to feel light-headed. She'd been fighting the condition all day, and she'd succeeded somewhat while still at school. But during this past hour, waiting for Jon to arrive, she'd grown positively flappy. She'd found herself putting milk in the china cupboard, forgetting her purpose when she walked into a room and, like a breathless adolescent, agonizing over which sweater to wear with what jeans.

It wasn't a good situation, and she was beginning to wonder what had ever possessed her to call and invite Jon to dinner. Had she actually believed that the attraction she'd felt during her weekend visit would simply disappear? It hadn't, and although Jon had no idea that she and Ivan had broken up, she still felt terribly open and defenseless in his company, her vulnerability as evident as the blush on her cheek.

"Hanging this won't take long, Angel," Jon said, laying the horn on the table by the door. "We only have to drive a couple of miles."

Angela scowled. "What are you talking about?"

He rocked back on his heels, fingers tucked into the front pockets of his snug jeans. "Are you ready for this? I've put a binder on the Thurgood house."

Angela's jaw dropped. "You're out of your mind."

At times, Jon's grin could turn so gleefully wicked she wanted to shake him. This was one of those times.

"Jon! What are you going to do with a five-bedroom house that's an hour away from Boston?"

"Live in it, I hope."

Angela sank into the nearest chair, her heart doing flip-flops. "I know your mind doesn't work like normal people's, Jon, but this...this has got to be the most harebrained, illogical... You can't buy a house just like that. Especially not that house."

He laughed, falling onto the sofa opposite her. "All our lives you've been saying, 'Jon, you can't do that,'" he mimicked.

Angela glared at him. She probably had. But just as consistently, he'd always replied, "Just watch me."

"But the cost..." she protested.

Jon shrugged negligently.

"The repairs. The size of the place. It's totally impractical."

"But I love that house, Angel."

"So? Does that mean you have to have it?"

He nodded without apology.

"You brat. You're spoiled so rotten a vulture wouldn't have anything to do with you."

Jon stood up and hauled her out of her chair. "Stop grousing and put on your coat."

Still flabbergasted, Angela rode with him to Elm Street and helped him hang the festive horn. It complemented the house's English architecture perfectly.

"Much better." Jon stood back and admired the door with a proprietorial glint in his eyes. Out on the lawn, the For Sale sign was now covered with a Sale Pending banner.

"Jon, it isn't even your house yet. You have no legal right..."

He turned to frown at her, exasperated. "Really, Angel, who cares?"

She shook her head, equally exasperated.

"Besides, it *will* be mine in a few weeks, once I get a mortgage." As he spoke, he pulled a set of keys from his jacket pocket and inserted one of them in the lock.

Angela's eyes widened into horrified saucers. "Jonathan! What are you doing? We could get arrested for trespassing."

He winked devilishly as the heavy door swung in.

The house was even more gracious than she remembered. Angela walked from one high-ceilinged room to another, fighting hard against her mounting excitement. By the time they'd climbed the dark carved staircase and reached the master bedroom, she knew she'd lost the battle. "Oh, Jon, this place is heaven."

Jon planted his elbow on the fireplace mantel and, taking a slow pleased survey of the room, smiled. "Isn't it just!"

"And you really plan to live here? You're moving back to Winston?" She swung toward a window, pretending interest in the view, but she feared Jon had already noticed the moisture gathering in her eyes.

"Yes. I've really missed the place, Angel."

She squared her shoulders and turned to face him. "You do realize how much work you have ahead of you. Everything's going to need repair."

"True. But it's surface work—scrubbing, painting, papering."

Suddenly Angela was overcome by the magnitude of what Jon was doing, so spontaneously, so without care. What a difference between him and Ivan, she thought. Where Ivan was as predictable as a block of cement, Jon was pure mercury.

But on the way downstairs, she grew pensive, because it began to hit her that maybe Jon wasn't as careless as she thought.

"How does Cynthia like the house?" she somehow got out over the jealousy clotting in her throat.

"Oh, she doesn't know about it yet. She's not coming home from her assignment till tomorrow. I'm supposed to pick her up at the airport."

Angela was glad her back was to Jon, because she was sure her expression was pained. Was he thinking of marrying Cynthia? Is that why he wanted to buy this big family house? Was he looking forward to filling it with a brood of little Stoddards? Angela's stomach cramped. And why Winston? Why the very street where they'd grown up? Did he expect her to come visit them in the future? Hadn't he done enough, or was he planning to make hurting her a lifetime pursuit?

"Before we leave, you've got to see the backyard, Angel." Jon fit his long fingers around her arm just above the elbow, hardly denting the thick sleeve of her white wool coat. Yet his touch, light as it was, still sent shivers racing through her.

He opened the kitchen door and led her out to a flagstoned patio strewn with wet leaves. Before them, a half acre of lawn, vine-tangled rose arbors, gardens and bare trees were shrouded in gray winter light.

"Lots of potential here," Angela commented, wondering if Cynthia liked to garden. She felt her mouth quiver and looked aside before adding, "I wish you all the best, Jon."

He gazed down at her, clasped the back of her neck and squeezed. It was a gesture anyone would recognize as merely friendly. But when he should have let go, his hand remained there, fingers tracing a shivery path up into her hair. Her pulse thumped, louder, faster. She tried not to misconstrue his intentions, but, Lord, he had to know what he was doing. Quickly she stepped away, molding her expression into as blank a mask as she could muster. "We'd better be heading back. I have to put our dinner in the oven."

He nodded, and the uncomfortable moment was dispelled. "Maybe we'll even have time to do something about that poor tree of yours."

Twenty minutes later, Jon was on his hands and knees, reaching for the tree stand. "You hold. I'll loosen."

Angela sighed unenthusiastically, reaching through the branches to grip the sticky trunk. "This isn't necessary, you know. The tree's fine as it is. I'm getting kind of fond of it, actually."

"Sweetheart, sweetheart, where's your Christmas spirit?"

"Out partying in somebody else's life, I think."

Jon made a small tsk-tsk of disapproval, and Angela cast a quick glance down at his crouched form, ready to tsk right back. But the next moment, she forgot her intention and became totally mesmerized by the strong curve of his back, the taut lines of his thighs, the crescent of still-tanned skin above his leather belt where his sweater had ridden up.

"What time's your interview tomorrow?"

Angela wrenched her gaze away guiltily. "Um... four."

"Are you ready for it?"

"Yes. Maybe." Actually, she'd been hoping to prepare today.

"Can you lift? I want to turn the stand so the screws won't sink into the same cockeyed holes you made."

She was glad Jon was oblivious to the nonsense that had been running through her mind. She didn't understand it herself, and Lord only knew what he would make of it.

Jon finally got to his feet and gave the tree a satisfied nod. "Much better. Now, where are the lights?"

With Jon's help, Angela spent the next hour stringing the old multicolored lights she'd known since she was a child, hanging the fragile glass balls that had traveled down the decades—and trying not to pay attention to their steadily growing mutual awareness.

Or was the problem just hers? After all, it was her fingers that fumbled with ornaments, her cheeks that flared at his slightest glance. Unfortunately he quickly became aware of her awareness, which only compounded the problem. He grew quietly constrained, moving as if he wanted to avoid touching her, and twice when she peeked through the branches, she was startled to find him peeking back, his brow puckered. The day was definitely taking on an uncomfortable feel.

"Dinner break," she announced as the oven buzzer sounded.

"Hold it, Westgate. You've got a branch stuck in your hair."

"A branch?"

"Well, twiggy things. Tip your head."

She did, and Jon worked his long fingers through her hair, the soap-and-cinnamon warmth of his body wrapping her in an intoxicating spell. She shivered under his gentle ministrations.

"Did I pull?"

She shook her head.

"Okay. It's out."

"Thanks." She didn't dare meet his eyes, but hurried off to the kitchen, instead. There she braced herself on the counter, hands splayed, and pulled in a steadying breath. She had to get hold of herself. It would be too humiliating if Jon guessed the effect he was having on her.

"Is there anything I can do to help?"

She swung around to find him watching her. "Uh, no. Table's all set. Well, yes. Here." She bumped awkwardly into a chair as she handed him the salad bowl.

She noted his confusion, then realized he was staring at the small kitchen table. "No, the table in the dining room." She pressed a dimmer switch, and a small chandelier brought the adjacent room to life. She saw Jon's eyes widen, saw him swallow.

"Somebody sure went to a lot of trouble."

Angela's cheeks blazed. She'd set the table before his arrival, deciding on a whim to use her grandmother's china, the Waterford crystal, linen napkins and tall white candles.

"What's the occasion?" Jon's voice was thick with apprehension.

She bit her lip, mortified. "Nothing. I just don't get to use my nice things too often."

He nodded guardedly, setting down the salad bowl. She handed him a bottle of wine and corkscrew, and hurried back to the kitchen. When she returned with the serving cart, he was pouring. In tense silence, she set out the chicken cordon bleu, rice pilaf and green beans with almonds, while Jon lit the candles. By the time they sat, she doubted she'd be able to swallow a single bite.

In all the years she'd known Jon, never had they gone through anything quite as uncomfortable as this. And the worst part was, she didn't even understand what *this* was.

"What are your plans for Christmas?" He cut into his chicken with a vigor more likely born of stress than of hunger.

Angela watched him chew, watched him swallow, wipe his mouth, sip his wine. She studied his long capable hands shifting utensils, noticed the candlelight flickering in his deep midnight eyes—all before remembering to answer him.

"I'm going to Peg's for dinner."

"You and Ivan?"

"No, Ivan won't be go—" Grabbing up her wine goblet, she took a swallow. She considered telling Jon the truth—that she and Ivan were kaput, and if he wanted her, she was his for the asking. All he had to do was crook his finger, give her one of his killer grins, and she'd be at his feet.

Oh, Lord, what was she thinking? She glanced across the candlelight to find Jon watching her, his dark head tilted, his curious gaze taking in her every facial tick and hand jitter.

"Ivan's...going to visit his mother in Cleveland." Cleveland? She popped a forkful of rice into her mouth and fell into a spell of coughing. Ivan's mother had passed away five years ago. "What are your plans?" she asked hastily.

"I'm flying down to Florida Christmas Day to be with my parents. My flight leaves around noon."

"Is Cynthia going, too?"

He was quiet an unusually long time before replying, "No."

They resumed eating, but questions lay so thick in the air she thought she would suffocate. Finally Jon looked up from his food.

"Cynthia and I...we're not as tight as you seem to think."

Angela's heart lurched.

"In fact, we've just about stopped dating." He tucked into his food again, grimacing as if he regretted this admission. Her silence eventually drew his attention. "What? Why are you smiling?"

She tried to wipe the expression from her face. "This is a crazy world. If you want to know the truth, Ivan and I aren't an item anymore, either."

A dozen expressions shifted in his eyes. "Oh, I'm sorry."

She accepted his condolence with a solemn nod.

"This *is* a crazy world." Jon seemed to be fighting off a smile, too. "So, it looks like we're both at loose ends this Christmas, doesn't it?"

"Looks like." Her breath had stalled somewhere in her throat.

Suddenly he leaned forward, face alight. "Angel, let's do it."

Her eyes snapped up. "Do what?"

"The climb. Remember our dream of camping out in the White Mountains on Christmas Eve?"

She lowered her knife and fork very carefully. Of course she remembered. The plan was they'd take their instruments with them, and as the sun rose on Christmas morning, they'd play a few carols. At sixteen, she'd thought the idea wonderful, the height of romance. But at twenty-seven, she saw it for what it was—pure adolescent folly. "You can't be serious."

"As an undertaker."

"But you've got a plane to catch and I..."

"We'll be off the mountain in plenty of time. Really, Angel, it's something we should do before we get too old. Some dreams shouldn't be put off."

"I'm afraid this one already has been."

"Don't say that. It's bound to be one the most moving experiences of your life, a moment out of time." His voice swelled with mock eloquence. "A direct communication with the sublime and transcendent. Besides, what else are you going to do Christmas Eve without a man in your life?"

Her look was dry. "Be warm. Be safe."

"Rrkktt!" Jon made a tight creaking noise deep in his throat, hunched his shoulders and contorted his hands.

"What are you doing?"

"An imitation. Of you—atrophying."

Laughing in spite of herself, Angela whipped her napkin across the table. He caught it in one deft hand and tossed it back.

"I'm going," he said with finality. "I wish you'd come along. It was *our* dream, not just mine."

"Was not. This is stamped with Stoddard eccentricity through and through." She paused. "You're really going?"

"Yes."

"Alone?"

"Apparently."

"You shouldn't. It's dangerous."

He leaned on his hand and cocked one dark eyebrow in a most enticing invitation. Angela was sure her toes curled.

Finally she threw up her hands. "All right! I'll go. But mark my words, Jon, it won't be what you think. All it's going to be is cold."

She picked up her fork and tried to resume eating. What had she just agreed to? Hike with Jon into the very mountains where they'd become lovers. Granted, it would be too cold this time to do anything but struggle to survive. Still, thoughts were bound to arise. As they were now.

Angela peered up warily. Jon was staring at his plate, his face gone serious. Her heart bumped wildly against her rib cage. Did he ever think back on that night nine summers ago, as she so often did? Did his blood stir, even a little, at the memory of their youthful passion? Is that what was giving him such serious pause right now?

His gaze lifted, and for one raw second she knew the answer. At this moment they were both back there, lying in a tent, locked in each other's arms, utterly lost in each other's eyes.

Jon cleared his throat, glanced away, turned back again. He seemed to be searching for something to say or do to rescue them from the moment. "Angel, look." He smiled and, linking his thumbs, positioned his hands near one of the candles, casting a shadow onto the wall—a bird, she surmised.

"Cute."

"Nothing compared to my rabbit."

But he didn't do a rabbit, and neither of them smiled. Jon dropped his head to his hands, burying his splayed fingers in his hair in a gesture of undisguised desperation.

"Help me out, Angel," he groaned. "I don't know how to handle it, either."

She froze, every inch of her instantly awake and pulsing. Was it possible? Had Jon been battling an attraction toward her, too? Is that why he'd been so quietly reserved?

She leapt to her feet and began to clear the table. Maybe if she got busy, they could let his comment pass. Obviously, he didn't welcome the attraction anymore than she did.

"Let me help."

"Sure." Her response was falsely bright.

For the next few minutes, the room was filled with such a clatter they might have been clearing tables in a major restaurant, instead of a simple dinner for two. Angela had no idea if busyness was helping him, but it was doing nothing for her. The faster she moved, the more aware of him she grew.

She was about to remove the breadbasket when Jon reached for it, too. Their eyes met, and in that one shattering look, she knew it was all over. Jon yanked the basket from her limp fingers, hurled it across the room, sending rolls bouncing off the walls and pictures, and caught her up in his arms.

"I've come to a decision," he announced. "This is how we should handle it." And the next moment he was kissing her.

He felt even better than she'd imagined. Far, far better. Suddenly a floodgate of restraint seemed to break, unleashing a torrent of desire too long pent up.

"Oh, Lord, Angel!" Jon came up for air with a gasp. She ran her fingers up his neck, sinking them into his luxuriant dark hair, hair she'd been longing to touch since forever. He dipped his head again, eyes closing, and brushed his open mouth over hers. Their breath mingled in a disbelieving sigh.

Was this really happening? she wondered, reeling in a happiness so profound it frightened her. "Jon?" The word was a tremulous whisper.

He opened his eyes, a languid sweep of black lashes. "Shh," he admonished, moving in to kiss her again. She didn't protest. Kissing him felt too good, too much like coming home. It was what she'd been burning to do all afternoon, and the miracle of the situation was he'd apparently been feeling the very same way.

As the first desperate moments passed, Jon's embrace relaxed, and he became more sensually aware of her, easing into slow, deep, lingering kisses that made her melt against him. He pressed his hands down her back, fitting her soft curves to every hard plane of him, and when she thought she couldn't get any closer, his hands slid into the back pockets of her jeans and pressed her closer still. The intimacy almost buckled her knees.

From what seemed a long distance away, a clock chimed its quarter-hour melody. With his mouth still moving over hers, Jon turned in the direction of the clock. Reluctantly he lifted his head.

"Time to go." Even his whisper sent curls of heat through her stomach.

Oh, this was truly a terrible situation! She'd known she was feeling a pull toward him, but the volatility and force of her response was something she couldn't have anticipated in a million years.

"Jon..." She touched his moist lips with fingers that trembled. He kissed them, took one between his teeth. "Jon, this can't happen."

But instead of sharing her trepidation, he only grinned. "Angel, babe, I think it already has."

CHAPTER EIGHT

REHEARSAL THAT EVENING passed in a blur. Angela remembered so little of it that, leaving the theater, she decided she must have spent the entire time out of body. What a dreadful dilemma she and Jon had created in a few short minutes of runaway passion.

"Well, Jon, I guess I won't be seeing you again until the concert." She tried to modulate her voice and pretend she was saying good-night to just any colleague.

Jon let the theater door fall shut behind them and gripped her arm tight. "Let's go for a walk." His face was grim.

With a pulse beating frantically at the base of her throat, Angela looked toward her car, parked across the street behind his. She'd suggested they come in separate vehicles to eliminate the necessity of his going back to her place. But all along she'd known they couldn't just walk away from what had happened.

They locked their instruments in their respective cars, then started toward the lighted windows of the downtown shops. Everything was closed at this hour, sidewalks deserted, garlands and Christmas lights swaying forlornly in a fine mist.

"Jon, I'm sorry." Angela had been rehearsing the words all evening, and now they poured out almost of their own volition. "I hope you can forget what happened back at my place. It was a mistake—I think we both know that—and I'd like to pretend it never happened."

Jon's footsteps slowed. "But it did happen, Angel, and it's not going to go away, no more than what happened nine years ago has gone away. We're going to have to face it sooner or later."

She closed her eyes tight. "No."

"But aren't you at all curious about it? Where it's coming from? Where it's going?"

"I know where it's going," she lashed back. "That's what I'm trying to head off. I don't want that to ever happen again."

Jon's left eyebrow lifted in an ironic curve. "Sorry it was such an unpleasant experience for you."

Angela's face reddened.

"What are you afraid of?"

"Don't be obtuse, Jon. You know as well as I what happened to our friendship the last time we . . . the last time."

Jon paused at a storefront window, staring with unfocused eyes at a mannequin dressed in holiday glitter. He rubbed his gloved hand along his jaw. "I've been thinking . . ." He spoke slowly, cautiously. "Maybe we'll be able to handle it now that we're older."

Angela glared at his profile, hardly able to believe his gall. For whatever mysterious reason, she aroused a physical need in him, and simply because he had that need, he assumed he had the right to satisfy it—like a child, suffering no thoughts of consequences, looking no further than the moment.

"Maybe you can handle it, but I'm not that sophisticated."

His brow knit. "I'm not sure I understood your objections."

No, he wouldn't. To him their lovemaking had been nothing more than a physical encounter, and apparently not a very important one at that. He hadn't shared any of her emotional turmoil, didn't have a clue how deep her heartache had run when she'd seen him just days later with another girl. Jon was a sensitive person in many ways, but when it came to sex and love, he was a moron.

"Let me put it this way, Jon. You've never been serious about a girl in your life, not for any length of time, anyway." They resumed walking. "I have a few theories why that's so."

"I'm sure you do." His sardonic tone made her hesitate. "Oh, please, don't let me stop you."

"Well, I have a hunch it's because you're afraid of serious relationships." She paused again.

"Go on," he prodded.

"You're afraid your career will bog down and you won't reach your potential. It's that, or else you just love the chase and get bored once you've made your conquest." She swallowed with difficulty. "So over the years they've come and they've gone, an endless parade of knockouts. But through them all, I remained because I was different. I was special to you, and by some stroke of dubious luck, we seem to have regained a measure of that closeness. And . . . and I think I like it. So you'll just have to understand when I say I don't want to be your girlfriend, Jon. I don't want to be . . . trivialized."

"Trivialized? You think I'd trivialize you?"

"Most definitely. I'd be put in a box marked Temporary Diversion, and then we'd have nothing, because after you lost interest, we sure as hell couldn't return to being just friends."

They'd reached the end of the block, crossed the street and headed back on the other side. The mist had thickened, spangling Jon's hair with silver droplets. He trudged along in silence, a frown darkening his handsome features.

"But we're friends now, after being lovers," he retorted.

"Yes, but it took nine years. Next time, I'm afraid forever won't be long enough to heal the breach."

Jon sighed, his lips pressing in defeat. "You're right. You're right. About everything, damn it."

Angela stopped dead. "I am?"

He nodded. "And I sure as hell don't want to lose you again." He tucked his hand under her coat collar, pulled her toward him and kissed the damp crown of her head.

Angela fought against a sudden weakening in her knees. "Wh-what did you say?"

He smiled. "I have a story I should tell you. Maybe it'll help you better understand what I mean. It happened one night about five years ago when I was traveling with that orchestra from Barcelona. We were in Prague at the time, and it was late, after midnight. We'd come in on the train from Rome that afternoon, performed that evening, and I was exhausted. I was turning down the blankets on the dormitory bed I'd been assigned when the guy in the bed next to me asked who I was talking to. I told him nobody, and he laughed. He said being on the road had finally gotten to me, because he'd definitely seen my lips moving.

"Well, I lay awake for a long time that night, and I finally realized I *had* been talking to someone. To you."

"Me?" Heat rose right up to Angela's scalp.

"Uh-huh. I'd been telling you all about the fifteenth-century palace we'd played in and about the food and the countryside. I also realized I'd been doing that for so long, keeping a running dialogue with you in my head, that I wasn't even aware of it anymore. It had become habit. My day wasn't complete until I did. Talking to you gave it order, validity. Do you know what I'm saying?"

The lights strung across the street blurred in the tears that suddenly welled up in Angela's eyes. She nodded.

"And, well, I don't want to mess with anything that important, Angel. I'm still not sure how we're supposed to take back what happened tonight. We had something really hot going there for a while." He grinned down at her briefly, maybe even self-consciously, before becoming serious again. "But if you say we have to, then we have to. As I said, I don't want to lose you again."

They'd come full circle and were back at the theater, its lights extinguished now, doors locked. Angela paused under the street lamp and dared a glance up into Jon's fathomless dark eyes. For all her show of clearheaded logic, she wasn't sure she knew what to do about what had happened, either. How *could* they go on, pretending nothing had changed between them? After those kisses, those embraces—how *did* you take back miracles like those?

But somehow they would have to. Otherwise, she was headed toward more heartache than she knew how to handle.

They crossed the street and while she unlocked her car he asked, "Do you still have your camping gear?"

"Yes." She was relieved that he considered the issue of their attraction closed and had moved on. "I packed it away in the basement of the condo."

"Good. I think my parents still have mine. I'll phone them tomorrow and ask them to ship it express."

Angela chewed on her lip. "Jon, do you really think it's wise for us to go on that hike?" Perhaps the best way to handle the situation between them and preserve their friendship was to spend as little time alone with each other as possible.

"Wise?" He turned from unlocking his car. "What do you mean?" He seemed genuinely unaware of her concern.

"Well, for one thing, it's dumb. And for another, it's dangerous, and I've been having second thoughts. I'd much rather stay home with my tree, maybe bake some cookies and listen to a Bing Crosby Christmas album. If I venture out at all, it'll be to midnight service."

Jon laughed. "Start getting your gear together, Westgate. You know where you're going to be Christmas Eve as well as I do." He folded himself into his car, laughed at her again in the rearview mirror and zoomed away from the curb.

Angela sat there long after he'd left. He was right, damn him. She'd probably follow Jon into the jaws of hell if he asked. What was the matter with her, anyway?

The drizzle had turned to unabashed rain, glittering like shredded cellophane in the bright illumination of the streetlight. She shivered and, wilting over the steering wheel, moaned a misery that rose from deep inside her.

He didn't understand, did he? She'd told him they couldn't pursue this mutual attraction because she didn't want to ruin their friendship, and he'd agreed she was right. But he didn't *really* understand.

Perhaps she should have talked about it. But how? How could she admit that their lovemaking was the most phenomenal experience of her life, an experience she hadn't even tried to duplicate with anyone else? And the deepest embarrassment of all—how could she confess that she'd been head over heels in love with him at the time? What a fool she'd make of herself. She didn't think she could bear his pity or contempt.

Angela turned on the ignition, adjusted the heat, glanced in the mirror—and glanced again. How wide and frightened her eyes appeared—and how clear their message. Yes, she was worried Jon would discover she'd been in love with him in the past. But she was even more afraid he'd discover she loved him *now*.

She shut her eyes tight and winced. She really did love him, didn't she? But then, had she ever stopped?

But he'd spurned her, rejected her in record time, and she didn't have the slightest doubt he'd do it again.

She pulled away from the curb, her chin tilted in defiance. No, there would be no more loving between her and Jon. She'd be his friend, she'd talk to him on the phone, go out for the occasional meal, and, heaven help her, she'd go on his hike. But never again was she going to let him break her heart.

THE WOMEN ON THE BOARD were already gathered around the conference table in the theater office when Angela arrived for her interview the next afternoon. Mr. Beech stood apart, gazing out the window. He turned.

"Good afternoon, Miss Westgate," he said in his usual brusque manner, but his hand drifted to her arm and squeezed in a private gesture of support.

She smiled her appreciation, wishing she were calmer and better prepared. This was the most important interview of her life, but recent events had completely derailed her from her purpose. On a fleeting wave of paranoia, she wondered if Jon had set out to do so on purpose.

Mr. Beech took a seat at the head of the table and motioned for Angela to sit nearby. It was then that she noticed how pale and tired he looked.

"Would you care for some tea, Miss Westgate?" The oldest woman on the board, Mrs. Fitzhugh, loved to entertain and evidently considered an interview excuse enough to cart out bone china and an antique silver service.

"Yes, thank you," Angela replied.

The women were a motley bunch. There was 190-pound Mrs. Conroy in her designer sweats, Mrs. Stevens wearing a Palm Beach tan and a condescending sneer, and Mrs. Estes who was trying to pretend no one knew she'd just returned from the Betty Ford Clinic.

A disparate crew, yet they all were friends, wives of prominent professionals, dedicated to charity and getting their picture in the paper as often as possible.

Mrs. Fitzhugh passed tea all around, and then they opened folders containing copies of Angela's application. For almost two full minutes the room was silent except for the turning of pages. Angela rubbed her damp palms along her thighs and tried to quell her nervousness. She looked at Mr. Beech, but he'd shut his eyes.

"So, tell us about yourself," Mrs. Conroy said, lifting a teacup in her plump white hand. "Why do you think you'd make a good music director with the Winston Symphony?"

Angela wrenched her concerned gaze from Mr. Beech, straightened her spine and plunged in. For the next few minutes, she reminded them of her training and work experience, but what she really tried to emphasize were the duties she'd fulfilled with the WSO.

"I've been with the group for seven years. I know the audience, know what pleases them. But more importantly, I understand the musicians, what they can do—and what they can't. I believe it's terribly important to choose music they can handle comfortably."

Mr. Beech sat forward. "I'd like to add that when they can't handle the music, as is often the case with the less proficient players, Miss Westgate gives most generously of her time to help them. She's been known to have people over to her house for extra practices, and she's a whiz at rewriting music for them, giving them a simplified version that dovetails so well with the original the audience is none the wiser."

"Really?" Mrs. Stevens looked offended, cheated perhaps, and Angela began to think Mr. Beech hadn't done her any favors.

"But what special vision will you bring to the ensemble?" Mrs. Fitzhugh inquired.

"Vision?" Angela blinked. Suddenly she wondered how Jon had answered that question. She could almost see him now, playing the tormented artiste, fulfilling their every warped expectation—and laughing up his sleeve while he did. "I won't be bringing any new vision. This isn't the Boston Symphony." The women exchanged glances.

"What a community ensemble needs," she went on, "is not a visionary but a common-sense, workmanlike teacher, a person who's patient, able to take music apart and present it in understandable, digestible segments. Someone who absolutely loves their work, too, and I'll defy you to find anyone who loves working with the WSO as much as I do."

Defy? Angela cringed. Emotion was getting the best of her. She was being too forceful, phrasing things badly.

Mrs. Stevens lifted her long pointed nose and sniffed. "I do believe you're serious about this application."

"Yes, I'm quite serious." Good Lord, did they think she wasn't? "Why?"

"Well, you must admit, it is a bit unusual for a woman to aspire to the podium."

Angela's fingers curled into her thighs. So, it *was* happening, just as she'd feared. They were ignoring her qualifications and zeroing in on her gender. "I...I can understand why you think that," she answered diplomatically. "In the seventies there were virtually no women conducting. But times have changed. Female conductors have definitely become figures to contend with. There's Marin Alsop, Catherine Comet, Joann Falletta..." She wished she'd brought along a few magazines to support her point.

"But how will you handle such a large group? How do you expect to project authority?"

Angela couldn't believe she was being torpedoed in such a sexist manner by other women. Still, she smiled. "I understand. There's an ingrained image of the conductor as the embodiment of leadership and authority, and traditionally those are qualities that the popular mind has reserved for men. But surely you must understand how the popular mind can change, and *has* changed over the past twenty years."

Angela was far from finished, but Mrs. Conroy interrupted, anyway. "What happens if you someday find yourself in the family way?"

Angela was sure steam was whistling from her ears by now. "Since I'm single, the issue is irrelevant. But just for the record, Gisele Ben-Dur made her debut with the Israel Philharmonic when she was nine months pregnant."

This remark elicited a series of sniggering oh-mys and good-heavenses.

"Miss Westgate, what ever would you wear?" Mrs. Fitzhugh inquired.

This sparked interest all around, except from Mr. Beech who cast her a helpless look of sympathy. Angela suddenly didn't care that she was in the middle of her interview. She leaned across the table and asked, "Are you okay?"

He nodded, fluttering his hand for her to pay no attention to him.

"What did you say, Mrs. Conroy?"

The woman was chuckling. "I asked what you'd wear, dear. The traditional tails?"

Angela fought to keep her smile in place. "I have two outfits that my superiors find quite tasteful. Clothing has never been a concern."

But evidently it was to this group. They wanted to know what the outfits looked like, the material, even their cost.

Angela eventually steered the discussion toward her plans for the future of the WSO—such as a children's concert series and combined productions with the local choral group. She also wanted to discuss new concepts for raising funds, but their faces had gone blank as soon as the discussion veered away from clothing.

Angela left the theater stewing. Conducting the Winston Symphony meant more to her than anything, and the board members hadn't taken her seriously! She slammed the car door and turned the key so hard the ignition ground. They simply hadn't *wanted* to take her seriously.

By the time she got home, however, her anger had plunged to despair. Her first thought was to call Jon. Her second thought was that it was Jon's fault she hadn't been better prepared in the first place, and she'd be hanged before she'd go running to him for sympathy. She should have spent yesterday preparing, anticipating the curves the board might throw her, rehearsing her answers until they sparkled. That was her usual method. Instead, she'd squandered the entire day on Jon. She really ought to have her head examined, she decided as she headed for the bathroom where she'd find consolation in a long hot soak.

But even as she turned on the tap, she knew her anger toward Jon was only an excuse not to call, not to admit that he *could* ease her burdens, *could* make her laugh, an excuse not to face the truth that Jon was very quickly becoming the center of her universe.

THE NEXT AFTERNOON Angela's phone was ringing when she unlocked her door. "Coming, coming... Hello?"

"Angela, it's Mr. Beech."

She dropped her canvas satchel on the kitchen counter, and Christmas cards, given to her on this, the last day of school before the break, spilled out. "Mr. Beech! How are you?"

"That's why I'm calling. Could you come by the house this afternoon? We have to discuss Sunday's concert."

"Of course. I'll be there right away."

Angela drove across town in record time. She hadn't needed to ask to know that something was wrong.

Mrs. Beech answered the door. She was a tall woman with patrician features and pure white hair pulled into an elegant twist—every inch her husband's counterpart.

"Henry's waiting for you in the study, dear."

Angela caught the woman's arm. "How's he feeling? He didn't look well during my interview yesterday. Did he...?"

"Have another heart attack? I worried about the same thing myself. I even took him into emergency last night, but the doctor in attendance said Henry was fine. His medication did have to be changed, though, and I must admit he looks better today."

"Thank heaven." Angela followed the woman down the hall. "I won't keep him long."

She found her mentor sitting by the fire, a green tartan blanket tucked up around his chest.

"Angela! Here already?" He laid aside the book he was reading. "Have a seat." He waved a hand toward the chair opposite him.

Angela unbuttoned her coat and perched on the edge of the seat, her eyes brimming with questions.

And he wasted no time in answering. "Angela, I need you to take my place Sunday."

Suddenly the room began to whirl. "What?"

"You're going to have to conduct the Christmas program. I thought I could do it, but..." He shook his shaggy white head.

"But the concert is only two days away. I can't!"

The old conductor pierced her with his most formidable look. "Nonsense. You've filled in for me on any number of occasions."

The metallic taste of terror rose in her throat. "Yes, but that was at rehearsal, bits here and there."

Mr. Beech spread his hands on the blanket, old spotted hands that trembled. "Angela, I can't do it." She'd never heard his voice so sad, so defeated.

"Can't you cancel?"

He gazed at the fire. "I could." Again that defeat. "But the Christmas concert is our biggest draw. We'd lose thousands of dollars if I did, and finances being what they are, we'd—" he swallowed "—go under."

"What?"

He nodded grimly. "After sixty-eight years, the WSO would have to fold."

The floor seemed to dissolve beneath Angela's feet. "I didn't know we were doing so badly."

"It's this damned economy." He sat forward, suddenly rigid with bitterness. "Priorities getting all turned around, cuts being made where they shouldn't..." As if exhausted by the effort, he sank back into the chair. "But even if money wasn't an issue, think of the musicians, Angela, all the hours they've put in just for the love of it."

Angela felt the corners of her mouth turning downward. And what about all *his* hard work? she thought. This was Mr. Beech's last concert. Is this how he was to be remembered—with a cancel? She closed her eyes, feeling trapped, wanting to cry.

As she did too often these days, she thought unexpectedly of Jon. Of course he wasn't responsible for this particular calamity, but still she found it odd; why didn't calamities of this magnitude happen when he wasn't around?

Jon! Good Lord, she'd be conducting Jon!

"If you won't do it for the good of the organization," Mr. Beech continued, "how about doing it for yourself? This is a golden opportunity to prove to the board exactly what you're made of."

Angela's head snapped up. That was the last thing on her mind. "But I might fall flat on my face and prove they're right. I don't know the score as well as you do. . . ."

"But you could. I'm not going anywhere for the next two days. Are you?"

Staring at her tightly knit fingers, she shook her head.

"Good. So what do you say? Shall we go for the glory?"

Angela groaned in painful insecurity.

"I'll take that for a yes."

Angela stayed with Mr. Beech for the rest of that day, fine-combing the music and listening diligently to his advice. Jon called her that evening, and when she told him what she was up to, the line buzzed with silence.

Then, "You're going to be doing *what* Sunday?"

"Conducting the concert. Oh, and I'm asking everyone to be there at noon for an extra rehearsal."

More silence.

"What's the matter, Jon?" She couldn't help smiling. "Having difficulty with the idea of me on the podium and you in the pit?"

"No, of course not."

"Are you sure? Our roles are usually just the opposite."

"No, it isn't that."

"Then what is it?" Her smile faded. "Oh. I see. You just don't think I can do it."

Jon cleared his throat. "Can you? I mean, it's such short notice."

"Thanks for the vote of confidence, pal."

"It's concern, Angel, concern. I know how wired you get when you don't feel prepared."

"I'll be prepared."

"I have another question." Jon's voice had an edge she couldn't quite define. "Why you?"

Her back straightened. "Why not me? I *am* Mr. Beech's assistant."

"But doesn't it strike you as just a bit unfair to the others who've applied for his job?"

"Like who, Jon?" she asked insinuatingly.

He groaned. "Angel, can we drop this? I've got a headache like you wouldn't believe."

"So, now I give you headaches."

"You got that right. Insomnia and indigestion, too."

"Good." She was relieved to hear him laugh. She hadn't meant to start an argument.

"I don't suppose you'd care to go skiing tomorrow?" he asked.

"The only thing I'm doing from now until Sunday is preparing for the concert."

Jon gave a low growl of frustration. "All right. I'll call tomorrow to see how you're doing. Take care."

As it turned out, Jon called her several times the next day, but Angela cut each of those calls short. During their last conversation he said, "Are you sure you don't want to take a break and go out for a quick bite?"

"Positive." Nothing was going to come between her and her purpose this time, especially not Jon. "I'll see you at the theater tomorrow."

"You don't even want me to come by and pick you up?"

"Uh-uh. I prefer to be alone till it's over."

"This isn't healthy, Angel," he said dryly.

"Wrong. This is how I thrive. You'll see."

She hung up, wiped Jonathan Stoddard from her thoughts, donned her earplugs to shut out distracting noises and once again mounted the makeshift podium before the mirror in her study. Then, raising her baton to cue an imagined orchestra, she proceeded to conduct the next day's program in the concert hall of her mind.

THE THEATER WAS richly draped in laurel garland caught up in deep swags by balsam wreaths. Their fragrance greeted Angela the minute she came in off the street. Two tall fir trees, heavy with decorations, stood on either side of the stage. The floors were unusually clean, the air pleasantly heated, everything about the place saying: this is it, show time.

Angela walked up the center aisle in a haze of unreality. As prepared as she was, her stomach still quivered. She paused halfway to the stage and took a few deep calming breaths. The worst thing she could do was impart her nervousness to the musicians. Given the circumstances, they were going to be skittish enough.

"Good morning." She smiled at five people who'd somehow managed to arrive before her. They returned wary nods. But then she'd expected that and tried not to take their wariness to heart. She hurried backstage and, after hanging her coat, ducked into the washroom to check her appearance.

Although she'd told the board that clothing wasn't an issue with her, this morning she'd dressed with inordinate care.

The results were gratifying. Looking back at her from the mirror was a young woman who projected strength and confidence. She'd elected to wear her black tuxedo today, complete with pleated shirt, white bow tie and cummerbund. But there was no mistaking her femininity, either. The suit was made of an elegant brocade and cut on lines that enhanced her figure. She'd applied her makeup carefully, arranged her hair in a glistening French braid, and finished off the look with pearl-cluster earrings and a lace-edged hanky tucked into her pocket. She smiled at her reflection, noting the nervous but eager excitement in her eyes.

"Yes," she whispered. "Let's do it!"

As she left the washroom, Jon was just hanging his coat. "Westgate!"

"Hello, Jon." She tried to quell the racing of her heart at the sight of him.

His admiring eyes traveled the length of her, up, down, then up and down again. For once in his life, he seemed speechless.

She beamed. She was definitely ready now. She *would* lead the WSO through this calamity. She *would* prove to the board she deserved the conductor's job. And finally, finally, she would show Jon that she could excel at something, too.

She stood at the podium and scanned the sea of guarded faces before her. Three hours until show time. Three measly hours to prove she could pilot this ship as capably as Mr. Beech.

But damn it all, she was better than Mr. Beech. She had more energy, broader understanding, clearer expression and, if she was really honest, far better rapport with the musicians. She lifted her chin and smiled with dignity and confidence. She loved this group, and for all the panic she'd suffered in the past two days, she absolutely adored being here.

Seventy musicians stared back at her, waiting, suspending judgment. One of those musicians was Jon. But she couldn't think about that now. She had to think of him as just another horn player, melding with the others.

"Thank you for coming to this hastily called rehearsal," she began. "I phoned Mr. Beech this morning, and you'll be happy to know he's feeling much better. However, his doctor still advised him to stay home today. So he told me to tell you he'll be watching us on cable, and in his words, we'd damn well and better be good."

The remark touched off a few nervous smiles, some twittery laughter.

"To which I replied, 'Mr. Beech, we aren't going to be good.'" She paused, gathering their attention. "'We're going to be *magnificent.*'" She gazed over the orchestra calmly, proudly, noticing smiles broaden. "And we *will* be. You've prepared well. So have I. Let's put it all together, shall we?"

SIX HOURS LATER Angela's once crisp shirt stuck in damp folds to her skin, and several tendrils had escaped her neat French braid. But she herself was radiant. She'd done it! She'd led the WSO through its crisis, and knowing the straits she'd been in, the audience had given her a standing ovation.

"Great job, Ange—I mean, Miss Westgate." The young flutist, whom Angela customarily sat next to, blushed.

Still trying to cope with the audience reaction, she choked out, "Thanks, Lynn. Great job covering for me."

"Oh, Angela!" Another musician overwhelmed her with a hug, while several others patted her on the back. "Excellent," she heard. "Wonderful job." She was surprised she didn't rise right off the floor with the happiness she was feeling.

Jon finally entered the backstage area, loosening his white tie. When their eyes met, his fingers stilled, as did her heart.

Jon was the person she most wanted to see now that the concert was over. She wanted to take him by his tuxedo lapels and cry out, "See, Jon? See? This is for all the awards I never won, for all the instruments I couldn't play, for all the ordinary dullness that used to be me."

She waited expectantly, staring at him across the noisy backstage crowd, the seconds spinning out. Finally he smiled and touched his fingers to his brow in a congratulatory salute. But then someone was reaching to shake his hand, and eye contact was broken. Angela waited a little longer, but more people approached him, and soon she realized she was waiting in vain. She'd received all the praise she was going to get from Jon.

Her smile dropped. She supposed there was nothing wrong with his response, but somehow she'd expected more. An exultant hug. A stunned admission that she'd been wonderful. But that brief salute left her feeling empty.

Eventually, everyone moved to the restaurant up the street for the annual Christmas party—musicians, guests, board members and special patrons. Angela, being the party's organizer, lost the first fifteen minutes to making sure the buffet was in order.

When she finally had time to look for Jon, he was already seated at a table, the most crowded in the room. She also noticed that two of his newest friends were women of the board.

"Miss Westgate?"

Angela turned, hiding her disappointment.

"We've saved you a place." Lynn stood and pulled out a chair. "I mean, unless you have to sit with the big guns now."

Angela cast another glance toward Jon's table. Nobody looked back. They were all too engrossed in whatever he was saying.

"I can't think of anyone I'd rather sit with than you guys."

The party went quite well, much to Angela's relief. For most of the evening, however, her attention was on Jon, who seemed intent on talking to each and every person at the affair. Angela felt slighted. Not that he avoided her exactly; he did seek her out a number of times. But the sense of hollowness stayed with her. She was riding on top of the world tonight, but the person she most wanted—and needed—to share her elation with was acting as if he barely even knew her.

"He's really something, isn't he?"

Angela turned at the sound of Mrs. Fitzhugh's voice. Had she been staring? "Uh, yes."

"Such talent! Such style! He really made the concert, wouldn't you agree?"

Angela sighed, suddenly very tired. "Yes, he was excellent." And he had been. Jon's solo performance had been pure magic, and the audience had given him a standing ovation, as well.

"You did a grand job, too, dear." Mrs. Fitzhugh's twinkling eyes caught and held hers meaningfully. "A grand job," she repeated before drifting off to continue her socializing.

Angela's mouth dropped in amazement. And then she smiled, a joyous warmth spreading through her. She *had* been grand, hadn't she? Even the board now acknowledged that fact.

Inadvertently, she gazed across the room to where Jon was laughing with some of the younger musicians. Why hadn't he noticed? What did she have to do to get him to *see* her? Had nothing changed since their youth? Was he still so wound up in his own accomplishments that he couldn't make room for hers even for one night? All the talent she'd pulled out of herself, all the grit, was it still not enough? *Oh, Jon!* she cried. Was it still not enough to make him love her?

Suddenly Angela had to get out of there. Though she'd scored the victory of her career, the taste was bittersweet.

CHAPTER NINE

"WESTGATE! WHERE ARE YOU off to so fast?"

Angela turned. As hurt as she was, a flame of hope still leapt to life within her. "What do you want, Jon?"

He ambled across the parking lot, his cashmere coat hooked negligently over one shoulder. "We have an expedition coming up day after tomorrow that we've hardly talked about yet."

"Oh, that." Her hopeful expression sagged. "For the last week you've done nothing *but* talk about that expedition."

He grinned. "So, are you ready?"

Her face hardened. "In case you haven't noticed, I've had a few other things to think about lately. But don't worry, I'll be ready."

"Would you like me to help you pack?"

"Uh-uh. I can manage."

"How about shopping? I have to go for myself. Do you—"

"No!"

Jon raised his palms. "Okay, okay. We won't go shopping. You're weird, Westgate, you know that?" And before she could retort, he added, "I'll call tomorrow to run through our old checklist to make sure we have everything we need. Okay?"

Angela knotted with frustration. Jon had to be aware of what a monumental task she'd faced today, but apparently he was choosing to ignore it. It was almost as if he couldn't accept this new adult side of her and so was going to skip right over it and blithely get on with their friendship as he understood it.

But then another thought struck her. Was it possible that Jon was secretly resentful she'd been allowed the opportunity to prove herself? Was he jealous?

Well, fine. Let him act like a child. It still wouldn't change the fact that she'd been good.

"Sure. Call. Whatever you want, Jon," she tossed off while heading for her car.

JON ARRIVED at her place early Tuesday morning, the very air around him ringing with his enthusiasm.

"Oh." Angela's voice sank. "You bought new clothes."

"Mmm. None of my old things fit anymore."

"Great." She cast a disparaging look over her shabby wools, purchased eons ago at the Salvation Army store. "You look like you just stepped out of a catalog, while I look like a bag lady from outer space."

"Nobody's going to see us."

"I don't care."

"The important thing is to be warm," Jon assured her, trying to hide his amusement. "Those clothes always served you well."

He turned to the mirror, and while he made a show of adjusting his new turtleneck, she stuck her tongue out at him. Since the concert, Angela had tried to lose her irritability, but this, his showing up in color-coordinated state-of-the-art outdoor wear, was doing nothing to help.

"What flute are you bringing?" he asked. "Nothing valuable, I hope."

"No. The old one I used in high school."

He nodded. "I rented a horn. Got extra socks?"

"Yes."

"Rain gear?"

Angela huffed. "We went through all this yesterday. Yes. I've got everything."

"Okay, then. Looks like we're ready."

Angela gave her snug warm condo a baleful glance and asked herself yet again why she was going on this hike. She couldn't come up with a single reason—except that Jon wanted to go, and, like the Angela of old, she'd let him bulldoze her into accompanying him.

"I ought to have my head examined," she muttered, locking up.

They followed Route 93 north, leaving the gently rolling landscape of southern New Hampshire for a world of ever thickening hills, which in turn grew steadily into craggy snow-capped peaks.

After two and a half hours of driving, they finally reached the Randolph Valley in the Northern Peaks region of the Presidential Range. They'd decided to tackle Mount Adams again, the second-highest mountain in New England. As often as Angela had visited the area, she still felt overwhelmed by its natural beauty—the dense pine and stands of graceful birch, the rushing streams and the fields glistening with snow. And the mountains, of course, the silent, wind-blasted mountains. In winter their beauty was a ferocious sort of thing she preferred not to dwell on.

But of course she did. How could she not, knowing that scores of people had died in these mountains, people who'd lost their way, or slipped off an icy cliff, or were caught in a surprise storm? The weather observatory on Mount Washington had once clocked the wind there at 231 miles an hour. Combined with temperatures that often dropped well below zero, the area had won the distinction of having the worst weather in the world.

Jon pulled into a parking area off the state highway just after eleven, his tires carving ruts in the four inches of new snow that had fallen the previous night. Behind a haze of cloud, the sun was now a dull white glare. Angela checked the heavy sky and then her watch. In good physical shape, she could make the climb in three hours. Out of shape, it might take five or six, and with the days being at their shortest this time of year, she only hoped they didn't run out of light before reaching the shelter Jon had chosen as their destination.

"Heaven help us," she whispered, regretting not having enrolled in aerobics class this fall.

"Put your gaiters on, Angel," Jon advised, opening the car door on his side.

"I am, I am," she said, slipping on the nylon protectors that would keep snow out of her boots. Then she tugged on her wool hat and glove liners. Her hands, she noticed, were trembling. So was her stomach, and she wondered again why she was putting herself through such agony.

Jon propped her frame pack on the fender, an old habit to make the task of slipping it on easier for her. "Great day for a hike, isn't it?" he said.

"Just dandy." She didn't even try to disguise her dread as she shrugged into the straps and buckled the pack in place. "Ugh! I feel like a beast of burden."

Jon's grin grew wicked. "I'll be right back. Just have to pay our parking fee."

By the time he returned her cheeks were beginning to feel the bite of the cold.

"Jon, the thermometer on that garage there reads fifteen degrees, and we're still at the base."

He merely winked, his eyes dancing with devils.

"You're crazy, Stoddard, you know that? You're crazy, I'm crazy, and we're both going to die... Hey, wait up."

They followed Lowe's Path across a logged area, over railroad tracks and into the rising woods. Angela remembered the trail as the easiest way to climb Mount Adams, with mostly moderate grades and inspiring views throughout. She and Jon had once hiked the trail right to the bare, jumbled rocks of the summit cone, but today they wouldn't be going quite that high.

Angela plodded on, snow-laden branches arching overhead, sometimes so thick and close she felt as if she was navigating a tunnel. The air was cold, but after a while, they had to stop to shed some of their layers. As Jon reminded her, it wouldn't do to perspire and dampen their clothing.

"How're you doing?" he asked while securing his sweater to his pack.

Angela flexed her shoulders. "I ache."

He cast her a mock-pitying frown. "Poor baby, come here." She did. "Turn." She did that, too, and with deep-kneading fingers Jon massaged the burning muscles of her shoulders. "There, that'll have to hold you for a while."

She faced him again, glaring her unhappiness with this whole undertaking. But Jon only chucked her under the chin. "Get your pack on, kid. We have miles to go before we sleep."

They trudged on, the snow getting deeper, the course rougher and more steeply pitched. Angela soon forgot the weight of her pack and simply lost herself in the rhythm of her walking, in the rhythm of her breathing. The air was blessedly still and fragrant with spruce and fir. Ahead of her, Jon whistled, his pace always intrepid. Maybe this wouldn't be so bad, after all, she thought.

A short time later, however, she developed a stitch in her side, which increased to a sharp pain. She broke out in a sweat, each step becoming an agony, and feared Jon would have to carry her back to the car. "Wait. Stop," she called out, gasping for breath.

Jon swiveled around, his expression filling with concern. "What's the matter?"

Brushing the snow off a fallen tree, Angela grunted, "I need to rest." She sank down onto the trunk and doubled over. "A cramp in my side," she explained to her snow-covered boots.

"Sorry. I was probably going too fast." Jon sat beside her and placed his arm lightly across her shoulders. "Just as well. I could use some hot chocolate right about now. How about you?"

Angela's throat tightened. She felt so inadequate, so like a failure—and so utterly frightened. What if this was appendicitis?

But of course it wasn't. By the time they finished their watery chocolate, the stitch in her side had disappeared, and she was ready to set out again.

Farther along, she interrupted Jon's singing. He'd been entertaining her with a medley that ran from a sublime "O Holy Night" to a ridiculous "Popeye the Sailor Man."

"Jon, will you tell me something?" she panted, catching up to walk by his side. "Why are we doing this?"

"Why? Aside from the fact that we promised ourselves we would a decade ago?" Jon squinted ahead, thinking. "Well...we need this, Angel. Personally, I've been working too hard, living in cities too long. The spirit gets dull. Life becomes so cluttered we can't see what's really important. Sometimes a person just has to simplify and reduce life to bare essentials in order to sort the wheat from the chaff and rejuvenate that old weary spirit. Know what I mean?"

Angela thought she did. "Okay. That's why you're on this hike. But what's my reason?"

He laughed, his breath billowing. "I don't know. That's for you to find out, but my guess is, your reason's pretty much the same." With that, he slipped his pack to the ground so he could put on his sweater again.

They were fairly high up the mountain now, and the temperature was dropping. Angela shivered, donning her discarded clothing, too. A wind was picking up, whistling through the thinning trees with a forlornness that made her long for home. Quickly, they zipped closed their parkas, tugged down their hats, pulled their neck guards up over their noses, and continued on their way.

Angela now ached from the small of her back all the way to her neck. Her chest was heavy, her head light from breathing so deeply for so extended a time, and the cold dry air made her eyes feel gritty. But it was her legs that concerned her most. They burned and quivered so badly she wondered how much longer she could stay on her feet.

Noticing that the sky was darkening, she checked her watch. "Oh, no! Jon, we're not making the time we used to."

"It's the snow that's slowing us down. You're doing fine. You'll hold up." Jon's dark eyes, all that was visible through his face mask, crinkled with a reassuring smile.

"So, how is everything with Ivan these days? Have you seen him lately?"

"No, and I probably won't for a very long time. Christmas break lasts five weeks. But he called."

"That so? Has he given you any trouble about your breakup?"

Jon had asked her that once before, but she answered anyway. "Nope. He's peeved but resigned." She knew they'd reached a point in their journey where it was important to keep talking as a check against disorientation—a sure sign of hypothermia.

They walked on, chatting inconsequentially for a few more minutes, and then Jon paused again, his eyes narrowed. Angela watched him peer in one direction, then another, and finally down to the compass he held in one hand and the map he held in the other. Suddenly her heart was beating like a metronome gone berserk.

"What?" she asked almost voicelessly.

"Nothing."

"You're lying."

"No, I'm just making sure we keep to the trail."

Angela scanned the snow-covered landscape and thought, *What trail?* They'd climbed clear to the tree line, a wild dangerous place where humans didn't belong. Here nothing existed except snow-encrusted granite and rock rubble. "We're lost, aren't we?"

"No, damn it. Will you stop moaning and let me think for a minute?"

Angela reared back. Jon rarely raised his voice, which only confirmed her fear: they *were* lost.

He whipped down his face guard. "I didn't mean to snap. Sorry." As he spoke, a snowflake drifted between them. Then another. Within seconds, the world had gone white.

"Oh, no! We're going to die."

Jon gripped her arms tight. "We are not going to die."

"Why not? People die in these mountains all the time."

"Hey..." Jon finally noticed she was trembling. "You're really frightened. I didn't realize... Oh, come here."

His jacket was as frigid as the air, but Angela didn't care. She nestled into him, needing his arms around her at this moment.

"Jon, I don't know where we are. We should've reached the hut by now, which means we must've veered off the trail. I'm sorry. I should've taken more interest...."

"Shh, shh. You're right. We did veer off the trail, but not by much. And you do know where you are." He tipped her face up to meet his confident eyes. "Grey Knob Trail is just a stone's throw away, back down in that direction." He pointed.

"It is?" Then why was his heart pounding under her hand?

"Yes. We'll be at the shelter before you know it." Jon pressed her face to his chest and turned against the wind as a particularly strong gust buffeted them. "Ready?" he asked against her wool-covered ear.

She gazed up into his dark eyes. This was the craziest, deepest trouble he'd ever led her into, and just as soon as they were home she was going to tell him so. But right now she was going to borrow all the courage and confidence she could from him. "Ready," she answered.

That "stone's throw" seemed interminable to Angela. The snow continued to fall, the darkness to deepen, and every step she took was a blind leap of faith in Jon's navigational instincts. She herself was totally disoriented.

Glimpsing the fear in her eyes, Jon finally stopped and patiently pointed out their location on the map. To her delight, she *did* know where she was. She felt better after that and even imagined a renewed vigor in her step.

By the time they reached the cabin in the designated camping area, however, darkness was fully upon them. Jon directed the beam of his flashlight on the latch, opened the door and let out a joyous whoop. "We made it!"

Stumbling in behind him, Angela wanted to cry, sure her toes were frostbitten. The air inside the wooden hut was as cold as the air outside, but at least now they were sheltered from the wind.

"Here, let me brush the snow off your clothes." Jon dropped his pack to the floor with a hard thunk. "Once we get a fire going, we don't want this stuff melting into the fabric."

A fire. Angela gazed toward the wood stove, took in the generous supply of chopped wood beside it and felt a ripple of hysterical laughter rise in her throat. "Yes. Let's get the snow off."

A lantern stood on a rough-hewn table in the center of the dark room. Jon pulled off his shells and mittens until he was down to his fingerless gloves, then pried a box of waterproof matches from his pack. Angela, stamping her feet nearby, noticed how stiff his fingers were, what difficulty he had holding a match and striking it. Finally he got one lighted and held it, shaking, to the wick. Soon the room swam with yellow light. But oh, Lord, in the illumination, how bloodless his face appeared. Angela's heart ached for him.

"What should I do?" she asked.

"Well, you could make us some hot chocolate. In the meantime, I'll try to get a fire going."

Angela was happy to do something useful. She set up her small propane burner on the table, poured bottled water into a tin pot, set it atop the ring and held her hands over the heat.

"I finally understand why cave people made such a fuss over fire," she commented, trying to contain the desperate joy she felt.

Jon laughed huskily. "This *is* rather primitive, isn't it?"

Angela watched him surreptitiously over her task. He didn't seem able to grip the kindling but had to shovel it up, instead, two-handed.

"Here, drink this." Angela handed him a tin cup and, squatting beside him in front of the stove, repressed a desire to put her arms around him and wrap him in whatever warmth she could provide.

Jon held the cup in two hands and leaned his face into the rising steam. "Thanks." As he sipped, the kindling inside the stove caught fire. Sighing in relief, Angela reached for a split log, carefully placed it atop the kindling, then picked up her own cup from the floor and took a comforting swallow.

For a long while they sat in worshipful silence, staring at the spreading flames. Finally, when heat began to radiate noticeably from the stove, Jon turned to her and smiled.

"Looks like we're going to live." He wound his arm around her neck and pulled her roughly against him. "So, where's my supper, woman?"

Angela scrabbled out of his grip, her mood lifting with his. "Woman? *Woman?* I am not amused, Jonathan."

"I can't help it. It's getting to me. You know, all this reducing life to bare essentials?"

Angela avoided his eyes, suddenly uneasy with the thought of reducing him to man, herself to woman.

Grinning, he helped her to her feet and together they emptied their bags of the dehydrated rations they'd packed. Soon they had chicken soup simmering on the ring burner and bread, wrapped in foil, warming on the stove. While that happened, they shook the cold from their sleeping bags and spread them on two of the wooden platforms built for that purpose.

"Before I get too cozy," Angela said when Jon removed his jacket, "I'm going to pay a visit to the, um, facilities."

"Take the flashlight, and don't go sight-seeing, okay?"

"You can count on that."

Angela couldn't believe how cold it was outside. And how dark! Not a single star glimmered in the inky blackness. But it was the sound of the wind that bothered her most, the low full-throated moan of it as it moved through ravines and resonated off granite walls; the wind, that up here hissed through the trees and slid the dry snow in ghostly veils upon itself with the same insidious hiss. Everything outside seemed alive with a patient malevolence, and Angela couldn't get back inside the hut fast enough.

She fell against the door, breathing hard, and feasted on the sight before her: a crackling fire, bowls of steaming soup, crude lantern light—and Jon.

"It's fierce out there." She removed her outerwear and hung it from a peg. "The hills are alive, Jon, and not with the sound of music." Though she joked, her sense of danger and isolation had deepened appreciably.

"Come eat."

"Gladly. Hey, what's that smell?" When she spotted the candle on the table, she laughed. "Bayberry? You carried a bayberry candle all the way up this mountain?"

"I thought I'd better. You reminded me often enough that you'd rather be doing something more civilized on Christmas Eve. Wait a sec." Jon bent over his pack, came up with a hand-size tape player, and within moments the cabin was filled with the sounds of Bing Crosby singing "Adeste Fideles"—wobbly sounds because the batteries were still quite cold.

"I also thought we'd top off our supper with these," he said, pulling out a small plastic bag of sugar cookies, mostly broken. "Followed by a reading of, voilà, *The Night Before Christmas.*"

Angela pressed her fingers to her mouth, muffling her astonished cry. Simultaneously, her eyes stung with tears. *Oh, Jon. How much I love you! And how thankful I am that we're still alive and together on this godforsaken peak.*

She sat down quickly and dug into her meal, trying to hide the emotion swelling within her.

"This soup is wonderful," she said after a few ravenous swallows. "Did you buy something new?" She scooped up another spoonful, lingering over its aromatic warmth, then savoring its saltiness and rich chicken flavor. Never had anything tasted so good or lent such comfort.

"No. What's new is we just survived one of the riskiest climbs we ever made."

She met his eyes slowly. "Damn you. It was risky, wasn't it?"

"And you're reaping one of the rewards—deeper appreciation of simple things." Jon smiled, his eyes burning with pride as they traveled over her wind-reddened features. "Thanks for being such a good sport and coming along. I wouldn't have done it without you." His face, made achingly handsome in the warm candlelight, became serious. "And I couldn't imagine doing this with anyone else."

Angela felt as if she were melting under his gaze. But she still managed to dig up one more scowl. "Don't thank me yet. This is the stupidest thing I've ever done, and I plan to be mad at you for a good long time."

Jon reached across the table and squeezed her hand. "I'm so glad you're having fun."

She glowered back at him, but all the while struggling with a smile. The heat from the stove was easing the tightness in her shoulders, the scent of bayberry filled her nostrils, and a profound sense of well-being suffused her soul.

She pushed aside her empty bowl and murmured hesitantly, "This doesn't make sense, but I feel really good right now. Heady. As if I could do almost anything."

Jon nodded in understanding.

"What's even crazier, I feel safe here."

Jon reached into her with his gaze. "You are safe. We're well equipped, we're experienced, and I let several people know our trail route. I'd never lead you into anything we couldn't handle. You know that, don't you?"

She swallowed. Yes, she supposed she did.

"So, what would you like to do with the rest of the evening? I brought a deck of cards...."

"I... brought something, too." She hesitated a moment, then brushed aside her reservations and presented him with a foil-wrapped box.

He blinked. "A present?"

She nodded. "Now, don't start feeling guilty or anything. It isn't much."

"Shall I open it now, or do I have to wait until morning?"

"Now's fine." In mounting anticipation she watched him peel back the paper.

"What the...!" The next moment he was howling with laughter. "Where did you ever find these?" he asked, holding up a pair of berry red boxer shorts printed all over with yellow French horns.

Angela beamed, delighted by his reaction. They'd started giving each other joke gifts when they were in elementary school, and the tradition had continued until they'd parted. She wasn't sure he'd remember.

When he dug into his bag and came up with a gift for her, her heart contracted. "What's this?"

"A little something to even the score."

Eagerly, she unwrapped the box and removed the top. A smile worked into her features and her shoulders began to shake. "Do you really expect me to wear these?"

"Absolutely."

Still chuckling, she lifted out a pair of sunglasses, each lens stamped with a bar of music. She put them on and, vision obscured, groped for her pack again.

The box she handed Jon this time contained what looked like an old-fashioned snow dome, but inside was a troll-like figure sitting at a piano. When the dome was shaken, tiny black notes swirled about, instead of snow.

This gift was followed by a pair of sterling silver earrings for her in the shape of treble clefs, and that was followed by a French-horn tie tack for him, followed by a T-shirt for her that read I Know the Score.

Angela smiled warmly at the array of presents heaped on the table between them, amazed that she had been on his mind as much as he'd been on hers during this shopping season. But her pack still wasn't empty. Biting her lip, she lifted out her last present.

Jon unwrapped it carefully, sensing it was special. When he unfolded the embroidered linen, his expression dropped. "Oh, Angel. Did you do this?"

Holding her breath, she nodded while he read the cross-stitch sampler. God Danced the Day You Were Born, it said.

"That's the nicest thing anyone has ever said to me." He swallowed, his eyes suddenly suspiciously bright. "But it must've taken you days...."

She shrugged his comment off even though he was right. "I'll have it framed for you, of course. It was just easier to pack like that."

"Thank you." Jon reached across the table, squeezed her hand and smiled. Then, without preamble he presented her with a final gift, too.

Angela didn't expect anything from him, not even the joke gifts. Now, folding back the tissue paper from this last present, she fought an urge to cry.

On a rosewood-and-mirror base posed an Austrian crystal angel playing a flute, its exquisitely cut facets afire in the candlelight. Angela was utterly speechless.

"It's a music box," Jon informed her softly. "Wind it up." She did, and a moment later the cabin chimed with the delicate sounds of Beethoven's "Ode to Joy," one of her favorite pieces of music.

"Well…" she said, her throat tightening. "Well…" she repeated helplessly, her eyes filling with tears.

Without speaking, they watched the angel revolve until the melody played out.

"Thank you, Jon," she finally managed to say. "I'll treasure it forever."

They spent the rest of the evening alternately admiring their gifts, nibbling sugar cookies and listening to the Bing Crosby tape. They even fit in a game of gin rummy. Finally, however, Jon got up to rebuild the fire, a prelude to turning in for the night.

Unexpectedly, Angela felt an awkwardness that had been missing most of the evening. She was still wearing three layers of clothing and knew that to sleep comfortably and avoid the danger of perspiring, she ought to be down to one—her underwear. But how to undress in front of Jon without turning ten shades of red?

She removed her boots and quietly placed them by the stove. Then she climbed onto the wooden platform and into her bag, fully clothed. There, she struggled with her sweater and woolen shirt, then grappled with her pants, feeling distinctly like a butterfly fighting its way out of a cocoon.

Meanwhile, having finished stoking the fire, Jon was standing by, watching. "Sweetheart, there's an easier way to do that."

She glared, quite aware that he was laughing. "I'm done." She fell back, panting, and stared up at the dark beamed ceiling, her sleeping bag tucked up to her chin.

When Jon pried off his boots, she turned her face to the wall. A moment later the cabin was filled with the rustling sounds of him undressing. Only after he'd settled did she dare look back. Their beds were at right angles, his feet to hers, so that their eyes met easily. She watched him tuck a shirt under his head, watched the light from the bayberry candle streaking across his chiseled face and swallowed over a dryness that wouldn't abate.

"Are you warm enough?" he asked.

"Yes."

He continued to watch her, his dark eyes gleaming like onyx stars. "Know something, Angel?"

"What?"

"This is the best Christmas ever."

She smiled, warmth flooding through her. "It isn't bad."

"Then you aren't mad at me anymore?"

"About what?"

Jon braced himself up on one elbow, a frown working across his brow. "Frankly, I don't know. Did I do something Sunday to upset you?"

A small current of tension zinged through Angela's body. "Uh, no," she said without conviction.

"Are you sure?"

She hesitated. "Well . . ." Then, riding a wave of remembered pain, she blurted, "Damn it, Jon! I was good. Why couldn't you be happy for me?"

He lay quiet. "You think I wasn't happy for you?"

She let silence answer for her.

Abruptly, Jon sat up and swung his legs over the side of the platform. Angela had seen him in thermals before, but not for a very long time. Good Lord, even in those the man was a dream.

"How could you think I'd be anything but happy? You were wonderful." He pushed himself off the platform and paced the floor, still looking very confused.

Angela stared at the ceiling over her bed, perplexed. "You didn't say much to me. You spent the evening schmoozing with the board ladies and anyone else you could buttonhole. What were you doing, Jon?"

His eyes narrowed. "What do you think I was doing?"

She shrugged, looked away, then mumbled, "Did you think I'd gained too much of an advantage that day in the race for Mr. Beech's job?"

Jon's face fell. A moment later he crossed the room and sat on the edge of her platform. She felt his closeness over every trembling inch of her body, yet willed herself to appear indifferent.

"That was the furthest thing from my mind. If I spent too much time talking to other people, I'm sorry, but I wasn't undercutting you. I was simply enjoying myself. It felt good talking to people from Winston, very good. We talked about real estate taxes, the high school hockey team, all sorts of things. What we *didn't* talk about was the WSO directorship or you." He reached over and framed her face with his hands, making her look at him. "No matter what you think, Angel, I'm not the enemy."

Her throat was so parched she couldn't swallow. "I'm sorry, Jon." She shook her head. "It's just..." Just what? she wondered. That he'd walked away from her once and she'd found it hard to trust him since?

Jon brushed the hair from her forehead, his hand tracing a path down the side of her cheek. "I don't know if this helps, but I wanted to be with you more. I just didn't know if you wanted to be with me. The day before you were so insistent we stay apart."

"That was while I was preparing."

"Well, I wasn't sure. And then there was the small matter of your looking so good. I thought if we were together too much, I'd have trouble keeping my hands off you."

Angela's cheeks turned to flame. "Knock it off, Jon."

"Knock what off? You looked great. Good enough to set atop a Christmas tree." His roguish smile sent tremors quaking through her.

She managed to cast him a wry glance. "An angel in a tux?"

"Depends on whose fantasy it is." He was leaning over her now, a hand planted on either side of her. Angela swallowed convulsively.

"Jon, I think you ought to get over to your own bed."

"I will, but in a while. I'm really in the mood to talk. Move over, will you?" Before she could protest, Jon slid his hands under her and lifted, sleeping bag and all, then settled her nearer the wall.

"What are you doing?" Her heart pounded.

"Shh." He stretched out on the platform beside her, his arm pillowing his cheek. Behind him, the cabin was lit only by the wavering bayberry candle. Angela, studying Jon's face, seeing it made achingly attractive by the mysterious backlighting, became frightened by the closeness.

"I know you feel uncomfortable talking about what happened between us nine years ago, Angel." Jon drew a line down her cheek with the back of his fingers, causing her breath to stop in her throat. "But I've got to return to that incident just one more time. For years I've been bothered by the thought that you misconstrued my reasons for making love."

Angela eased onto her back, away from his hot earnest gaze. A heaviness returned to her heart. What was to misconstrue? His behavior after that trip had explained everything.

Jon cupped her hot cheek and turned her to face him. "Making love to you wasn't the simple physical encounter you seem to think it was." His thumb traced the curve of her lips with drugging slowness. Angela wondered how she could feel so languid while her heart was racing away. "It was much more. If you remember, we'd been talking about leaving Winston and meeting new people...."

Angela wet her parched lips. "Yes. I remember."

"Hmm. But what you don't know is how upset I was by your going away. You were special, my forever friend, my Angel...." He breathed her name with the same reverent passion she remembered from that day nine years ago. She closed her eyes, melting under the heat of his dark gaze.

"And the idea of sharing you and ultimately perhaps of losing you drove me crazy, especially when we started talking about your...well, you know, your having sexual relations. Suddenly I wanted to tuck you into my pocket, take you wherever I was going and shield you from all the insensitive jerks of this world. I wanted to *keep* you, Angel, even though I knew we both had to part."

Angela couldn't believe what she was hearing. If time could take on color, this moment would be all spangly silver, and at the center of that moment would be Jon.

"Why...why are you telling me this?"

"Well, initially I wanted to explain what I was feeling when we made love nine years ago. I thought you might feel better if you knew I wasn't just running on rampant teenage hormones."

This made her smile.

"But somewhere along the way, I began to realize that this conversation has more to do with wanting you right now. All the reasons I'm giving you are just words, air spun into rationalizations to make sense of the simple fact that I want you."

Angela wasn't sure if she was about to laugh or weep. She suspected there was reason to do both.

"Angel, I'm not going to tell you that you were the only reason I returned to New England. I was tired of traveling and missed home.

"And you had Cynthia."

His sardonic laugh left no doubt how much influence Cynthia had exerted on his decision to return. "But I will say this. I was curious about you, curious about this feeling I'd been living with that something had been left undone. There was an incompleteness to our relationship, a disturbing lack of closure."

"Closure? You need closure?" Dismay pressed down on her.

Jon lifted himself up over her. "What I need, my Angel, is to find out why I never stopped thinking about you or why nothing in my experience has ever come close to that one night of heaven we shared on this mountain nine years ago."

"Jon, no..." She tried to lift a staying hand, but his lips were already touching hers. This couldn't be happening, she thought, even as her body curled helplessly into the heat of his. She'd been devastated by his desertion of her nine years ago. What would it do to her now? And he *would* leave her, just as soon as he'd satisfied his curiosity and acquired his sense of closure.

"Jon, please, we promised we wouldn't do this. We agreed our friendship was worth too much to risk."

His lips, warm and parted, brushed over hers and down the soft underside of her chin. Angela's senses reeled under the tender assault.

"I've heard all your reasons, and when I think about them rationally, sure, I agree. But right now, sweetheart, my reasoning powers aren't working too well. Right now I'm all intuition and nerve endings." His intoxicating gaze seemed to be drawing her into him. "Just for once, join me, Angel. Don't think. Just for this night, stop analyzing, stop trying to control things, and let your feelings go."

Angela felt a quake deep inside her, like a bastion weakening. She gazed into Jon's midnight eyes, eyes she'd known all her life. He was such an important part of her. Opposites, yes, but fitting so well that together they made a complete circle—halves of a whole who needed the other for balance. A smile curved her lips as the words "yin" and "yang" passed through her mind.

"What are you smiling about?" Jon tilted his head.

I love you, she thought with her heart. *I love you so very, very much.*

What she whispered aloud was, "Come here." Lifting her arms, Angela felt the last of her defenses tumble.

For a moment, she thought he'd changed his mind. He pulled back, his whole body stilled. "Yes?" he whispered.

"Yes. Come here."

His eyes darkened as he moved closer, and when he pressed his lips to hers, they positively smoldered.

He tasted sweeter than her wildest fantasies. She touched his face, his hair, the corded muscles of his neck; she pressed her hands along his neck and over his chest, desperate to know that he was real and really with her.

Somewhere on the edge of her consciousness, a zipper whispered open—a long, slow coming-apart sound—and then Jon was with her without the barrier of the sleeping bag. Her body ran molten from the moment they touched.

What was happening was crazy, she thought through the thickening fogs of passion. It was bound to lead to heartache, was bound to ruin their friendship. They'd be left with nothing. And then he'd leave....

No, don't think, Angela. Just for tonight, let yourself go....

And she did.

CHAPTER TEN

ANGELA AND JON made love in a white heat, a blinding whirlwind that left her lying in his arms in a floaty semiconscious rapture. Outside, the wind still hissed through the trees, and the inky night, one of the longest of the year, pressed down on the vast primeval wilderness of ice and granite. But inside the hut, the world had once again become an Eden. Angela snuggled against Jon's side, feeling warm, safe and at perfect peace.

They awoke simultaneously to the tiny beeping sound of Jon's wristwatch alarm. The cabin was dark and cold. They groaned and, hugging each other, huddled deeper into the warmth of the down-filled bag.

"Do we really have to get up?" Angela murmured groggily against his smooth shoulder.

He shifted, wrapping her under him. "We don't have to do anything we don't want to." In the dark he kissed her forehead, her cheek, her ear.

"Are you perchance looking for my lips?"

She felt him smile. "I know where they are. After last night, there isn't an inch of you I don't know how to find. Ha! You're blushing. Good. Keep it up. It's mighty cold outside this bag."

In an abrupt move, he threw the covering off them. Angela shrieked, but when she reached to pull it back up, he swung her off the platform and set her on the ice-cold floor.

She was still wearing her wool socks, but she felt the chill nonetheless. "You're a sadist. I hate you," she gasped, dancing about and groping for clothing.

Jon laughed, lit the lantern, and with a casual disregard for his nudity, caught her in his arms and kissed her. Helpless against him, Angela whimpered, and the kiss that had started out as playful soon became a long intimate exploration.

Jon shuddered as he finally set her away from him. "Aw, no. If we start that again, we'll never get out of here." He took a deep breath, then laughed. "You're thinking the same thing I'm thinking. No, Angel." He patted her backside. "Get dressed, and while you're at it, try to keep jumping around and get the blood flowing."

Jump around? Angela grinned. This morning she felt sure she could fly.

They left the hut in the predawn gray, dressed as if for an Arctic expedition, each carrying an instrument case. Angela walked along in relative comfort, despite the fact that the thermometer outside the hut read only six above. The air was blessedly calm and dry, and overhead the morning star burned bigger and brighter than she'd ever seen it; her special Christmas star, she decided.

They climbed a short distance above the tree line. "How's this?" Jon asked.

From the open ledge facing southeast, Angela gazed out over countless miles of peaks and valleys, feeling as if she was standing at the heart of creation. "This is fine."

"Glad you approve." Small lines fanned out from the corners of his eyes, and her heart flooded with warmth, remembering again the closeness they'd shared through the night.

"Would you like to sit?" Jon laid his horn case on a flat granite slab. "It shouldn't be more than a few minutes."

They brushed away the snow and sat, eyes directed toward the horizon. Time ticked on, but the sky looked as dark as ever.

"Such a long night. Is the sun never going to rise?"

Jon stretched out his legs, arms folded calmly over his parka. "Patience, sweetheart. The sun always rises. Hey, that sounds like a good title for a novel."

The morning stillness was silvered with Angela's soft laughter.

They fell into companionable silence again, watching the horizon, waiting the long winter's wait for the sun. After what seemed an age, Jon looked at her and droned, "I know, I know, this is crazy."

She shook her head solemnly. "Don't think it even for a second."

Gradually the sky took on an orange-pink wash. She glanced at Jon, a question in her eyes, but he still shook his head.

She sat closer, beginning to feel the cold, and continued to watch the panorama before her. She waited while the sky washed to peach and the morning star gradually disappeared. When the horizon went to white, Jon finally pulled off his mask and opened his horn case.

"Okay, I figure we have about five minutes before condensation shuts down this gig," he said.

Angela felt her pulse quicken. "Then let's do it in style."

She raised the cold flute to her lips, and just as they had agreed when they were dreamy-eyed teenagers, they began to play "What Child Is This?" And as they played, the sun rose over the far horizon, bleaching out the snowy peaks and flashing off the rich brass bell of Jon's horn.

Vaguely Angela wondered if anyone heard them. A scientist perhaps over at the weather station on Mount Washington. Or a farmer deep in some sleepy valley rising to milk his cows. She wondered what miracle they thought they were waking to.

But she and Jon hadn't come here to play for anyone else, and if no one heard, which was probably the case, that was all right, too. They'd come here simply for the experience.

Something about the moment reminded her of a print Jon used to have in his room when he was young, Michelangelo's *Creation of Man.* But in his inimitable way, Jon had tinkered with the masterpiece. Right over the almost-touching fingers of God and man, he'd drawn a quarter note. She'd never asked him to explain, but now she thought she understood what he'd meant.

She put her flute down before the song ended, unable to continue for the tightness in her throat, leaving Jon to finish alone. And as he played, tears slid down Angela's cheeks. Whatever music was capable of doing, Jon's music did it. He touched the soul and lifted it to touch the sublime.

Jon finished the song and lowered the horn to his knee. Angela wiped her eyes and watched the sun pour its cold wintry light over his solemn face. His eyes were hard and fixed, his chin jutting, sure signs that he was shoring himself up against a tide of emotion. She had so much to say—how the experience had surpassed her wildest expectations, how thankful she was that he'd given her this moment—but knew she didn't have to, for he understood. He took her hand and together they sat in silence for a few minutes more, watching the sky fill with sunlight.

Finally they got to their feet.

"Merry Christmas, my Christmas Angel," he said, framing her face with his hands.

"Merry Christmas, Jon." Her smiling lips trembled, and when he kissed them, they trembled even more. She thought she'd never been so happy.

He sighed contentedly and kissed her forehead. "Let's go have some breakfast."

ANGELA LEFT THE HUT reluctantly. If time could be measured by the depth of emotion experienced within each minute, then she and Jon had spent a lifetime here. But he had a Florida-bound plane to catch, and she had a long drive to her sister's. So they hiked back down the mountain, a journey that went surprisingly fast, and returned to her condominium in Winston.

Yet, when it came time to part, Jon couldn't seem to let her go. Standing at the door, he held her in his arms and continued to kiss her passionately, repeatedly, despite her occasional reminders of the time.

Finally he stepped back. "Okay, you're right. I'll miss my plane if I don't get moving." He took a deep breath and, tearing his gaze away from her flushed face, hurried out the door.

But a moment later he was back and kissing her so thoroughly her knees turned to water. When he eventually lifted his head, he was grinning in pure male satisfaction. "Hold that thought till I get back," he said. As he jogged down the walk, Angela fell against the doorframe, laughing in something close to rapture.

Two days later, she was racing the vacuum cleaner around her living room when the doorbell rang. Jon was due back from Florida, but not for another hour at least. She looked out the window, then threw open the door.

"Mr. Beech!" She cast aside propriety and gave him an exuberant hug. "Come in. How are you feeling?"

"Much better. How was your Christmas?"

She smiled beatifically. "Transcendent."

His expression made her laugh. "Transcendent. Well, you can't do better than that."

"Can I get you something to drink?"

"No, thank you. Please, could we just sit a moment and talk?"

"Sure. What is it? You look . . . This is something important, isn't it?" The next second, it hit her. She'd been so wrapped up in her happiness she'd actually forgotten.

"The board has made a decision regarding my replacement."

She drew a breath. "And?"

"And I felt I ought to come over and deliver the news in person. Angela, I'm so sorry."

She closed her eyes, feeling weak and dizzy. "I...I didn't get it?"

"No, I'm afraid not."

"Then, if I didn't, w-who did?"

Mr. Beech reached for her hands and held them tight. "Jonathan Stoddard."

CHAPTER ELEVEN

"ARE YOU ALL RIGHT?" Mr. Beech peered at her with concern. "Can I get you some water?"

Angela's voice, when she finally answered, was remarkably calm. "Thank you, no. I'm fine. I'm sure Jon will be wonderful. He always is."

The old conductor eyed her more sharply, and though it would have been bad form for him to admit she would've been better, the thought passed between them nonetheless. "I'm so sorry, Angela. I tried."

His sympathy was almost her undoing. Her throat closed and her eyes stung. "I understand, Mr. Beech, and I appreciate everything you've done."

He hesitated. "I haven't talked to Jonathan myself yet. Mrs. Conroy was in charge of delivering the news to him. But when I do, I intend to recommend he keep you on as directorial assistant, if that's all right with you."

Assistant to Jon? Second best again? "I'm not sure what I want right now, Mr. Beech."

"Of course. You'll need time for the news to settle."

"Could you tell me one thing? What is it about Jon that swayed the board? What does he have that I don't?"

"I think the word was 'panache.'" Mr. Beech rolled his eyes. "I don't mean to diminish his talent. It's immense, and he probably will be wonderful once he grows into the position. But what struck the board most was Jon, the personality. They felt that here was someone who would draw a crowd, attract new patrons and, in short, keep the WSO solvent."

Panache! After Mr. Beech left, Angela slumped to the half-vacuumed rug in front of her tree and in a daze stared at the ornaments. How did you fight something as indefinable as panache? Suddenly the shiny decorations swam out of focus as the realization sank in: she'd lost the WSO directorship. Good Lord, she'd lost! What was she to do now? There was no place else she wanted to be, nothing else she aspired to. She buried her face in her hands and, refusing to cry, merely shook for a few unsteady seconds.

All along she'd feared not getting the position, yet secretly, deep down, she'd believed she would. Some steady little flame of hope had always burned. But apparently she was a fool. Jon had kept his application in, and when Jon was in a race, no one else stood a chance. "Damn him!" she cried.

On a sobering wave of guilt, Angela knew she was being unreasonable. It wasn't Jon's fault. After all, he had offered to withdraw from the contest and she had told him to stay.

But even as she thought this, the pain of her disappointment welled up inside her, drowning her objectivity, and the next moment she ached to lash out at the world once again.

"Damn him!" she cried again. He could have chosen to withdraw. As her friend, he *should* have chosen to withdraw. But he hadn't. Why had she let herself think he'd be so gallant? Had she begun to believe him when he said he didn't want the job?

She should've paid stricter attention to what she *knew* about Jon rather than what she *felt*. He loved facing new challenges, loved taking center stage, and if that meant riding roughshod over a friend, well, so be it. Friend, move aside.

Damn, damn, damn! He'd been a contender all along, even while wooing her friendship and trust and ultimately her love. He didn't care one bit about her goals or feelings. She felt used and lied to, her friendship betrayed, a victim once again of Jon's ambition and arrogance.

Angela closed her eyes and moaned. She didn't like feeling this resentment, this rage, and part of her knew she was reacting irrationally. Good heavens, she loved the man. But she couldn't help herself.

The doorbell rang and her heart leapt. This time it had to be Jon. She considered swallowing her pain and congratulating him as warmly as she knew how. That would be the adult thing to do. But almost instantly she knew she'd never be able to pull off the act.

Deciding to face the problem head on, she swung open the door. But she wasn't ready for the emotional punch that came with just seeing Jon again.

He strode in and, before she could say a word, pulled her to him, one strong arm encircling her waist, his other hand burrowed into her hair. Then he was kissing her as if he'd missed her as much as she'd missed him these past two days.

Oh, Jon, don't do this, she thought. But as his soft warm lips moved over hers, plying their usual magic, as memories of their Christmas Eve swirled through her mind, she couldn't resist kissing him back.

But no, this couldn't happen. Gathering up her willpower, she pushed him away. "Stop."

He seemed stunned, then hurt. "Angel, what's the matter?"

"What's the matter? How can you show up here pretending nothing's happened?"

"Pardon me?"

She smiled icily. "The WSO directorship?"

"What about it?"

Angela fell quiet for a long embarrassing moment. "D-didn't you talk to Mrs. Conroy?"

"Uh-uh. I drove here straight from the airport." His eyes narrowed, and then he said, "Oh, hell."

Realizing what she'd just done, Angela spun away. "I'm sorry. It isn't my place to give you this news."

He gripped her shoulder and turned her to face him. "Angel, I'm really sorry."

She crossed her arms stiffly. "I'm sick to death of that word 'sorry.' You don't mean it, never have, and I don't want to hear it anymore."

Jon sighed heavily. "This isn't the way things were supposed to work out."

She laughed, trying to pretend her heart wasn't breaking. "Of course not. You didn't count on my being upset, did you? Simpleminded little Angel was supposed to be overjoyed for you. She was supposed to greet you with hugs, hallelujahs and a brass band, wasn't she?"

Jon hooked his hands on his hips and stared at her with intense searching eyes. "What's this all about?"

"What it's about, Mr. Stoddard, is the fact that you've run roughshod over me once again."

His color deepened. "But I told you weeks ago that I didn't want the position."

"Words are cheap, Jon. If you really didn't want the position, you could've withdrawn your application."

"You told me not to, damn it! You said you'd never speak to me again if I did."

Even while she understood his exasperation, her pain and anger drove her on with their own peculiar logic. "So? Did you have to listen? Couldn't you see how much the job meant to me?"

Jon thrust his fingers through his hair in frustration. "The reason I kept my application in was I never for a minute doubted you were better qualified and would get the position. I'll admit I did want it at the very beginning, but the night I slept over I saw your résumé. I saw the score you were preparing, and I realized you were far and away my superior. *You're* the one with the inferiority complex, Angel. I have no idea why, but *you* created it, *you* perpetuate it. I kept my application in for your sake. I wanted you to feel better about yourself when you were awarded the position. I wanted you to know you'd beat everybody, fair and square, including me. I was so sure you'd get it."

Angela's throat grew thick with pain. "Well, I didn't. Thank you for being so considerate!"

Jon gripped her upper arms. "Look, I don't want the damn job. I have every intention of refusing it."

"It doesn't matter anymore. Don't you see?" Her voice cracked. "You've already proved your point."

"Which is?"

"That you're better than me at everything."

"Don't be ridiculous. The only thing that's happened is a handful of women made a grossly stupid decision. I plan to turn down their offer, so the job's yours."

"As I said, it doesn't matter. There's no joy in being the orchestra's consolation prize, Jon. You've spoiled it for me. You've spoiled everything."

He let her go with a harsh little shove. "Oh, grow up!" He walked away, his hand clasped to the nape of his neck.

"Me, grow up? Now, there's a laugh."

He swiveled around, and suddenly Angela was struck by the depth of hurt in his eyes. "I've had enough of this. I'm cutting out."

Her head jerked back. "What do you mean?"

"Just what I said. I told you my reasons for applying for the job and keeping my application in, but apparently you just don't want to believe me. For some reason, you insist on believing the worst. Well, I've got a flash for you. Friends don't do that." He zipped up his jacket. "There used to be a time when trust was the basis of our friendship. I've tried to get it back, but I guess it's just not there anymore."

He smiled ruefully. "You said we'd changed. I didn't want to believe it, but now I see you were right." He paused a moment, his eyes pained as he took one last look at her. Then, "Goodbye, Angela." The next moment he was gone.

HE'D BE BACK, Angela told herself, lying awake that night. The WSO would be reconvening in two weeks, and he'd be there, taking the podium and loving every minute of it, because that's just the way Jon was. In spite of what he'd told her, she had no doubt that leading the WSO was exactly what he wanted. He'd banked on it, in fact, going so far as to actually buy a house here in Winston.

But one thing was certain: when the WSO did reconvene, Angela Westgate would not be there. How could she continue to sit in the trenches when she'd been so close to being on the podium? It would hurt too much. But what would hurt even more was having to face Jon every Wednesday night, the very nature of the meeting a reaffirmation that she'd lost to him.

Before she got up the courage to hand in a formal resignation, however, Mr. Beech called to ask if she would help him straighten the music library at the theater. She said yes, met him at the theater and, after twenty minutes of sorting through dusty files, finally broached the subject.

Mr. Beech dropped a sheaf of yellowed *1812 Overtures* into a drawer and turned, stunned. "You're not serious, are you?"

"Absolutely." She lifted another stack of jumbled files off a shelf and set them on a table.

"But, my dear, you can't quit the orchestra."

"I'm sorry, but I have to."

He frowned. "Have I missed something? Has someone declared this National Resignation Week without telling me?"

Apprehension trickled down her back. "Why?"

"Well, just yesterday Jonathan Stoddard called the board together and handed in his resignation, too."

Angela gulped. "Jon did what?"

"That's right. We met right here, in fact."

"Jon resigned his brand-new position?"

"Well, since he'd never actually accepted it, I suppose what he was doing was refusing it. Throwing it in the board's collective face, actually. Gave them a sound thrashing, too, I might add."

Her eyes widened. "For what?"

"For not choosing the right candidate for the job. I'm so glad I showed up. It was priceless." Mr. Beech laughed one of his rare raspy laughs. "That's why you can't quit. Mrs. Conroy will be calling you any time now."

Angela felt for the chair she knew was behind her. "To offer *me* the position?"

"Of course, as she should've done in the first place."

Angela's jaw hardened. "Well . . . I won't take it."

"Why not?" When she didn't answer, he asked, "Pride? Is that it, Angela?"

She rose and scrambled up the stool, away from his disconcerting gaze. "It's . . . complicated, but okay, you could call it pride."

"And you think by refusing the board's offer, you'll be hurting them? Oh, Angela, don't you realize the only person you'll be hurting is yourself?"

"Me?" She handed him a stack of old concert programs.

"Yes, you. There's an expression for what you're doing. It's cutting off your nose to spite your face."

"Well, for heaven's sake, Mr. Beech, what would you do in my situation?" She came down off the stool.

"No question about it. I'd see the board members for the fools they are, accept the position and enjoy it to the fullest. I wouldn't measure my worth by their standards, and I certainly wouldn't sit home sulking like a child."

This last remark brought a sting to her eyes. He was the second person to comment on her lack of maturity in almost as many days. "I'm sorry you feel that way." Her voice wobbled.

"Angela, buck up. This isn't like you, and quite frankly, I don't understand your behavior. Is something going on that I don't know about?"

"It's . . . personal. Between me and Jon."

"Ah. I see."

Angela frowned, wondering precisely what it was he saw. "It's a long-standing rivalry," she explained.

"Really? Hmm. That's strange."

"What is?"

"Well, if Jonathan is what you call a rival, I wish I had a few like him. If I did, I'd never want for a friend."

She blinked rapidly. "As I said, it's complicated."

Mr. Beech smiled. "Yes. Love usually is."

Dumbfounded, Angela stared at the old man as he hobbled off to a hot plate where earlier he'd prepared a pot of tea. "It doesn't have anything to do with love, Mr. Beech. What it's about is Jon's big fat ego."

"Oh. And you don't have an ego problem yourself?"

Under his sharp eye, Angela's color climbed.

"Angela, my dear, I think I need to tell you something about Jonathan." He handed her a cup of tea. "He requested I keep it a secret, but . . ." He shrugged. "The first time Jonathan and I talked was late August. He called."

"About the directorship?"

"No. He was looking for you."

"M-me?"

"That's right. He wanted to know if you were a member of the WSO. He said you were an old friend he was trying to locate. It was only after I assured him you were indeed a member that he applied for my job. Call me romantic, Angela, but I'd say the guy did so just to have an excuse to become part of your life again."

The teacup rattled as she set it in its saucer. "That's ridiculous!"

"Is it?"

"Then, you mean . . . ? Oh, hell! What've I done?"

"Yes. What have you done, Angela?"

"Cut off my nose to spite my face?"

"Hmm. I thought you were looking a little peaked today."

"Mr. Beech, do you mind if we continue this later?"

"Not at all."

"Thanks." She was already pulling on her coat.

Angela drove aimlessly for more than an hour, trying to sort her muddled thoughts. For the most part, they remained muddled. But as the miles accumulated on her odometer, one realization did emerge: Jon and Mr. Beech were right; she *was* acting childishly. She'd been hurt and had gone off to sulk. And why? Because she'd felt unloved. But by whom? Who did she think didn't love her? The board?

As always the answer was Jon. She'd wanted to excel at something so he could admire her. But she'd failed. It was nine years ago all over again, and he was about to discover she wasn't as interesting as he thought. She was just ordinary, mediocre Angela with nothing to hold him here.

She suddenly felt an overwhelming need to apologize. What a terrible load of guilt she'd dumped on him, accusing him of robbing her of her joy. Spotting a phone booth, she pulled off the road.

The phone rang four times before he picked it up.

"Hello?"

Angela frowned. "Jon?"

"No. This is Anthony. Jon is out at the moment."

"Anthony?"

"Yes, the person Jon sublet the apartment from. I just returned from England."

"Oh. Oh, of course."

"Jon will be gone most of the day. He's out apartment hunting."

"Apartment hunting? Where?"

"Let's see. Today he's doing Back Bay, I believe."

"That's in Boston?"

"Yes. Would you like him to call you when he gets in?"

"No. That's all right. I'll call again later. Thank you." Quickly, before he could ask her name, Angela hung up.

Apartment hunting? In Boston? She walked back to her car in a daze. Why would Jon be doing that when he was on the verge of buying the Thurgood house?

Suddenly her stomach bottomed out. She raced back to town, flew up the hill to Elm Street and, filled with foreboding, pulled to the curb in front of the gracious English Tudor she'd spun so many dreams about of late.

"Oh, no!" she whispered, her worst fear confirmed. The Sale Pending banner had been removed, so that the sign on the lawn again read For Sale. When Jon said he was cutting out, he really meant it.

But could she blame him? What had she ever done to make him want to stay? She'd fought their friendship every step of the way, arguing and complaining throughout, even on their dream-come-true Christmas hike. She'd also made it impossible for him to accept the WSO conductor's job, whether he'd wanted it or not. She still wasn't certain of his true feelings in that regard, but she did know he'd wanted to come back to Winston. And how better than by becoming an integral part of a community institution?

Odd, she hadn't realized it before, but everything in Jon's behavior pointed to the fact that he'd matured and was here to settle. He'd told her how tired he was of traveling, how much he'd missed New England and longed for a place to call his own. But she hadn't taken him seriously.

And now he'd given up. She gazed at the house, shimmering in her tears. She'd pushed him once too often.

Angela tried to fill the next few days with chores. She went grocery shopping, cleaned the house and washed her sweaters. But all the while she continued to think about Jon and mourn his absence.

When Mrs. Conroy finally called and offered her the conductorship, Angela surprised even herself. "Could you give me a couple of days to think about it?" she replied.

Suddenly being conductor of the Winston Symphony didn't seem all that important anymore. She'd come to realize her life wouldn't end if she turned down the position. She had her teaching jobs, and what was to stop her from applying to some other orchestra? True, she loved working with the members of the WSO, but perhaps she'd placed a little too much value on them, making them a substitute for family after her mother died.

In the meantime, she had to do something about Jon. She could live without the WSO, but she couldn't live with knowing she'd hurt Jon and disrupted his life. If he wanted to return to Winston, it was high time she did something to help.

It was New Year's Eve when Angela made up her mind to drive down to Cambridge and apologize to Jon in person. He might not accept her apology, but she had to offer one, anyway. That was the least a friend could do.

She remembered his mentioning that he would be playing with his jazz group that night, which suited her just fine. That was probably the best way to approach him, when he was relaxed and in good spirits.

She applied her makeup with care, then slipped into a sheath of a sapphire color that accentuated her eyes. She brushed her hair until it crackled and, as a concession to the festive night, caught it up in two rhinestone combs. A touch of subtle cologne behind her ears, a change into higher heels, and she was ready. Then, knees knocking, she headed for the door.

Angela wasn't aware that traffic would be so heavy and only belatedly remembered that Boston celebrated First Night in such lavish fashion. It was late when she finally walked into the club. The place was crowded, all the tables taken, and for a moment she felt self-conscious, standing alone at the bar. Everyone else was with somebody on this special night. But then a waiter led her to a small table that had just been set up to one side. As she sat he placed a silver party hat and a noisemaker before her and smiled diffidently.

She ordered a schnapps to chase away the chill of the night, then sought out Jon on the stage. As always, her heart soared just at the sight of him.

The group finished the number they were playing and announced a break. Angela wrung her hands as Jon walked off the stage. Abruptly she stood, and even though she didn't say a word, he turned in her direction. When he recognized her, his head jerked back.

Please don't turn away, she prayed with all her heart. *Please, hear me out.*

Slowly, he approached her table, everything about his demeanor held in check. "Westgate! Well, well." His mouth, usually so sensual and relaxed, looked hard, his eyes cold as steel.

"H-hello, Jon."

"What brings you here?"

The waiter arrived with her drink, and Jon took the opportunity to order an ale.

"Would you care to sit?" Angela offered.

He eyed her guardedly, then hooked a chair out and sat it astraddle. "So?"

"So." She ran her sweaty palms along her thighs. Where did one begin? For days she'd been trying to sort her thoughts, and finally she'd believed she had everything figured out, all the answers and explanations and reasons for her behavior. But now her mind felt like a jumbled attic. Suddenly the only thing she could think to say was, "I messed up."

His eyes drilled into her. "Yes, I know."

Angela felt her color deepen. "That's why I'm here. I'd like to apologize for the horrible things I said to you." She ducked her head. "They were childish and unfair, and I hope you didn't take them to heart."

Jon's ale arrived and he took a long sip before answering. "What did you expect? A guy tends to sit up and take notice when he's been told he's just taken all the joy out of his best friend's life." He set the glass down and again eyed her narrowly. Oh, he was hurt all right. She'd never seen him so reserved.

"The reason I said those things..." She paused, unsure of her ability to explain, because at the bottom of everything was the simple fact that she loved him.

"Suffice to say I've spent the last few days sorting priorities, and I'll be damned if..." Her eyes grew hot. "I'll be damned if you didn't come out right on top."

Jon started to say something.

"Please, let me finish before I lose courage." She sipped her drink. "It only occurred to me this week how serious you were about wanting to move back to Winston. I also realized how difficult I made that move. So I've tried to make amends."

He scowled. "Amends? How?"

"Well, I put a binder on the Thurgood house again, in your name. If you really, really don't want the place, fine, let it go. But, Jon, if you do, please, don't let someone else snatch it up."

Jon's eyebrows arched so high they practically disappeared under his hair.

"The second thing I did..." Here she took a much bigger sip of her schnapps. "I called Mrs. Conroy yesterday and asked if the board would reconsider your application for the WSO directorship."

"You what?" Jon stood up and turned his chair around.

"Poor woman got pretty confused. She'd offered me the job just the day before. But in the end she said yes. So..."

Angela left the sentence open, but her meaning was obvious. The position was his for the taking.

Jon clutched his head in his hands, his eyes trained on hers. Was he angry? Was he about to tell her to get lost?

"Oh, Angel," he finally breathed. Just hearing him say her name flooded her with relief. "I told you I don't want the job, and I mean it. I'm perfectly happy with the one I've got. As you once said, I'm a musician, not a conductor. But the house—" he smiled unexpectedly "—now that's another matter. I will take you up on your offer—on one condition."

"What?" She'd agree to anything to make him happy.

Jon leaned closer. "That you move in with me."

Angela nearly toppled her drink. "What?"

"Give all that great old furniture you own a proper home."

"Oh. It's my furniture you want, is it?"

Jon's amusement deepened. "Yes. You know I don't have any, myself."

"You're making fun of me. I'm sorry. I came here in good faith, but maybe I should leave."

When she attempted to get up, however, Jon grabbed her wrist. "Angel, I'm making fun of both of us, not just you."

She searched his face, startled, confused.

"Sit down, sweetheart," he said tenderly. He moved his chair around to her side of the table and, turning his back to the room, carved out a private little space for them to talk. Then he took her hands in his, forcing her to face him squarely. "You see, you're not the only one who knows how to mess up, and when I do, I aim high. Mess-ups on a cosmic level."

Angela frowned. "What are you talking about?"

He sighed. "I was a fool for running off nine years ago. I should have talked to you, should have called or written and told you how much you meant to me." He looked aside, swallowed. "But I didn't."

"It's perfectly understandable. You were young. You were frightened and confused by what we'd done, and you had four years at Juilliard ahead of you, dreams to follow after that..."

"No. I made the wrong choice. I chose to chase a career, thinking it was a me-or-you situation. If I didn't put myself first, I thought, everything I'd ever dreamed of doing or becoming would go up in smoke."

"That just might've happened, Jon. Can you honestly say you'd be the same person today if you hadn't done what you did? The teachers you learned from, the broad range of musical experiences you enjoyed..."

Jon's grip on her hands tightened. "But there was no excuse for not staying in touch with you. I should've realized that a career and a love life are not mutually exclusive. But I didn't, and as time passed it become more and more difficult to call. For that, all I can say is I'm sorry.

"If it's any consolation, I was miserable. Memories of you wouldn't give me peace. Through nine years and four continents, I couldn't get you out of my mind. Finally I knew I had to return and find out what those memories were all about." He lifted one of her hands and pressed his lips to her palm.

Sitting on the edge of her seat, Angela shook her head, stupefied. "I don't believe this."

A frown troubled Jon's brow. "I'm sorry to hear that, but it's probably only what I deserve."

"No. When I say I don't believe this, I mean this is too good to be true."

A smile warmed his eyes. "Yeah?"

"Yeah."

He smiled more confidently. "Good. Because I finally figured it out." Oblivious to the people behind him, Jon threaded his fingers through her hair and pulled her closer. "What those memories were about, of course, was the fact that I love you. Always have. Always will." He moved in and kissed her lips.

Angela was sure she floated clear into the air, like one of the pretty balloons he'd given her. "Well, that's good to know, Mr. Stoddard," she replied dreamily, "because I happen to love you, too."

"Are you sure?'

"Very."

"What about this competitiveness you've driven me crazy with lately?"

"Oh, that." She wrinkled her nose. "Well, the long and short of it is, there is no competition, Jon. I only wanted to excel at something so you'd consider me your equal."

"Oh, Angel." Jon's expression was pained. "When have I ever not—"

She placed her fingers over his lips. "I know. If anything, you've always believed I could do far more than I actually could. There was only that one incident of rejection, and at eighteen, it cut deep. I thought if I'd been prettier and smarter, you wouldn't have left."

Jon was about to say something, but just at that moment, the saxophone player appeared at his side. "Sorry to interrupt, but it's that time again."

Jon sighed, his broad shoulders slumping. "Don't run off, sweetheart. We still have a lot to settle."

Angela watched him walk away and join the other musicians. When they began to play, she tried to pay attention, but she was wound much too tight with everything that had been said.

Jon, too, seemed unable to concentrate. His brow remained knit, his eyes troubled, and time and again he looked toward her table.

When the number finally ended, he got up from his piano and stepped over to the other musicians. They leaned in, nodding as he spoke, and watching them, Angela frowned. What was Jon plotting now? For a moment she tensed, thinking he might have another flute tucked under his piano. But no, he couldn't. He hadn't expected her tonight.

Jon returned to the piano and adjusted the microphone. Simultaneously the others stepped back, instruments lowered, like soldiers at ease. A hush fell over the audience as Jon gathered their attention, the silence deepening while he continued to stare at his hands poised over the keys. Finally, he said quite simply, "This is for Angel."

Angela sucked in her breath. For Angel? What was he doing? She was still confused when he began to play.

She recognized the piece immediately. How could she not? It was "The Angel Waltz," Jon's dubious tribute to her, pretty much as it had sounded the first time she'd heard it when she was sixteen—simple, predictable and sweet. Angela couldn't believe Jon was playing it in public.

But almost imperceptibly the steady one-two-three rhythm began to change, the simple melody became layered, and before long Angela realized she was listening to an extremely complex jazz number—beautiful and intense and full of surprises. By the time Jon finished, she'd gone through three tissues, and her tears were still flowing.

Jon stood up and, ignoring the applause that broke over him, strode off the stage straight to Angela's table. "Come on. Let's get out of here." He held her coat for her.

She sniffed. "But the band..."

"Never mind the band. Let's go." He gripped her arm and escorted her to the door, earning the smiling curiosity of everyone they passed on the way.

Once outside, he wasted no time in wrapping her in his arms and covering her mouth with his. He was trembling—arms, chest, thighs. Even his lips had a certain desperation about them as they moved over hers.

"Angel, my Angel," he whispered.

"Yes, I'm here." She slipped her arms under his sports jacket and, working them up his muscled back, moved into him until they were a snug fit.

He drew in a sharp breath, closed his eyes and ran his parted lips along her hot cheek. "Sweetheart, we've got to do something about this friendship of ours."

Shuddering under his touch, she replied, "Do you have any suggestions?"

A slow sensual smile eased across his face. "What do you say we slap a license on it?"

"What sort?" Her voice was suddenly breathless. "Hunting? Fishing?"

"Maybe later. Right now I'm thinking more in terms of marriage."

"Marriage." She closed her eyes, wanting to cry all over again. "You mean the kind with a house and a dog and . . . and children?"

"Oh, at least enough children for a string quartet."

Her throat worked convulsively. "I think we can work something out."

Jon stood very still. "Is that a yes?" All his flippancy was gone.

So was hers. "Yes."

Jon closed his eyes and held her so close she could barely breathe. "Thank God. I never want to be apart from you again."

"You won't be, I promise," she somehow got out.

"Good, because without you..." Jon pulled back, smoothing her long hair from her flushed face. "Oh, my Angel, my soul..." He leaned in and kissed her again, a long possessive kiss that made her forget they were standing on a public sidewalk.

"I know," she murmured. "Without you, I feel empty, too, as if half of me is missing."

"We're really fortunate, aren't we? What we share is a very special love."

She smiled, another tear slipping down her cheek. "One of cosmic proportions is my estimation."

"At the very least."

In the distance across the river, fireworks had been booming for some time.

"Must be close to midnight," Jon murmured.

"Mmm. Can we see the fireworks from here?"

"I'm not sure." Jon drew her to his side and walked to the corner. From there they discovered they could indeed see the display, at least the uppermost splashes of it. But despite the sky's filling with brilliant jets of color, Angela and Jon remained absorbed in each other.

"You haven't told me what you think of the completed 'Angel Waltz.'"

Angela purposely hemmed and hawed. "It's okay." When she saw how crestfallen he looked, she laughed and hugged him close. "It was magnificent, and I'm not just saying that because I was flattered. Jon—" she was filled with wonder "—you've become one heck of a composer."

He winked. "The best is yet to come."

"I haven't a doubt."

"For you, too, sweetheart. You're one heck of a conductor." Grinning mischievously, he kissed her forehead. "You know—"

She laid a hand on his jacket. "Stop. I don't like the sound of that 'you know.'"

The sky began to pulse with a series of explosions so thick and frequent it could only mean the grand finale was under way.

"You know," he persisted, the fireworks reflected in his deep midnight eyes, "I play with this little band over in Boston, and I was just thinking..."

"No, don't think, Jon."

"I was just thinking that someday I might be able to wrangle an invitation for you to lead that little band as guest conductor."

"No, Jon. I'm not interested in conducting the Boston Symphony Orchestra. The only group I plan to conduct from now on is the WSO. You're out of your mind. You always have been...."

Before she could say another word, he kissed her. "Happy New Year, Angel."

From behind restaurant doors and apartment windows drifted the muffled jangling of noisemakers, cheers and sentimental strains of "Auld Lang Syne."

Angela's eyes misted. "Happy...First Night, Jon," she whispered.

With his arm around her shoulders, they slowly walked back toward the club. "What do you say I grab my coat and we cut out now?" suggested Jon.

"Sounds good to me. Where do you want to go?"

"Well, how about you help me pack my things—it shouldn't take long—and then we head up to Winston?"

Angela beamed from ear to ear.

At the door to the club Jon paused to kiss her one more time. When he finally lifted his head, he smiled at her, his eyes sparkling with love. Angela returned his smile, aware of how blessedly happy she was. Life with this wonderful man was never going to be dull. Of course, she'd probably never feel surefooted or in control of anything again. But then, who ever did? Life was uncertain, surprises and challenges at every turn—if you were lucky. The best a person could hope for was to find someone to join hands with while taking the glorious ride.

"I love you, Angel," Jon whispered in her ear.

"Love you, too," she replied.

Then he opened the door, and with fingers reaching to intertwine, they walked through.

She aimed to rope herself a cowboy—
and haul him in for Christmas!

A COWBOY FOR CHRISTMAS

Anne McAllister

Chapter One

If there was any animal stupider than a cow, Jess Cooper didn't know what it was. Unless, he thought grimly, it was the cowboy who had been trying unsuccessfully for the past hour to outthink one.

He scowled at the empty meadow, the untouched salt lick, the grassy slope edged by oak brush where he'd expected to find the half dozen black Angus cattle that Mike Gonzales had said he'd seen over that way yesterday.

He should've known better.

He sighed and reached up to remove his hat, then rubbed his fingers through his hair. Settling the hat back on his head, he reined his horse around and headed up the valley the other way. His bones ached and his stomach growled. He'd been too far from the ranch house to go back for dinner, and the couple of sandwiches and thermos of coffee he'd brought along had disappeared hours ago.

But these few cattle were all that was left up this way. He'd brought the rest down over the past two days so they'd be available to be checked over and sorted before shipping. If he didn't get them today, it would just mean coming back tomorrow.

He straightened, ready to head down when a gleam, sudden and unexpected, caught his eye.

He blinked. There, glistening against the velvet green backdrop far across the valley, the wide front window of the ranch house reflected the fiery brilliance of the setting sun. It stopped him mid-movement, made him settle back in the saddle and smile.

"Like a diamond," he said aloud, though if he'd been able to think of anything more precious than diamonds to compare it to, he would have. Because, had Jess Cooper seen mere jewels, he could easily have turned away.

Diamonds were just sparkly stones. Distant and unreal. Meaningless.

Not like the ranch.

The Rocking R Ranch was real. It was almost four thousand acres of southwestern Colorado: mountains and valleys, meadows of timothy and clover, forests of aspen and spruce. It was Nathan Richards, forthright and stubborn, Jess's boss. It was half a dozen horses, a couple of dogs and just over three hundred head of black Angus cattle, some stupider than others.

It was "home." He said the word softly, barely breathing life into it. He felt funny saying it, as if not only the word but its implications were alien to him.

And if he was honest, they were.

He'd been Nathan's right-hand man at the Rocking R for nearly three years, the longest he'd been any one place in his thirty-four-year life. Until now he'd never thought of any place as home. He wasn't exactly sure when he'd started thinking that way about the Rocking R.

It wasn't *House Beautiful,* that was for sure.

"House Functional," Nathan called the two-story log house he'd built twenty years ago when the first frame house on the land had burnt to the ground.

It was functional, Jess conceded. But it was something more. There was something special about it that drew him back whenever he was down in Texas at a cattle auction, up in Denver selling their own beef, or even spending a Saturday night in town.

Used to be he didn't care where he laid his head or where he woke up in the morning. Now the Rocking R was in his blood. Now he wanted to be here.

He'd even begun having hopes of owning the spread someday, making the old man an offer, putting his name on the dotted line.

But to dare to call it *home*—to actually say the word out loud—still seemed to be tempting fate.

"Presumptuous," his eighth-grade English teacher, Mrs. Peck, would have called him.

And about this Jess was afraid she would have been right.

Nathan disagreed.

Nathan Richards had had his share of dreams in seventy-nine hard-living years. "Gotta have 'em," he'd told Jess the day he'd hired him.

They'd stood facing each other in the coffee stall at the cattle auction, the old man and the young one, the dreamer and the cynic, and Nathan had taken a deep swallow of the lukewarm brew and nailed Jess with his pale blue stare.

"Gotta have dreams," Nathan repeated. "A man ain't alive without 'em."

Jess wasn't sure about that. Dreams had done more damage than good to his own father. Les Cooper could never let go of the notion that he was destined to be the world's champion steer wrestler. And he'd wrecked his marriages, all three of them, and his family in the pursuit of that dream.

Jess wanted nothing so grandiose. Generally he tried not to think about what he wanted in life. It seemed like asking for trouble.

"Don't got any dreams?" Nathan had challenged him. "Young feller like yourself?"

"Not really," Jess had replied at last.

"Damn shame, not to have hope," Nathan said. His pale eyes had regarded Jess thoughtfully. "What's it like to be hopeless?"

Jess's chin had come up. "I'm not hopeless," he said, a rough edge to his voice.

"No?" Nathan shrugged. "'Pears so to me. What's your future then? What do you want?"

Jess wrapped his hands around the coffee mug, clenching it really, not daring to think about his future, his dreams. It was like wishing on a star. Childish. Foolish.

It was enough, he reckoned, to get from day to day.

But when Nathan continued to wait for his response, he ventured gruffly, "Own me a few head of cattle. Have a place to graze 'em."

"Come work for me and you got it."

Jess simply stared. It was too simple. Too impossible to be that simple, he told himself.

Jobs—especially jobs like the one Nathan seemed to be offering—didn't just drop like roast ducks into the mouths of cowboys drinking coffee at a café. Least of all to washed-up rodeo cowboys on the mend from four cracked ribs and a broke-in-three-places leg.

But Nathan Richards meant what he said. And he had a habit of making things happen.

"'Sa matter? Don'tcha think you can do it?" he'd challenged.

And Jess, never proof against a dare, had replied, "Damn right I can."

And over the past three years, with Nathan's blustering encouragement and continual needling insistence on the necessity of looking with hope toward the future, Jess had dredged up a few dreams of his own.

Small ones to start with. That'd been hard enough.

But by the end of that first day's auction, Jess had had the start of his herd. Seven yearling heifers. Black Angus, like Nathan's.

"Put your own brand on 'em," Nathan said to him. "Got a brand figured out?"

What young boy hadn't? Jess wondered. He'd doodled his own on more schoolbook covers and carved it into more trees than he could remember.

"You bet," he replied. Now there were seventeen of them branded with his JC.

Yeah, Nathan had a way of making things work, of inspiring a guy to look ahead, to plan, to figure, to hope.

Jess still wasn't comfortable with it. But now and then he dared.

But he was still surprised when Nathan hadn't thought he was crazy, when he'd broached the subject of the ranch last week.

"Buy me out?"

Jess had been afraid the old man would laugh and tell him that some dreams really were too big, especially for men like him.

"Not right away, I don't mean," he'd protested quickly. "I know you got a lotta years left."

But Nathan's blue eyes had got that faraway look in them, the one that Jess had learned to wait on, to sit quietly and expectantly while Nathan thought things through. So he shut his mouth and waited.

The old man stretched and stuck his sock-clad feet out toward the fire, then folded his hands on top of his flat belly. His blue eyes met Jess's. "Don't see why not."

Don't see why not.

The rest of the world would have had a million objections: Jess's past, Jess's present, Jess's prospects.

God bless old Nathan Richards, Jess thought. He didn't have a one.

"Mine," he said softly now, trying out the word as he looked around him. "My ranch."

He looked over his shoulder, almost expecting to see the ghost of Mrs. Peck scowling at him. But all he saw was the empty meadow behind him. That was comeuppance enough.

"And I gotta find *my* cattle," he said to Dodger, for they were in fact his, the ones up in this pasture. And with shipping day barely two weeks away, he needed to bring them down and look them over, get them shaped up and ready to sell. Putting his heels lightly to the horse, he rode on.

If he hadn't passed them on the way up, they'd headed round the hill toward Sutter's place. It'd take him another hour before they reached a fence so he could round them up and herd them home. Provided they'd stayed together, of course. And what were the odds on that?

His stomach growled, reminding him of the time. It was getting close on toward supper. He hoped Nathan wasn't cooking anything that would burn.

The old man was a surprisingly good cook when he wanted to be.

"Course I am," he'd said, offended, when Jess had first commented on it. "What'dya think? Was your grandmother taught me."

Jess smiled now as the horse threaded his way through the aspen and down the slope. His grandmother, Ella, had cooked and kept house for Nathan until her death eight years ago. Jess had been surprised to find out that Nathan had never replaced her.

"Couldn't," the old man said simply. "She ran the show."

Jess didn't believe that, but he admired Nathan's loyalty. He'd learned in the meantime that Nathan was a better cook than Ella had ever been. He'd never said so.

Wouldn't do to give the old man a swelled head.

He was luckier this time. He'd gone scarcely more than a mile before he spotted the cattle—five in all, with four of them standing there looking at the fifth who'd got her head stuck between two strands of the barbed wire and couldn't pull back out.

"Damn fool cow."

It wasn't the first time. It wouldn't be the last, unless he made some sort of rough contraption that would prevent her from poking her head in where it didn't belong. He could sell her, of course. Serve her right to wind up on somebody's Sunday platter. But she was a damned fine-looking cow, sleek and fat. Hers had been the best of this year's calves.

"Beautiful but dumb," he told her. She couldn't even turn her head to look at him.

He dismounted and slipped between two bovine bystanders. "Think the grass is greener over there, do you?" he asked as he eased the barbed wire over her ears.

She chewed stolidly on, stepping back when he nudged her with his shoulder. "C'mon. Move it."

Freed now, she did, giving her head a little shake, then turning and ambling up toward the creek, her companions following.

"Not that way!" Jess swung back into the saddle and headed after them, cutting them off and herding them downstream, Scout the dog helping. They balked, then moved, disgruntled, going at last the way he wanted them to go.

It was another forty minutes before he'd brought them down into the hay meadow with the rest of the herd.

The wind came with just a little nip now that the sun was gone. September days were warm, but the nights cooled off quick. A guy could feel winter coming, but it was still a ways off. No snow in the air for a while yet.

He shut the gate, then took his time, enjoying the peacefulness, the sense of belonging he felt every evening now as he headed back toward the house, prolonging the anticipation.

There would be warmth there, a fire, a meal and Nathan.

After supper, while Jess leaned back and propped his feet on the hassock, Nathan would grumble about the events of the day. Later, while they played checkers, he would tell Jess what letters had come in the mail, where his far-flung family was and what they were up to now. Nathan talked about them so much that sometimes Jess felt as if they were his family, too.

The best kind of family. One that you could enjoy secondhand without having to be responsible for.

He smiled, thinking about them as he led Dodger into the barn and took off his saddle. Hell of a family Nathan had—only son in the foreign service in Sri Lanka or some damned place, grandsons in London, in Florida and L.A. His only granddaughter was a librarian in New York. Nathan had gone to visit her in July.

"What's the matter? Can't she bear to leave the big city and come out here?" Jess had asked him the day he'd taken Nathan to the airport in Durango.

He'd worried about the old man making the trip on the little plane to Denver, then having to go miles in the airport to get the jet to New York.

"I reckon she could, but she's pretty busy. I'm not."

"She oughta come here," Jess insisted. "She used to when she was a kid."

"You remember her?" Nathan lifted one white brow.

Jess shrugged. "Seen her once or twice."

"Pretty little thing, wasn't she?"

Another shrug. "Don't remember."

"Ayuh." Nathan's scepticism was obvious, but Jess ignored it.

Yes, he remembered Alison Richards. And yes, she had been pretty, with her long shiny dark hair, her wide grin and her deep blue eyes.

But she'd been no more than fifteen the last time he'd seen her. And far above his touch besides. A diplomat's daughter had little in common with a cowboy. Even if the age differential hadn't existed, he'd never have approached her. They were from different worlds.

She'd had a bit of a crush on him that summer, and he'd done his share of daydreaming about her. But he was smart enough to know nothing would come of it. Intelligent, worldly girls like Alison Richards never got serious about men like him.

In any case, getting serious about a woman wasn't something Jess ever intended to do. He'd seen enough of marriage in his childhood to know that.

He wondered, though, as he coped by himself during the weeks Nathan was gone, if the old man had mentioned to his granddaughter who his hired hand was.

He wondered if Alison Richards would remember him, if Nathan had.

He hoped not, since the last time she'd seen him, he'd been sprawled in the dust and bleeding. The mere memory of that could still make Jess squirm.

He'd waited for Nathan to say something about his visit, about Alison after he got back. The old man never did.

"So, did you have a good time?" Jess was finally forced to ask several days later when Nathan didn't volunteer anything.

"Informative," Nathan said. "Good thing I went."

Jess waited for him to elaborate, but he never did, just started talking about a bull he'd heard was for sale down El Paso way.

Jess sighed, but didn't ask anymore. A guy didn't pry. Nathan's granddaughter wasn't his business. He didn't care about her at all.

But if Nathan's granddaughter didn't come up in the conversation again, the bull did. Just this morning the old man had brought it up again. "Maybe we oughta go down after shipping this fall, take a look at 'im."

"What do we want another bull for?" Jess wanted to know.

"Always gotta look to the future, Jess. We might give it some thought."

Maybe they would, Jess thought now, unbridling Dodger and rubbing him down. Maybe they'd buy the bull and bring him home. Maybe they'd find a few head that Jess could use as well, if he could afford it.

But maybe, he thought, smiling and flexing his shoulders, he'd have all his money tied up by then.

Just as he was going out the door this morning Nathan had said they'd have to talk about putting together a land contract, too.

He gave Dodger one last stroke, filled his bin, then headed for the house, Scout at his heels.

The reflected brilliance of the sun was gone now, but in its place he saw the warm glow of light from the kitchen. His pace quickened as his stomach growled again, anticipating one of Nathan's thick stews or a slab of beef and potatoes.

He stamped up the steps, one last cue for Nathan to put the meat on, just in case he hadn't seen Jess ride in. Then he opened the door to the porch, took off his boots and rolled up his sleeves. He ran hot water in the sink, splashing it over his face and arms, then ducked his head under the faucet. Groping for a towel, he rubbed his hair briskly and mopped his face, scowling at himself in the splotchy old mirror as he did so.

His hair needed cutting again. Used to be he got it done regular. On the rodeo circuit he'd had an image of sorts and a desire to impress the ladies. Now, with only Nathan to impress, he didn't bother.

But Nathan could cut it. Better than playing checkers again and losing. He had a snowball's chance in hell of ever winning a game against the wily old fox. Nathan always had something up his sleeve, and even when you thought you had him cornered, he'd distract you.

"Got a letter from Ali today," he'd say and pat his pockets futilely. "Now what'd I do with it?" Or, with a glance at the kitchen, "Cathy Lee baked us an apple pie. Sure would like a piece. How 'bout you?"

And so Jess would ferret out the letter or cut each of them a piece of pie, and when finally he could get his mind on the game again, damned if he hadn't forgotten his well-planned move.

It was only a matter of time until Nathan captured the last of his pieces and chuckled with satisfaction.

Letting the old man hack at his head seemed a better bet all around.

Jess stuffed his feet into a pair of old moccasins, ran a comb through his hair, and, whistling softly under his breath, opened the door to the kitchen, sniffing hopefully, trying to guess what dinner would be. He didn't smell anything.

"Nate?"

He could hear the television in the living room. Nathan didn't like television. He swore he never watched it, but Jess had his suspicions.

"Thought you didn't like TV," Jess had chided him just last week after Nathan had treated him to a long discourse on Peter Jennings's story about the latest situation in the Middle East while he washed up after supper.

"Don't," Nathan huffed. "Infernal idiot box."

"So where'd you hear all this stuff you're tellin' me?"

"National Public Radio, of course."

"Of course," Jess said diplomatically, then gave Nathan a bland smile. "When did Peter Jennings go to work for National Public Radio?"

"G'wan, get out of here," Nathan grumbled. "'Less you wanta dry these dishes."

Laughing, Jess had left. Now he grinned. It would be hard for Nathan to claim National Public Radio was on the idiot box tonight.

He crept quietly into the living room, spotting Nathan's thinning white hair just visible over the top of the lounger that faced the set.

Peter Jennings had long since gone home. Whatever was on now had a laugh track and a very silly girl in a tutu doing pirouettes across a kitchen floor.

Jess shook his head. Boy, would he give Nathan a hard time about this!

He advanced stealthily until he stood directly behind Nathan's chair, then cleared his throat. "What's this? A rerun of 'All Things Considered'?"

Nathan didn't reply.

"Come on, Nate. 'Fess up. I caught you."

Nathan didn't move.

Jess frowned. "Nate?" He moved around the side of the chair, touched Nathan's shoulder. *"Nathan?"*

But Nathan didn't hear him. He didn't see Jess or the girl in the tutu who pirouetted right out the door and into a commercial for laundry detergent. He didn't feel Scout's cold wet nose nudge his hand or Jess's trembling fingers touch his cheek, then frantically grope for a pulse.

Nathan Richards was dead.

JESS COOPER could rope a steer with the best of them. He could brand a calf, ride a bull, break a horse.

He couldn't talk on the telephone worth a damn at the best of times, and he sure as hell couldn't call up Nathan's family and tell them something like that.

"You tell 'em, Charley," he pleaded with the doctor who'd met the ambulance at the hospital, examined Nathan's lifeless body, then had shaken his head sadly and told Jess what he already knew.

Charley Moran clapped a hand on Jess's shoulder. "Better coming from somebody who knows them."

"I don't!"

"Never even met them?"

"Yeah, well, once or twice, years ago. But I—"

"I've never met them at all. People don't want to hear about the death of a loved one from a stranger. Believe me, Jess."

People didn't want to hear about the death of a loved one from anyone. Jess knew that.

He twisted the brim of his hat in his fingers, damning Charley silently with his eyes. A nurse bustled past with a patient in a wheelchair. Charley squeezed his shoulder sympathetically.

"He was a swell old man. The best."

Jess nodded miserably.

"We'll all miss him."

Another nod.

Charley's hand gave one more squeeze. "No one more than you."

"Ain't that the truth." Jess looked away. He still couldn't swallow the awful lump in his throat.

"Dr. Moran?" The nurse beckoned to Charley, and the other man gave him one last sympathetic look and hurried away.

Jess stayed right where he was. He still couldn't believe it. Less than two hours ago he'd been whistling and contemplating a haircut as an alternative to letting Nathan scalp him in checkers. It hadn't been more than an hour and a half since he'd called the ambulance.

There had been no hurry by that time, of course, and he'd known it.

Jess had seen death before. His mother. His father. The old lady at the boarding house in Grand Junction. Pete Cummins, gored by that bull down Gallup way. Countless cattle and horses.

A guy ought to be used to it by now, oughtn't he? Be able to accept the inevitability?

But, God Almighty, *Nathan?*

He'd never known a man more alive than Nathan, with his guileless blue eyes that belied his devilish grin. It was Nathan, not Jess, who always talked about the future, for crying out loud. It was Nathan who had always insisted on dreams, hopes, plans.

Jess had just gone along with them, echoed them. He tried again to swallow, rubbed a hand across his eyes.

"Damn you, Nathan," he muttered. "How could you go and do something so stupid as die?"

He found a phone booth near the door of the hospital, went in, leaned against the wall and picked up the receiver.

He didn't dial. Couldn't.

He walked back out again. Charley was just coming down the corridor.

"Ah, good. You called?"

Jess shook his head. "Don't have the number," he mumbled, heading toward the door.

"Directory assistance," Charley suggested to his back.

But directory assistance was beyond Jess right now. Talking rationally to a bunch of Nathan's far-flung relatives was impossible. He got into the pickup and flicked on the ignition.

"Boleyns' will be calling you. Got to get things started," Charley said from the doorway.

Boleyns' was the undertaker, efficient as hell. Jess had no doubt but that they could get Nathan buried without the advice and consent of any relatives at all. He shoved the gearshift into reverse and whipped out of the lot.

"You can't stall around on this," Charley called after him.

But Jess was already gunning down the highway, throat tight, eyes blurred. He had some grieving to do and, as far as he was concerned, grieving came first.

•

HE CALLED Sri Lanka at three in the morning. It was as soon as he felt he could say the words. It also seemed a safer bet than calling anyplace in the States—more likely to be daytime for one thing, and more likely to have a bad connection for another.

Jess knew he couldn't tell anyone without his voice breaking. Nathan's son half a world away didn't have to know that.

The connection was better than he'd hoped it would be.

David Richards was shocked. His own voice broke, his pain apparent. "I'll come as soon as I can," he said. "I won't get there in time to make the arrangements. Ali can do that."

Jess hoped to God he wouldn't be expected to call her. He was vastly relieved when David said he'd take care of it.

"She'll be devastated," he told Jess. "No one loved him like Ali did."

I did, Jess thought, but he didn't say so.

"No, sir," he said quietly. He stood barefoot in the darkened living room and stared unseeing out the window into the night.

"She'll take care of everything. I'll let you know when we'll be arriving," David went on.

"I'll be expecting to hear from you."

The connection crackled. "You can...handle everything on the ranch?" David asked worriedly.

The ranch.

Jess had tried not to think about the ranch.

More than Nathan had died last night. Jess's dream had died as well. But it didn't seem fair to think of that now.

It seemed selfish, rotten. He felt guilty the instant the thought crossed his mind. His dreams didn't matter. Never had. It was Nathan who mattered, Nathan who'd been like a father and grandfather to him, Nathan who'd been for the past three years virtually all the family Jess had.

"I've never been much of a rancher," David went on shakily, his voice still ragged. "I guess you know that."

Jess struggled to keep his own emotions out of his. "Don't let it worry you, Mr. Richards. I can handle the ranch."

YOU CAN'T go home again.

Alison Richards, like any good librarian, was familiar with Thomas Wolfe's sentiment. And she believed he was right. Which was why she hadn't been back to the Rocking R Ranch in twelve long years.

She knew her father would be surprised to know she thought of the Rocking R as home. After all, she'd only spent a few summers there while she was growing up. She'd spent far more time in Beirut, Mexico City, Hong Kong and Athens.

But it was in southwestern Colorado that she'd invested her soul.

It was here in these mountains that she'd first given her heart.

Foolishness, she thought now, as she turned the rental car onto the narrow gravel road that led off the county highway and up into the hills where her grandfather had his land.

The foolish act of a foolish child. And no one save herself had ever known she'd done it.

"Just as well," she said aloud. She shook her head at the folly of the fanciful young girl she had been. She'd read too many fairy tales.

"And too many Westerns," she told herself, smiling wryly now.

She obviously hadn't watched enough television. Everyone knew that cowboys never hung around. Most of them made their careers out of riding off into the sunset at the end of the show. Why should reality be any different?

Besides, Alison had grown up now and made a career of her own. She'd made hers by going to library school. A prosaic, if fitting, end.

She'd wanted to bring to other children the same enthusiasm for reading, for learning, for understanding and enchantment, that she had known.

She was a good librarian, too. She kept up on new titles. She tried to remember her patrons' tastes in reading. She encouraged the young, sympathized with the old and stayed late to shelve books if the pages hadn't got it done by the time the library closed.

And if her life wasn't exactly what she'd dreamed it would be when she was five or ten or fifteen, well, whose was?

She was happy enough. She had a good job, a steady boyfriend, a neurotic cat. She was a grown-up now. And she'd do well to remember it, she thought, coming back, as she was, to the scene of her youthful dreams.

She'd never imagined she'd come back like this.

She'd just seen Nathan two months ago. He'd been hale and hearty, as opinionated as ever, poking his nose in every aspect of her life, looking down it at her boyfriend, Gary, scratching it at the antics of her cat.

She'd taken a week's vacation to be with him. They'd gone to Ellis Island, to a Yankees game, to lunch in the open-air pavilion at Rockefeller Center. In the daytime they'd enjoyed New York. At night they'd talked about the ranch—not the way it was now, but the way it had been.

"You oughta come back for a visit," Nathan had told her, smiling, his feet stretched out and crossed at the ankle, one toe wiggling to tease the cat.

But Alison had shaken her head. "No." She didn't want to. It was perfect just the way it was, a memory to be taken out and cherished, not a reality to be faced as an adult.

But reality had a way of intruding, no matter what. She'd just been going off to work yesterday morning when her father had rung her with the news.

"I'll get there as soon as I can," he'd said. "But if you can make the arrangements, I'd appreciate it."

"Of course."

There was only one funeral home in town. It hadn't been hard to track it down. She'd done as much arranging as she could over the phone. Nathan had, she discovered, done a lot of it himself.

"A great planner, your grandfather," Horace Boleyn had said. "Had the format of his funeral all figured out. And, of course, he'll be buried at the ranch in the family ground next to your grandmama."

"Of course."

"So, visitation Friday noon to nine. Funeral at St. Francis Church Saturday at ten? How's that suit you?"

"I think that should work."

"Call with your flight time and Cooper can pick you up at the airport."

"Cooper?" Just for a moment Alison stopped breathing.

"Jess Cooper. Your granddad's man."

Alison couldn't have said how long the silence lasted. Boleyn broke it finally, saying, "Shall I tell him to pick you up?"

"I'll rent a car. We all will. Th-thank you, Mr. Boleyn. I'll see you Friday."

She hung up and stared unseeing out the window. Jess Cooper.

Not *her* Jess Cooper.

It couldn't be. Of course it wasn't.

There were bound to be a dozen Jess Coopers in the west, maybe more. Nathan had never mentioned him, for heaven's sake! Surely if his hired man were the same cowboy who'd worked for them all those years ago, Nathan would have said.

No, she thought now as she shut the last gate and climbed back into the car to head up the narrow track toward the ranch house, it couldn't be the same Jess Cooper.

A minute later she found out it was.

Chapter Two

She was taller than he remembered. More slender.

Prettier, too, damn it.

He'd seen pictures of her since she was fifteen, of course. Nathan had taken a couple of rolls of snapshots in July. He'd caught her laughing at an outdoor café. He'd taken one of her cooking spaghetti in her apartment and another playing with some flea-bitten cat. But they hadn't done her justice.

They hadn't caught the red highlights of her long brown hair as it drifted in the breeze or her casual grace as she got out of the car or her shapely bottom as she opened the trunk.

Jess stood inside the barn and watched as she brushed her hair back from her face and looked around slowly. She wore sunglasses, so he could only guess when her gaze rested for a moment on the barn. But he felt a flicker of discomfort, wondering if she might be able to pick him out in the shadows watching her, even as he was sure she could not.

She turned then and faced the house, squared her shoulders, lifted her suitcase and headed for the door.

It was unlocked. She could get in without him. He wouldn't have to follow her, talk to her. Not yet.

But to avoid it was just postponing the inevitable. And there wasn't much point in that.

Odds were she wouldn't even remember him. And if she did, well, so what?

He rubbed his hand through his hair and settled his hat back on, jerking the brim down a bit more than usual. Then, taking a breath, feeling sort of like he felt when he was just letting himself down on an unknown bronc, he set off toward the house.

She had already disappeared into the kitchen by the time he got to the porch. He hesitated a moment on the steps, then pushed open the screen and went in.

She was standing by the table, one hand clenched on the red gingham oilcloth that covered it. In the other she held a photo that Nate had tacked up on the bulletin board—one of him and Jess, laughing together at the barbecue after the branding in the spring.

His steps made the floorboards squeak, and he stopped just inside the door.

She heard him, of course. But she took her time turning, and even when she had, he felt off balance because she was still wearing her sunglasses, and he couldn't see her eyes as her head lifted from looking at the photo to looking at him.

"Jess Cooper," she said at last.

And he knew she remembered him. He felt a tide of hot blood creep up his neck and hoped she wouldn't notice. Her voice was different than he remembered it, deeper, smokier. Of course, he told himself. It would be. She'd been a girl then. She was every bit a woman now.

He cleared his throat and bent his head acknowledging their acquaintance. "Ma'am. I just...I want to say... I'm...really sorry about...about Nathan."

He saw her swallow, then she managed a small smile. "Yes. So am I."

And then neither of them said a word.

Up the valley Jess could hear the mooing of the cattle. A jay was racketing in the branches of the pine just outside the window. He could even hear the refrigerator hum. He shifted his weight from one foot to the other. "Shall I...take your bag up...ma'am?" he asked at last.

"I'll do it."

"The bedroom—"

He started to gesture, but she said, "I thought I'd use the one I used to have. If that's all right?"

"Of course. I mean, it's not my house."

But it had been his bedroom, the one she was talking about. Yesterday evening he'd moved his gear back out to the old bunkhouse that hadn't been used since his grandmother had died, maybe before. From the first Nathan had invited him into the house, and he hadn't argued. Maybe that was what had made it seem like home to him, made him feel as if he belonged.

But Nathan's family wouldn't expect to find him there. He was only the hired hand, after all.

"You suit yourself, ma'am. I'd best be getting back to work. It's a busy time of year." He backed toward the door. "If you need anything, you let me know." He pivoted on his heel to make his escape.

"Jess?"

He turned. She had taken off her sunglasses and he felt trapped in the brilliant sea blue of her gaze. "Ma'am?"

Her lips quirked. "I know I'm older than the last time you saw me, but I didn't think I'd aged that much."

He blinked.

"You used to call me Alison."

He shrugged, feeling foolish. It wasn't her age he was stressing, for heaven's sake. It was the distance between them. But he could see she didn't understand.

"Sorry. Alison," he muttered.

"Thank you." Then as he started to leave again, she stopped him again. "How long have you been here, working for my grandfather?"

"Close on to three years."

Her eyes widened slightly as if she found it hard to believe. "He never said. Never mentioned you."

God bless Nathan Richards, Jess thought. "Prob'ly didn't think it was important." He hesitated. "Is that all, ma'am?"

She just looked at him, one brow lifted.

He scowled. "Alison," he amended at last.

She smiled. "That's all. My father should be here by suppertime. So should Doug and Peter. Chris can't get here until late. I'll have supper ready by seven. I know it's kind of late, but Dad's plane doesn't get in until late afternoon. Will that be all right?"

"You don't have to fix me supper, ma . . . er, Alison."

"But it's expected. We'd like you to come and—"

"No, thank you. I'll eat on my own." And he was down the steps and heading toward the barn before she could say any more.

It was all right to sit at the table and eat with Nathan, to listen to Nathan's plans and dreams. Nathan was his sort of person. Nathan took a man as he came, didn't expect dazzling conversation or informed world views, wouldn't think a guy was an idiot if he couldn't direct dial Sri Lanka on the first try.

But he wasn't about to eat with David Richards, hotshot diplomat, and his sophisticated offspring. Jess didn't need people looking down their noses at him.

And even if they were polite enough not to, even if they kept their conversation limited to what they had in common with him, he wouldn't be able to do that, either. What they had in common was Nathan, and there was no way in hell that he was ready to talk about Nathan Richards.

Anyway, he thought angrily, as he led his horse out of the barn and swung into the saddle, he didn't have time to talk about anyone or anything.

He had the ranch to see to.

The ranch was both Jess's pain and his salvation. He tried not to think about it as his any longer. There was no point. He didn't expect he'd have a chance to buy it now. Those who would be able to "see why not" would undoubtedly scotch it.

But he'd told David he could manage, so he did, caring for it, doing whatever needed to be done.

God knew David was right: there was a lot of work. But doing it was better than sitting around feeling sorry for himself, feeling miserable about Nathan.

Nathan couldn't have picked a worse time to die. For most of the year, he stayed at the house, planned and dreamed, did the cooking for the two of them, doctored whatever cattle Jess brought down, kept the barn mucked out.

But in fall he made decisions.

Nathan spent most of the year listening to Jess tell him about the cattle, noting which ones had good calves, which ones were sickly, which ones gained well. He would sit for hours asking questions, scratching his nose, nodding his head.

Then, in October, Nathan put everything he heard together with what he could see and decided which cattle were going to be shipped for sale in Denver and which were staying on.

In two weeks, the big trucks would be pulling in, expecting Jess to have a hundred head of cattle ready to go to the sale barn in Denver.

So he couldn't be bothered with David Richards or his clever professional sons or his beautiful grown-up daughter, Alison. This year the decisions were going to be up to him.

Surely David wouldn't sell the ranch before then.

Would he?

ALISON WAITED until he was gone, till she heard the sound of his boots hit the dirt, and then she breathed again. Slowly, tentatively, as if she wasn't quite sure she remembered how.

The second breath came easier and then the third.

It was the shock, she told herself, that made something as simple as breathing so hard. It was her astonishment at encountering Jess Cooper again face-to-face.

As a teenager she had dreamed about him nightly. A young hired man on her grandfather's ranch, he was the man on whom she'd hung her fantasy of the perfect hero.

Six feet of lean, whipcord strength, with dark shaggy hair, tanned, work-hardened hands and mysterious dark brown eyes, Jess Cooper had attracted her from the moment she'd first seen him.

Maybe it was the way he sat a horse, or maybe it was the way he wore his hat. Maybe it was his cool, quick competence in the saddle and his slightly shy awkwardness when she'd met him later in the kitchen. Maybe it was simply the physical Jess Cooper with his lean, rangy, hard-muscled body and his soul-melting eyes. Heaven knew, just that would have been enough.

But whatever it was, he was the one she thought of whenever she read about knights in shining armor. He was the one she dreamed of whenever romantic heroes were mentioned.

In all the books she'd read, Alison had never had another fantasy hero affect her the way Jess had. She hadn't been able to look at him without her heartbeat quickening and her palms becoming damp.

It had been twelve years since she'd seen him, and she had never completely forgotten.

He must think she was a total idiot, she fumed now, her cheeks warming at the memory of the past few moments. She had acted almost as tongue-tied and foolish this time as she had whenever she'd been around him all those years ago.

Except that last time...

The last time had been different.

It had been the day before she was to leave Colorado and go back to Mexico City. She had been out for a ride, hoping against hope that she would run into Jess.

She wanted to give him one last chance to say all those things she'd dreamed of him saying, to tell her he cared, to ask her to write to him and to promise that he would write to her.

She had headed up toward the north meadow because she'd overheard the foreman telling her grandfather that there was a break in the fence up there. But, though she rode for two hours, Alison had never found the fence break, and at last she gave up, convinced that she'd missed him.

She'd been following the creek down through the woods toward the lower meadow near the road when she'd heard voices, hard and angry, and the sounds of scuffling. Curious, she'd urged the horse forward.

Coming into the clearing, she'd halted only for an instant to take in the scene. She'd found Jess, all right.

He was lying on the ground, fighting for all his worth against the three men who were pounding him into the dirt.

Alison didn't even stop to think. She just kicked her heels into the horse's sides, riding right towards the men, yelling, "Quit that! Stop! Leave him alone! What do you think you're doing?"

The men glanced up, took one look at her on horseback bearing down on them and stepped back. One of them reached out to try to grab the reins of her horse, but she evaded him, hurtling past, relieved that Jess had rolled out of the way.

"Get out of here! Leave him alone!" She wheeled the horse around, heading back toward them.

"Another one of your women?" the tallest one spat at Jess. He went after him again, taking one last swing, connecting full force. Jess fell back sprawling in the dirt, blood streaming down his face.

"Come on, Wes," said the fat one. "I think he got the point."

The tall one turned to Jess. "If you don't, we can make it again." He smiled. "It'd be a pleasure."

"Get out!" Alison yelled at him, heading the horse in his direction.

He aimed a kick at Jess, then jammed his hat onto his head and followed the other two through the trees to where Alison could see a truck parked by the side of the road.

She waited only long enough to see them get in before she slid off her horse and ran to Jess's side. "My God, are you all right? What happened?"

He swiped at the blood on his face, spitting into the dirt. "Nothing. It's all right."

"*Nothing?* Why were they—?" She couldn't even find the words to express the horror she felt. She pulled out a handkerchief and used it to stanch the blood still coming from his nose.

He tried to get up, winced at the pain and tried again.

"Maybe you've broken something." Alison slipped her arm around his back, helping him to his feet. "Are you sure you should be doing this?"

He shook her off. "I'm okay." He looked around, then muttered under his breath. "My horse ran off."

"You can take mine. We can ride together," she said quickly. "You should see a doctor."

"I don't need a doctor!"

"But—"

"I'll be all right." He limped over to a fallen log and lowered himself gingerly, grimacing as he did so. Alison followed. He looked awful. One of his eyes was almost swollen shut. His nose looked broken. There was an ugly abrasion along the line of his jaw.

"Give me your shirt. I'll get it wet in the creek and you can wash."

He'd looked as if he would protest, then apparently thought better of it. When he shrugged carefully out of his shirt, she saw that his ribs had taken a beating, too. She hurried to the creek and came back with the shirt dripping. He reached out to take it from her, but she wouldn't let him.

"I'll do it. I can see."

"And I can't?" he'd said gruffly.

Alison smiled slightly, lifting her hand to brush a lock of hair away from his swollen eye. "Not very well."

She knelt between his knees and began dabbing carefully at the cuts on his face. He tensed, trying to hold still. She worked slowly and efficiently, marveling at the steadiness of her hand.

Every other time this summer that she'd come within two feet of him, she had nearly had heart palpitations. Now she was kneeling only inches from his bare chest, while she gently washed his face. She licked her lips, trying to think of him as no more than a collection of cuts and bruises. Yet at every moment she was aware, always aware, of the physical Jess Cooper.

Jess sat stoically waiting until she was finished and sat back on her heels. The moment she did so, their eyes met and Alison's breath caught. She licked her lips nervously.

Would he kiss her?

The thought came unbidden, and, without even realizing it, she leaned almost imperceptibly toward him.

He hesitated, then, "Come on," Jess said, straightening and trying to get up so that Alison had to scramble backward to avoid being knocked on her rear. "It's getting late. You need to get back." He stepped past her, brushing at the dust on his jeans, then limped toward Alison's horse.

"Wait a minute." She hurried after him. "Why were those guys beating on you?"

He shrugged, holding out the reins to her horse for her. Alison didn't take them.

"What was going on, Jess? Pops will want to know."

"Nathan doesn't need to know anything," Jess said sharply.

"He's going to have a hard time not knowing," Alison pointed out, "with you looking like you've been dragged through a thicket backward."

"I'll tell him I fell off my horse."

"You think he'll believe that?"

"I don't give a damn what he believes, it's not his problem!" Jess dropped the reins and stalked off toward the woods.

But Alison followed him. "What happened, Jess? Tell me. Tell me or... or I'll tell Pops exactly what I saw."

He turned and glared at her. "Why?"

"Because... because they shouldn't be allowed to get away with it."

He grimaced. "Doesn't make any difference. It smartened me up, that's all."

"What do you mean?"

"Damn, but you're a nosy little kid."

"I'm not nosy. And I'm not a kid! Am I?" she challenged him, slapping her hands on her hips. The act made her breasts strain against her shirt.

Jess scowled at her, then shrugged. "I guess you're not," he muttered, looking away.

"So tell me."

He gave her an exasperated look. "Why should I?"

"Because... because I care... about you."

"Don't bother. I'm not worth it. Ask Cindy Brinkmiller." He started to turn away again.

Alison caught his arm. "Who's Cindy Brinkmiller?"

He pulled his arm out of her grasp. "Oh hell, leave it, will you? She's the reason her brother and cousins were beating me up."

Another woman? She'd never thought about Jess with another woman. He belonged to her. "Why?" Her voice sounded hollow.

"Because she's pregnant, damn it, and she told them the baby's mine."

Now Alison did feel like the child she'd just denied being. She felt out of her depth, floundering. Sex was something she fantasized about. Babies were part of another world. And to think of Jess...

"Is it?" she whispered. "Yours?"

He gave a scornful laugh. "As if I'd ever got close enough to do more than kiss her."

Alison felt almost giddy with relief. She beamed. "Thank heavens."

Jess gave a hard look. "What's that supposed to mean?"

"I just meant . . . I meant . . . you're a little young to have children."

"I'm not having children," he told her gruffly. "Ever."

"But when you marry—"

"And I'm not getting married, either."

"But surely when you—" *When you know how much I love you,* she'd been going to say. But even Alison knew better than that. "But when you meet the right person," she began hesitantly.

"I'm not lookin'." He took the reins out of her hands. "Come on. Get moving. The old man'll be sending out the posse soon."

"But you—"

"I've got to find my damned horse."

"I'll take you."

"No." He jerked his head toward the sorrel. "Get on. And when you get home forget all about this."

She wanted to argue with him, but he was looking at her impatiently, and she knew words wouldn't do any good. She touched his arm, felt it tense under her fingers.

"Jess?" She spoke his name. It was a question, but even she wasn't certain what she was asking.

He shut his eyes. A muscle in his jaw ticked. When he opened his eyes again Alison read torment in them. She waited. And finally his control broke.

His hand came up and touched her hair, stroked her cheek. And then his lips touched hers.

The kiss couldn't have lasted more than a few seconds before he jerked back, some rational part of him regaining control. His teeth snapped together. He rubbed a hand over his face, then winced.

"I shouldn't have done that."

But Alison didn't agree. Rationality hadn't regained any control over her. She'd dreamed about those lips touching hers every night all summer long. She'd fantasized about those rough fingers caressing her skin. She looked at him lovingly.

"Thank you, Jess," she whispered. She raised her hand and touched her lips lightly, then touched his.

He pulled away. "Damn it, Ali. Quit that. I told you, I shouldn't have done it. Get on your horse and get outa here. And forget everything that happened this afternoon."

She hadn't, of course.

That kiss had given her a year's worth of daydreaming. The husky way he'd called her "Ali" had provided many marvelous nights.

She loved him. And she was sure, from his kiss, that he loved her, too. She'd gone back the following summer, confident that things would develop between them.

He'd been long gone.

She'd felt betrayed. And foolish.

She felt foolish now. She was twenty-seven, not seven. It was time to grow up.

It was nothing she hadn't been telling herself for years. And nothing that her father and brothers hadn't told her as well.

Just two weeks ago her brother, Peter, had flown in from L.A., and had introduced her to three eligible lawyer friends in the space of three days.

"You're not by any chance matchmaking, are you?" Alison had asked him, a wicked glint in her eye.

Peter grinned just as wickedly. "Just helping nature out a bit."

"You'd hit the roof if I did the same for you."

"You know any eligible women? Bring 'em on," Peter had challenged her.

But Alison didn't know anyone she thought was good enough for her favorite brother, and she said so. "But you seem quite willing to fob just any old man off on me," she complained.

"They're not old," Peter said, still smiling. Then he sobered. "No, I know what you're saying, Ali. But maybe your standards are too high. You might be sitting here till you're eighty if you're waiting for Prince Charming."

"I'm not waiting for Prince Charming," Ali had protested. In fact, she was seriously considering marrying Gary. He hadn't asked, but she suspected he would.

Gary was a middle management man for a computer software firm. She'd met him playing softball in June. He'd asked her out. She'd gone. She liked Gary. He was comfortable, stable, friendly. Not a dream man.

But Alison was beginning to think that dream men were just that, ephemeral, insubstantial figments of her imagination. She wanted a home and a family. She wanted a man to love and children to cherish. But at this rate she wondered if she would ever find them. Maybe it was time to stop telling herself that the right man was out there, and that she'd know him when she saw him.

The way, all those years ago, she'd known Jess Cooper.

"And that was such an enormous success," she mocked herself.

She should have forgotten him. It was her own folly that she never had.

Actually, she thought now as she picked up her bag and headed for the stairs, it was probably a very good thing she'd run into him again.

It would be a salutary experience, meeting up with her childhood dream lover as an adult.

If she was ever going to get on with things and meet the real man who was out there waiting for her, she would have to come to terms with Jess Cooper as he really was, not the way her youthful fantasies had imagined him.

She would see him the way an adult would see him...and be cured.

HE ATE baked beans out of a can, sitting on his bunk and pretending he was reading *Livestock Weekly.* There was another rental car parked next to Alison's when he'd come back from bringing down more cattle that afternoon. He'd seen a light on in the kitchen, people moving around. He'd turned his back and walked to the bunkhouse, a confused but willing Scout at his heels.

"You don't need to follow me," Jess told him gruffly. "Your grub is up at the house."

But Scout wasn't going unless he did, and he ended up sharing the beans with the dog. Before he finished them off, he heard another car growling its way up the hill.

He got to his feet and peered out the corner of the window, watching as it stopped next to the others and two men got out. Alison's father and brother, undoubtedly. They took suitcases out of the trunk and started across the dirt toward the house. Jess saw the door open and Alison standing there silhouetted in the light.

He turned away and flung himself down on the bunk, staring down at a fascinating article on new vaccines.

It didn't hold his interest any more than the one on the relative merits of feeding alfalfa hay or clover. He flipped to the back, scanning the ads. That was what he should be reading—the Help Wanted section.

Lord knew there was a good bet he'd be needing a job before long. There wasn't a chance in hell that David Richards would hang on to the ranch and let him run it. And sure as shooting, when he sold it, whoever bought it would either run it himself or bring in his own man.

So much for his dreams.

It didn't do to get tied to a place, that was certain. It only made it harder to leave.

THE BEDROOM was almost exactly the way Alison remembered it. The same narrow bed, same chifforobe of bird's-eye maple, same desk with a bookcase above that she'd used all those years ago. It felt lived-in, too, as if she'd slept here last night and the night before.

She ran her hand lightly over the old log-cabin quilt. That was the only change she could see: its blues and grays were more faded than she remembered.

She stood quietly listening as her brothers and father settled in for the night, remembering other similar nights, thinking how much the same everything was.

And how different.

She had, as her kindergarten teacher friend, Donna, would say, stayed "on task" all evening. She hadn't let her thoughts stray to Jess at all. She had talked with her father about his trip from Sri Lanka, she had listened to Peter describe the gorgeous redhead he was dating now. She had tried to make sense of Douglas's careful evaluation of the worth of ranch land and had even been able to report coherently the call from Nathan's lawyer, Mr. Kirby, which had precipitated it.

After dinner she had sat in front of the fire Peter had made and reminisced with them all about Nathan, and when Jess's name had come up, she'd talked easily and sensibly about Nathan's ranch manager.

There, she told herself as she climbed the stairs to get ready for bed. See? You can handle it. You were just spooked when you saw him this afternoon. It was just shock.

The next time she saw him, it would be fine—like seeing Kenny Loggia, who worked with her in the library, or Dan Hernandez, the CPA she used to date. No big deal.

She put on her nightgown, brushed her teeth and slipped beneath the covers. And couldn't sleep.

Gradually the rest of the family quieted down. She heard her father close the door to Nathan's room where he was sleeping. She heard Peter and Chris go up to the loft, heard the soft murmur of their voices for a while, then silence. Down the hall she could hear the rhythmic squeak that was undoubtedly Doug doing his nightly regimen of sit-ups on the old wooden floor. And then, nothing.

She should be exhausted. She should have gone out like a light the moment her head hit the pillow. She hadn't.

She tossed and turned, sighed and punched her pillow. Finally, despairing, she got up and started back downstairs.

She heard a soft creak. She froze for a moment, then moved on. She must've been wrong about Doug. He was sometimes wakeful, too. And now that she was down she could see a small light on in the kitchen. He must be making some warm milk. She pushed open the door.

"Can I have some, too?" she began. Then, "Oh, it's you."

It wasn't Doug at all, but Jess who stood in the middle of the kitchen.

Alison was suddenly acutely conscious of her thin nightgown, of her rapidly reddening face. "I saw the light. I thought it was my brother. I didn't know—"

"I—I'm sorry I disturbed you. I just came to get...that." Jess pointed past her at a shabby looking blanket on a bench in the corner.

"You should have stayed in the house," Alison said. "You must be freezing out there. There's plenty of room."

"No. It's not for me. It's...it belongs to Scout. He was...restless." Was it her imagination or was his color deepening, too?

"He can come in, too."

"He's all right," Jess said gruffly. "We both are." He moved past her to get the blanket. His sleeve touched her bare arm. She quivered.

"Sorry," he muttered, grabbing the blanket and edging past her again. "Night." And he was out the door without another word.

Standing there barefoot and shivering on the cold linoleum, Alison knotted her fingers against her breasts and watched him go, watched with rapt attention as his lean-hipped, broad-shouldered silhouette vanished into the darkness.

And she knew for a certainty that she wasn't as immune as she'd hoped.

Chapter Three

Jess talked to David Richards at the wake. They talked about cattle and land prices and prospects and such like. It had to be done, Jess knew, and it was easier than talking about Nathan.

David didn't seem to mind. He had to get back to Sri Lanka as quickly as he could, which meant leaving late on the afternoon of the funeral.

"I met with the lawyer today and got everything taken care of that concerns me. I know Dad would have understood. He believed in taking care of one's obligations to the living." David paused and ran a hand over his face. "He was a wonderful father."

Jess nodded. "I reckon he was."

"He thought very highly of you. I'm glad you were here to be with him. You'll sit with us tomorrow at the funeral."

"I—"

"He'd want you there. We do, too. He's left something for you, too. Kirby will talk to you about it." He gave Jess's arm one last squeeze, then turned to speak to another mourner.

Jess, feeling dismissed, still couldn't leave. He needed to ask one more thing, the thing he'd been leading up to from the start, the thing he was almost afraid to put into words because the answer meant he would have to start making other plans. "Mr. Richards. I was just... wondering... what... what about the ranch?"

David turned back to Jess, blinked, then smiled, his blue eyes gentle and uncannily like Nathan's for just a moment. "Don't worry about the ranch, Jess. The ranch will take care of itself."

NATHAN'S FUNERAL was short and sweet. The minister spoke briefly about the inspiration Nathan had provided for his family and friends, for all those whose lives he had touched. Then, while the morning sunlight streamed in the narrow stained-glass windows, everyone listened while Jimmy Rodriguez, the town's musical pride and joy, played a haunting English folk tune, Nathan's favorite, on his guitar.

Afterward David got up to speak. He shared a couple of family memories that communicated once more the openness with which Nathan Richards had faced the world, the enthusiasm that he'd brought to it, the joy with which he encouraged his only son to embrace it as well.

"He could have kept me tied to the ranch," David said. "But he believed that every man has to choose his own destiny. Despite the fact that it has taken me away from him for most of my adult life, I will always be grateful that my father had the generosity to allow me to choose mine."

Jess, listening, shut his eyes, felt an ache in his throat.

He was startled into opening them a few moments later when he heard Alison's hesitant voice.

She stood at the podium, her face pale, her eyes bright, as she looked out over the full church.

"My brothers," she said slowly, "who have never been shy about grabbing the limelight in the past, have been more than willing to allow me my share on this occasion." Her expression became fondly wry as she went on, "In fact they have generously allowed me to speak for all of us. I suspect it's because they don't mind if I cry in public, but they're embarrassed to."

She spoke haltingly about her first memories of the ranch, about how no matter where her father's job took them, that it was the place she held in her heart as home, and that even more than the ranch, home meant her grandfather.

"I always knew, in the back of my mind, that he was here." She smiled a watery smile. "It's silly. It's irrational. It's the way I felt. No matter what, he was there behind me, supporting me, understanding me, believing in me. Loving me." She blinked rapidly and swiped at her eyes.

"Tomorrow I'm supposed to meet with the lawyer to find out what inheritance my grandfather has left me," she went on. "But I already know what he's left me. A legacy of love."

Jess put his hand over his eyes and in his mind rode the wiliest bronc he'd ever ridden, then braved the toughest bull he'd ever faced. He had to, or he'd make a fool of himself bawling in front of God and everybody.

He didn't watch, only heard Alison come back to the pew and take her seat next to her father.

Then the minister introduced the last musical piece, a baroque trumpet solo that Dan Grissom, the high school band director, sent soaring to the heavens.

As a send-off it was pure Nathan all the way. Jess knew he would have been pleased.

THERE MUST HAVE BEEN three hundred people who came back to the ranch afterward.

But not Jess.

Alison knew because all the time she was sharing recollections with Nathan's friends and neighbors, all the time she was pouring coffee and smiling her best, she kept an eye out for Jess.

He'd sat in the same row she did at the church. He'd driven back home in the car behind hers. He'd stood shoulder to shoulder with her while Nathan's body was lowered into the ground at a small family plot on the hill behind the house.

Then he disappeared.

The most she saw of him came in the middle of the afternoon when she caught a glimpse through the window. There were still ten or twelve people milling about in the living room when she spied him outside just beyond the front gate.

He was still wearing the suit he'd worn to church, and the light breeze mussed his hair. This morning Alison had thought the suit had made him look serious and remote. Now, incongruous against the backdrop of the rugged mountainside, it simply made him look lonely.

Was he?

In her dreams, of course, he had been—lonely for the love of a good woman, satisfied only with her.

In reality she'd never believed it was true. She didn't think she'd ever encountered a more self-sufficient man in her life than Jess Cooper.

But now, watching the man who stood so still looking up at the house, she wasn't sure.

IT WAS EARLY EVENING by the time Alison took a breath that she felt she could call her own. The last of the funeral dinner guests had departed shortly after four. After they did the washing up, she and Doug and Peter went through Nathan's scrapbooks sorting out the few that her brothers would take with them. Most they seemed quite willing to leave for her.

"You're the one who used to love the place," Doug reminded her. "You're the one who got us dragged back every summer."

Alison looked at him, shocked. "You didn't want to come?"

He shrugged. "Well, when I was a kid, yeah. But later on, not really. The wide world beckoned, you know—" he gave her a grin "—like it did to Dad."

Alison understood, but was surprised nonetheless. She smiled at him. "Then thank you for being so forbearing."

He reached over and tousled her hair. "No problem. It's what big brothers are for."

"And twin brothers," Peter chipped in. He was tossing the last of his gear into his duffel bag, preparatory to driving to the airport.

Alison turned to him, astonished. "You didn't want to come, either?"

"Till we got to be about fourteen, yes. Then things changed. You started making calf's eyes at Cooper."

"I never!"

Peter laughed. "You used to tag after him everywhere he went."

"He was... nice to me," Alison said lamely.

"I didn't think he ever even talked to you," Peter said frankly, zipping the bag shut.

"Sometimes he did."

Peter flicked her a glance over his shoulder. "Oh, yes? So passion wasn't completely unrequited?"

Alison rolled her eyes. "I was a kid." She wasn't about to admit how little her feelings seemed to have changed.

"And now you're not. Has he this time?"

"Has he what? Talked to me? Of course."

"He didn't show up today."

"He was at the funeral."

"But not here after."

She shrugged. "I'm sure he has lots of work to do."

Peter was still looking at her. "Maybe." He grinned at Doug. "Or maybe it was like old times. Maybe he's still dodging Ali."

Mortified, Alison felt her cheeks flame. "He didn't! Did he?" she asked worriedly after a moment. It was all too possible, seen from afar.

Peter turned his grin on her. "No. I just know how to get a rise out of you. And I noticed you were looking."

Alison shook her head. "Not for him," she lied.

Peter just looked at her, but Doug breathed a sigh of relief.

"Good," he said. "I'm glad you've grown up."

"Right," Peter said. He glanced at his watch. "Ready, Doug? It'll take an hour or better to get to the airport. We'd better leave now."

Douglas clicked his suitcase shut and slipped on his coat. "All set." He paused and looked at his sister. "Sure wish you were coming, Ali. I don't like to think of you all alone up here."

"I'll be fine. I was fine before you got here," she reminded him as they walked to the door.

"She's a big girl now. Besides, she has Cooper to protect her," Peter said with a grin.

Doug stopped quite suddenly so that Alison almost ran into him. He scowled. "Not funny," he said to his brother.

"Wha—?"

"Remember Cindy Brinkmiller?"

Peter's grin faded. "You don't think—"

"That had nothing to do with Jess," Alison said abruptly.

Doug's eyes widened. "How do you know?"

Oh, hell, Alison thought. She had done what Jess had asked, never telling anyone about the fight, about what he'd told her that afternoon. She didn't want to break her word now. "I just know," she said stubbornly.

"I don't think you knew anything. You were a kid."

"I knew," she insisted. "Anyway, I'm not a kid now."

"And you think that makes me feel better," he said grimly.

"I'll be fine, Doug, honestly. I won't let him seduce me. I promise." She gave him a cheeky grin.

Doug sighed, dropped a kiss on her forehead and got into the car. Peter stowed their gear in the trunk, then stopped beside the door of the car and turned to look at her. His expression was grave, his blue eyes concerned.

"Would he have to, Ali?" he asked.

TRUST PETER.

She could always buffalo Douglas. He never saw beyond

his balance sheets or his stock quotes. She could put off her father and Chris by noncommittal nods and vague replies followed by questions about their pet projects.

She could never deceive Peter.

She stood in the silence, long after the car carrying her brothers had disappeared down the dirt road and out of sight around the bend. She thought about what he had asked her.

She didn't know how long she stood there before a tiny self-mocking smile crept onto her face. The question was moot. Jess Cooper was no more interested in her than he had ever been.

She had just turned to go back into the house, when she heard the phone ring. It was Gary.

"How are you? I've missed you."

Alison smiled at the eagerness in his voice. "I'm okay," she told him. "I've missed you, too," which would have been truer if she'd had more time.

"When are you coming home?"

"Tomorrow night. I have to see the lawyer in the afternoon."

"Want me to pick you up? Where are you coming in and when?"

"LaGuardia, around midnight. You don't need to, really. I'll take a cab."

"No trouble," Gary insisted. "I'll be there. Seems like you've been gone an age."

It seemed to Alison as if she'd been out of real time altogether, as if she'd somehow slipped from the present into the past.

"Gotta run now," Gary was saying. "I'm off to lift weights. See you tomorrow. Count on me."

"Yes," Alison said, but he had already gone. She set down the receiver, then went to the door, intending to latch it for the night. But behind her the radio Doug had left on was still playing, and the stillness in the yard seemed to beckon her.

She opened the door again and went out.

She stood still, letting the tranquillity settle over her.

It wasn't really all that quiet. It was simply an absence of human and mechanical noises that she experienced. No laughter, no music, no taxi horns or car alarms. Nothing save the gentle sighing of the western wind through the spruce and, off in the meadow, the lowing of the cattle as they settled in for the night.

There was no light, either, other than the narrow sliver of moon and the canopy of stars she never set eyes on in the city. She tipped her head back now, marveling at this universe that might as well not exist back in New York.

She turned slowly, relishing it, then lowered her gaze to the even blacker bulk of the mountain peaks surrounding her. She remembered doing the same thing years ago, opening her arms and turning in slow circles, embracing the natural world that most of the year, when she was in Beirut and Paris, had seemed so remote.

It was equally remote most of the time now. Even when she stood out on her terrace and stared up at the sky, picking out the few visible stars, she never lost the sense that the city was pulsating beneath her feet.

She remembered the night she'd got the news about Nathan. She'd stood there on the terrace, listening to the hoot of horns, the wail of sirens, the scritch-scratch of her downstairs neighbor Ginger, who was repotting a bonsai on her patio. Ginger's bonsai was twenty-seven years old. Older than Ginger.

Ginger loved it. Nathan hadn't. "Nature in a pot," he'd groused when Alison had taken him down to meet Ginger.

And so it was, but what was wrong with that?

The whole world couldn't live in the wilds of western Colorado, as lovely as it was. She remembered Nathan urging her to come out and visit him again, get in touch with all the things she had loved as a young girl.

And she had declined.

What was the point? All those wild desperate longings of her teenaged self had no place in her life now.

She looked back at the house, then turned and walked slowly up the hill toward the family burial plot. There she stopped and looked down at the newly turned sod.

"Thank you, Pops," she said now. "Thank you for bringing me back one more time. But I can't stay. Really I can't. There's nothing for me here."

She lifted her gaze and looked down the hill toward the bunkhouse. It was dark. Silent.

Jess was no doubt sound asleep. He was, she was sure, every bit as busy as she'd told Peter and Doug he was, and would no doubt be up at dawn tomorrow to work again.

Jess.

Her cowboy. Her hero. Her fantasy.

But reality was Gary, her job, her life in New York. There was no future for Ali Richards and Jess Cooper. Never had been—except in her heart.

HE COULD SEE her standing there in the moonlight. With the lights off in the bunkhouse, there was just enough illumination outside to make him aware of her as she stood in the yard, turning circles, her arms wide.

He swallowed, dropped the curtain and turned away.

He wasn't getting any sleep standing there watching Alison Richards. And damn it all, he needed his sleep. He had work to do and plenty of it, as soon as the sun came up tomorrow.

He sat down on the edge of the bed, started to lie down, then, as if drawn, he lifted the hem of the curtain again.

She was still there, moving up the hill slowly. He could just glimpse her slim figure moving through the darkness. Sweet, tender, caring Alison.

He shouldn't be watching her now. He hadn't seen her since the burial. He's stayed well away from the house afterward. There'd been plenty to do. More cattle to bring down, a bit of doctoring, some fence work.

Life was for the living. That was what Nathan had always said. Nathan would have understood why he'd stayed away today.

Jess's mouth quirked at one corner.

Sure he would, he mocked himself. Nathan would have looked right square at him and called him a coward. Nathan would have said he was running from his dreams, from his fantasies. From Alison.

Nathan would have been right.

Jess let the curtain fall from his fingers, lay back on the bed and folded his arms beneath his head.

So what? he said to himself. Dreams weren't all they were cracked up to be.

He only had to get through twenty-four more hours. Then he could worry about the things that really mattered in life. In twenty-four hours Alison Richards would be on her way back to New York.

FRANK KIRBY couldn't see Alison until four in the afternoon.

"He's tied up in the morning," his secretary apologized, "and then, well, you know, once you get going, you don't want to stop until you have to."

Alison could only vaguely decipher the meaning of that theory. She supposed it meant that Mr. Kirby, once committed to some pursuit became single-minded and wouldn't likely be free until then.

"You couldn't just maybe tell me what's mine over the phone," she suggested hopefully. "I'm right out here at the ranch, you know. I could simply pack it and catch the earlier flight."

"Oh, no. Mr. Kirby wants to see you," the secretary said.

So Alison spent the morning packing her bags and collecting the few things from the bedroom she'd been using that had been hers all those years ago. Then she walked out to the corral and leaned against the fence, letting the early-autumn sun warm her back as she rested her arms on the top rung and stared out across the corral and the valley, soaking up last impressions.

They would have to last her a lifetime, for she wouldn't be back. The ranch would be sold. Her father hadn't said so, of course. David Richards was the consummate diplomat, even in family matters. He would never have broached the subject of selling the Rocking R with Nathan barely in his grave. It would have been too hard on them all.

But Alison didn't delude herself.

There was no way her foreign service officer father was going to abandon his career to come back to a remote corner of southwestern Colorado and raise cattle.

No, the ranch would go. The cattle, the horses, the barns. Everything would go.

Even Jess.

And all she would have would be her memories.

She stored up as many as she could that morning. She never saw Jess, which wasn't surprising. He'd been gone since daybreak. She'd awakened to hear him riding away, but she'd deliberately lain in bed instead of going to the window to watch. There were some memories she didn't need.

Now she drew a deep breath and opened the door of Kirby and Ransom Law Offices, prepared to hear Mr. Kirby's reading of her grandfather's will. Then she would go back to the ranch once more, take whatever he left her and be on her way.

She didn't expect to see Jess.

He was sitting in the office.

Alison stared, then turned to the secretary. "Did I mistake the time? I thought my appointment was at four."

The secretary smiled. "That's right. Mr. Kirby is just finishing up his previous appointment now. Please have a seat. He'll be with you in a moment." She motioned Alison toward the seat next to Jess's. He was no longer slouched.

His booted feet were planted firmly on the floor. He had begun to strangle his hat in his hands. He didn't look at her.

Alison moved to sit by him, remembering Peter's comments, knowing her cheeks were reddening as she did so. How he'd laugh if he could see her now. The secretary went back to her typing. Alison sat silently, noting out of the corner of her eye the muted plaid of Jess's shirt, the soft denim covering his thigh, the way his fingers creased the brim of his hat.

She cleared her throat. "I thought you had work to do today." She knew she sounded almost accusing, and that made her cheeks burn even more.

Jess rolled the hat's brim between his palms. "Kirby said he needed to see me."

"That's right. Dad said Pops left you something, too."

"Nothing valuable, I don't reckon," he said quickly, as if she might be thinking he'd been trying to steal her inheritance.

Before Allison could say that she had no such fears, the door to the inner office opened and Mr. Kirby ushered out his previous client and shook hands with him. Then he turned his attention to Alison and Jess.

"Sorry I'm running late. Come on in."

Alison, confused at which of them he'd been speaking to, looked at Jess. He looked back at her.

"Which of us did you want?" Alison asked finally.

Kirby looked over his shoulder. "Which? Why, both of you, of course." He sat down in his big leather chair and began shuffling through the papers in front of him. At his nod, she took the chair across the desk from him. Jess hovered in the background.

"Shut the door and sit down," Mr. Kirby said. "Pull over that chair and we'll get down to business."

"Don't you want to talk to her first, then me?" Jess suggested, which would have been Alison's suggestion, too.

Mr. Kirby aligned papers on his desk, folded his hands on top of them, then lifted his gaze and met Jess's scowling one with a wide smile. "Nope."

He cocked his head and waited expectantly. Reluctantly Jess dragged over the other chair and sat.

Mr. Kirby picked up the sheaf of papers. "Pity you couldn't have come in earlier," he said. "It's going to take a while to spell out all the conditions and ramifications."

"I could have been here anytime today," Alison said sharply. "I told your secretary that."

"Yes, but Jess had work to do, and there's no sense in going over it twice, is there?" He gave them another happy smile.

Alison frowned.

"Go over what?" Jess asked cautiously.

"Nathan's bequest to you."

They looked at each other again.

"Me?" Jess asked. "Or her?"

"Both of you."

Alison didn't look at Jess this time. She looked at Mr. Kirby, her eyes wide. "What did Nathan leave us?" she asked him quietly.

"You mean the old devil really didn't warn you? Ah, Nathan." Kirby chuckled and raised his eyes to heaven where his dear departed client was no doubt at this very moment sharing the joke. "He's left each of you half interest in the Rocking R Ranch."

Chapter Four

Half the ranch?

Jess stared. He heard the words. Minutes later they were still echoing around his head like pebbles in a saucepan, making sound but not sense. Not yet.

"—stipulations, of course," Frank Kirby went on. "Not too difficult, though, as I'm sure you'll agree."

"What sort of stipulations?" Jess heard Alison ask. He couldn't have formed the words himself. He felt cold and shivery, as if he'd just been tossed into an icy creek. It was a shock.

Half the ranch.

He said the words over slowly in his mind, testing them, probing them for meaning. Intellectually he had no trouble. Emotionally he was lost.

He shook his head numbly, then bowed it and held it in his hands, staring down between his booted toes at Kirby's worn carpet. Solid wool reality. Slightly fraying. Standard office tweed, not even rose-colored as circumstances might have warranted.

A man can't live without dreams. Jess could hear Nathan now. He could see the old man, see him sitting there at the coffee bar, fixing Jess with those deceptively mild blue eyes and asking, *What's your dream?*

His wildest dream?

The Rocking R.

And Nathan had given it to him.

Correction. Nathan had given *half of it* to him.

Slowly Jess lifted his head and focused on the woman sitting next to him, the woman leaning forward earnestly with her attention wholly fixed on whatever Frank Kirby was saying, the woman who owned the other half of his dream: Alison Richards.

"Then what you're saying is, we can sell it?" he heard Alison say, and this time the words were registering.

"I'm saying that Nathan was prepared for that eventuality, yes," Frank Kirby replied. He tapped his pen on the desk. "But he doesn't want it broken up."

Jess found his voice at last. "Which means what?" He thought he sounded rusty, as if he hadn't spoken in years, but no one else seemed to notice. *Sell it?* Hell, he'd just got it! But Alison . . .

He shot her a quick glance.

Of course she'd want to sell it. What would a New York City librarian want with half a Colorado cattle ranch, for Pete's sake?

"It means," Frank said, "that you have three choices. You can keep it." He smiled at them both. "You can, either of you, sell your half to the other. Or you can decide to sell together. But individually you can't sell your half to anyone else."

He folded his hands again and looked at them. "Very simple, really. Very clear."

"Very," Alison said hollowly after a moment.

And Jess, letting the ramifications sink in, thought it was no wonder that Nathan had always beaten him at checkers. The old coot had always had something up his sleeve. The question was, what was he trying to pull now?

Was it a simple bequest or was there more to it than that?

With Nathan a guy never knew.

"Well, I'm sure you'll want to discuss it just between the two of you," Frank said, standing up and rubbing his hands together briskly. He looked hopefully at them.

Jess got to his feet, then reached out instinctively to catch Alison when she stumbled getting to hers. His hand brushed against the soft cotton covering her breast. He pulled back as if he'd been stung.

"If you need any advice, you can call on me," Frank went on, oblivious, ushering them to the door.

"Thank you," Jess heard Alison say in a voice barely above a whisper.

"Much obliged," he said, following her out.

He was almost out the door when he felt something touch his arm. "This is for you."

He turned. In Frank's hand there was a one-hundred-dollar bill.

Jess scowled. "What's that for?"

"From Nathan." Frank smiled. "He gave it to me when we made out the will. Said I should give it to you when I told you about the ranch. He figured the two of you could go out, have dinner on him and . . . talk about your future."

THEIR FUTURE?

Her future with Jess Cooper?

Alison wanted to laugh. She would have if she hadn't thought she would end up crying instead.

Oh, you foolish, crazy old man, what have you done to me now? she wailed silently as she followed Jess's truck down Main Street and around the corner on Aspen toward the Hitching Post. It was scarcely a fifty-dollar-a-plate restaurant, but they'd have had to drive clear to Denver for that.

She hadn't really wanted to go at all, and she had known from his expression that Jess hadn't, either. But he hadn't said so. He'd simply walked behind her in silence all the way out to the street. Once there he'd said, "So where do you want to go?"

"Home?" she'd said with a tight little smile.

And Jess had grimaced before holding out the money between two fingers. "Yeah, right, but then what are we supposed to do with this?"

Alison sighed. "I guess we'd better use it. He wouldn't like it if we didn't. But we'd better use it fast. I have a plane to catch."

Jess murmured something that sounded distinctly like, "Thank God," under his breath, then told her to follow him to the Hitching Post.

He was waiting for her now, leaning against the door of his truck as she turned into the parking lot and pulled in alongside him. He didn't even wait until she got out of the car before turning and heading toward the restaurant. Hurrying, muttering imprecations against her meddling grandfather, she followed him.

The Hitching Post was the nearest thing Bluff Springs had to a fancy restaurant. Catering to hunters in fall, skiers in winter and locals the rest of the year, the notched-log lodge specialized in game dishes half the year and in pasta the rest. Since it wasn't hunting season yet, linguine seemed the order of the day.

"Our specials are clam linguine or linguine with marinara," the hostess told them as she sat them at a table by the huge stone fireplace and handed them menus. "The waitress will be here to take your order shortly."

Alison glanced around the spacious room with its round tables and deep armchairs. The Hitching Post hadn't existed when she'd last been in Bluff Springs.

Except in her dreams. She remembered a fantasy in which a doting Jess had taken her to just such a place for their first date.

She flushed now, remembering the idiocies of youth. Yet she couldn't help a small ironic smile as she did so. Here they were, after all. And by stretching her imagination, she could even call it a first date!

And last, she reminded herself. One glance at Jess told her he'd never be the doting swain she'd dreamed of. He sat across from her stiffly studying the menu with intense scrutiny. He hadn't looked at her once, nor had he directed a word to her since they'd left Kirby's office.

The waitress came, smiled at Jess, mostly ignored her. Taking their orders, she disappeared again, leaving them alone. Alison sat back in her chair, studying the man across from her, memorizing him, recalling all her adolescent fantasies.

The notion that Pops had actually given her a "future" with Jess amused her. And yet somehow it made her ache as well.

Had he had any idea of what he was about, throwing the two of them together like this?

Had Nathan suspected her childhood crush?

Even to Alison's fanciful mind, it didn't seem likely. And yet...

"—have to get an appraisal," Jess was saying.

Allison looked at him blankly. "Why?"

"So I can pay you what it's worth, of course." He grimaced and eased his collar away from the nape of his neck. "By rights I should be paying you for the whole ranch," he said after a moment. "I never expected him to—" He looked away out the window, and Alison could see that he was embarrassed by Nathan's bequest.

"I didn't imagine that you did," she said quietly.

"He never said."

"No. He wouldn't." She gave a wry smile. "Pops liked his surprises."

"I'll say."

The waitress brought their salads, poured Jess a beer and gave Alison the glass of red wine she'd ordered. "Enjoy," she said brightly, giving Jess another winning smile.

He didn't smile back. His gaze never left Alison's. His fingers drummed on the tabletop. Finally he reached for his glass and raised it. "To Nathan." There was an ironic twist to his mouth.

Alison smiled. She wanted to reach out and lay her hand over his, tell him not to worry, that everything would be all right. She wondered if she was losing her mind.

She lifted her own glass and clinked it lightly against his. "To Nathan," she echoed softly and lifted the glass to her lips. The wine made her head feel light and fuzzy.

"Simmons at the bank can do it," Jess went on between bites of his salad.

Alison, watching him chew, had to drag her mind back to what he was saying. "Do what?"

Jess gave her an impatient look. "Give us an appraisal."

"Oh, right. I suppose he can."

"I don't know how I'll be able to come up with the money. Maybe we can do a land contract. If you're willing..."

"Mmm."

The waitress reappeared with their meals. Jess dug right in. Alison didn't. She watched Jess.

His head was bent, and Alison noted, not for the first time, that his hair needed cutting. She had to sit on her hands once more, this time to keep from reaching across the table and brushing back the dark locks.

It was odd, this temptation she'd always had, to touch him. She didn't ever remember feeling it with any other man. Even Gary. She and Gary held hands, of course. They even kissed. But she never needed to reach out to him. At least she hadn't yet.

Jess rubbed a hand around the back of his neck, then took another bite of his steak. "It's going to have to be a long-term loan," he said slowly. "I...I talked to Nathan once about maybe buyin' the place off him sometime. I had...hopes...but...I sure as hell didn't think it'd be this soon."

Alison listened and yet she didn't. She heard his words, understood that he expected her to sell to him, knew that indeed that was what she would do.

And yet...

And yet she found herself wondering just what Nathan had had in mind when he left half the Rocking R to her.

Her thoughts went back to the bonsai tree, to Nathan's disparaging comment about it. She knew Nathan hadn't been enchanted with her New York life-style. She knew he'd sensed her own unspoken restlessness. But had he really thought coming back to the Rocking R was the answer to her questions?

Or was it just his way of giving her options?

New York, the Rocking R or the money from its sale to pursue her dreams.

Or. . . Jess?

No. Surely not.

"Reckon I can get Simmons out sometime next week," Jess was saying. "When he's taken a look around, checked the books, totaled everything up, I can get in touch with you. All right?"

"Fine."

"Or we can wait until after sale day."

"Whatever." She needed to leave, to stop these crazy speculations, to get back to Gary, to her job, to her life. She pushed back her plate. "I have to get going. You can stay if you like."

"No problem. I have to get up before five." He beckoned to the waitress. "Can we have the bill?"

They had enough change left over from Nathan's hundred dollar bill to go out again. And again.

Jess offered her half of what he got back when he'd paid.

Alison shook her head. "Don't be ridiculous."

"I owe you, then."

"No."

He stuffed the bills into his wallet and tucked it into the back pocket of his jeans. He held the door for her and she slipped out past him, careful not to brush against his shirt.

The sun was below the mountains in the west, already casting a soft golden glow that heightened the color of the aspens. Alison, looking at it, couldn't help thinking how beautiful it was and how much she'd like to be around to see it.

You don't have to go. The words seemed to come out of nowhere, teasing, tempting.

She shook her head. She did have to go.

It was wishful thinking to imagine that she could just walk away from the life she'd made for herself. It was foolishness to think that she'd have anything to stay here for.

There wasn't a chance in the world that Jess Cooper was going to stop by the side of her car and beg her to stay, declaring his undying love.

The very thought of it made her smile.

"What's funny?"

She shook her head. Then she lifted her gaze and smiled at him, grateful for the chance to look at him this one last time, to smile at this man who had been her fantasy in person for so long, to wish him well, to—

"Will you kiss me goodbye?" The words were out of her mouth before she realized it.

The moment she said them, she was horrified. Her hand flew up to cover the exclamation of dismay that followed.

"I didn't mean—" she began, then shook her head helplessly because, in fact, despite her better judgment, she did. She wanted his kiss.

Why not? If she was growing up, turning her back, kissing her fantasies goodbye metaphorically, why shouldn't she do it literally as well? If this was as close as she was going to get to her dreams, surely she ought to take it. Take it and be finished.

Jess just stared at her, then blinked. He was looking at her as if she'd grown another head. His stupefaction fortified her bravery.

"Don't tell me you're afraid to?" she said recklessly, lifting her chin.

"Afraid?" Now the stupefaction was in his words.

She nodded, managing a cheeky, challenging grin. After all, what difference did it make?

In five minutes she'd be gone, never to see him again. They'd talk, of course, about the sale of the ranch. Or maybe Mr. Kirby and Mr. Simmons could do it for them. She didn't know. She didn't care.

She only knew she wanted this, even more than she'd wanted his kiss twelve years ago.

"It's a yearning for closure," Ginger the amateur psychologist would have told her.

Alison supposed it might be. It might also be no more than a desire to slake her ancient lust.

"Why not?" she said, shrugging carelessly, and smiled at him, wondering even as she did so if that one glass of wine hadn't been one too many.

Jess hesitated. His fists clenched and unclenched as he struggled with her request.

In another moment Alison knew she'd feel the veriest fool. How could she have said it?

But then he reached for her, pulled her close, wrapping those strong hard arms around her. And with a mutter that sounded very much like, "What the hell, why not?" his lips came down on hers.

It was a stunner of a kiss. In her life Alison had never had another one like it, had never even imagined there could be kisses like it!

Lips were lips, after all. One mouth was pretty much like any other.

Except Jess Cooper's.

She remembered his first kiss, the quick hard touch of his lips against hers. She'd hoped for at least that, but had expected a half-hearted indifferent brush of his lips across her cheek.

What she got was warm and eager, demanding, not a perfunctory peck at all.

It was everything Alison had ever allowed herself to dream of.

No, it wasn't. It was more.

Alison had kissed her share of men. She'd read her share of love stories, told her share of fairy tales. She knew about passion, about promise, about need.

This went beyond those things. This was something so deep, so elemental that she felt touched not just on the lips but to the depths of her very soul.

Her arms came up to clutch his back and she clung to him, dizzy and mindless.

If this was goodbye, she wondered shakily, what would happen if they ever kissed hello?

She supposed she should feel relieved that when at last Jess pulled away, he looked as shaken as she felt. His chest was heaving, his fingers dug lightly into her arms.

"That's what's known as playing with fire," he said hoarsely.

Was he warning her? Or himself?

"Yes." Trembling, Alison reached down, fumbling open the car door, and got in. Only when she was safely inside did she look at him again. His eyes met hers, dark and stormy.

"Nathan should have known better." He scowled, stuffing his hands into his pockets. "And so should I."

He turned on his heel and stalked to his truck.

HE SHOULD NEVER have kissed her.

He worked from dawn until dusk the rest of the week and all the week after. It took a hell of a lot of work to shape up a herd for shipping: three hundred odd cattle to check over and sort; yearlings and dry cows to cut out and stick in one pasture for the sale; the rest to drive down the valley to the winter pasture where they'd remain. Nathan usually hired an extra man to help out. Jess did it all himself.

Because he should never have kissed her.

He branded five summer calves besides. Treated some pink eye. Did some worming. Mended fence. Cleaned out cattle guards. Chopped wood.

And it didn't do anything to help him sleep at night because he should never have kissed her.

He'd see a flash of glossy chestnut foreleg, and he wouldn't think what a good piece of horseflesh it was. He'd think of how much the color reminded him of Alison's hair.

He'd pass Nathan's grave on his way up the hill in the morning, and he'd remember the night he'd seen the silvery outline of her curves as she'd stood there.

He'd burn his lip on scalding coffee early in the morning, and all he would recall was the heat of Alison's mouth on his.

Dear Lord, why had he kissed her?

He was thirty-four. Old enough to know better; far past the age when he'd needed to take a dare.

And it had been a dare; he could see that in her eyes. They were more wicked then he'd ever believed possible. The same sparkling blue of a deep mountain lake, just begging him to drown himself. They'd taunted and teased him unmercifully, making his whole body react.

She'd wanted it. And yet underneath he'd sensed she was just as afraid of it as he was.

And heaven knew they'd had reason to be!

It had been a humdinger of a kiss. Whoever would've thought it?

Not Jess.

Sure, he'd always found Alison attractive, even back in the days when she'd been curvy as a fence post and leggy as a colt. But he really wasn't given to dreaming, despite Nathan's best efforts.

He spent far more of his time in the here and now or thinking about the past than he did dreaming about what never had been nor likely would be. Consequently he hadn't really considered what it would be like to kiss Alison Richards.

He should've left it that way.

Knowing was hell.

At night he lay awake in bed, tossing and turning, remembering. It might have helped, he told himself, if he'd had the good sense to stay in the bunkhouse where he belonged.

But oh no, he'd had to act like the lord of the manor and move back into the house. Back into the room he'd used before Nathan had died. Back into the bed where Alison had slept.

Jess sleep?

Not on your life.

He'd spent almost three years in that bedroom, in that bed, and he couldn't have dreamed about Alison Richards more than once. Or twice. Now he couldn't stop dreaming about her—even awake.

Damn it, why had he kissed her?

"—hear what I said, Jess?" Alvin Simmons's impatience broke into his reverie.

Jess blinked, looking around, saw Alvin tapping his foot on the porch. The older man's asperity meant he'd said whatever he'd been saying more than once. "Sorry. I...got a lot on my mind."

"Reckon so," Alvin agreed with a bit more equanimity. "Not the best time to be doing this, day before the sale. But if you want all the figures on hand before the sale, we've got no choice."

"I want 'em." Even if it meant showing Alvin around the house when he wanted a shower and something to eat. Even if it meant he would be up half the night attending to last-minute details. The sooner he had Alvin's appraisal, the sooner he could contact Alison, make her an offer, get her once and for all out of his life.

"Well, fifteen, twenty minutes at most and we'll be done," Alvin promised. "You gonna sell out?"

Jess shook his head. "Buy her half," he said, crossing his fingers that the bank would agree.

"Funny business, the way old Nathan set it up, you and that granddaughter together. Coulda knocked me over with a feather when I heard."

Me, too, Jess thought. He followed as Alvin paced around the kitchen, making a note on his pad.

"Nathan always was a sneaky old buzzard." Alvin shot Jess a speculative look. "Sure you wouldn't rather make a go of it with the girl?"

Jess snorted. "Me and some big-city girl? Don't even think it."

"Reckon Nathan did," Alvin said cheerfully, heading into the living room.

Jess shook his head. "No way."

"Why'd he do it, then?"

Jess had wondered that, too. He'd been thinking long and hard about it since the day they'd been to Kirby's office. He remembered Nathan returning from New York that last time preoccupied and muttering. "Probably thought she needed to get in touch with nature again. Or maybe he wanted to put her in touch with her dreams," he said wryly. "Nathan was big on dreams."

Alvin grinned. "Then maybe she won't sell."

"She will. She took off the day after the funeral. Reckon she couldn't wait to get back to the bright lights."

"Some women are like that."

"Yes," Jess agreed. And he would do well to remember that fact instead of her scorching kiss.

It took Alvin longer than fifteen or twenty minutes to finish, mostly because he stopped every few minutes and talked. Jess followed him, dutifully answering the questions as well as he could.

He was tired and hungry. He needed a shower. He'd been late coming in, and Alvin's truck was already outside the house when he'd got back. He felt dirty, grimy and sweaty. His bad leg ached. His ribs were sore.

He leaned against the doorjamb to the attic, swaying slightly, his eyes closed, listening to Alvin poke around, tapping on rafters, knocking on the chimney pipe. Every once in a while Alvin would send a question floating down and Jess would try to come up with coherent answers.

"All done," Alvin said at last, thumping back down the steps. "I'll give you a call later tonight when I've got it all figured out." He trotted down the stairs and out to his truck, leaving Jess standing on the landing. Just as well, Jess thought wearily. Then he wouldn't have to trudge back up to take a bath.

His stomach growled, but he ignored it. Most days he wanted a shower, quick, brisk and invigorating. Tonight he wanted to soak, to lie back and let the hot water soothe his aches.

When the tub was half-full he lowered his aching body into the steamy water, sighing as the heat eased tired muscles, settling back and closing his eyes. Bliss.

He drizzled a washcloth full of hot water over his head, then sank lower, letting the water lap against his neck. By tomorrow night he would be in Denver and almost home free.

The cattle would be in the stockyards awaiting Monday's sale, he would know how much he needed to make in order to give Alison an offer, and Sam and Mal, the truck drivers, would be ready to party.

When he'd gone to Denver with Nathan, partying had been the last thing on Jess's mind. He'd been too interested in plaguing Nathan with questions about the business side of ranching to bother.

"Ain't natural for a young fella like you to be hanging around a motel on a Saturday night. Leastwise, not with me," Nathan had complained. "G'wan, get outa here."

To humor him, Jess had gone. There was always plenty of action in Denver's various bars, and plenty of willing women if a guy wanted them.

This year Jess thought he might.

One woman was as good as another, his father'd always said. And while there wasn't much Les Cooper said that Jess believed, if he was going to forget about Nathan Richards's granddaughter, he needed to prove his father right.

Yeah, he was looking forward to Denver tomorrow night. He needed to do some serious partying.

He pulled the plug and stood up. Water ran down his torso as he stepped out of the tub and reached for a towel. His stomach growled again and he sighed, anticipating dinner. He rubbed his hair, blotted his chest, then cocked his head as he heard a creaking sound on the stairs.

"You already ate, Scout," he said, slinging the towel around his neck and jerking open the door. "Don't pester."

It wasn't Scout.

"I'm back," said Alison Richards.

Chapter Five

The door shut smack in her face. Fast.

But not fast enough. Not nearly fast enough to prevent her unimpeded observation of a lean male torso, lightly matted with damp, dark hair. Not at all quick enough to shield from her sight the most essential part of Jess Cooper's masculinity. And certainly not soon enough to eliminate her clear view of his shocked face.

"What the hell are you doing here?"

Alison heard more rage than embarrassment in his voice, and that, thankfully, gave her the gumption to reply determinedly, "Moving in."

The door jerked open again. This time he was standing behind it, only his outraged face appearing around the edge of it. "Moving in?" he yelped. "Here? The hell you are!"

"The hell I am," Alison said firmly.

It had taken her three soul-searching days to come to that conclusion, another eight to get her affairs in order, take her accumulated vacation time in lieu of notice, quit her job, find someone to sublease her apartment, gather her most important worldly possessions, say goodbye to Gary and come west.

She wasn't going back now.

The door banged shut again. "Hang on. Don't do anything." She could hear him scrabbling around for his clothes. "Don't move. Just wait there. We've got to talk."

"I'll put my things in my room. It's only—"

"No!" There was a crash and he was back, poking his head out again. "No," he said in more moderate tones. "I mean, you can't. Use Nathan's room," he commanded. It was the least welcoming offer of accommodation Alison had ever heard.

"But my room is—" Fine, she was going to say.

"Mine," said Jess.

Their eyes caught and held. A dark flush lined his cheekbones. He glared at her defiantly.

His room? Her room was *his* room?

Alison smiled faintly, hugging her cat against her chest. "Fine," she said mildly. "I'll use Nathan's room."

Her grandfather's room was across from hers—Jess's, she corrected—and once she got inside, she dumped the cat on the bed, then slumped down beside him and pressed cool palms to suddenly overheated cheeks.

"Oh, my," she murmured. "Oh, my. Oh, my. Oh, Jess."

Jess. She smiled. Ah, Jess.

Jess naked. Promising.

Jess enraged. Not so promising.

But she hadn't been expecting him to welcome her with open arms. Not right away. Even she wasn't that big a fool.

Still, she'd had to come back. She'd been thinking about him since she'd left.

How could she not, given that kiss?

She'd envisioned a hundred scenarios for her return. But never Jess naked with only a towel around his neck. She grinned, then giggled, then took a deep, shuddering breath.

Get a grip on yourself, Ali, old girl, she counseled herself.

She tried. Really, she did. But the memory of his lean naked body wasn't the stuff of which indifference was made.

Still, she told herself, she'd better not dissolve into a puddle of either desire or laughter the next time she faced him. Not if she wanted her dreams to come true.

And that was, she admitted, what she wanted.

She'd lived on the memory of Jess Cooper's kiss since he'd stalked away from her at the restaurant eleven days ago.

At first she'd tried to get him out of her mind.

No such luck. As far as kissing Jess Cooper went, reality beat fantasy hands down every time. But if she'd thought the kiss was devastating when it happened, it was nothing compared to the way it made her feel later that night when she dashed off the plane and into Gary's arms.

She had run to him, thrown her arms around him, touched her lips to his and felt . . . nothing. Not a thing.

There was no hunger. No passion. No need.

Just lips, warm and pleasant. Not unlike Nathan's grandfatherly pecks. Alison felt a shaft of cold slip down her spine. She took a trembling breath. Gary seemed to notice nothing at all.

He took her bag in one hand and her hand in the other and led her out to his waiting car, all the while telling her about his newest software program, inquiring casually about her trip, not even particularly interested in her news about Nathan's amazing bequest.

"Wouldn't you even like to see it?" she'd asked him.

And he'd shaken his head. "To misquote one of our former national leaders, 'If you've seen one aspen, you've seen them all.' And, honestly, Ali, I doubt if cattle are much different."

She'd fallen into silence then, wondering, looking at Gary through new eyes. She liked him. She'd always felt comfortable with him. She'd never really expected the sort of desperate passionate yearnings with him that she'd felt about Jess all those years ago.

After all, she'd reasoned, they were the product of her age.

Now, unfortunately, she knew she was wrong. They were the product of the man.

And could she even think about marrying Gary when she knew for a fact that another man could wreak such havoc in her soul?

Gary had chatted on amiably all the way back to her apartment. He'd expected to come in. She'd stopped him at the door. "I'm really exhausted. Why don't I call you tomorrow?"

"It is tomorrow," Gary had said with a perplexed grin.

Alison nodded. "Later then, all right?" She had looked at him pleadingly and he had taken pity on her, dropping another of his dispassionate kisses on her forehead.

"All right, love. You get some sleep."

She hadn't slept. She had lain awake thinking, remembering. She had known for a certainty that she wasn't his love, nor was he hers.

And Jess?

What about Jess? a niggling little voice inside had plagued her.

Jess had been her dream. Ah, yes. But Jess was also real.

And so was his kiss.

"Pops always told me to follow my own rainbows," her father had once told her when he was explaining how he had chosen to leave the sheltered valley in southwestern Colorado where he'd been raised.

It seemed to Alison as if Nathan had handed her this one.

Was she going to hand it back to him? Turn her back on it?

Was she really going to share a kiss like the one she had shared with Jess Cooper and then simply walk away?

Could she settle for Jess's cold hard cash when she could possibly have so much more?

She began making plans to come back.

Gary thought she was crazy.

"You're moving to Colorado and becoming a cowgirl?" He had stared at her, aghast.

"Rancher," she'd corrected. "I'm becoming a rancher."

He'd taken her hands in his. "What about us, Ali?" he'd asked.

And Ali had had to admit that there really wasn't an "us." She'd considered marrying Gary not because she couldn't live without Gary, but because she'd come to see him as a means to achieving her dream of home and family. It wouldn't be enough.

She still wanted a home, she still wanted a family. But she also wanted desire, hunger, love. She'd tasted those things on Jess's lips, or hoped she had.

She aimed to find out.

She didn't say any of that to Gary. She hemmed and hawed, mumbled about needing space and trying to find herself. Gary, no fool, got the point.

"Don't expect me to sit and wait," he'd muttered. "There are other fish in the sea, Alison."

Alison nodded. "No doubt."

Ginger had squealed and clapped her hands over her mouth when Alison had broken the news to her. Then she had looked deeply into Alison's eyes and, no fool either, had asked bluntly, "What's his name?"

But Alison wasn't saying. She wasn't sharing her hopes with anyone. It could all come to nothing.

Still, she began to think perhaps Nathan had had a reason for leaving her the ranch. He must have, or he would have left her money like he'd left her brothers.

Was that reason Jess?

It seemed fanciful to think so. But she couldn't help it. Maybe it was sheer rationalization. But the dream had not died, and try as she might, she could not seem to shut it out.

So she made her excuses to Gary, ignored Ginger's questions, smiled enigmatically at her co-workers, all the while working feverishly to tie up all the loose ends in her life and return to Colorado.

Her goal had been to come and help get things ready for the sale. She hadn't really made it in time for much of the work, though she hoped that she might be of some use tomorrow morning. But from here on out, she planned to do her share.

She and Jess would learn to work together.

But if she kept seeing him in a towel and nothing but, she thought with a smile, it was going to be a little hard to keep her mind focused only on cattle.

She heard footsteps now, and Jess appeared in the doorway, barefoot and clad in jeans and a long-sleeved plaid shirt, which he was still in the process of buttoning.

His eyes went from her to the cat. He scowled. "What's that?"

"My cat. He's called Kitten. Kitten," she said, "this is Jess."

Jesse didn't look pleased at the introduction. Man and cat stared at each other, sizing each other up. Jess looked away first. Kitten sat down and began to clean his tail.

"What's this nonsense about moving in?"

Alison mustered her most optimistic look. "Just what I said. I quit my job, sublet my apartment, and here I am." She spread her palms and gave him a sunny smile.

It was a good thing, she thought, that she hadn't expected him to throw his arms around her and declare his everlasting love.

He looked horrified. "Quit your job? What the hell'd you go an' do a stupid thing like that for?"

"Because I wanted to. Because I don't have to work there anymore. Because—"

"You own half a ranch and you think you're a woman of leisure now?"

"Of course not, Jess. Don't be an idiot."

"*I'm* an idiot? What do you think you're going to do around here?"

She gave him an impatient look. "I'm going to help you with the ranch."

He had nothing to say to that. His snort of disbelief said it all.

Alison slapped her hands on her hips. "What's wrong with that?"

He pressed his lips together and looked away. "You got an hour or two, I'll tell you."

"Don't be obnoxious, Jess."

"Me? Obnoxious?" He paced an irritated circle in Nathan's small room. "You come bargin' in here right before sale day and you call *me* obnoxious?"

"I came to help," Alison said with all the patience she could muster. "Now, what needs to be done?"

He raked his fingers through his hair. "I don't believe this." He stalked another circle, kicked the bedstead, sending Kitten scurrying for cover.

"Believe it," Alison said.

HE DID.

He didn't want to, damn it all, but he did.

She had that same earnest, determined look about her that he remembered so well from when she'd been barely more than a kid. That I'm-gonna-do-this-if-I-bust-my-head-tryin' look. It was one of the things that had attracted his attention clear back then.

When all the other girls had been content simply to bat their eyelashes and simper at him, she'd wanted to learn how to rope. She'd followed him around, not saying anything, just watching, emulating, messing it up, hauling the rope back in and trying it again. And again.

Dogged. Determined.

In the end he'd taught her. Showed her how to make the loop, how to hold the rope so that the coils would slip out freely as she threw. And he'd watched her practice—her teeth biting into her lower lip as she concentrated, her nose wrinkling in disgust when she missed, her shoulders squaring determinedly as she tried it over and over.

She was looking at him with just that same determination now. He gritted his teeth.

"Hell," he muttered under his breath. He slapped his hand against the doorjamb. His stomach growled again, and he remembered he still hadn't eaten any supper. Not that he felt much like it now.

"Come on," he said gruffly over his shoulder. "You can tell me about this hare-brained scheme while I eat. If you think you're going to be the next Dale Evans, we've got some talking to do."

"Does this mean you're going to be Roy Rogers?" Alison asked him as she gathered Kitten into her arms and followed him down the stairs.

He banged a pot on the stove and reached down to yank a can of stew out of the cabinet. "Like hell."

"I'll make it," Alison volunteered.

"You won't." He jerked the opener out of a drawer and ground open the can. He didn't want her doing things for him, playing Mrs. Rancher. "It's insane, you know," he went on. "You movin' back here." The stuff of his worst nightmares.

"I don't know."

"You sure as hell don't. You don't know the first thing about ranching. You're a librarian, for cripe's sake." He slapped the bottom of the can and the congealed stew thudded into the pot.

"I can learn."

He snorted. "Yeah, how?" He paused, a possibility occurring to him. His head snapped up and he glowered at her. "You're not followin' me around all day."

"Fine," Allison said shortly. "Then I'll find out other ways."

"What other ways?" He jabbed at the stew with a fork, stirring it, making the pot bang against the burner.

"Asking questions—"

"Not me."

"—of willing people, observing *willing* people, reading books."

"Reading books?" He looked at her, incredulous.

Alison lifted her chin. "You'd be amazed what a person can learn from reading books."

"I would," he agreed. He slanted her a nasty grin. "I sure as hell would like to see you learn to rope a steer by reading a book."

"I don't have to read a book to learn how to rope," Alison reminded him. "A formerly nice person once taught me."

"The more fool he," Jess growled and slapped a huge spoonful of stew onto his plate. He kicked out a chair, sat down and, ignoring her, began to eat.

He could feel Alison's eyes on him. Doggedly he stabbed a piece of beef and stuck it in his mouth and began to chew. It tasted like his saddle.

Abruptly Jess stood and dumped the stew back into the pot.

"What's wrong?" Alison asked nervously.

"It's cold."

Which was true, of course, but which was the least of his problems.

His biggest was sitting at the table, watching him with those wide blue eyes and smiling at him with that warm, kissable mouth.

It wasn't just another bad dream. It was Alison, in the flesh, sitting mere feet away, talking about moving in, talking about taking part in the day-to-day operation of the ranch, not selling, but in fact invading his very life!

Hell's bells, Nathan, he wondered desperately, what were you thinking of?

Did the old man have a clue as to the mischief he'd wrought with his stupid will?

Of course not.

He couldn't possibly have known how Jess felt about his granddaughter. Not once had Jess betrayed more than a fleeting interest in her whenever Alison's name had come up. Not once had he admitted his attraction.

So why did he feel as if Nathan was sitting up in heaven chuckling right now?

Jess adjusted the flame and poked irritably at the lumpy mass in the pot, trying to think of something sensible to say, something that would make her realize what she was proposing was a mistake. "Nathan wouldn't expect you to go haring off doing something idiotic like this," he began.

"On the contrary, I think it's exactly what Nathan wanted me to do."

He stared at her. "You do?"

She nodded complacently.

"Why?"

She hesitated. She sat back in the chair and pulled her knees up against her breasts, wrapping her arms around them. It made Jess conscious of the length of her, of the subtlety of her curves, of how much of a woman she'd become. He sucked in his breath.

"I think," Alison was saying, "that he thought I'd be... happier here. When he came to New York to visit, we spent most of the time talking about the ranch."

"Hardly a reason to move here," Jess said gruffly.

Alison brushed a lock of hair away from her cheek. "No. At least I certainly didn't think so at first. But—" she looked up and gave him a smile that started his insides to melting "—I do feel freer here, happier."

He scraped the bits of burning stew off the bottom of the pan and dumped the whole mass onto his plate again. "You haven't had to do any work yet."

She smiled again. "That's true. But I'm quite willing."

He wasn't. He scowled. "And that's why you came back?" It seemed pretty vague and stupid to him. He doubted her resolve would last. He hoped it wouldn't.

"Not... entirely."

"So why else?" He wanted all the cards on the table, wanted to know what had prompted her, so he could do his best to undermine her.

"The kiss."

"The *kiss?*" He felt as if she'd just punched him in the gut. "Holy Mary, Mother of—" He raked his fingers through his hair. "You quit your job on the basis of a kiss?"

He shut his eyes. This couldn't be happening.

Even in his best—or worst—dreams, sane and sensible, intelligent city-bred women like Alison Richards didn't do things like this!

"It's not as idiotic as you're making it sound," she said irritably. Her blue eyes were stormy as they glared at him.

He sat down and took a bite of stew. "It isn't?" he said around the chunk of beef.

"No. Not unless you kiss every woman like that."

His head jerked up. She was looking straight at him. "Do you?"

He choked. Coughed. Alison leapt up and smacked him on the back. Finally he swallowed. She handed him a glass of water. He drank it. His eyes were watering. Damn, even eating with her was dangerous!

"Better?" Alison asked him when he'd settled back in his chair and was breathing normally. She sat down again.

He nodded, still not trusting his voice.

"Then answer my question." Blue eyes met his implacably.

"What question?" he tried.

She just looked at him.

Oh, hell. He rubbed a hand against the back of his neck, scowled, shrugged, wanted desperately to lie to her. Couldn't. Quite.

"It was only a kiss," he muttered hoarsely, knowing she could easily hear what he wasn't willing to say.

She beamed. "Not 'only.' It was quite a kiss."

He made an inarticulate sound deep in his throat.

"So," she went on guilelessly, "I thought, for Pops's sake, we ought to see where it might lead."

It was his turn to stare.

"You wanted to see where it might lead?" he rasped finally. He shoved back his chair so hard it fell over. Scout and Kitten looked up, startled, then vanished around the corner. Jess came around the side of the table to stand over her.

Alison looked up at him. "Well, I—" She gave him a helpless little shrug.

But Jess was beyond being stopped by helplessness. He reached out and took hold of her hand, pulling her to her feet, hauling her against him, touching his lips to hers.

"Here," he muttered, his mouth on hers. "Here's where it will lead."

The kiss was long and hard and left him aching. He wanted to grab her and haul her upstairs to bed and thanked God he wasn't fool enough to do it.

He stepped back, breathing hard, staring down into her astonished, wide eyes.

"Any more questions?" he said raggedly. Then he turned around and stalked out the door without looking back.

"NOT AN AUSPICIOUS beginning, was it, Kitten?" Alison said to the cat. She sat huddled in Nathan's high feather bed and stared dismally into the darkness.

It was now nearly midnight and Jess still had not come back. She had followed him to the door, but he was walking fast in the direction of the truck. So she stopped where she was.

She'd heard the truck start up and had watched him through the window as he whipped it around in the yard and gunned the engine, scattering gravel behind him as he roared off down the hill.

And that was the last she'd seen of him.

She'd washed the dishes, scoured the pan he'd burned the stew in, then carried the few things she'd brought with her up to Nathan's room.

She stayed there, hoping that if she kept a low profile for a time, things might improve. But there was no chance of them improving if Jess didn't even return.

She sighed and lay down on the bed, curling around Kitten, hugging his unresisting body against her, trying to will herself to sleep. Seconds later she sat up again.

She couldn't sleep not knowing where he'd gone. What if he'd been in an accident? What if he was lying somewhere hurt?

The memory of what the Brinkmillers had done to him was vivid in her mind.

There wouldn't be any Brinkmillers tonight, she told herself firmly.

Still she couldn't sleep. She got out of bed and padded into the hall, flipping on the light. Kitten blinked at her.

She continued along the hall to Jess's room, then stood in the doorway, looking in.

It made sense now, why the room had felt lived-in when she'd been back for Nathan's funeral. It had been Jess's room even then. He must have moved out right before they came.

Why hadn't he said? Why had he pretended otherwise? Had he felt that uncomfortable around them?

She wished she understood him better. He was such an enigma. So intense and yet so private. She had dreamed of him forever, and yet she had very little notion of what had made him the way he was.

Why did he kiss her so hungrily, then thrust her away?

She started to go into his room, wanting simply to look around, to learn more about this man who'd haunted her for so many years.

Then, far off she heard the sound of an engine. She flicked off the light, then padded quickly into his room, not looking around, but simply crossing the floor to look out the window.

She pulled back the shade and saw, down the valley, a pair of headlights moving this way.

"Thank heaven," she breathed, relieved that all her worst fantasies had come to naught.

She stood watching until he drove into the yard, cut the engine and quietly shut the door of the truck. Then she turned and ran quickly to Nathan's room, jumping into bed and pulling the covers up to her chin, pretending to be asleep.

He didn't come in.

Finally, when a quarter of an hour passed and he still didn't come in, she eased herself out of bed again and crept across the hall to his room.

The yard was empty except for the silent truck. She frowned, peering into the darkness, trying to discern movement.

There was none.

But something was different. A light in the bunkhouse.

And the very moment she noticed it, it shut off.

So he was hiding out, was he?

He'd deny it, she was sure. But that was what he was doing, as sure as she was Nathan's grandchild.

Alison sighed. It wasn't the homecoming she'd wished for, although it had had its moments, she thought with a smile, remembering him coming out of the bathroom in his birthday suit.

Still, things had gone right downhill from there.

She walked slowly back to her bed and slid beneath the covers, asking herself exactly what Jess Cooper was afraid of.

THE TRUCKS CAME up the hill at dawn. It felt as if they were rumbling right through his head. Great honking semis grinding their gears in the grooves of his brain, peeling out against the backs of his eyeballs, letting go with roaring blasts of their air horns, loud enough to explode the inside of his head.

Jess ground the pillow against his face and groaned.

What in the hell had he done to feel this way?

He wasn't so far gone that he didn't remember. He'd panicked and run. He'd taken one look at Alison Richards's smiling, hopeful face, remembered the kiss they'd shared, heard her wonder aloud where it might lead, and he'd bolted like a bronc with a burr under his saddle.

He'd started at the Silver Dollar, moved on the Moriarty's, and finished at the Blue Heeler.

"Whatcha doin' here? Ain'tcha shippin' tomorrow?" Denny the bartender at the Silver Dollar has asked, curiosity wreathing his bulldog face.

Jess had scowled into his beer. "What of it?"

Denny took a step backward, picked up a towel and began to dry another glass. "Just wonderin'," he said mildly, and when a customer called for a gin and tonic, he'd moved gratefully away.

Nearly the same had happened at Moriarty's, where old Gus had shaken his head and said, "Let it go to hell that fast, didja? Poor ol' Nate."

"Nothing's gone to hell," Jess had snapped. Except maybe him. "The ranch is fine. The cattle are fine."

"Uh-huh," Gus said. And the skeptical look on Moriarty's face had sent Jess to the Blue Heeler within minutes.

The Blue Heeler was primarily a tourist joint. Hunters with an eye for an elk or a ten-point deer hung out there. There were no hunters yet, it was too early in the year. But a busload of German tourists on their way from Phoenix to Denver were stopping for a night at the springs and a little local color.

They watched with silent respect as Jess drowned his miseries.

"You are a real cowboy," one of them said with wary admiration, looking him up and down as if he were a tiger on the loose.

"*Ein* true American hero," nodded another. He smiled at Jess hopefully. "Can I take your picture, *Herr* Cowboy?"

Jess wished he had a six-shooter.

If he had one now, he'd think about putting himself out of his misery. He sat up on the edge of the bunk and held his head in his hands. God, how could he have been so stupid as to drink that much the night before shipping day?

How could he not, he asked himself, given the prospect of Alison's smiling, wide-eyed face?

Where would it lead? He knew damned well where it would lead. That was why he'd had to get out of there!

He staggered to his feet and pulled on his boots, then stumbled to the sink and stuck his head under the faucet. The stream of icy water on his skull nearly accomplished what a six-shooter would. He yelped, pulling back. Then, cautiously, he ducked his head again, letting the water beat against his skull so that now the outside felt as if it were being as soundly hammered as the inside.

The first truck rumbled into the yard as he was toweling off his hair. He grabbed a jacket and headed for the door.

Alison was there before him, all bright-eyed and cheerful as she talked to Sam Wiley, the driver.

Sam grinned at him. "Mornin', Jess. See you got some new help." His gaze flickered to Alison approvingly.

Jess strode past without stopping. "Hell of a lot of help she'll be. Come on. Time's wastin'."

Sam's brows lifted and he gave Alison a wink. "Got up on the wrong side of bed, did he?"

"If he even went to bed at all," Jess heard her reply behind him. He gritted his teeth and headed toward the corral.

The cattle were restless, aware that today was different, that things were about to change, and it took all Jess's concentration to get them moving toward the chute. He turned to shout at Sam or Mal to open the gate.

Alison was already there, anticipating him.

He sighed. His head hurt.

"Give her some credit, Jess," Sam said. "She's not half bad."

Jess grunted and went back to his work.

But Sam was right. She did have a pretty fair sense of what needed to be done, and she was right there, opening this gate, closing that one, trying her best to do it. He had to give her credit for that.

Still it didn't mean she ought to give up librarianing for ranching. Especially not here.

So what if she owned half of the ranch? Hadn't she ever heard of absentee landlording?

Presumably she had. And she'd been going to do it until he'd kissed her.

And what had he done last night except kiss her again?

Damnation! What was the matter with him?

Jess scowled, wiping a hand across his grimy forehead. He turned, watching the quick, efficient way she moved, appreciating the way she filled out her jeans. He wished some cow would do its worst all over her shiny new boots. He wished she'd catch a dirty wet tail across the cheek.

It wasn't going to work, him and Alison Richards being partners, working together; no matter what fuzzy little idea she had in her pretty head. She was too damned tempting, too desirable.

He wanted her.

He'd used Nathan's memory and a good dose of solid common sense to mind his manners when she'd been around for the funeral. He'd done fine for three days, thank you very much.

But he wasn't a big enough fool to believe he could keep it up indefinitely.

The hell of it was she didn't seem to want him to. "I figured we owed it to Pops to see where it would lead," she'd said.

Did that argue for a platonic relationship?

Not on your life!

And after they became lovers, then what?

"You got a problem, you gotta step back and look at it from all angles," Nathan had always said. "Get yourself a little distance, some perspective."

Jess had the mother of all problems.

"Come on, Denver," he muttered, urging the cattle toward the chute, hoping against hope that three days and three hundred miles would give him the perspective he sought.

THE CATTLE WERE LOADED by eight. Jess left Sam and Mal locking up the last of them and went into the house to get his gear.

He tossed his bag onto the bed and threw shirts and jeans into it indiscriminately. Then, grabbing his shaving kit out of the bathroom, he headed back downstairs.

Alison was just coming up.

He moved aside giving her wide berth. Only when she was safely past did he say, "When I get back from Denver, we're going to have a talk."

"Why don't we talk en route?"

"What?" He stopped dead, his hand on the newel post. "What do you mean, 'talk en route'? You're not coming with me!"

"Of course I am."

"Like hell!"

"Then I'll go with Sam."

What he said then was even ruder. "Who's going to take care of things here?" he demanded.

She shrugged. "Who was going to take care of them if I hadn't come back?"

"Brian Gonzales."

"Well, then," she said lightly, "I guess Brian Gonzales will." And she turned to head back up the steps again.

Jess, furious, strode after her, taking the stairs two at a time.

"Listen to me, Miss Dale Evans Richards, if you're gonna be responsible for half of the things that happen on this ranch, you need to do your share! You need—"

"As a co-owner I need to find out as much as I can about the livestock we're selling and about getting the best deal possible," Alison said with quiet authority. "The bottom line is what we make on the cattle, isn't it? Well, then I need to come, too." She paused. "I don't have a steady income anymore, remember?"

"That's not my fault," Jess bit out.

She just looked at him, then smiled that damnably maddening, tempting smile. "Isn't it?"

"Oh, hell." He turned on his heel and stomped down again.

He was sitting in the truck fuming when she came out a few moments later.

Sam had already headed down the hill. Mal was starting after him. Jess would bring up the rear.

Ordinarily he would've ridden with either Sam or Mal. But he wasn't letting Alison in a truck cab with them for a whole day.

Once, he'd have figured she'd keep her mouth shut and smile politely. But since she'd asked for that goodbye kiss, he realized there was no telling what she'd do.

He sat with his hands clenched on the steering wheel, knuckles whitening as he watched her come out the door. She turned back for a moment, bending down, patting something.

The cat, he thought irritably.

What on earth were they going to do with a cat?

He muttered an expletive under his breath. Then, reaching over, he jerked open the passenger door. "Come on if you're coming," he yelled. "We haven't got all day."

She came at a run, tossing her bag into the back before she scrambled in and settled down beside him, grinning. "All set."

Jess gunned the engine and they shot off down the road. She bounced forward, and he reached over and thrust her seat belt at her. "Use it."

She put it on, then leaned back against the seat and smiled at him. She'd been herding cattle since sun up and damned if she didn't smell like flowers.

He thought he'd lose his mind.

A WHOLE DAY in a truck, just her and Jess Cooper. It was the stuff of which Alison's adolescent dreams had been made.

Reality was a far, far different thing.

In her dreams Jess had taken advantage of the opportunity to declare his undying love, to hold her hand, to steal kisses whenever the switchback curves permitted.

In reality he turned on the radio, kept both hands on the wheel and never said a word.

No, that wasn't quite the truth. He would speak if spoken to. But he didn't seem to be jumping into this talk that he'd said they were going to have, though Alison allowed him plenty of time.

That being the case, she decided to bring up the subject herself. "You wanted to talk to me?"

He grunted.

"Well, I thought you said—"

"I'm trying to figure out how to say it. How to be tactful."

"Why start now?"

He ground his teeth and turned up the radio.

THE TRIP TO DENVER took fourteen hours. It seemed to Jess like four hundred years.

He should've been concentrating on the cattle, on how he needed to shape them up when he got them there, on what he needed to tell the commission man before Monday morning.

He thought about Alison and about how to get her out of his life.

He wasn't used to talking to women, especially not about personal feelings, and most especially not about sex, but he didn't see any way around it.

She wasn't leaving him any choice.

"All right," he said finally when they'd reached the Interstate without him being able to find the words. "Let's put it this way. Pure and simple, it wouldn't work."

Alison, who had been looking out the window for the last hour in complete and unnerving silence, looked at him and blinked. "What wouldn't work?"

"Going to bed with you." His face burned even as he said the words.

Alison blinked. Her face reddened a bit, too. Then she gave him a saucy grin. "How do you know unless you try?"

Jess sputtered. "Geez! What in hell would your grandfather say?"

"I don't know. But I rather think he'd have more to say to you than to me," Alison told him.

Jess snorted. His thumbs tightened on the wheel.

Alison turned sideways in the seat so she could look at him. He felt like a bug, pinned to a board.

"Let me get this straight," Alison said conversationally. "You have been sitting here contemplating the prospect of sleeping with me for almost three hundred miles?" She sounded almost amused.

His hands strangled the steering wheel. "Well, what d'you expect. You suggested it!"

"I!"

"Who said, 'Let's see where it might lead'?" He turned a glare on her. "That was you, wasn't it?"

"Yes, but—"

"Well, damn it all, that kiss I gave you yesterday, that's only where it would start, and you know it. I'm sure you're terrific in bed and all that, but—"

"Thank you. I think," Alison cut in.

"But I think if you really give it some consideration," Jess went on, determined to get it out once and for all, "you'll decide it isn't what you want, either."

"It isn't."

"But you said—"

"I said what I said because I felt like something was happening between us. That did not mean I was simply angling to go to bed with you!"

"It didn't?" He looked at her narrowly. "Then what the hell did you mean?"

Alison stared for a long moment at her hands in her lap. Then she lifted her gaze and met his. "Think about it," she suggested quietly.

Jess did.

That was more terrifying yet.

Chapter Six

"Ho, no. No way."

She couldn't mean what he thought she meant. Could she?

It took one swift glance to tell him that, yes, indeed she did.

"M-marriage." Even to him his voice sounded rusty. "You're thinking about *marriage?*"

"It's a possibility."

"Huh-uh." Jess shook his head. "Talk about things that wouldn't work."

"How do you know?"

He stared at her, incredulous. "You're serious? You think that just because Nathan has stuck us together on a ranch in the middle of nowhere we ought to get married?"

"Nathan has nothing to do with this."

"You mean if you hadn't inherited half of the Rocking R you'd have shown up to propose to me, anyway?"

"Don't be an idiot."

"I'm not the idiot here," Jess muttered. Marry? *Marry Alison Richards?* He couldn't fathom it.

"I'm not proposing to you."

"Sounded like it to me," he muttered, still shaken.

"Still, you have to admit, after a kiss like that—"

"Kisses aren't proposals, either!"

"No, but you're a man, I'm a woman. We're within a reasonable age of each other."

"And you think that's enough?"

"Of course not. Love is necessary, too."

"Love." He snorted. If there was ever an emotion he doubted, it was love. "What's that?"

"You don't know?"

"I'm asking, aren't I?"

"It's wanting to share, to care. It's when someone else's good, someone else's happiness matters to you more than your own."

"And you read all that into a kiss?"

"It wasn't indifferent."

"You've never heard of plain, simple lust?"

Her fingers clenched. "Of course, but—"

"That was lust."

"Oh, Jess." She sighed and shook her head.

"I'm not getting married."

"You said that once before."

"When?"

"The day the . . . the Brinkmillers were . . ."

She didn't have to finish. He remembered now. Too well. God, why had she been there that day?

He gritted his teeth. "And I meant what I said."

"Why?"

He shot her an exasperated glance. Damn it. Couldn't she leave well enough alone? "Some people aren't cut out for marriage. Me, for instance."

"How do you know?"

"What the hell is this, twenty questions?"

"I'm . . . curious. What made you decide? Is it for religious reasons? Did you take a vow?"

"You think it's funny?"

"No," she said quickly. "I don't know what to think, Jess. Really. I'm trying to understand."

He rubbed his hand against the back of his neck.

"Family history." He stared straight ahead waiting for her to ask what he meant by it. But she just looked at him, and he found himself explaining without the question.

"My family doesn't do marriage. Or when they do, they don't do it well."

"Your parents divorced?" she asked quietly.

"No. But stayin' together until my mother died doesn't mean what they had was good."

His hands tightened briefly on the steering wheel as he remembered the arguments, the tears, the upheavals during which his mother had moved them from relative to relative, dragging him and his sister along while his father took off rodeoing again.

"My ma died when I was ten. Dad married again. And again. Those marriages didn't work, either. One lasted six months, the other barely two years. Hardly world records. And after that, he stopped marryin' 'em and just lived with 'em. Not exactly a role model for fidelity, would you say?"

"No, it isn't." She looked at him earnestly. "But that's just one man, Jess. And he wasn't you."

"Maybe not, but he handed it down. Did you know my sister, Lizzie? She used to work at Cutter's ranch as a hired girl."

"Long wavy dark hair, beautiful big brown eyes. She used to sing. Didn't she have a . . . a child?"

Jess's mouth twisted. "Yeah. Patsy. She's got two more of 'em, by last count. All with different men, and she never married any of 'em." He lifted one brow almost mockingly. "See what I mean, Ms. Richards? It's in the blood. So don't talk to me about marriage." He stomped down on the accelerator, moving out to pass a truck.

Alison didn't answer. She sat quietly, looking down at her hands, and he felt faintly guilty about the intensity of his outburst.

"Sorry," he muttered.

"I'm sorry, too," Alison said softly.

"I don't need you feeling sorry for me."

She just looked at him. He roared past three more cars before cutting back in sharply.

"No," she said. "I won't."

They drove on without speaking, the road was wide and straight as it headed up the eastern edge of the Rocky Mountains toward Denver. As Jess drove, he glanced over at her from time to time, trying to guess what she was thinking. He hoped she wasn't thinking too badly of him, but it wouldn't have surprised him. He didn't exactly have a background to put on a résumé. She might as well know it before she got any more damn fool ideas.

Just north of Colorado Springs, he cleared his throat. "If you want to fly back from Denver, I can send your gear on to you."

"Fly back?" She looked at him, puzzled. "To Bluff Springs? Why would I want to do that?"

"Not Bluff Springs. New York."

"I'm not going back to New York. I told you that."

"But you can't stay on."

"Why not?"

"By all that's holy, woman, we just discussed that! It won't work!"

"Like marriage won't work?" Alison smiled at him. "A detached observer might say you're protesting a bit too much. Don't worry, Jess. I won't pressure you, I promise. I just said I wanted to see where it would lead. If it doesn't lead to marriage, fine." She gave a negligent little shrug and went back to looking out the window.

It made Jess want to shake her.

"You're as bullheaded as your pesky grandfather," he muttered.

Alison nodded. "Thank you very much."

SHE DOUBTED he meant it as a compliment, even though she took it as such.

He probably thought she was crazy. Maybe she was. But why not spell it out, or at least admit she'd considered marriage as a possibility.

What could he do? Throw her out?

Hardly. She owned half the ranch.

Of course knowing what she was thinking could make him uncomfortable. But he was uncomfortable now. For better or worse, her presence seemed to have accomplished that.

In any case, coming out here again was taking a risk. She knew it. And she wasn't about to increase the risk by fostering misunderstandings.

She was no longer a starry-eyed adolescent content to live on a raft of fantasies for the future.

The future was now.

And if it was foolish to lay all her cards on the table with Jess, it would have been more foolish to pretend that all she wanted was a roll in the hay.

She had no doubt that a roll in the hay with Jess Cooper would be well worth remembering. Her cheeks warmed at the very thought. But that wasn't all she wanted.

She didn't honestly know yet if she wanted marriage, either. But she was at least willing to consider the idea.

Why couldn't men accept marriage as a possibility to be explored rather than a gun to run from?

Well, she consoled herself, it had got her one thing, this honesty of hers—it had encouraged Jess to open up to her for the first time.

All she'd ever known about his family before had been what she'd heard from his grandmother all those years ago. Ella hadn't told her much, mostly that her grandchildren worried her. Lizzie was wild, with crazy dreams of being a singing star that Ella was sure would bring her to ruin. And Jess was the opposite.

"He's so quiet. I never know what he's thinking. He's not like Lizzie. He's gentle, my Jess," Alison remembered Ella saying. "He won't hurt no one. People take advantage of him and he lets them. It will get him into trouble someday. I know it will." The old lady had shaken her head.

Alison had believed in Jess's gentleness then. She told herself it must still be in there now. Only she had the feeling that perhaps Ella had been right. Somewhere along the line, Jess had lost that gentleness—or had hidden it.

He was very well defended now.

He wasn't about to let anyone in—certainly not Alison.

She turned to him now. "What do we do when we get to Denver?"

"*I* get the cattle settled in, then find me a hotel room, go out to dinner with Sam and Mal, have a few drinks, then come back and get a good night's sleep. *You* can do whatever you damned well please."

She blinked at his vehemence, but didn't argue. "Fine. I will."

She heard a soft curse and looked over at him. "What?"

"Never mind. Come with me if you want." He was scowling at her.

Alison smiled slightly, then thought of his grandmother's words. "I don't want to take advantage. I don't want to ruin your trip."

"You already ruined my trip."

Alison looked at him. He gave her a ghost of a grin.

"I meant everything I said about us. And about marriage. Just forget that. But—" he sighed irritably "—oh hell, we are partners." He seemed to hesitate over the word for a split second, but then he went on doggedly, "Half of these cows are yours. You have a right to be there, too."

Alison placed her hand over her heart and gave him her best Girl Scout salute. "I promise I'll be good."

His expression was glum. "You'd better be."

IT WAS DARK by the time they got to Denver. Alison was glad that unloading the cattle didn't take as long as loading them had, and she was delighted when Jess drove her and Sam and Mal to a downtown hotel where they all got rooms.

"Dinner in an hour," he told her briskly in the lobby, handing her a room key. He turned to Sam and Mal. "You don't mind if she tags along?"

Mal looked astonished. "Mind? Why would we mind? She's a damned sight prettier than you are."

"Better conversationalist, too, I'll bet," Sam added, grinning.

Jess scowled. "So long as all you want to do is talk."

Mal and Sam looked at Alison, then gave him identical innocent smiles. "What else?"

Jess opened his mouth, then apparently thought better of whatever he might have been going to say. "See you in an hour," he muttered and stalked off toward the elevators.

Sam looked at Mal. "He look a little green around the edges to you?"

Mal grinned. "Just a tad." He gave Alison a wink. "Your fault?"

"You mean he isn't always this cheerful?"

Mal laughed. "See you at supper."

They ate in the hotel restaurant, a dimly lit, dark-paneled room with thick burgundy carpet and hunt club prints on the walls. The chairs were leather and the tablecloths linen. It was a far cry from the pine ladder-backs and faded checkered oilcloth in Nathan's kitchen.

"We like to live right once a year," Sam told her with a grin as they sat down.

"You come to Denver every week," Jess objected.

"Yeah, but we pretend we don't. Wouldn't want to make you feel bad." Sam grinned at Alison.

If she'd worried about feeling out of place having dinner with the three of them, she learned quickly that Mal and Sam were more than willing to welcome her. And if Jess ignored her, Mal and Sam were easy to talk to. They were eager, when she asked, to regale her with stories of Nathan and the Rocking R's earlier sale days.

"Topped the Denver market twice," Sam told her over a thick slab of prime rib. "Nathan was damned proud."

"Should've been," Jess put in abruptly. "Means he did things right. I'd like to do it again." His dark eyes met Alison's, challenging her. They were the first words he'd spoken since they'd sat down, and she heard the faint stress on the singular pronoun.

Mal, oblivious to the tensions between them, grinned. "Reckon you got your work cut out for you then. Ain't gonna be easy."

"I'll do it," Jess said quietly.

"Yes," Alison agreed. "We will."

After supper all Alison wanted to do was go back upstairs and fall into bed. Sam and Mal had other ideas.

"Thought we'd take in a little of the bright lights," Sam said as they were heading back toward the lobby. He gave Alison a hopeful, encouraging look.

She shook her head. "Go right ahead. Don't let me stop you," she replied. "I'm tired. I plan on going straight up to sleep. I'll see you in the morning."

He looked disappointed, then shrugged. "Another time, then. You comin', Jess?"

Alison looked over at Jess. He'd complained in the truck about how tired he was. She knew he hadn't slept much the night before. He was looking at her, his expression brooding. But when Mal asked, he didn't even hesitate.

"Sure. Why not?"

HE MEANT to have a high old time. Certainly Sam and Mal, released from the constraint of being gentlemen for Alison's benefit, were set on having one.

It didn't take them more than fifteen minutes to find a bar with a live band, a mechanical bull and a bevy of willing women. Perfect, Jess thought.

So why the hell was he sitting at the bar drinking orange juice by himself?

Because this morning's hangover was all too recent and well recalled. Because he needed to be sane and sensible when he went to the stockyards in the morning. Because he didn't have Nathan here to make the final decisions this year. And he sure as hell couldn't count on Alison, not for advice on shaping up the cattle. She probably thought she could, though. She seemed intent on infiltrating his life.

Damn Alison.

A woman with the looks, personality and education of Alison Richards could have her pick of men. So why was she fooling around with him?

Marry Alison?

Didn't he wish!

But he hadn't been lying when he'd said marriage wasn't for him. There was no way he wanted to end up like his father with a wife he couldn't satisfy and children he didn't give a damn about.

Jess Cooper knew there was only one way for a guy like him to relate to women, and it didn't take a preacher to do it.

"Kinda glum tonight, aren't you, honey?"

He looked up as one of the willing women slid onto the bar stool next to him and gave him a smile.

He shrugged, looking her over as he did so, wishing the sight of her would light some fire deep inside him. She was pretty enough. Big dark eyes, a puffy cloud of equally dark hair.

But there was knowledge in those eyes, a kind of unspoken calculation that instead of warming him actually made him feel cold.

"Not real talkative, are you?"

He hunched over his glass. "Got a lot on my mind."

"Bet I could distract you." Her voice was soft, almost a purr.

He wished it were true.

"Probably you could," he told her gently, "if I wanted you to." Inclining his head slightly, giving her a faint smile, he set his glass down and backed away, then turned and headed for the door.

Maybe he was a fool. She would have provided some solace. It had been a long time since he'd held a warm and willing woman in his arms. But there was only one woman who interested him that way right now.

The irony was, he could have her if he married her. And the even bigger irony was that in a more perfect world he would do it in a minute.

But Jess knew better than to believe in dreams like that one.

A ranch, well, yeah, maybe he could get that with hard work, determination and Nathan's blessing. But Nathan and all the hard work and determination in the world couldn't correct his past, couldn't change the family he'd grown up in, couldn't give him the courage to try the impossible.

That said, for the moment at least, he was going to have to learn how to accomplish the extremely difficult—living day by day with Alison, at least until she'd satisfied her curiosity and once more gone away.

In the past whenever things had got too tight, whenever he'd felt commitments closing in, he'd been able to take the time-honored cowboy's retreat and ride off into the sunset without looking back.

A rancher couldn't do that.

You couldn't roll up a ranch like you could a bedroll, toss it in your truck and be on your way. You stayed where the ranch was.

Or you sold out.

Could he sell out? Walk away and leave the one dream that finally seemed to be within his grasp?

Walking away had never been a problem in the past. He'd never tried to hang on to anything, and he'd left without looking back.

You never had anything worth hanging on to, he reminded himself.

But now he did.

One time, in the first year he'd worked for Nathan after he'd come back, he and Nathan had had a disagreement.

Jess, angry and feeling misunderstood, had packed up his gear and headed out the door.

"Chicken?" Nathan had called after him.

Jess had spun around, fists clenched. "Who're you callin' chicken?"

Nathan had been sitting calmly at the kitchen table, the Sunday papers spread out in front of him, looking as calm and unruffled as a sleepy hen as Jess had glared at him. He'd looked up with those mild blue eyes and challenged him. "Well, if you're afraid to stay and fight for what you want..."

"It's your ranch," Jess retorted, stung.

"And it's your life." A corner of Nathan's mouth had lifted slightly. "What're you gonna do with it, son?"

Jess had stayed.

He'd slung his bag down, stalked over to the table, glowered down at Nathan and once more argued his point. Nathan had listened, then insisted that Jess listen to him. Jess couldn't even remember which of them had prevailed. He only knew that he'd taken a deeper interest in the ranch after that.

It had really begun to matter to him.

It still mattered.

Sure, he could sell out. But he never would. Not now.

So that meant he had to stay and fight. Fight his attraction to Alison. Learn to get along with her until she left. Pray every night that his desire would fade or that the siren call of the big city would lure her away before the temptation became too much.

HE'D AGREED to call for her when he was going to the stockyards Sunday morning. He hadn't wanted to, she could tell, but she'd been adamant. "Like you said, we're partners, Jess. I need to be there, too."

So now Alison hurried to get ready, not wanting to keep him waiting. In fact she wondered if he'd show up on time.

If he'd had a hard night out on the town, perhaps he'd sleep right through his alarm. Or maybe he had stayed out so long, he wouldn't have been to bed at all. That thought made her wince.

Whichever the case, just as she finished braiding her hair, she heard a knock on the door.

He was wearing his customary jeans and long-sleeved shirt, with his sheepskin jacket hanging open, his hat in his hands. He looked surprisingly well rested for a man who had been so eager to party last night.

Or maybe, Alison thought, he wasn't so much well rested as well satisfied. The notion made her teeth clench. She drew a fortifying breath.

On the way to the stockyards Jess was all business, telling her how he intended to shape up the cattle he was selling, what size lots he figured to let them go in, what sort of prices they would be hoping for.

He was as talkative as she'd ever heard him, but at the same time he seemed distant and professional and formal. Perfectly proper. Very aloof.

Alison listened carefully, trying to digest everything he was telling her as they parked and she trailed after him, knowing as she did so that she'd forget a lot of it and have to ask again.

"Jess!"

Alison looked up to see a dark-haired man hurrying toward them. He was tall and broad-shouldered, like a football player, and, somewhat incongruously, wearing a suit. His white shirt cuffs peeked out below his spotless navy-blue sleeves, and a small blue sapphire sparkled in the center of a burgundy and navy tie. He looked like a Wall Street broker except for the boots.

Jess turned to Alison. "This is Steve Sudmeier, our commission man. This is my new partner—" once more Alison heard the fleeting hesitation "—Alison Richards. Nathan's granddaughter. From New York."

"Formerly from New York," Alison qualified with a smile. "Now I'm from Bluff Springs." She offered Steve her hand.

"I was sorry to hear about your grandfather. He was a good friend. A fine man."

"Thank you. He was. And a bit of devil, too, leaving Jess and me half the ranch."

Steve grinned. "I don't think you'll have any trouble selling it. Will she, Jess?"

"But I'm not going to. I've decided to come west instead."

Steve looked surprised. "To live at the ranch?"

Jess was shifting his feet, making impatient tapping noises with the toes of his boots.

Alison smiled. "I didn't realize how much I missed it until I came back for the funeral. And—" she shot a mischievous glance at Jess "—there were other enticements, too."

Steve's brows lifted.

"You can waste time chatting if you want," Jess said abruptly. "I got work to do." He turned to Steve. "You come over when you're finished socializing, and I'll show you how I want the cattle sorted and shaped up."

Without giving Steve a chance to answer, he turned on his heel and stalked off.

"Been working hard, has he?" Steve asked her as he watched Jess leave.

Alison sighed. "Oh, yes."

Steve slanted a glance in her direction. "I guess I ought to be, too," He hesitated. "Are you... spoken for?"

"I beg your pardon."

"You're not married? I didn't think you were, but enough women keep their maiden names these days that a guy can't be sure." He gave her a disarming grin.

"I'm not married."

"But that doesn't mean you don't have somebody interested. Jess, for example?" The brows lifted again.

"He says not," Alison admitted, which was putting it mildly.

"He ought to have his head examined," Steve said. "But—" he grinned "—all the better for me, I guess. Would you join me for the afternoon, then? Once we get work taken care of, I'll show you some of the bright spots of Denver."

"Thank you. I'd like that."

Why not? Steve Sudmeier seemed a nice man. And there was no point in sitting in her hotel room and pining away while Jess was out having a good time.

She might have her fantasies, but she wasn't a total fool.

IT WAS WORKING. He could handle it.

If he mentally stuck Nathan's bushy white eyebrows and thinning hair on her, padded her with thirty-five pounds and imagined she was eighty-two, it was a piece of cake.

If he talked business, speculated on prices, discussed bulls' bloodlines and the cost of feed, it was no problem at all.

Jess was feeling positively cocky by the time they got back to the hotel.

"We don't have to meet Mal and Sam for dinner this noon," he told Alison as they boarded the elevator together. "There's a good French place about half a mile from here. I'll take you to Henri's," he offered, pleased at his own ability to cope.

"Oh," she said, a tiny frown creasing her forehead. "I'm really sorry. I can't. I have a date with Steve."

"The commission man?" He should've moderated his tone a little bit. The other people in the elevator were looking at him.

"He said we'd have the afternoon free. Don't we?"

"Sure. Of course we do," he said, his tone clipped. He shoved his fingers through his hair. "Do what you want."

The doors opened on their floor. They walked down the hall together in silence, halting when they got to her room.

"I'm sorry."

"No problem. Have a good time," he managed.

Alison gave him a bright smile as she went into her room. "I'm sure I will. You have a nice day, too."

Yeah, right, Jess thought.

And how in hell was he supposed to have a nice day thinking about her going out with Steve Studly?

Chapter Seven

He had time on his hands.

He should've told Sam and Mal he'd take them up on that extra ticket to the Broncos' game. It would have been a far better way to spend the afternoon than sitting around his hotel room wondering what Alison was doing with Sudmeier.

What was so great about Sudmeier, anyway?

Sure he was good-looking and he had that toothpaste-commercial smile. But he wore a suit with his cowboy boots, for crying out loud. And his hatband looked like he never sweated at all.

Probably didn't, Jess thought glumly. And that was probably the attraction.

He ought to be glad. Alison was hankering after big-city men already. If that was true, she wasn't really all that serious about digging in at the Rocking R.

He ought to have hope.

Telling himself that, he decided to go look up the only person he knew who lived in Denver. His sister Lizzie.

He and Lizzie weren't what you'd call close. There was nothing "Leave It To Beaver"-ish about the family he'd grown up in. He'd thought "Father Knows Best" was a joke.

Les Cooper had always been on the move, trekking from one rodeo to another, one dead-end job to another, one unemployment line to another, while Jess's mother tried to keep the home fires burning. She hadn't had much success.

After his mother died and his grandmother had taken them in, Jess and Lizzie had spent even less time together. Lizzie, at thirteen, had better things to do than hang around her kid brother. She'd had dreams clear back then, and Jess had already seen the harm such dreams could do.

If they'd had little in common growing up, they'd had even less the last time he'd seen her.

That had been two years ago when he and Nathan had come to Denver for the sale.

He'd been out on the town with Sam and a couple of other guys, making the rounds of a variety of country-western bars, and to his amazement, Lizzie had been singing in one of them.

She'd cut her hair and lost weight. Her eyes were enormous. She looked like one of those paintings on velvet that Jess sometimes saw in pawn shop windows.

He'd waited for her afterward to drive her home, but she'd refused. "Tom comes to get me."

"Who's Tom?" It had been Hank, last he knew.

"My one true love. He writes gorgeous songs. They make me want to cry." She'd looked at Jess with her brown eyes sparkling. He remembered Hank as her one true love. Or had it been Danny?

"He living with you?" Jess had asked her.

"Of course."

"You marry him?" He hadn't known whether to hope she had or not.

"Marriage isn't important, Jess," she'd said, tossing her head defiantly. "Love is what matters. And Tom loves me. He says he can get me an audition in Nashville. Wouldn't that be super, Jess?"

"Super," he'd echoed, but Lizzie wouldn't hear the skepticism in his voice.

"Tell you what, sweetie," Lizzie'd patted his cheek. "You come around tomorrow and we'll have a good ol' sister-brother chat." She scribbled an address on a piece of paper.

So Jess had come around. He'd found her tiny duplex, had climbed rickety steps to ring the bell, then had shifted impatiently from one foot to the other. He was about to leave, pretty sure she'd forgotten or was avoiding him, when he saw a curtain twitch.

Moments later the door opened. A little girl looked out. "Who're you?" the child asked.

"My name's Jess. Is your mother here?"

"She's sleepin'. Are you her brother? She said you might come. You can come in. I'm Sue. I'm four." The girl stuck out her hand. Solemnly Jess shook it and followed her into the sparsely furnished living room.

A few moments later a sleepy, disheveled Lizzie had appeared. "Oh, it's you."

Lizzie had wanted to know what he was doing, and when he told her, she'd told him he ought to go back to rodeoing.

"I like what I'm doin'."

She'd looked at him long and hard. Then, at last she'd shrugged. "Livin' in one place, chasin' little critters all day? You're a strange one, Jess," she told him, but she was smiling. "You always have been."

"No stranger than you," he'd countered with a grin.

"I'm gonna get there," Lizzie had told him stubbornly. "I believe, Jess. I'll make it. You just see if I don't."

Jess had smiled faintly and stood up, moving toward the door. "Good luck to you."

His eyes had flicked from his sister, with her bloodshot eyes and smoke-roughened voice to the school photo of Lizzie's older girls stuck on the refrigerator, then to Sue who still hadn't taken her eyes off him. "Good luck to all of you."

It was probably a mistake to go back to see her again this afternoon.

Still, what else did he have to do? And if he ever got tempted to actually think marrying Alison was a good idea, seeing Lizzie ought to go a long way toward curing him of that.

There was a fresh coat of paint on the duplex when he got there. Someone had repaired the front steps. He felt a faint flickering of hope as he rang the bell.

The door opened and tall thin man looked out. Tom? Jess wondered. Or his replacement.

"I'm looking for Lizzie Cooper," Jess said.

"Don't know no Lizzie Cooper."

"She doesn't live here?"

"Nope. We been here a year. Don't know who was before that. Guess you could ask the landlady." He jerked his head toward the other side of the building.

But the landlady didn't know anything, either.

"Lizzie Cooper? She moved well over a year and a half ago. She an' the kiddies. Went east, I think. Nashville, maybe?"

"Probably." Jess gave her a ghost of a smile. "Yeah, I reckon it was. Did she leave a forwarding address?"

The woman shook her head. "Nothin' to be forwarded." She looked him up and down. "You the father of one of them kiddies?"

"No. I'm her brother. I just came up from Bluff Springs for a cattle sale, thought I'd look her up."

"Wish I could help you, but she's long gone now."

"Thanks." Jess settled his hat back on his head and made his way back down the steps.

He shouldn't have been surprised. Moving on had always been a habit with Lizzie. And every move, she hoped, would bring her one step closer to her dream.

For her sake—and that of her kids—Jess hoped it had, too.

He got into the truck and drove back to the hotel. He tried not to wonder where Alison was. At least there was football on television.

IT WAS THE DAY of Alison's dreams—lunch at one of the restaurants in the Larimer Square area, a leisurely wander through the historic district and around the botanic gardens, followed by an elegant dinner at the Brown Palace with a handsome, charming, witty man.

The wrong man.

It wasn't fair, Alison thought as Steve brought her back to the hotel that evening. He was better educated, more loquacious, tons more charming and at least as good-looking as Jess Cooper. It shouldn't have been a contest.

And it wasn't—because he wasn't Jess.

"You're very quiet," Steve said as he escorted her to her room.

"I'm tired. It's been a long day. But a very pleasant one."

"I hope we can do it again."

"I'm not likely to be in Denver again. Until next year."

"Maybe I can persuade you. Or—" he shrugged "—maybe I can come out your way."

Steve followed her to the door of her room, his hand still holding hers.

Alison smiled. "Thank you very much for a lovely day." She raised her hand and touched the front of his jacket, just as his lips began to come down.

"I don't think—" she began softly.

"Ah, good, you're back." Jess's voice sounded louder than she'd ever heard it. Steve's nose collided with hers as Jess slapped him on the back.

"Have a good time?" he asked cheerfully.

Steve rubbed his nose, stepping back. "Just fine, thanks."

"Too bad you can't hang around any longer. Alison and I have business to discuss."

"Business?" Alison and Steve said in unison.

"We are partners, aren't we?" Jess looked right at her.

Alison smiled slightly. "Yes."

"Then we have business to discuss." He put a hand on her arm.

"I can go down to the bar and have a drink until you're through," Steve suggested.

Alison felt Jess's hand clench against her arm.

She turned a smile on Steve. "Thanks very much, but I really am tired. I'll see you tomorrow."

Steve grinned. "Count on it."

Jess hauled her down the hall and into his room before she could say another word.

The door banged shut behind them. "Don't you know better than to encourage guys like him?"

"Encourage? Guys like him?" Alison stared at him, then started to laugh. "You're . . . are you jealous, Jess?"

He was pacing back and forth, but her question stopped him dead. "Of course not!"

"Well, then . . ." She spread her hands, still smiling.

"It's damned near eleven o'clock!"

She looked at him wide-eyed. "I have a curfew?"

"You were gone hours!"

"If you're not jealous, what do you care?"

"We're partners, as you're forever reminding me. What if something had happened to . . . to the cattle?"

"The *cattle?*" Alison did laugh then. "Like they all ran away or something?"

He glared. "You know what I mean."

"Ah, Jess." She crossed the room and put her arms around him, felt him tense as her hands locked against the small of his back. She touched her lips to his. "Yes. I know what you mean," she said softly.

"Damn it, Alison."

Her tongue ran lightly along his upper lip, then teasingly dipped into his mouth. Her lips rubbed gently, tantalizingly against his. "Hmm?"

He started to say something, then stopped, unable to speak and kiss at the same time. And he was kissing her. It was no longer a one-way street. Alison could feel the need in him, the hard press of desire.

And then he was pushing her away, taking deep lungfuls of air, shoving his fingers through his hair. "Cripes! That's exactly what I mean."

She looked at him perplexed. "What's what you mean?"

"Why we can't work together! Blast Nathan anyway!" Jess slammed his hand against the door. "I don't know why he ever— What the devil could he have been thinking of, saddling me with you?"

"I don't know, Jess," Alison said quietly. "What do you think he was thinking?"

The words fell into the silence and stopped him dead.

Their gazes met. Jess seemed to halt, mid-glare. And as she watched, Alison saw his expression undergo a subtle change, from anger to awareness to confusion. He sighed and jammed his hands into his pockets. He scuffed his toe on the rug.

"That manipulating son-of-a-gun." He looked at Alison, his gaze stubborn. "It won't work," he said.

But Alison wasn't so sure about that.

IF FOR MOST PEOPLE a good defense was a good offense, mending fence seemed to Jess the best defense of all.

He set out the morning after they got home.

"I'll be gone all day," he told Alison. "But I'll be in tonight to move out my gear."

"That is ridiculous." She was standing at the sink, cutting a grapefruit, still wearing her bathrobe, her hair tousled and tempting.

Jess knew it wasn't ridiculous at all. And if he didn't, seeing her in her robe, knowing how little must be under it, would have proved it to him. "Think what you like."

"I feel as if I'm driving you out," she complained.

"You are."

"Thanks very much."

"You're welcome." He started back out the door.

"Don't you want some breakfast?"

"I'll be fine."

"You'll die from hunger before noon if you don't eat something. You ate with Pops, didn't you?"

"Sometimes."

"How many times?"

He scowled. "Most of the time."

She smiled and held out half a grapefruit. "Then you can eat with me. We're partners, remember?"

Jess didn't see how he was supposed to forget.

He did his best. He stayed away at noon. He kept busy all day. There was always something to do.

And while he was gone, he pretended that nothing had changed. He imagined Nathan back at the house, puttering around, reading the livestock journals, making his soup.

He didn't let himself think about Alison.

Much.

When he did, he tried convincing himself that she'd get bored, find ranch life confining, hanker after big-city lights and yearn for all the things she'd left behind in New York.

Maybe when he got back this evening, she'd have seen how ridiculous her ranching notion was. There'd be nobody to talk to, no books to check out, no magazines to catalog. Maybe she'd have gone stir crazy in one afternoon.

Maybe she'd have her bags packed and her cat under her arm and be waiting for him to come back, so she could offer to sell out.

THE MOVERS BROUGHT all Alison's worldly goods later that morning. She had, in the course of following her father's career all over the world, become used to traveling light. But she had learned long ago that, while most things didn't matter, it was helpful to have a few favorite things to carry along, to provide continuity, to make a house seem like a home.

Consequently she was delighted when the big white van trundled up the road and left fifteen large packing containers and her few beloved pieces of furniture on the porch.

"You sure you don't want us to move 'em in, lady?" the mover asked her. "It's part of the deal."

But Alison shook her head, signing the receipt and handing it back. "I don't know where I want them yet. I have to make room."

There was considerable cleaning and weeding out to do. While Jess had kept the rooms painted and fresh, the furniture had seen better days, the oilcloth and the curtains all had been washed more often than they'd had any right to expect, and Nathan's tendency to save everything gave the house a more-than-lived-in look.

Alison had her work cut out for her.

The mover tucked the receipt in his pocket and gave her a smile. "Good luck, then."

Alison, standing on the porch with Kitten weaving between her legs, watched him drive away and knew she would need it.

As the dust from the van finally settled and the sound of the heavy-duty engine no longer reverberated in her ears, she knew that there was no going back.

"Come on," she said to Kitten, "we've got work to do."

She didn't know whether to expect Jess for noon dinner or not.

He'd eaten the grapefruit and the oatmeal she'd forced on him. He'd grabbed a couple of apples and some carrots from the refrigerator without comment. He'd said, "See you," as he'd stuffed them in a saddlebag, and he'd gone out the door without looking back.

Probably she should have asked. She hadn't dared.

She'd pushed Jess just about as far as she could. Any more and he would bolt, she was certain.

So for the time being she would handle him the way she'd seen Pops handle a skittish horse—taking things easy, moving slowly, letting him get used to her.

"You don't 'break' horses," Pops told her. "You gentle 'em."

Alison figured the same would be true of Jess.

So she hadn't asked and now didn't know if she should fix anything or not.

Better to err on the side of preparation, she decided. So she made a stew and baking powder biscuits, fixed a fresh lettuce salad, then took some corn on the cob out of the freezer and put water to boil it in on the stove.

Then while the water heated, she carried a couple of her boxes of books into the living room and set about finding them shelf space.

At two o'clock she ate the stew and salad alone. Then she went out to the barn and fed the biscuits to the Belgians that would pull the hay wagon when the tractor couldn't handle the snow. The boiling water sat cooling on the stove awaiting supper. The corn she put in the refrigerator.

After she ate, she unpacked her stereo. It was nothing compared to the high-tech quality of Peter's, but it was far superior to the tinny radio she found in Pops's kitchen. Then she uncovered the box in which she'd shipped her tapes and CDs, and before long she was wrapped in music to suit her mood.

She spent the afternoon weeding through Nathan's bookshelves, getting rid of old stock guides and yellowing issues of long-defunct magazines, accompanied first by soft rock, then by a reggae beat. She scrubbed and dusted, waxed and polished, then, humming and tapping her feet, she shelved her books alongside Nathan's own.

She stopped in the middle to stretch her back and run up and down the stairs. She used to do it in her brownstone every evening after work, for exercise. She had no doubt that she'd get lots more real exercise out here, but it didn't look as if she'd get it this afternoon. So she started on the first floor, ran up to the second floor and the attic, then went down again clear to the cellar.

That was where she discovered the shelves of home-canned fruits and vegetables. She recalled Ella having kept similar shelves, but she hadn't imagined Nathan and Jess canning anything. A little further snooping revealed that they hadn't.

The jars all had neat little labels with kitty cats or rainbows on them, and they all said, "Made Especially for You by Cathy Lee Parsons" or "From the Kitchen of Mabel Kirby" or "Yummies by Diana Lee."

Obviously Nathan and Jess hadn't starved.

On her last trip down, Alison plucked off a jar of Mabel Kirby's peaches for a pie.

The pie was sitting on the counter cooling, the leftover stew was simmering once again and fresh water was boiling for the corn, and Alison was wondering whether she'd be eating supper alone, too, when at last she heard the screen door to the porch bang shut.

In the midst of returning the last pile of books to the shelves, she stayed right where she was. She would take her cue from Jess.

He appeared in the doorway between the kitchen and the living room a few minutes later, his face freshly scrubbed, his hair still damp. His gaze found her where she sat cross-legged in front of the bookcase, a book on equine diseases in her hand.

She smiled up at him. "I'm just putting away some books. My stuff arrived today."

"So I see." He didn't sound thrilled.

"I thought I'd move in slowly, sorting things out as I go."

"Suit yourself. It's your house."

"It's also half yours."

"In name maybe. I won't be here." He shoved his hands into his pockets.

"I still think you're crazy."

He just looked at her, long enough and hard enough to make her squirm. "Crazier to stay in here," he said gruffly and turned to go back into the kitchen. She scrambled to her feet and followed him.

"I won't jump your bones if that's what you're worried about, Jess."

He shot her a dark look over his shoulder. "It's not."

"Then what is?"

"That I might jump yours."

She felt heat surge into her face. "Such a compliment."

"Not a compliment. A statement of fact."

"But you're interested—" she began hopefully.

He cut her off. "In sex. I'm interested in sex. Not marriage." He gave her a sardonic smile. "So unless you want sex with no strings attached, you won't mind me moving, will you?"

She hated his sarcasm. It wasn't like him, not the way she remembered him, not the way she'd dreamed him.

Her fists clenched, but she moderated her tone. "Well, if you can't control yourself..." she said lightly, giving him a playful smile, trying to make him smile, too.

He didn't. "Want to find out?"

She swallowed. "Not if it's only sex, Jess. No."

"Well, it is. So if you want this 'partnership'—" his voice gave the word a bitterly ironic twist "—to work, you'd better be glad I'm going." That said, he turned away and lifted the lid on the stew pot. "Smells good."

Alison, staring at him, realized that the discussion, as far as he was concerned, was finished.

Her heart was still pounding, her fists still clenching and unclenching. Deliberately she made an effort to steady herself, to tell herself that he was still running scared, that she had to wait him out, let him relax around her before she did anything else.

She smoothed her hands down the sides of her jeans. "Are you hungry?"

"Starved," he said and began ladling the stew onto his plate.

He didn't seem to be exaggerating by much, either, Alison thought as she watched him eat.

She had only a small helping of the stew. He finished it off. She ate an ear of corn. He ate three and looked hopefully around for more. He made short work of the salad and finished up with several slices of bread and butter. Through it all he never said a word. She wondered if he was still angry, but he didn't seem to be.

After he'd finished with third helpings and she got up to bring the pie to the table, she ventured, "You weren't kidding, were you?"

He was as lean as he had been twelve years ago. There wasn't a spare ounce of fat on him anywhere. Gary had to work out constantly and eat sparingly or in weeks he'd sport a spare tire.

Jess looked faintly embarrassed. "You're a good cook. And . . . apples don't go too far."

"You could have come home for dinner."

"I was clear up in the top meadow," he said gruffly. "A waste of time comin' all the way down." He frowned. "Did you fix dinner?"

"I had the stew ready then. And the salad. Also biscuits."

He looked around hopefully. "Biscuits?"

"I fed them to the horses."

"A whole pan of biscuits?" Jess stared at her, horrified.

"I don't think it will hurt them," Alison said quickly.

"Not them. Me. How could you get rid of them like that? A whole pan," he muttered, dismayed.

"Biscuits aren't good cold." She cut a large wedge of pie and set it in front of him.

"I'll take 'em any way I can get 'em."

"You sound as if you've been starved for weeks." She gave him an arch look.

He looked up, still chewing. "Nathan brag about his cooking, did he?"

"No. I didn't mean Pops. I found all those jars in the cellar from Mabel Kirby and . . . and Diana somebody—"

"Lee," he offered helpfully.

"—and Cathy Parsons and, for all I know, Betty Boop!"

He grinned. "Nathan had quite a fan club."

"I don't suppose it was Nathan they were trying to impress," she said irritably. Then, because she couldn't help herself, she asked, "Are they part of the 'no strings attached' brigade?"

Jess grinned. "Not Mabel Kirby. She's attached to Frank."

Which didn't answer Alison's question about the other two. She got up, turned her back and began scrubbing the plates fast and furiously.

She didn't want to feel this shaft of pure jealous rage, but she couldn't help it. She had no doubt that whatever interest Jess had in them, it went no further than his interest in her. But even that knowledge didn't help.

"Aren't you gonna have a piece of this pie?" he asked her. "It's good."

"I'm not hungry. I'll get fat eating this much every day."

"A body's got to eat. This isn't library work, you know. D'you miss it?"

"No. But I've only been away from it a week. Why?"

He shrugged. "A man can hope."

"You're not getting rid of me. I'm here to stay." Alison sat down opposite him again. "Speaking of which, we need to talk about a fair division of labor."

"I suppose you're gonna herd cattle now?"

"I don't know. You tell me." She looked at him hopefully.

He scowled. "I told you to go back to New York. Look how much good that did."

Alison dismissed that. "You should be getting a salary for what you're doing. I know Nathan paid you for your work around here, and now you're doing it for nothing."

"I own half the ranch," he reminded her. "Anyway, I didn't get paid much in money. I took most of it in cattle. A fair bit of that herd is mine."

"So I don't really own half."

"You own half of the property and half of about two thirds of the herd. I should be paying you rent for pasture."

"Don't be silly."

He lifted one brow. "Weren't you?"

"I just don't want to take advantage, Jess. I know Nathan cooked, and I can do that. But what else do you want me to do?"

He hesitated, a faint flush crept into his face. He looked away.

"He kept the books and made notes," Jess said after a moment, a rough edge to his voice. He nodded toward a file cabinet in the corner of the kitchen. "It's all in there. Not that he needed to refer to it. He had it all up here." He tapped his head, then sighed. "Helps when you're deciding which to keep and which to sell. How many calves they've had, how those calves have done. He was a master at that. You can go through the files. See if you can make heads or tails of 'em."

"I'll put them on computer."

"Computer? Why?"

"It's a wonderful analytical tool. It can make all kinds of comparisons."

Jess grunted doubtfully.

"Come help me unpack it," Alison suggested, "and I'll show you how to use it." And maybe that way he would see that she could be of some use. Maybe that way he'd begin to get used to her.

"Can't. I got work to do."

"It's dark."

"Not field work. Movin'."

LATER THAT NIGHT, after he'd moved, she had unpacked the computer by herself. She set it up in the living room and entered the first file. Then she shut off the light and climbed the stairs to go to bed.

But instead of going into Nathan's room, she turned the other way, going into her old bedroom. The room that Jess had just moved out of.

From the window she looked out over the yard, across to the barn, the shed, the bunkhouse.

There was no light now. He was asleep, just as he had been asleep twelve years ago when she'd stood here, a young and dreamy teenager, staring down at the place where she knew Jess lay.

Then she had wanted to lie with him, to sleep with him, to love him and to wake up in his arms.

She wanted that still.

He wanted it, too. Tonight he'd said so in no uncertain terms.

The problem was, for him that would be the answer to everything; for her it would never be enough.

Chapter Eight

She was getting under his skin. It was harder every day to pretend that nothing had changed.

Oh, the thick dark greens of pine and spruce stayed the same. The aspens turned ivory and gray as they did every year. Barbed wire was barbed wire, any way you looked at it. The cattle still took up most of Jess's time.

But at night when he came in for supper, Alison was there.

Changes were being made. She interspersed the beef and potatoes that he was used to with chicken stir-fries and hearty French stews. When he came in at night the house was redolent with a variety of exotic and enticing smells.

The wide pine plank floors were waxed until they shone. She uncovered a pair of Navajo rugs in the attic, aired them and spread them on the living room floor.

Pictures appeared one by one, in the living room and up the stairs into the hall. Some were photos of her parents and grandparents, her brothers and herself. But one day he was startled to see the photo of himself and Nathan framed and hanging alongside her parents' anniversary photo.

Another day he came home to find she'd been digging through Nathan's clippings and had found several about Jess's rodeo career. Jess winced, watching her pore over them. The next day he hoped to find them in the trash. Instead they were framed and on the wall in his former bedroom. Alison took him by the hand and dragged him up to see.

"It's a memorial," Alison told him cheekily and dug her fingers into her ribs. "All I have of you until you come to your senses and move home."

"I am home," Jess told her gruffly.

She laughed and ruffled his hair.

He could still feel the touch of her fingers that night when he went to bed.

She hung art prints, as well. Alison's taste was more eclectic than Nathan's Kentucky Derby winners. It ran to R.C. Gorman prints and others of sailboats and tropical-looking stuff that Jess thought she said were done by someone called Homer Winslow.

Jess thought it was an improvement, but he didn't tell her.

He didn't comment at all. Not when the prints went up, not when the floors got shiny, not when new yellow gingham curtains and place mats appeared in the kitchen and the oilcloth disappeared.

But he noticed, and at night he lay in the bunkhouse and touched his hair, remembering her fingers there, touched his mouth and remembered her lips.

It was like being tortured.

All he could do was hope that when she finished the house, she'd get bored and restless, and decide she'd had enough.

She got a job.

"A job? Where?" he demanded. She'd sprung it on him in the middle of the meal. He had his mouth full, and he almost choked demanding an explanation.

"Not full-time," she said patiently. "Just three afternoons a week. I'm helping set up a library in town. We're taking book donations to start it. I'm donating a lot of Nathan's, a lot of the fiction, a little of the husbandry and some of the stud books and magazines, too. If you don't mind," she added quickly.

"Me? Why should I?" She could donate any damned thing she pleased, including her time, if she'd just leave.

"They're half yours," she reminded him. "We're partners."

He shut his eyes.

He didn't see how he was going to make it. He was so damnably aware of her. And day after day, week after week, the awareness didn't go away.

It grew.

He sat in the kitchen eating supper as quickly as he could, knowing he needed to get out of there, if he was going to keep from touching her, kissing her. It didn't keep her from touching him.

Nothing blatant. Nothing he could take and hold up and say, "You're coming on to me!" making it an accusation. And maybe, he conceded, she wasn't. Not intentionally.

But it was happening nonetheless.

The casual touch on his arm when she wanted to show him something. The way they seemed to always end up passing each other in narrow doorways, so that her hair brushed his shoulder or her breasts brushed his chest. It was enough to drive a man to drink.

So was the way she could provoke him with a mere comment. She said the damnedest things.

Tonight, for instance. It was Wednesday. Alison had gone into town to spend the afternoon helping with the fledgling library and then picking up some new curtain rods. Jess had agreed to mount them after supper.

He was standing on the counter, with his back to her, screwing the rod into the wall, grateful that there could be no accidental physical encounters here, when she said, "We got an unusual donation for the library today."

"Mmm." He didn't turn around.

"All about men's buns."

The screwdriver slipped and gouged into the wood.

"It was quite interesting," Alison went on conversationally. "There was the usual, the swimsuit sort of thing, and underwear, of course. Slacks don't do much for a man, you know. But jeans—" there was a pleasurable sigh coming from the other side of the room, moving closer "—some of them were pretty impressive."

"Al-i-son," through gritted teeth.

"Not as good as yours, though."

He heard the teasing lilt in her voice. He tried not to react. It was like trying not to breathe. His whole body tightened—notably, among others, the part he was sure she was studying. He fitted the screwdriver back into the screw and gave it a savage turn.

"You're especially nice in chaps," she went on. She was so close he would swear he could feel the heat of her breath against the back of his leg.

"We're thinking of having a money-raising benefit to get the library off the ground. Cathy Parsons suggested we take our own set of local photos like the ones in the book, then auction them off. What do you think? Want to be my model?"

He glared down at her. She was standing right below him, her hands on the counter, looking up and grinning her head off.

He stepped on her hand.

"Jess!" she howled. She tried to yank her hand away, catching his pants hem, twisting and pulling.

"Damn!" He turned, slipped, then skidded, and landed hard on the floor facing her, breathing hard. Their noses were scant inches apart. He clamped his jaw shut. His fists clenched.

"I suppose you're going to say no," Alison said after a moment.

It was the last straw.

He grabbed her forearms and held her so they were almost nose to nose. They didn't touch.

"What do you want from me, Alison?" he demanded. "Just what the hell do you want?"

He hoped his fury would scare her. He hoped she would back off, say, "Nothing," shrink away.

She didn't move, didn't even seem to be breathing hard, though her pupils were dilated and her eyes had never seemed so blue. She was so close he could even smell the lemony scent of her shampoo. She just looked at him, her gaze steady. That was bad enough.

It was worse when she smiled. It was a sweet smile, a wistful smile, a gentle smile that he was sure would undo the best intentions of any man who didn't run from it.

"You don't have to ask, Jess," she said in a voice as gentle as her smile. "You know."

SHE'D JUMPED the gun.

She'd pushed too hard and sent him running in a panic. Jess had bolted the house after their encounter last night, and had taken off in the truck, spraying gravel every which way. And, though she'd stayed awake until two, she never heard him come back.

She'd spent the evening cursing her tendency to overplay her hand.

"Slow and easy," Pops used to say. "Slow and easy."

She should have known better. She must've been behind the door when patience was passed out.

But, damn it, she'd had enough.

For days she'd felt him watching her every move, and not with antipathy, but with awareness. She'd seen brief flickerings of desire in his eyes when they'd passed too closely in the hall, had heard the quickening of his breath the evening she'd shown him the clippings she'd framed and hung in the bedroom.

She knew he wanted her. She knew he liked her. She suspected sometimes that what he felt even went beyond liking.

But he never gave in.

He hedged, he stonewalled, he ran.

She was at the end of her rope.

He didn't come in for breakfast. She went out to the barn and found him saddling Dodger. He looked hollow-eyed and miserable, with bloodshot eyes and unshaven cheeks.

"I suppose you're not hungry," she said.

He glanced at her. "I'd barf."

"Found too much solace in the bottle, did you?"

He looked at her, his expression haunted. "Too much bottle and not enough solace." His voice was rough. He finished saddling Dodger and brushed past her, leading the horse out of the barn.

She followed him. "We're two human beings, Jess. We have needs, feelings."

His mouth twisted. "You do. Not me."

"No feelings? No needs?"

He swung into the saddle and sat looking down at her. His jaw was tight. "None I can't handle if you let me be."

"Oh, Jess."

"Oh, Jess," he mocked. "Don't push me, Ali. We're partners. No more, no less."

DINNER WAS an awkward meal. Jess was quiet. Alison was hurt. She didn't believe his protestations, was certain he felt more than he said; but his words were painful nonetheless.

And though she knew she would challenge him in time, she didn't feel tough enough to tackle him over them yet. They ate in silence, Jess hurrying, though whether it was to get into town to get the welding done, as he said, or whether it was simply to get away from her, Alison didn't know.

He was putting on his jacket when she said, "I hesitate to ask you, but there are a few things I forgot yesterday at the grocery store."

"Of course I'll get them."

"I wasn't sure you'd want to be bothered."

Jess's jaw tightened. "Don't be stupid, Ali. We're—"

"Partners," Alison finished for him dryly. "Yes, I know." Their eyes met and held.

There was no telling how long they might have simply stayed looking at each other, no telling where the discussion might have gone from there, for at that moment they heard a car coming up the road.

Jess looked at her quizzically. Alison shrugged. He pushed back his chair, going to the door to see who it was.

"A friend coming for tea?" he said archly. "Or perhaps more 'interesting' donations for the library."

Alison, dishing up blueberry cobbler, joined him at the door. "No one I know."

"A tourist, then," Jess said, opening the door. "Little late in the year for fall color now." It was the first week in November, and they'd already had several light dustings of snow.

The car door opened and a woman got out.

Alison thought she was about her own age, with an ash-blonde pageboy haircut, a neat business suit and high heels. Not common attire among visitors to the Rocking R.

Jess went out on the step to meet her. "You lost? Can I help you?"

"Mr. Cooper? Jess Cooper?"

He looked surprised. "Yes, ma'am."

She smiled. "Then I'm not lost. I'm Felicia Darrow from the Department of Social Services. You're Elizabeth Cooper's brother?"

Jess nodded warily. "Lizzie? Yeah. What's she done?"

The woman gave him a sad, sympathetic smile. "She hasn't done anything, Mr. Cooper. But I'm afraid I have to tell you—" she hesitated, then plunged in baldly "—she's dead."

The color drained from Jess's face. He took a step back, and Alison found herself holding on to his arm.

"Dead?" The word came out as a croak. "What happened? When?"

"In March."

"Where? How? She wasn't sick?"

"No. She was in Nashville. It was an accident. She must have been preoccupied or something. She was crossing a street against a light..."

She didn't have to say anything more.

Jess didn't speak, simply stood there as if he'd been turned to stone. Yet Alison could feel the rapidly beating pulse in his arm, felt him tense, then quiver as a shudder passed through him.

"What the hell'd she think she was doing?" Jess muttered. "Was she drinking?"

"Not a drop. I gather she was simply euphoric and not paying attention. I understand she'd just been offered a recording contract."

Jess stared. Then, "Jesus Christ," he murmured. It was more prayer than blasphemy, and Alison felt him almost sag against her.

"Lizzie," he muttered. "Damn it, Lizzie..." He turned hard eyes on the social worker. "That was months ago," he protested after a moment. "How come nobody told me before now?"

"We didn't actually find out your whereabouts until last Friday. We'd been looking for several months. One of our regular case workers was doing a follow-up and managed to contact a Mrs. Blodgett, Ms. Cooper's former landlady. She said you'd dropped by looking for Lizzie. She remembered where you were living. And—" Felicia Darrow shrugged and smiled "—here I am."

"Yeah." Jess shook his head, clearly still having trouble comprehending. "Well, thanks. I'm obliged, your comin' all this way just to tell me about her."

"You're welcome." Felicia Darrow smiled again. "But that isn't precisely why I came. It was because of the children, really."

"The children? Oh. Yeah." He straightened up, running a hand through his hair. "Lizzie's kids. Who's takin' care of Lizzie's kids?"

"It seems," said Felicia Darrow, "that you are."

THERE WAS NOTHING, Jess found, like inheriting three children to take one's mind off one's loins. Suddenly his preoccupation with Alison seemed the least of his problems.

He walked around in a daze the rest of the day, not going to town, not doing the shopping or getting the welding done, just thinking—or trying to.

But he couldn't make sense of it. Felicia Darrow was like a bad dream who had got back in her car and driven away. By nightfall he had himself almost convinced that he'd hallucinated the whole thing.

He was even seeking out Alison in the hope that she would confirm it. He'd left the house once, right after supper. But sitting down in the bunkhouse by himself, mending tack, had been torture. All he could see in his mind's eye were miniature versions of Lizzie, staring up hopefully at him. All he could imagine is how ill equipped he was to fulfill that hope.

Facing Alison, enduring the temptation of being around her, seemed, for once, preferable.

"She isn't seriously going to show up here tomorrow with the girls, is she?" he asked, coming back into the kitchen.

Alison was sitting at the computer. She'd been typing when he came in, but she stopped now and looked up. "Miss Darrow?" She gave Jess a sympathetic smile. "I think she is."

He raked a hand through his hair. "I can't believe it. What in the hell am I going to do with three girls?"

"Raise them?"

"Me?" He'd said the same thing to Felicia Darrow. "You've got to be kidding," he'd said to her.

But she hadn't been. And when he'd continued to protest, she'd shown him a copy of Lizzie's will. It had been right there in black and white, staring him in the face. Three pages of legalese. But what it boiled down to, in Jess's eyes, was one line: "I leave the custody, care and supervision of my minor children, Patricia, Dorothy and Susan, to my brother, Jess Cooper."

"It doesn't make sense." He'd said it to Felicia Darrow then. He said it again to Alison now.

"She must have thought you were the best person," Alison said.

Jess snorted. "The only one, more likely."

"What about their fathers?" Alison rested her fingers on the keyboard. "She could have named them, couldn't she? But she didn't."

"Those jerks?" Jess felt angry at the very thought. "They never even hung around to see their kids, not one of them! I could do a better job than they could!"

Alison gave him a gentle smile. "Lizzie must've thought so, too."

Jess just stared at her. She was looking at him with such confidence, such faith.

"God!" He dragged his palms across his face. "This is insane. I don't know anything about girls!" He shoved himself up on the counter and banged his heels against the cabinet below.

Alison smiled. "That's not the impression you like to give."

He looked at her sharply, then groaned. "Oh, hell, and I suppose I have to worry about men like me now, too!"

"I suppose you will."

"I think I'm going to throw up."

"A tough guy like you?" she chided gently. "Come on, Jess."

"Three girls? I can't!"

"Sure you can." She hesitated. "I'll help you."

He looked at her suspiciously. "Why?"

"We're partners?" She said the words softly, almost warily. There was a faintly teasing lilt to her voice as if she were throwing his words back in his face, but she seemed serious, too.

He hunched forward, resting his elbows on his forearms, linking his fingers. "Hell."

She got up and he heard her moving toward him. "What do you want to do?"

He gave a short half laugh. "Take off and never look back?"

"Realistically."

"Cripes, I don't know." He shook his head. "All I know right now is that there are only three people in the world I feel more sorry for than for myself—Patsy and Dottie and Sue. I can't imagine getting raised by me."

"You don't think you can do it?"

For just a moment Jess stiffened at the challenge in her tone, then he sagged again.

"I don't know," he said, his voice low. "I just don't know."

"You can do it, Jess," she told him. "Together we can."

Together?

Like a couple, did she mean? Married? Is that what she was getting at?

He tensed. "I'm not getting married!"

Alison stepped back as if she'd been slapped. "Don't be an ass, Jess. Did I ask?"

He rubbed a hand against the back of his neck. "No, of course not. I'm sorry. It's just . . . I don't know. I'm not thinking straight."

"No, you're not." Alison's tone was clipped, and he knew he'd really offended her.

"I'm . . . sorry," he said again. He bowed his head. She was standing scant inches from him. And though, minutes ago, he'd been anxious for her presence, now he wished she'd step back, move away, give him some space. It was too tempting, having her standing there.

He wanted to reach out to her, hold her, have her arms around him, holding him.

He wanted to hang on. Tight.

He didn't dare.

"They're not your problem," he said gruffly at last.

"They're girls, not problems, Jess." Her voice had lost some of its edginess. She sounded gentler. "You've got to believe that, if it's going to work."

"Fine for you to say. You can take the next bus out of here."

She reached out and grabbed his hands, holding them tight, her action and her touch so astonishing him that he looked straight at her. "For the last time, Jess Cooper," she said with steel in her voice, "I am not leaving."

A corner of his mouth twisted. "You must be a glutton for punishment, then."

She shrugged. "Maybe. But I've made up my mind. I have no intention of leaving. Especially now. From what I gather, your nieces have had a pretty rough year. They're going to need some stability and security. I can help you try to give them that."

"Yeah? And when you get fed up? When you decide it's time to—"

"Don't say it, Jess."

He sighed, said a rude word, chewed his lip. "Okay." He lifted his eyes and met hers. "But how?"

"By getting involved with them, by caring about them and showing them that you do. That *we* do. By making them feel like they belong."

"And that's gonna be enough?"

"It's a start."

Jess bent his head, looked at her hands holding his, thought about his past, about the way he'd envisioned his future. He thought about Alison, all that was sweet and warm and womanly, thought about those three little girls he didn't even know. He thought of a million potential disasters that lay ahead. He understood better than he ever had the old adage about being damned if he did and damned if he didn't.

"What if we blow it?" he said. "What if *I* blow it?"

"I thought cowboys believed in 'try,' Jess. Is it better not to try?"

"This isn't bronc ridin', for cripe's sake!"

Alison shook her head. "No." Her hands were still clasping his, her thumbs rubbing gently along his wrist bones. Her touch was undermining him, lessening very reasonable fears.

"I've never—"

"They need you, Jess."

He shut his eyes. His fingers tightened around hers. But what about what *he* needed? Had anyone ever thought about that?

He lifted his gaze and met Alison's. Her eyes were warm and blue and very bright.

He sighed. "Maybe you're right."

SHORTLY BEFORE NOON he saw Felicia Darrow's car barreling up the road. Jess held his breath for a split second, hoping against hope that she'd be alone.

She wasn't. She pulled up next to the gate, shut off the engine and got out.

Slowly the other car doors opened, too.

Lizzie's daughters got out, looked around, saw him, hesitated. Then the tallest took the hand of the youngest and the three came toward him.

He remembered the littlest one, though she was taller now. The other two had been only faces in photographs the last time he'd seen them and scarcely more than toddlers the time before that. The oldest, he was startled to note, was almost a woman.

Felicia Darrow came with them.

"This," she said briskly as they reached him, "is your uncle Jess. Mr. Cooper, these are your nieces. Pasty," she nodded to the eldest, who looked at him in unsmiling assessment, "Dottie—" the middle one seemed to be eyeing him with frank curiosity and perhaps a bit of hope "—and Sue."

They all stared at him.

Jess stared back, hoping desperately to find some rush of family feeling, something that would make these girls less than total strangers to him. He felt, except for a surging sense of panic, curiously blank. His fingers clenched and unclenched, wrapped suddenly in other fingers, warm and supportive. Alison's. He hung on.

"Sue," he said, looking at the littlest one. He found his voice a bit rusty, "Remember me?"

Dark hair swung back and forth emphatically. "Nope."

"I'm sure you'll make lots of new memories," Felicia Darrow said optimistically, turning toward the car. "Go get your things out of the car, girls. They don't have a lot," Felicia Darrow confided to Jess and Alison. "They've moved around so much, poor dears. It's been so hard on them."

"I'll help you," he heard Alison say, and he felt her fingers give his own a brief squeeze before letting him go. She followed the girls toward the car.

Felicia Darrow laid her hand on his arm. Probably, he thought, because she must have sensed he was ready to bolt. "I know you haven't had much time to prepare, Mr. Cooper, but—" she smiled earnestly "—believe me, it wouldn't be easy if you had a month."

He rubbed a hand against the back of his neck. "I guess," he muttered.

"They're lovely girls. I've enjoyed knowing them. I know you will, too. You'll do just fine." She fished in her handbag and handed him a card. "If you have problems or questions, feel free to contact me. I'll do whatever I can to help."

Jess stood there, watching helplessly as she moved to say goodbye to the girls, giving them each a handshake and a brief hug. He saw her tell them something that made them look over at him. Then she shook Alison's hand, smiling, and Alison nodded and smiled in return.

When she reached the car, Felicia Darrow turned and gave him a wave. "Bye, Mr. Cooper. Bye, girls. Good luck."

Jess and his nieces looked at each other and knew they were going to need it.

PERHAPS SHE'D BEEN overconfident. Believing that strong, tough, capable Jess could do anything had been a way of life for Alison.

She'd never seen him like this.

Even battered and bloody, after the Brinkmillers had pounded him into the ground, he hadn't had the stunned, desperate expression on his face that Alison saw now.

She shepherded the girls right past him into the kitchen, saying, "You must be hungry. I'll bet you'd like some dinner."

She opened the cupboard, handing down plates. "Here, Dottie, you take these over to the stove. Patsy, you can dish things up. Sue, wash your hands after petting the dog."

The girls, all apparently willing to do something if it meant feeling less awkward, moved to do what she said.

Alison wiped her sweating palms on her jeans, saying, "Help yourself to the milk and start eating. I'll be right back."

Jess hadn't moved an inch. He still stood in the dirt by the fence, looking dazed. When she came up to him, he turned slowly to look at her, but his gaze was unfocused. He looked numb.

"Jess?"

"I can't!"

"Damn it, Jess. Grow up! These girls are depending on you. They need you!"

He shook his head. He was looking at her as if he wasn't even seeing her, as if he were somewhere else altogether.

"Come on, Jess!"

And when he still didn't move, she did the only thing she could think of. She grabbed him, pulled his head down and kissed him. Hard.

If the kiss Jess had given her that night after their dinner at the Hitching Post had awakened her, this one, she hoped, would wake him.

It wasn't a gentle kiss. It didn't seek, nor did it ask. It demanded. Her tongue thrust into his mouth, teasing his, her teeth nipped his lips, her hips pressed into his, and she didn't let up until she felt him respond.

When she stepped back, he was glowering at her, breathing hard. Alison glowered back at him.

"You're playing a dangerous game, Ali," he growled.

She lifted her chin. "This isn't a game, Jess. This is our life. And it's their life now, too. It's time for dinner. Come on."

She turned on her heel and walked back to the house, not waiting, pretending not to see the three faces in the window peering from behind the curtain, pretending not to care if Jess followed or not.

When she got back in the house she found that the girls had arranged themselves around the table where they were eating, whispering quietly among themselves.

She got her own plate and joined them, smiling, crossing her fingers of the hand that lay in her lap. At last she heard the sound of a boot heel on the steps.

When the door opened and Jess entered, the eating stopped.

The girls all looked up, watching, waiting, their eyes on Jess.

Alison tried to look unconcerned as she smiled at him. She got to her feet and moved toward the stove where she dished up his food.

He hesitated in the doorway, then sat down. She put his plate on the table in front of him. He picked up his fork, but he didn't eat.

Slowly he lifted his gaze and looked from one girl to another. "I'm sorry about your mother." His voice was low and ragged, as agonized as Alison had ever heard. She hated herself for having forced him, even though she knew she could have done nothing else.

Patsy met his gaze, then nodded solemnly. "Thanks."

Jess swallowed, then went on, "I don't have a clue about raising kids, which I suppose I probably shouldn't admit." He shrugged. "I reckon you'll find it out soon enough," he added with a ghost of a grin. "So we'll just have to do the best we can. You guys, er, girls, and me."

Sue nodded her head, hair flopping in her eyes which went from him to the woman at the other end of the table. "And Alison," she said with a little smile.

Jess's gaze lifted and met Alison's for a long moment. She still ached from their kiss. She wondered if he did. His expression gave nothing away.

"Yeah," he said quietly. "And Alison."

HE WAS A COWARD and he knew it.

Bu he couldn't hang around. He got through dinner because there was food to eat, an excuse not to talk, something to do with his hands. The moment the meal was over, he was on his feet and moving.

"I'm off for town," he said quickly, heading toward the door. "I got that welding to see to and all."

"Today?" Alison was staring at him as if he'd grown another head.

He jammed his hat on his head. "Damn right, today. There's work to be done."

The look she gave him told him he wasn't fooling her. It made him mad. "You need that shopping done, too," he reminded her.

"We won't starve if you wait a day."

"No, but the cattle will if I don't get the welding done, and we have to wire that piece again." So it wasn't precisely the truth. It was close.

"D-d'you feed a lot of cattle?" Dottie asked. It was the first question either of the older girls had ventured. Jess looked at her, startled.

"About three hundred."

Her eyes widened. She reminded him of Lizzie when she looked like that.

"Maybe Dottie would like to come along," Alison said.

Jess glared at her. He looked with dismay at the girl still sitting at the table.

"If she likes cattle. Do you, Dottie?" Alison gave the girl an encouraging smile and got Dottie a tentative one in return.

"Yeah," the girl said quietly. "But I don't know much about 'em."

"You'll learn," Alison said. Her gaze shifted and she looked at Jess expectantly.

He scowled at her, hating her for trying to back him into a corner. He hadn't asked for this, damn it. He took off his hat and rubbed his hand against the back of his neck. "I reckon it'd be kind of boring for a kid."

Alison gave him an arch, disapproving look.

Jess didn't care. He backed toward the door. "I'll be home before supper." And he let the door bang shut behind him.

He didn't turn around to see if anyone was watching as he headed for the truck. He whistled for Scout, started the engine and took off as fast as he could.

The truck jounced from one rut to another as he took the road far too rapidly. He'd have yelled at Alison if she'd driven it that fast. But he couldn't help it.

He needed some of that distance and perspective Nathan had always been talking about.

How in God's name was he going to raise three girls? Girls who reminded him of a past he wanted to forget and a future he never wanted in the first place!

He thought about Felicia Darrow and her blithe, "I know you'll do just fine. Give me a call if you have any questions or problems," and his foot stomped down on the accelerator even harder.

Hell, yes, he had questions! A heap of them. And didn't she think being saddled with his sister's three kids was a problem?

And talking of problems, what about Alison?

Damn Alison, anyway!

What a time to kiss him!

It was like kicking a guy when he was down. He didn't have any defenses left!

The truck bottomed into a pothole with a resounding crack.

Jess winced. All the more so, seconds later when, back on the road again, he could hear the tinny clanking of his muffler dragging against the gravel.

By the time he'd reached Bluff Springs, five miles away, he still didn't have perspective and he doubted if he ever would!

"I DON'T THINK Uncle Jess likes us much," Sue said as she sat at the table and watched Alison and Patsy do the washing up after supper.

"The hell with him, then," Patsy said, thumping the glass she was drying onto the counter with such force that Alison cringed. "We didn't ask to come here."

"It isn't that he doesn't like you," Alison began carefully, feeling as if she were stepping into an emotional minefield. "I'm sure he does. It's just been a shock for him. Hearing about your mother, getting used to the notion that he has new responsibilities."

"That he doesn't want," said Dottie flatly. She tipped back in her chair, making it balance on two legs.

"I wouldn't say that," Alison protested, not because it wasn't true, but because she hoped he'd change his mind.

He hadn't come back from town until almost supper time. Before Alison could even raise an eyebrow at the length of time his supposedly short trip had taken, he thumped seven bags of groceries on the kitchen table, muttered something about damned potholes and new mufflers, and took himself off to put some newly welded widget back on his tractor.

"That's a lot of groceries," Alison had said to his rapidly retreating back. A lot more than had been on her list.

"Reckon they'll get eaten," he replied over his shoulder.

"Supper's almost ready. Don't you want to eat?"

"Nope. Got work t'do."

They hadn't seen him since.

Alison and the girls had soup and sandwiches for supper. For dessert Alison had made them sundaes with the ice cream and chocolate syrup that hadn't been on her list.

It was the ice cream and syrup that gave her hope.

She knew enough about Jess now to know that he did care about his nieces, that he wanted to welcome them, even to love them, but that he didn't have any idea how to go about it.

She remembered what he'd said about his background and guessed that he didn't have a lot of experience along those lines.

She did. And there was nothing more she would like than to show Jess how it was done, to share in the doing of it with him.

Sue seemed to accept Alison's explanation about Jess's reticence with equanimity, wanting to believe. She knew that Patsy and Dottie were frankly doubtful.

"How's he gonna get used to us, if he isn't around us?" Patsy asked.

Alison smiled. "Give him a little time."

It wasn't until after the girls had gone to bed that Alison expected him to reappear. He hadn't had any supper, after all.

She waited for over an hour, sitting at the kitchen table, using her grandmother's old treadle sewing machine as she put pleats in the new living room curtains.

Every few minutes she got up and peered outside, hoping to see him coming, checking at least to make sure that the light in the barn was still on.

Just past eleven the barn was dark when she looked. And even as she watched, the window in the bunkhouse lit up.

"Ah, Jess," she murmured.

She put her sewing away, made two meat loaf sandwiches, filled one thermos with hot soup and another with cold milk, then dished up a bowl of ice cream and drizzled chocolate syrup on top.

Nudging open the door with her knee and closing it with her elbow, she carried the tray of food across the porch, down the steps and across the yard.

She kicked the door of the bunkhouse. "Jess?"

The door jerked open. "What's wrong?"

"I brought you some supper." She didn't give him a chance to object, stepping past him into the room, setting the tray down on the bare wooden table, then busying herself laying out the silverware and straightening the napkin.

He was bare-chested and barefoot, and the top button on his jeans was undone. She stared at it, then dragged her gaze away to meet his eyes.

He looked away. For a moment she thought he was going to ask her to leave. Finally he closed the door. "You didn't need to bother," he said gruffly.

"I needed the excuse."

"Why? Because I took off and left you with my problems?"

"Not exactly."

He snagged his shirt off the hook by the door and pulled it on, but he didn't button it. He looked at her warily. "What, then?"

She swallowed. Their gazes locked. And Alison knew she was looking at him with her heart in her eyes.

He groaned, then reached for her, pulling her into his arms. And she came willingly, needing his touch, starved for it. And he seemed equally starved. His hands were all over her, gliding down her back, pressing her against him, moulding the line of her hips, her bottom. Her hands slid up beneath the tails of his shirt, rubbing against the rough hair of his chest, learning the shape of his muscles, the firm strength of his shoulders.

"This is crazy," he muttered against her mouth, even as he kissed her again. Harder. Longer.

"No," Alison insisted. "It isn't."

"It is. Nothing's changed." His face was in her hair, his thumbs caressed the line of her jaw. He was trembling.

Alison shook her head. "It has." She sought his mouth, traced his lips with her tongue, felt a tremor run through him, then another, felt his hips surge against hers.

"I love you, Jess," she whispered.

He stopped cold.

She could feel his heart pounding a hundred times a minute. His chest was heaving. His muscles clenched and unclenched spasmodically as he pulled back and fought for control. He shook his head, the look he gave her dazed yet fierce.

"No!"

She touched his cheek. He winced and pulled away, crossing the room, bracing his hands against the window frame, staring out into the blackness. Alison could see through his shirt the quick rise and fall of his back.

She came to stand behind him, touched him lightly, traced a line down the length of his spine. "I do, Jess. It's true."

He shook his head. "Don't."

"I can't help it." She slipped her arms around him from behind, clasping them together just below the waistband of his jeans, touching him there. "I love you." Her lips touched the nape of his neck. She flicked out her tongue. He trembled violently and pressed himself against her hands.

Then his own hands dropped and caught hers, holding them tight against him, not moving them. She could feel the heat of his desire, could feel the urgency of his need and the quick, shallow gasps of his breathing.

"No," he said through clenched teeth. "Don't. Please, don't, Alison. I... don't... love... you."

Chapter Nine

He shut her out. He shut them all out.

But it wasn't because he didn't like them, Alison realized. Jess was afraid.

At first she didn't believe it. It was hard to think of a man like Jess being afraid of anyone—especially a woman who loved him and a trio of little girls. But as the days went by, there was nothing else she could think.

For the most part she deliberately kept her distance from him, talking to him as little as possible, generally leaving rooms when he came in. She couldn't pretend that his words hadn't hurt.

She didn't want him hurting the girls, though, the way he'd hurt her. So at times she overcame her own better judgment and stayed to speak to him. Then she took him to task.

"They think you don't like them," she challenged him after the girls had been there nearly a week and he'd barely said more than a dozen words to each of them. She followed him to the sink after dinner, making her point.

"Of course I like them," he snapped, ignoring her while he washed his hands.

"Then prove it."

He glared at her. "How?"

"Talk to them. Show an interest."

"You're doing that."

"*I'm* not their uncle! Ask them what they're working on, what they're interested in. You could ask Sue about the kindergarten field trip to the fire station. You could give Patsy a hand with her algebra. Heaven knows, I'm no good at it. And, as for Dottie, you could show her the tractor or take her to feed the cattle."

"The tractor?" He stared at her as if she'd lost her mind.

"She loves anything to do with the ranch. Especially what makes it work. Like tractors. And horses. And you."

Dottie watched Jess far more than her sisters did. Alison recognized in her a kindred spirit, not only in her absorption with Jess, but also in her determination to be a part of the life of the ranch.

Dottie was always up first thing in the morning, coming downstairs to feed Kitten and Scout even before Alison did. She wanted to feed the horses, Alison knew, but given no encouragement by Jess, she hadn't dared.

"Let her feed the horses and hang around a bit."

Jess glanced at his watch and headed for the door. "I'll try."

Alison watched him go and hoped he remembered, hoped, for Dottie's sake at least, that he dared.

He did better than she could have hoped.

"I thought I'd sort through Pops's *Western Horseman* magazines this afternoon," Alison said when Dottie banged in from school. "Want to help?"

"Can't," Dottie gasped, eyes shining. "Uncle Jess gave me a ride up from the bus on his horse, an' he asked me to help him put the salt licks in the pasture!"

The expedition to set out the salt licks was a success, better even than Alison had hoped. Dottie was beaming when she came back, and after supper it emboldened her enough to ask if she could help feed the horses that night.

Jess was already headed for the door. His eyes flicked for an instant to connect with Alison's, read the challenge in them, then came back to his niece.

He nodded. "Don't see why not."

Dottie was on her feet like a shot.

Alison knew it wouldn't be quite as easy with the other girls.

Patsy was the least willing to accept his interest or his help. As the oldest, she was the one who had always been responsible for maintaining the girls' sense of identity as a family, keeping them together. She wasn't ready to relinquish her role until she trusted that someone else was going to do it as well or better.

Jess's taciturnity meant to Patsy that he didn't care. When he finally did show some interest, his questions, awkward and hesitant as they were, got only monosyllabic answers.

"I can't force her to like me," he told Alison late one night when the girls had gone to bed and he'd come back to the house to get a roll of tape.

"She already does like you. She's just defensive."

Like you, Alison wanted to add. She didn't. He was doing the best he could. He and Dottie fed the horses together every evening. He even came in some nights and played checkers with her.

Alison got the tape out of the cupboard and set it on the table. She expected him to pick it up and leave.

He didn't. He picked it up, spun it on his finger, shifted from one foot to the other, then asked if she'd heard an evening weather report.

"Snow," she said. "And more snow." She went back to the file she was putting onto the computer.

Jess moved toward the door, then stopped. "What're you working on?"

Alison looked up at him, startled. It was the first time he'd expressed even the slightest interest in what she put on the computer. "The cattle. I'm putting Pops's records in."

"Yeah?" He really did seem interested.

She hesitated. She hadn't encouraged him in the least since that night at the bunkhouse. There was just so much rejection a woman could take.

She looked at him closely, saw something in his expression that made her wonder. "I'll show you what I've got, if you like," she offered after a moment.

She saw his Adam's apple work. His tongue slid over his lips. His eyes met hers, then flicked instantly away.

"Not tonight," he said, turning and hastily opening the door. "See you."

"Jess!"

He looked back.

"Don't forget the tape."

SHE WAS ANGRY with him. Probably she had a right to be. But damn it, Jess thought, wouldn't she be angrier if they made love and that was all there was to it?

Women wanted protestations of love. They wanted rings and weddings and happily ever afters. He couldn't promise anything like that.

So it was better to resist.

But now she was angry.

He could tell from the way she was avoiding him. She barely spoke to him directly—except to chew him out about the girls. She never smiled at him anymore. She acted as if she wished he was dead.

He hated it.

He wanted her smiles. He liked her laughter. He missed their conversations, their arguments, the little daily things they shared.

But he was afraid of them, too. He wanted them back. He wanted *her* back. But she said she loved him.

Jess didn't think he could handle love. But if they got back on their earlier footing, would he still be able to resist?

AFTER THE NIGHT with the tape, Alison started once more to hope.

"I'm an incurable optimist," she told her reflection in the mirror that night as she went to bed. "Or a damned fool."

She wasn't sure which.

Not until the night Jess finally connected with Sue.

If Patsy was difficult to reach, Sue presented a different set of problems. Jess had little in common with a kindergartner. Sue's interests centered on whatever current holiday or field trip her class was preparing for and the ongoing saga of her well-traveled dolls.

Sue loved her dolls. They were the part of her universe that she could control. Sue gave them adventures that would have made Indiana Jones cringe. They always had plenty of cliffs to climb, rivers to ford and problems to solve.

They also had happy endings, the sorts of endings, Alison began to realize, that Sue wanted in her own life and was determined to provide.

Within days of her arrival, the dolls had moved to a ranch, worked transcribing files onto a pretend computer, loved to read books and spent a lot of time feeding cattle.

They also argued some and kissed a lot.

"They're gonna get married," Sue told Alison, "an' have a family. Isn't that a good idea?"

Alison agreed that yes, it was.

In fact, as the days went by, Alison found herself becoming more engrossed in the lives of Sue's dolls than she ever had in any soap opera. Sometimes she wished she had a set of her own.

One night during the week before Thanksgiving, Jess came in to play checkers with Dottie. Patsy was making clothes for the dolls out of remnants Alison provided, and Alison was hemming a skirt. The two of them were sitting side by side on the couch while Jess and Dottie sat at the table and Sue spread her dolls out on the floor below.

The checkers game went quickly, Dottie taking them all.

"You were letting me win," she accused Jess.

"I was not!"

"Humph," Dottie snorted. "You beat me last night."

"Last night Alison and I had gone shopping," Patsy put in without looking up.

Alison caught a glimpse of Jess just then. He got quickly to his feet, raking his fingers through his hair. "I gotta get going."

"How come you never play with me?" Sue asked.

He hesitated. "I could play you at checkers tonight," he offered wryly.

"I can't play checkers. You want to play Alison and Jess?"

Alison froze.

"Play *what?*" Jess asked, frowning down at her.

"Alison and Jess. My dolls. That's what their names are," Sue said. "They got a ranch, too, so you'd know how. You can be Jess if you want to."

Jess's gaze jerked up to meet Alison's. A tide of red flooded his face.

Alison's own cheeks were hot, but this wasn't her fault. She looked back at him expressionlessly.

"Here." Sue handed Jess a dark-haired boy doll. She tugged on the hem of his jeans. "Come on. Sit down."

"Don't do it," Dottie warned. "She'll make you kiss her."

Jess's eyes widened. "What? Kiss who?"

"The dolls. Course they kiss," Sue said firmly. "They're gettin' married. Come on." She jerked his pants leg once more. "I'll show you."

Jess hesitated. He looked from the disapproving Dottie to Alison. There was speculation in his gaze.

She hoped her embarrassment wasn't showing. She wished he'd say no, and knew that for Sue's sake she should be wishing the opposite.

Jess sat, folded himself cross-legged on the floor, holding the doll gingerly as if it might explode in his hands.

"Now what?" he asked his niece.

"First you gotta put him on his horse. Mama bought me this horse for my birthday last year." She handed Jess a glossy plastic white stallion. "Isn't he be-yewt-i-ful? His name used to be Whitey. But now it's Dodger," she said proudly.

Jess cleared his throat. "Like... my horse?"

"Course," Sue said.

She waited patiently while he fitted the doll onto the horse and ventured a quick, desperate glance at Alison, who did her best not to giggle. He looked at Sue for further instructions.

"Now you gotta feed the cattle."

"Oh. Right." Jess looked around for the cattle, confused.

She pointed toward the area at the base of the sofa right by Alison and Patsy's feet. "Over there. You gotta pretend some things, Uncle Jess. The toy people don't make cows, you know."

Jess edged himself over, carrying the horse as he went.

Sue, watching, sighed. "Not like that. Jess rides better than that," Sue told him. "Do it right, so's he's real."

Jess did his best to gallop the horse until he was sitting practically on Alison's toes. He shot her a quick sideways glance. She swallowed. His eyes narrowed. He picked up her sock clad foot.

"Jess!"

He ignored her. "Is this the food?" he asked Sue, a grin quirking one corner of his mouth. His thumb tickled the ball of Alison's foot.

Alison wiggled her toes, trying to pull away and tuck her feet under her. "Jess," she protested again.

Sue giggled. "Yes, that's it."

"How do I feed it to the cattle?" Jess asked. "Shall I saw it off?" His finger drew a line across the base of Alison's toes, sending a shiver up her spine.

"No, silly, you just grab it and pull," Sue advised.

In a second Alison's sock was off and Jess's warm callused fingers closed around her bare foot. "Like this?"

Sue nodded, her eyes like saucers.

"Now the other one," Jess said and, before she could move, Alison found her other foot had been captured and that sock stripped off as well. Jess's fingers played with her foot making the horse nudge her toes.

"He's nibblin' you," Sue exclaimed, delighted. She bestowed an approving smile on her uncle. "Dodger likes the cattle's food, doesn't he?"

"You bet," Jess agreed, his hands still holding Alison's feet. "It's great stuff." He shot Alison a wicked glance. "Maybe I should try it, too."

Alison felt herself blushing even more hotly. "I don't *think* so," she said, still trying to tug her feet away.

Sue danced the girl doll up alongside the one Jess was holding. "Here's Alison to help you," she said.

Both dolls then started tickling Alison's feet. She gave a tiny shriek and managed at last to pull away.

"I think the cattle have all been fed," she said, tucking her feet up under her.

"Too bad," Jess said solemnly. "Now what do we do?" he asked Sue.

"Well," the little girl thought about it a moment, started to speak, hesitated, then went ahead. "You should kiss her."

Jess froze.

Alison did, too. There was such a thing as pushing too far, too fast.

"Sue, I don't think—" she began.

"Listen. Sue, I—" Jess said at the same time.

Sue gave a mighty sigh. "The dolls, I mean. I tol' you that. Alison helped him, and he wants to thank her. So he kisses her. See?"

She gave the real Alison an impatient glare, then turned her gaze onto her uncle. The look she gave him was only slightly less exasperated. "Come on," she said.

Jess fumbled with the doll then angled it toward the one Sue was holding, touching its face briefly to hers.

"Not like that," Sue said. "Here. I'll show you."

She took the doll from him and stood them on the ground, pressing them together, doing her best to wrap their arms around each other. Their lips met. Sue held them that way. It was a long and, if her expression was to be believed, supremely satisfying kiss.

"Oh, yuck," said Dottie, making gagging sounds.

Patsy gave a long, low wolf whistle.

Alison wished the earth would open right where she sat.

Jess swallowed, stared, swallowed again and didn't say a word.

After a a considerable interval Sue looked at Jess, pulled the dolls apart. "See?" she said to her uncle. "Like that. Get it?"

Jess cleared his throat. "Got it."

HE HAD IT, all right. Bad.

And every day it was getting worse.

He couldn't stop it.

He and Brian Gonzales, Mike's son, would take the tractor and the wagon out in the morning to feed the cattle, and instead of paying attention to what he was supposed to be doing, he'd be daydreaming about Alison.

He'd ride along the fences, checking things out in the afternoons, and he'd remember kissing Alison with the same abandon that Sue's dolls showed. He'd be trying to chivvy a cow out of a thicket, and he'd be thinking about the way her hair had smelled, the way her lips tasted, the way her hands had touched him.

He should've known his daydreaming would get him into trouble.

It was late on the Monday afternoon before Thanksgiving that it happened. He was riding Dodger through some oak scrub, trying to get some cattle out, thinking about Alison, the way he'd left her, rolling out gingerbread dough on the kitchen table.

She'd worn a dish towel apron tied around her waist. The sleeves of her navy plaid blouse were pushed up to her elbows as she bent over the pastry board. The top two buttons were undone, giving him a tantalizing glimpse of a lacy white bra and creamy flesh beneath.

The kitchen was warm, and she had a flush on her cheeks and a smudge of flour on her nose. He'd wanted to kiss it, kiss her. Wanted to undo the rest of the buttons, let his fingers slide down the softness of her curves and learn—

"Ow! Hell!"

He guessed it was a rabbit that made Dodger start, jerking to the side, then lunging forward, knocking him against the oak scrub.

Whatever it was, one moment he was in the throes of red-hot passion, and the next his left knee—his bad knee—was consumed with a white hot pain.

He swore, gritted his teeth, wanted to howl. He jerked back hard on the reins. "Stay put, you stupid fool! Oh, damn. Oh, hell."

He held himself absolutely rigid until the sharpest edges of the pain began to recede a bit, then tested his knee gingerly, running his fingers over it, feeling the almost immediate swelling. He put a little weight on it in the stirrup and winced.

Still, nothing was broken. He wouldn't have been able to put any weight on his leg at all if it had been.

He should go back to the bunkhouse right now and put ice on it. But it would only feel worse before it felt better, and he had the rest of this section to do.

He urged Dodger forward. "Keep your mind on your work," he muttered to the horse, then recalled where his own mind had been. "And I will, too," he added roughly.

It was a good thing he kept going.

There was a break in the fence near the top of the pasture. If he'd left it overnight, there was no telling how many cattle would've been gone by morning. Three were already up into the national forest land, standing in the trees looking down at him as if daring him to do something about it.

It took him longer than he would have liked to get them back. They were balky, perverse, intractable cows. The sort that always found their way through the fence and didn't take kindly to being brought home.

His knee was swollen stiff by the time he finally got them back on their own side of the fence, dismounted, repaired the fence and tried to swing back into the saddle again.

He couldn't do it. Bending his knee was a near impossibility. Putting all his weight on it while it was bent, then using it to lever himself into the saddle was an actual one. He shut his eyes momentarily, waiting for the pain to abate, then went around to the other side. Dodger shied nervously, unused to such goings on.

"Hold still, you stupid horse."

But Dodger didn't. He made nervous noises, stepping sideways, dragging Jess as he attempted to put his right foot in the right stirrup.

"Damn it, I said, hold still!"

Clenching his teeth, anchoring his right foot as well as he could, Jess heaved himself into the saddle. Dodger whinnied, pulling madly.

"For God's sake!"

It took him until well past six to make it back down to the ranch. Dottie was standing at the gate, waiting for him in the dark.

"Where were you?"

"Some cattle got loose. I had to bring 'em back, then mend the fence." He eased his foot out of the stirrup and slid carefully to the ground.

"You should've waited for me. I could've helped."

"You can do me a favor now, if you want." He handed her the horse's reins. "Take care of Dodger."

"All by myself?" She stared at him wide-eyed.

"As long as you do a good job."

She beamed. "You know I will!" She turned and started leading Dodger toward the barn, then stopped. "Will you tell Ali where I am?"

"I'm not goin' up to the house tonight. I'm not really hungry."

Dottie looked disbelieving, then shrugged. "If you say so." She tied Dodger to the gate, then took off running toward the house.

Jess hobbled his way toward the bunkhouse. He knew he couldn't get past Alison without limping. And he knew she'd fuss if she saw his knee.

He might have been able to handle her fussing other times. Not now. He was too vulnerable, and he knew it. A few sympathetic murmurs, a kiss to make it better—he grimaced—and he wouldn't stand a chance. He had to stay away completely.

He winced as he removed his boots with the bootjack, then unzipped his jeans and eased them over his knee. It was bigger than the biggest grapefruit he'd ever seen.

He probed the swollen discolored flesh gingerly, tried to bend the joint, shuddered and limped over to the sink. He should use ice, but ice meant going up to the house. He soaked a cloth in cold water, wrung it out and wrapped it around his knee. Then he hobbled back to the bed and lay down.

God willing it would be better by morning. God knew it had to be. There was work to be done.

SO HE WASN'T hungry, huh?

Alison almost snorted when Dottie gave her the news. More likely he was not up for another evening playing "Alison and Jess."

She'd seen his face that night. She'd seen the way he'd avoided the house after dinner every night since.

"Oh, Jess," she sighed. "Just when you were getting through to them."

The problem, she was fairly sure, was that they were also getting through to him.

Well, fine. But if he was just doing it to avoid the latest Jess and Alison episode, it would serve him right to go without supper.

The dolls hadn't kissed once tonight. "Alison" had taught "Jess" how to make gingerbread men.

"Should we take Uncle Jess one?" Sue asked. She was thrilled with the little cookie men and had bitten their heads off with great relish.

"Not if he hasn't eaten his supper."

"But, Ali—"

"No," Alison said firmly. "He can have one after breakfast."

But Jess didn't come in for breakfast, either.

"Was your uncle in the barn when you went out this morning?" she asked Dottie on the way to the bus.

Dottie shook her head. "I thought he'd come in early for breakfast."

Maybe he had. Jess was unpredictable. He did things in his own time on his own terms.

It didn't do to pressure him.

At least that's what she told herself until he didn't come up for dinner, either.

Alison stood staring out the kitchen window down toward the bunkhouse. The tractor was back. She could see the rear end of it just peeking out from the barn. They had finished a little later than usual, she'd noted. But Brian's truck was gone, so they must be done.

"Maybe you should take him a gingerbread man after all," she said to Sue.

"Even though he didn't eat?"

"Even though."

Sue grabbed two off the plate and took off running. Ten minutes later she was back. "He said thanks, they were good."

Alison frowned. "And that's all?"

"He tol' me not to be late for school. Is it time to go?" Sue looked at the clock. "The big hand is on the nine."

"It's time," Alison said as she shrugged into her coat and handed Sue her book bag. Normally she dropped Sue off at kindergarten on Tuesday, then worked on the library until school was over. "What was he doing?"

"Sittin' in bed."

"Just sitting on the bed?" That didn't sound like Jess.

"Not on the bed. In the bed."

"*In* it?" Alison stomped down on the accelerator, shooting them out of the yard and down the gravel road toward the highway.

Sue nodded. "He said he was restin'. I didn't think big people took rests."

Alison didn't think Jess did. "I'll look in on him."

"You can take him another gingerbread man, if you want to."

Alison didn't bother.

She dropped Sue off at school and came right home, stopping the truck in front of the bunkhouse.

She knocked, waited until she heard, "What is it?" then opened the door and went in.

Jess was, in fact, in bed, a stockman's journal in his lap. He scowled at her. "Why aren't you at work?"

"Why aren't you?"

"I'm resting. Any law against it? Don't you think I work hard enough for you? It's half my ranch, too, remember? I can take a break if I want."

Alison folded her arms across her chest and looked down at him, waiting until he stopped and looked at her, a faint flush on his high cheekbones.

"Are you quite finished now?" she asked.

He scowled. "I'm finished."

"Then tell me what's wrong."

"Nothing's wrong."

"Liar."

He glared at her. She stared impassively back.

"Get out of here, Alison," he said finally. "I don't come bustin' into your bedroom, tellin' you what to do."

"You can if you want." It just popped out. She hadn't meant to say it.

But, having said it, she wasn't sorry.

"Look, I don't know what your problem is, but you won't solve it sulking down here. If you're really afraid of Sue and her dolls again—"

"I'm not afraid of Sue and her dolls!"

"Then what?"

He stared out the window, trying to ignore her. She didn't go away. Finally he plucked irritably at the blanket. "I hurt my knee."

"Your knee? Let me see it. How did you hurt it? What happened?" Alison was reaching for the blanket even as she spoke.

"Damn it. That's exactly why I didn't come up to the house. I knew you'd make some big blasted deal out of it."

"It's not a big blasted deal? Then let me see it."

She didn't wait for him to comply, just pulled the blankets and sheet back.

He wasn't wearing any jeans.

Wouldn't you know, Alison thought. Every time she saw him bare-legged, she never got a chance to appreciate it. She began unwrapping the plastic-wrapped damp towel. When she finished, she winced.

"Oh, Jess."

"Oh, Jess," he mimicked in a mocking tone. "I knew you'd fuss."

"Call it what you want. You need to see a doctor."

"A doctor can't do anything. It's not broken. It's the same knee I hurt bronc ridin' three years ago. It's sore that's all."

That wasn't the word Alison would have used.

"You shouldn't be walking on it."

"I'm not."

"You went out and fed the cattle."

"Brian did most of it."

"Dottie and I could have done it."

Jess snorted.

"Dottie and I *will* do it," Alison said, "until you're well again."

"You're not strong enough."

"You'd be surprised. Come on." She reached for his arm, trying to help him up.

He stayed right where he was. "I'm not going anywhere."

"You're going to the doctor, Jess. And then you're moving into the house. Unless you end up in the hospital."

"I'm not going to any damned hospital."

"Fine. The house, then."

"There's no room."

"Sue can move in with Dottie, and Patsy can have the attic. She'd love it."

"But—"

She gave him a saccharine smile. "Chicken?"

He glared. "Dumbest thing I've ever heard."

"Dumbest thing I ever heard is you saying that you're staying down here." She tossed him his jeans. "Put your pants on. I'll carry your clothes while you're getting dressed."

"I don't need—"

"I don't need an argument. Put your damned pants on, Jess, or I'll do it for you."

He gritted his teeth. "Get the hell out of here, Alison."

She picked up his clothes and left.

When she got back, he was dressed and coming out the door. She moved to slip an arm around his back for support, but he brushed her away.

"I'm fine."

"Of course you are. That's why you're limping, you stubborn cuss."

"I never denied it." Grimacing at every step, he moved slowly across the bunkhouse porch.

"Stop at the truck," Alison said. "I'll take you to see the doctor first."

"I told you, I don't need a doctor."

"You will if you don't stop at the truck."

He turned to glare at her. Her gaze moved pointedly from her foot to his knee.

He went white. "You wouldn't."

"Want to bet?"

JESS WAS RIGHT about one thing—the doctor couldn't do much.

"Banged it up good, didn't you?" Charley Moran said, shaking his head as he looked at it. "With a knee like yours you oughta be paying closer attention to where you're going."

Jess muttered something under his breath.

Charley grinned. "But then, I reckon I can see where you might have your mind on other things these days. Hell of a lot of swelling. Didn't you put ice on it?"

"Didn't have any."

"Refrigerator not working?"

"I'm staying in the bunkhouse."

Charley gave him a long assessing stare. "And nobody'd bring you any?"

"I didn't ask."

Charley rolled his eyes.

He took X rays, then shrugged. "Nothing visible, which doesn't mean you're imagining it," he said with a grin.

"It's just the same old thing," Jess said gruffly.

"Probably ligament damage, yes. When the swelling goes down we'll take a closer look."

"Here." He handed Jess two fat pills and a cup of water, waiting while Jess swallowed. "That's for pain," Charley said. He scribbled out a prescription. "They'll help with the swelling, too. And take them, you damn fool. Don't be some macho tough guy. Get out of that damned bunkhouse, too. Somebody needs to keep an eye on you."

"I can take care of myself."

"Right," Charley said. He didn't mean it.

He opened a closet in his office and fished out a pair of crutches. "Use these for a week or so." He fitted them under Jess's arms and walked with him back out to the waiting room where Alison sat.

"Keep him off it completely until the swelling is down."

"I've got work to do," Jess argued.

"And a family to do it," Charley said unsympathetically. "Lucky you. Bed, fella. Rest. Lots of it. In the house. Got it?" he asked Alison.

She nodded. Jess glared.

Charley turned to his nurse. "Give Jess an appointment in three weeks." He handed the prescription to Alison. "Make him take them."

"I will," she promised, holding the door for Jess, who swung himself out on the crutches like a man who knew well how to use them.

"He didn't have to give it to you," Jess grumbled as they headed for the truck. "I'm not a child."

Alison looked at him doubtfully. "You must've done a good imitation of one, then."

But she let him prove it by allowing him to maneuver the crutches and negotiate the step and the door by himself.

It was difficult as hell. His knee was killing him. He wouldn't admit it.

Still, he waited in the car while she filled the prescription. Then he looked at her with surprise when she drove to Bluff Springs's only fast-food place. "I'll be right back."

Moments later she came out with a hamburger, a soft drink and French fries. She handed him the bag. "I thought you might be able to use this."

He took it, letting it sit in his lap, untouched. He felt ill-humored and sulky and he wished he could get mad at her, but it was hard when she wasn't bullying him.

His stomach growled. But he lasted until the edge of town before he opened the sack.

"Thanks." It wasn't very gracious.

"You're welcome," she said.

Alison drove up as close to the house as she could get. She took the groceries and opened the gate. She didn't help him. He wouldn't ask her to, even though the pain killers were beginning to make him woozy and he almost fell up the steps.

She left the groceries in the kitchen, then went ahead of him up the stairs, stripped the sheets off Sue's bed and was beginning to put on clean ones when he finally hobbled, exhausted, into the room.

She glanced up. "It's a pity all the bedrooms are upstairs. I'll have the bed ready in just a minute."

He leaned on the crutches, his knee throbbing. "What's Sue going to say when she finds out I've stolen her room?"

"Yippee, I imagine," Alison said dryly. "You have no idea how many times she's asked why you stay in the bunkhouse."

She straightened the quilt, then folded it back and patted it. "All set."

He didn't move.

"Jess?"

"All right," he said irritably. "I'm coming." But he almost stumbled when he did.

In an instant Alison was at his side, helping him maneuver so that he could ease himself down onto the bed. He leaned the crutches against the wall and lay back, his eyes closing.

"Come on, Jess." Before he could react, she was helping him move sideways, lifting his legs onto the bed.

He let her. He felt too fuzzy to protest. Even when her fingers deftly unbuttoned his shirt and slipped it from his shoulders, he just looked at her.

Not until she pressed him back against the pillows and set to work unfastening his jeans did he finally rouse himself.

"I knew you'd be having your wicked way with me if I came up to the house," he muttered, looking up at her as she bent over him.

Alison licked her lips. She made him raise his hips so she could slide the jeans down his legs. "Is that what I'm doing?" she asked. He thought her voice sounded a little breathless.

"Isn't it?" he asked hoarsely.

"What do you think?"

Chapter Ten

It was the effect of the pills, of course, that was causing this euphoric haze through which he was experiencing the world. At first he tried to fight it, blinking his eyes, muttering imprecations at Charley for having prescribed them.

But then it was too much trouble. It didn't seem worth the effort. Besides, his knee didn't hurt so much anymore. If she wanted to fuss, let her. Maybe if he slept . . .

When he woke, the haze was still there, making him feel warm and well cared for. Voices sounded soft and slurred, and colors blurred a bit around the edges.

Alison came in and offered him a glass of water, and he could hardly seem to lift his head. When she put her arm around him and helped him up, he couldn't find the words to protest. His head lolled in the curve between her arm and her breast.

He felt lighter, happier. He even smiled sleepily at the girls when they came to check on him after dinner.

"Don't worry, Uncle Jess," Dottie assured him. "Alison and Patsy and I can take care of everything."

You can't, he wanted to tell her. But she looked so earnest, so sweet, that all he could do was mumble. Then he shut his eyes and slept again.

He didn't remember anything else until Sue, clad in fuzzy cat pajamas, came padding in to say good-night. She kissed him solemnly and said, "I'm glad you came in to stay, Uncle Jess. I wanted you to."

He saw Alison standing behind her, watching them, smiling. He smiled back muzzily, even when she said quietly, "I told you so."

SHE WATCHED him sleeping. Crept in after the girls were in bed and stood just inside the doorway looking down on him, afraid to go closer for fear of waking him.

He had drifted off with the light still on, a book on cattle diseases open beside him on the bed.

She was surprised he'd even made an effort at it. The pills Charley Moran had prescribed had done a stunning job of making Jess woozy and amenable.

So amenable, in fact, that she felt faintly guilty every time she touched him, as if she were taking advantage. Imagine being able to undress Jess Cooper with no more protest from him than one faint wisecrack and a smile.

When the girls got home, they had further undercut any moves he might have made to reassert his independence. Horrified to find out that he'd been hurt, they went rushing upstairs to hover over him, wanting to know how they could help, what they could do.

If Uncle Jess needed a glass of water, he had it before he could move his toe. If Uncle Jess wanted to listen to the radio, it was beside his bed before he'd finished saying the words.

After an initial protest or two, Jess had given in, seeming to relax, allowing them to wait on him. In fact, Alison realized, he seemed almost amazed and a little awed by their concern.

She had to admit that she was concerned, too. She hoped he would rest now, doing what Charley told him he needed to do to get well.

She leaned closer, trying to see if he really was asleep at last.

He was lying on his back, the comforter bunched down near his waist. His navy T-shirt outlined in dark relief his muscular chest.

Two day's worth of stubble shadowed his cheeks, highlighting his high cheekbones and the lean lines of his face. Jess's face was still tough, even in sleep. Only the dark rumpled hair that ruffled across his tanned forehead and the equally dark, thick half moons of lashes against his cheeks lent softness to his features.

Alison slipped closer. Reaching down, she picked up the book, marked his place, then set it on the bedside table. All the while she never took her eyes off Jess.

It seemed strange to think about how many times she'd dreamed of him here in her room.

How many times had she lain awake at night and imagined what he would look like unguarded, asleep?

And now it was happening.

Did dreams come true? Did the lives of librarians and cowboys really meet?

Deliberately she pinched herself on the arm. It hurt. Smiling at her own foolishness, she reached out and brushed the hair back off his forehead.

His brows drew together slightly. His lips parted. He sighed.

And Alison couldn't resist the temptation.

"Playing with fire," Jess had called it.

But Alison wasn't playing. She hadn't been playing since she'd moved back from New York.

She leaned down and touched her lips to his. Gently this time. She didn't want to wake him. She only wanted to tell him that she understood.

She wasn't hurt any longer. She knew that it wasn't that he didn't love her. It was that he was afraid to.

It was going to be up to her to teach him not to fear love, up to her to wrap him and his nieces in the warmth and love with which she'd been raised.

"I'll do it, Jess," she promised him. She touched his cheek, rested her palm against his stubbled jaw, saw his mouth curve slightly.

Her own curved, too. "I love you, Jess. And whether you believe it or not, you love me. I'll show you."

HE SLEPT LATE. Later than he ever remembered sleeping in his life. The sun was halfway up in the damned sky and he was just coming around.

He flung back the comforter and swung his legs around, wincing as he did so. But his knee felt better, not as stiff, nor as swollen. He reached for his jeans.

"What do you think you're doing?"

His head jerked up. Alison was standing in the doorway, hands on her hips, smiling at him. He yanked the comforter back over him.

"Getting up, obviously. What the hell were you thinking of, letting me sleep this late? Those cattle need to be fed!"

"They have been."

"They aren't just gonna stand there politely waitin'—What did you say?"

"I said they'd been fed. Brian and I fed them."

He stared at her, shook his head slowly, disbelievingly.

"I told you we would."

"Yeah, but—" He stopped and frowned at her.

"Brian knew what to do."

"Who drove the tractor?"

"Me."

"*You?* Since when do you drive tractors?"

"Since this morning at six-thirty."

"You just went out there, flipped the ignition on and took off."

"Well—" she grinned "—it was a bit more complicated than that. More gears than I'm used to."

"Brian taught you?"

"I'm a librarian, damn it. I read the manual!"

He stared at her, dumbfounded. "You learned to drive the tractor reading a book?"

"Amazing, isn't it?"

"Mind-boggling."

"In any case you don't have to worry about the cattle. Get back in bed and I'll bring you some breakfast."

He hesitated, mind still reeling at the thought of Alison, manual in hand, figuring out the tractor, then helping Brian load up the bales and taking them out to the stock.

"You were... all right? I mean, you got back all right? You didn't wreck anything?"

She sighed. "No, I did not 'wreck anything,' thank you very much. Honestly, Jess." She gave him a long-suffering look.

"You could've. You could've got yourself killed," he grumbled. "Tractor accidents happen all the time."

"I read that in the manual, too. Rest assured, I was very careful. But I'm glad to know you care," she added with a smile.

He muttered something under his breath.

She grinned. "Stay in bed, Jess. I'll bring you some dinner."

"I'll come down."

"That's not what Dr. Moran said."

"Charley's an old woman."

"Not to my way of thinking."

Jess's brows drew together. "What's that supposed to mean?"

"Charley Moran is a good-looking man."

His eyes narrowed, his scowl deepened.

"Not as good-looking as you are, though," Alison winked. "I like dark, grumpy men best."

"Hussy," he muttered.

She grinned.

She brought him dinner and more of Charley's miserable pills, hovering over him until he'd swallowed them. Later she brought him the mail, then a computer analysis she'd done on the growth of their yearlings.

And all the while his good sense and his firm resolution about staying clear of Alison Richards were turning to mush.

He lay there watching her adjust the curtains, the sunbeams outlining her blue-jean-clad curves, and he wished he could slide them right off her.

He dozed intermittently as she read him a letter from her brother, Peter, detailing a date he'd gone on with his latest lady friend, and Jess dreamed that he and Alison were dating, too.

His mind fuzzed. He tried to talk logically, think coherently. He said something that made Alison laugh. He didn't know what. He only knew she had the sexiest laugh he'd ever heard.

After she'd read him the letter she made him take a nap.

"A nap?" He looked at her, horrified.

She pulled the curtains shut. "A nap. And if you take a good one, maybe you can watch Mickey Mouse Club reruns with Sue when you get up."

She blew him a kiss and went out, shutting the door, leaving him only Kitten for company.

They stared at each other doubtfully from opposite sides of the room. Then Kitten got bored and went to sleep.

Within minutes Jess did, too.

He did get to watch a Mickey Mouse rerun with Sue. Afterward he ate supper in bed, while Dottie sat at the desk, eating hers and keeping him company.

"We drew straws to see who could come up and eat with you," she told him. "I won."

Jess stared at her. "You lost, you mean," he joked, but she shook her head.

"Nope. We all wanted to, but Alison said you probably didn't need that many people all at once. Alison takes very good care of you, doesn't she?"

Yes, Jess thought. She did.

She was back after supper with another pill.

"Haven't I had enough of these today?"

"Last one," she said. "To get you through the night."

While he was in the bathroom, she straightened his sheet and plumped his pillow and folded the comforter back. When he came back, she was standing in front of the dresser, her hands knotted in front of her, watching him, smiling.

In his hazy afternoon dream she'd been waiting just like this, eager yet apprehensive, wanting him. The way he wanted her. He shook his head.

Sue poked her head around the corner of the door. "You wanta play 'Alison and Jess'?"

Alison and Jess? Oh, God, yes.

Jess looked at Alison. "How about a little Alison and Jess?"

"Not tonight." Alison smiled. "It's time for your uncle to go to bed."

"I've been in bed all day."

Alison ignored him. "He's had quite enough stimulation."

"He could always use some more," Jess said hopefully.

Alison gave him a baleful look. "Not tonight." She touched Sue's shoulder. "Uncle Jess needs to sleep."

"No, 'e doesn't," Jess tried to protest. But the damned pill was already taking effect.

He could barely keep his eyes open. He slumped sideways onto the pillow, letting Alison lift his feet and turn them under the comforter while Sue patted his hand.

"'S'your fault," he mumbled to Alison. "Knockin' me out like this."

She smiled. "It's the only way I can control you," he heard her say. "And me."

SHE HEARD A YOWL, then a crash. Her feet hit the floor before she was fully awake.

"Damn!"

It was Jess's voice, furious, pained. She ran into the hallway. Jess was on the rug, struggling to get up.

Alison knelt beside him, mind still fuzzed by a dream—a dream of Jess. "Are you all right?"

He managed a sitting position, but stayed there, clutching his knee. "Swell," he muttered.

Alison began patting him in the dark, trying to see how badly he was hurt. "Can you get up, Jess?"

"Of course I can get up."

"What happened?"

"Ask the damned cat."

"Oh, heavens. I forgot about Kitten. He usually sleeps on the hall rug," she said apologetically.

Kitten wasn't a snuggler. He liked to be where people were, but he also liked to keep his distance. "Here, give me your hand." She began hauling him to his feet.

He seemed taller in the moonlight, more imposing. Alison's hands were more than ever aware of the muscles beneath the soft cotton of his T-shirt. She'd been dreaming when she'd heard the noise. A warm dream. A wonderful dream.

Pieces of it floated through her head now as she helped him. She had been touching him then, too. Soft touches. Loving touches. Touches that she'd been dying to give him all day. All month. Ever since she'd returned.

They stood scant inches apart now. Alison felt her pulses quickening under his scrutiny. She was suddenly conscious of her thin nightgown, of his state of undress. She swallowed, brushed her hair back from her face and looked directly into his eyes.

Abruptly Jess shook his head as if trying to clear it. "I need a drink."

"I'll get you a glass of water."

"I didn't mean water," he said hoarsely.

"Well, water's all you're going to get. Go back to bed and I'll bring it to you."

He didn't go. "Bein' thirsty's not the only reason I'm up, Alison," he said at last.

"Oh." She looked away, even more flustered. "Of course. I'm sorry." She stepped out of his way, and he swung past her toward the bathroom.

She stood and watched as the door shut. She ought to go back to bed. She ought to turn on her heel and vanish into her room.

But she couldn't.

She had lived with him for weeks now. She had learned his strengths and his passions. She had become his partner, his friend.

But it wasn't enough; she wanted more.

She wanted what she had dreamed of since she was fifteen, what she saw in his eyes, but never yet had heard from his lips.

She wanted Jess Cooper's love.

Of course, he might send her away. He already had. He'd lied—to protect himself. Because, although Jess had been fighting her from the start, he was fighting himself, too, far more than he'd been fighting her.

Something existed between them, something strong and vibrant and growing. Something that all the resistance and stubbornness and determination he could muster still hadn't killed.

She waited for him.

He swung out into the hallway and stopped when he saw her standing there.

She didn't back down.

He swung past her toward the bedroom, careful not to hit anything. She followed.

He leaned the crutches against the bedstead, then sat down. Wincing, he swung his legs in. Only then did he look up at her, his eyes challenging. "I suppose you came to tuck me in?"

Alison ran her tongue lightly over her lips, drawing courage, then nodded. "By all means," she said.

With great care, she drew the comforter up around him and smoothed it across his chest, then tucked it in around him. She let her hands linger slightly as they brushed his shoulders. Then, just before she straightened up, she shoved an errant lock of hair off his forehead.

His eyes were dark, heavy-lidded, watching her every move. She felt momentarily awkward and foolish. She licked her lips, then dared to smile at him.

Then he tilted his head. His eyes narrowed. "No good-night kiss?" His tone was sardonic, almost as if he was daring her.

He should have known better.

"Damn it, Alison! Wait a—"

But Alison had waited long enough.

The dream would not be denied. Her lips came down and touched his, hard and warm.

She felt his initial resistance, felt his tension, his desperation. And then he was kissing her, too.

And it was like the other times he'd kissed her, hungry and demanding. And yet it was more.

Those had been kisses under protest, kisses that promised an end almost before they'd begun.

This wasn't a goodbye kiss. It was hello.

It was a promise, an acknowledgment, an omen of things to come.

And Alison rejoiced in it, gave herself over to the sensation of it.

This was the Jess she'd been waiting for, the man she'd been dreaming about. And, even as she knew it, she knew her dreams hadn't held a candle to the real man.

He was leather and soap and horses and something purely, indefinably Jess. And she drank of his kisses with a thirst unimaginable. She felt as if she'd been in a desert for a lifetime, as if she'd been parched for years. And Jess seemed to feel the same.

When at last she pulled back, purely to breathe and for no other reason, her heart was slamming against her ribs. She'd never felt so desperate. She wanted more, wanted . . .

But before she could even begin to articulate it, Jess was kissing her again, drawing her close, pulling her onto the bed beside him, kissing her the way she'd always imagined being kissed.

And Alison thought, yes, oh, yes. Like this.

Exactly like this.

She snuggled closer still. Her hands touched his dark hair, stroked through it. Her fingers shaped the curve of his ears, her thumbs brushed against his temples, wanting to memorize them all.

Jess's hands found her shoulders, flannel soft, slid down her back and drew her closer, tracing the curve of her spine, sending goose bumps in their wake. Her breasts pressed into the comforter between them, and she heard him groan. Then he reached up and dragged the comforter away.

Now only the softness of her nightgown separated them. She could feel the hard muscles of his chest beneath her nipples. Pressing closer, she sensed the pounding of his heart against her own.

He nipped gently at her lips, then, as they parted, teased them with his tongue, letting it slip inside her mouth, and she shivered at the pleasure of it. She returned the favor and smiled at the shudder that coursed through him.

It was odd how she felt so right doing this with Jess. It wasn't something she'd done with Gary or any of the few other men she'd dated in her life.

She supposed she should have felt nervous. She wasn't a bit, because she'd been here before—in her dreams.

With anyone else she would have bemoaned her lack of experience, would have hesitated, feared making a fool of herself, feared panicking at the last moment.

With Jess she was not afraid. It was right.

She framed his face with her hands. Her thumbs caressed his cheekbones, her lips touched his nose, his brows, his eyelids.

"Ah, Jess," she murmured. "My Jess."

She'd said the words in her mind for years. And in her mind he had agreed.

In reality, since Nathan's death, he'd denied her. He'd argued, resisted, walked away.

Not tonight. He didn't walk away. Nor did he argue.

He just looked at her, his eyes dark and wondering. His hand touched her cheek almost hesitantly.

She looked down and her lips curved in a tiny smile. "You're all untucked again. You'll get cold."

A corner of his mouth twisted. "Not likely."

She moved away, starting to pull the comforter back around him. His hand shot out and caught hers. "Don't go." There was a ragged edge to his voice. "Stay...awhile."

Forever, Alison thought. *I'm staying forever.*

"Yes," she said softly. And she kissed him with such hunger, touched him with such abandon, that she broke his control.

He wasn't made of stone, damn it.

He'd tried. Oh God, he'd tried.

Ever since Alison Richards had come back into his life, he'd been resisting her. She hadn't made it easy, with her smiles and her enthusiasm and that curvy little bottom of hers. But he'd done it, and he'd survived.

Until now.

Now he was finished. He couldn't fight her any longer. Didn't want to.

He wanted her. Needed her. Now. Not in his daydreams. Not in his fantasies. In his bed. Tonight.

He'd done his best to think about the long term. God knew he'd tried.

But the long term had always been hard for Jess, and never worse than now. With her body toe to toe and nose to nose with his, their hearts pounding in unison and their lips touching, the long term had ceased to exist.

He could feel her cheek, her breast, her knee. Her leg moved up his thigh, nudging him.

He made a sound deep in his throat, then reached down and took hold of her gown, drawing it up over her hips, past her waist.

The backs of his fingers brushed against the narrow band of lace at her hips. He paused, imagining the way it looked, letting his fingers find out. The lacy panel curved on around toward her belly. And as his fingers followed, he felt her take a quick breath. He waited a moment, feeling tremors in his own fingers as he deliberately slowed the pace.

Then, when he felt her move restlessly against him, he continued, stroking the soft firm flesh of her belly, letting his hand slide beneath the fabric, moving lower, touching the soft curls there.

Alison swallowed, tensed, then her own hands began to move on him. One played lightly across his chest, drawing tiny circles around his nipples, then dancing down farther, brushing against the elastic of his shorts. The other, the one lying against the bed, managed to begin a subtle exploration of the back of his thigh.

Jess shifted, lifted his knee, gave her room, gave himself over to the sensations she was evoking.

He didn't know how much more he could take, how much longer he could last.

But her soft, gentle explorations were too exquisite to resist, too heady to deny, too rare to push away.

He'd never made love like this, so slowly, so tenderly. He'd never known a woman like this.

Alison.

He was afraid to believe it, afraid he would wake up and find out he was dreaming the way he'd been dreaming all day, except that now his dreams had reached new heights, surpassing his wildest imaginings.

But it was no dream.

She was here in his arms, warm and willing. And though it might be the stupidest thing he'd ever done, he couldn't stop. He wanted her too badly, had wanted her too long.

He left off touching her just long enough to skim the nightgown over her head and the lacy underwear from her hips. He struggled to remove his own shorts, winced as he moved his knee and felt Alison's hand on his, stilling him.

"Careful," she murmured. "Let me."

Her fingers hooked inside the elastic and eased them down his hips, slipping them gingerly past his knee. When they were off completely, she knelt on the bed at his feet, looking up at him.

Slowly, carefully, he drew her up and over him, looking all the while deep into her eyes. He felt her tremble, knew he was trembling himself.

"Jess," she whispered again. "My Jess."

And he knew she was right. He did belong to her the way he'd never belonged to another woman.

Then moving just as slowly, carefully and tenderly as he had, she brought him home.

He shut his eyes. His teeth clenched. He felt a fine sheen of sweat break out on his forehead. His fingers bit into her hips, lifting her, then lowering her.

He saw her own teeth clench, her body tense, her breathing quicken. Her dark hair tossed as she caught his rhythm and began to move.

The pace quickened, sweeping both of them along together, pulling them apart, driving them on. And then, at last, when he thought he could stand it no longer, they became one.

It took an instant... and an eternity.

It shattered him and made him whole. It wasn't what he had imagined. It was far, far more.

Jess folded Alison against his chest and heard her wildly beating heart echoed by his own. He stroked still-trembling hands down her damp back, drew the comforter up and settled it around both of them, making them their own little cocoon against the world.

He wished it could be like this all the time, wished that he would never have to let her go, that morning would never have to come.

He had tasted wonder moments ago. He had felt magic. Alison Richards had touched a part of him that until now he'd never known.

Alison lifted her head from his chest, looked at him in the silvery light. Her eyes were wide, concerned. "Are you...all right?"

"All right?" The words came out sounding rusty, as if he hadn't spoken for a very long time.

"Your knee, I mean."

He'd never noticed. He flexed it slightly. "It's fine. Don't worry." He hesitated, smitten with sudden worries of his own. "Are you? All right? Was it...?"

She smiled at him then. It was an angel's smile, pure and sweet. She touched her lips to his. "I've never been better in my life, Jess, believe me."

And Jess lay back and shut his eyes, felt them sting slightly and didn't know why.

He swallowed, drew one deep, steadying breath and then another. He folded one arm under his head and listened to the gradually slowing rampage of his heart.

He tried to tell himself that nothing had changed, that life was exactly the same as it had been half an hour ago. But he knew, even as he tried to convince himself otherwise, that this was new territory, alien and uncharted.

He didn't know what to say, what to do. He only knew one thing: how he felt. It amazed him.

Gently he stroked Alison's hair with a still-trembling hand. "Neither have I."

Chapter Eleven

Bliss. Serenity. Gratification. Wholeness.

One word alone couldn't begin to describe the feelings Alison had when she awoke the next morning at the sound of the alarm.

On two and a half hours sleep she should have been feeling miserable and exhausted.

She felt perfectly splendid, if you please.

She yawned and stretched luxuriously, wriggled her toes and flexed her shoulders. Then she simply lay quite still and let the events of the night play through her mind again. And as she did so, she reveled in the unaccustomed tenderness in her body, in the pure contentment of her mind, in the peaceful satisfaction of her emotions.

She had crept back to her own bed shortly before four, leaving Jess reluctantly. He didn't awaken as she left. He'd been holding her close, his arms wrapped around her as if he didn't want to let her go. She hadn't wanted to go, either. But she knew she had to.

It wouldn't do for Dottie to stumble in on them together if she got up before the alarm. There would be a time and a place to share with Jess's nieces the new developments in their relationship, but Alison wanted it to be one of their choosing, not an accidental morning discovery.

Now she sat up, still smiling as she did so, feeling as if she was hugging a very wonderful tiny secret to herself. She scrambled out of bed, dressing quickly in jeans, a shirt and a pullover sweater. Then she ducked into the bathroom long enough to wash her face and teeth and comb her hair.

She caught a glimpse of her face in the mirror and actually grinned. Yes, she did look as if she had a secret. Her cheeks were rosy, her eyes bright.

She drew a deep careful breath and went back out into the hall. The door to Jess's room was open a crack.

Unable to resist taking a peek, she eased it open farther. He was lying on his side, facing the door. One arm was curved around the pillow, holding it the way he had held her. She longed to slip back under the comforter with him, to love and be loved by him once more.

She lingered a moment longer, then blew him a kiss. "Tonight," she promised him—and herself. Today she would show him her love in another way, by helping him and his nieces grow together as a family.

She had the dressing made and the turkey stuffed by the time Dottie appeared, tucking in her shirt and looking at Alison through sleepy eyes. "Whatcha doin'?"

"Putting the bird in the oven. If we're going to be out in the pasture all morning, I won't have time later. Besides, I'll need to make the cranberry sauce then, and the pies."

"All that?" Dottie looked taken aback.

"Of course. It's Thanksgiving." Alison finished stowing the bird in the oven, then turned and gave Dottie a hug. "Come on. Let's get Patsy up, too. If she helps, we can get done that much faster. There's lots to do."

Brian was already loading bales of hay onto the wagon, when they got to the barn. He was, as always, quick and efficient, and today, at least, Alison had a fair idea of what she was supposed to be doing.

Dottie, of course, already knew, and Patsy learned quickly.

It was hard work, heavy work, sweaty work, even in freezing temperatures. But once they got out in the pasture, they developed a sort of rhythm with Alison driving the tractor, Dottie cutting and stripping the twine, while Patsy separated the bales into leaves and Brian lifted them and tossed them down to the waiting cattle.

It took them three trips to carry and distribute all the hay. It was almost eleven o'clock by the time they got back to the barn.

"Would you like to come in for pumpkin muffins?" Alison asked Brian as they finished.

"You can tell Uncle Jess we're doing a good job," Dottie added.

Brian grinned. "You got yourself a deal." He fell into step with Patsy. "I hear you're going to the dance with my brother."

Patsy smiled a little shyly. "He asked me," she admitted.

"What dance is that?" Alison asked.

"They call it the Snow Ball," Brian told her. "It's the high school Christmas dance."

"Sounds like fun," Alison said. "When is it?"

"Two weeks from tomorrow," Brian said. "Luke's talking about renting a tux."

Patsy started to say something, then sighed and chewed her lip. Alison took a couple of quick steps and caught up with them.

"We'll have to make sure your dress is pretty special then, won't we?" she said to Patsy.

Patsy gave a helpless little smile and shrug. "I guess so."

"Brian," Dottie broke in, "Davy says you've got a lot of horses. Can I come over some day and look at them?"

Davy was another Gonzales brother, one who was Dottie's age. Brian shrugged. "Sure. Just get off the bus with him after school."

Dottie turned to Alison. "D'you think maybe Uncle Jess'd let me get a horse? I could help him even more if I had one."

"That's something else you'll have to ask him."

Brian drank two cups of coffee and ate five pumpkin muffins while Alison rolled out pie crust and Patsy, following her directions, made the cranberry sauce.

She wanted to forget it all and run up the stairs to see Jess. Yet at the same time she felt strangely reluctant.

She wondered how he felt about it—about her—now.

What if he regretted it?

He had been so determined, had resisted so long that she couldn't help worrying. This morning, when she'd peeked in on him, she hadn't given it a thought.

Now, having had four hours to contemplate the issue, she felt unaccountably nervous.

Dottie appeared in the kitchen. "Uncle Jess needs a cup of coffee. I told him I'd bring it, but he said he was coming down."

And when Alison looked up, there he was.

He wasn't smiling. He stood leaning on his crutches, looking at her, and she saw in his expression all the worries and nervousness she'd felt herself.

Seeing that, all her own worries fled. She smiled. She loved him, and she was glad she had finally shown him how much. She hoped—prayed—that he was glad, too.

"Jess?" she said softly. She offered him her heart with her eyes.

He hesitated, swallowed, licked his lips, bit down for a moment on the lower one. Then he smiled, too.

Alison felt as if she might laugh aloud, might dance around the kitchen, might make a complete and utter fool of herself. She started grinning, wanting to go to him and hug him, to show him her joy.

But Jess wouldn't thank her for that.

He was a private man. Last night he had loved her and she wanted to tell the world. But that was risky. For the moment it was enough to tell him in silence, with only her eyes and her smiles, that she loved him too.

She nudged out a chair with her foot, waving floury hands in his direction. "Come in. Sit down."

He hobbled over to the table. Dottie poured him a cup of coffee, and he sat nursing it and eating a muffin, while Brian sang their praises, assuring Jess that his cattle were being well fed.

"Good," Jess said. He gave his nieces an approving look. "You've done great." Then his gaze lifted and his eyes met Alison's. "Thanks."

She finished crimping the crust on the pie, blew the flour off her nose and a lock of hair out of her eyes. "You're welcome."

Always welcome, she told him with her eyes, *in my bed, in my life, in my heart.*

Carefully she washed her hands and dried them, stepped over Sue who was playing with her dolls on the floor and as casually as possible reached out and took Jess's coffee cup and filled it again. He looked up at her. She took a sip from it, then set it down in front of him.

His hand lay still on the tabletop for a long moment. Then carefully he picked it up, cradling it in his palms, breathing in the fragrance. He looked up at her. Their eyes met. He touched the rim to his lips, drank where she had drunk, his gaze never leaving hers.

"Do you think these cranberries are cooked yet?" Patsy asked.

"What? Oh, let me see." Alison went to look at them.

Jess still talked to Brian, listened to Dottie, sat with one arm around Sue who'd come to lean against him. But wherever she moved, Alison felt his eyes on her, and she thanked God, because she knew it was just a matter of time until once more she felt the touch of his lips.

IT HADN'T TAKEN her long to figure out that, as far as Jess and his nieces were concerned, Thanksgiving was a holiday that had been celebrated in social studies class, not at home.

Last week when she'd asked Jess whether he wanted the meal at noon or in the evening, he'd said, "What difference does it make?"

"I want to do what you're used to." She thought it would help to preserve whatever traditions his family had observed.

"I'm used to feeding cattle and eating beef stew out of a can."

"For Thanksgiving? But surely Pops—"

Jess shrugged awkwardly. "Oh, the last couple of years we've been invited out and he insisted that we go, but it doesn't matter to me. I don't care."

"Well, I do," Alison told him.

Patsy and Dottie had shown about as much enthusiasm as Jess.

"We could get hamburgers at the take-out," Dottie had suggested. "Then you won't have to cook."

"I'm going to cook," Alison assured both of them. "We're all going to cook. It's part of the holiday. Part of the sharing. It's important."

Sue had been enthusiastic at first, when she'd thought it had something to do with the Indians eating the Pilgrims. Once her misconception was corrected, her interest waned.

Alison didn't let their indifference discourage her. It took time to develop appreciation for a holiday like Thanksgiving, she told herself philosophically... time and the experience of love that went with it.

Personally she relished the holiday.

Ever since she could remember, in whatever corner of the world they'd found themselves, the Richards family had made a point of celebrating this very American tradition, though they hadn't always done everything the traditional way.

She remembered a Thanksgiving in Mexico when they'd had turkey *mole* and another in Bangkok when they'd had a chicken, peppers, and water chestnut stir-fry.

But while the food often changed, everyone pitched in, and the Thanksgiving spirit always remained the same.

Her parents had taught them that Thanksgiving was a time to remember the past with gratitude, to look toward the future with hope and, most especially, to give thanks for the joys of the present, for the people one found oneself sharing it with.

Alison had never felt more grateful than she felt this year as she prepared to celebrate with Jess and the girls.

She had known it wouldn't be simple for the five of them to become a family.

But slowly, surely, things were coming together, figuratively and—she smiled at the memory of last night's loving—literally.

She got down her grandparents' best silver and set Dottie and Sue to polishing while they watched the football game with Jess. Then she went back into the kitchen to help Patsy wash the seldom-used, slightly dusty wine and water glasses, and all the while she marveled how far they had come.

"Five of each?" Patsy asked her dubiously, holding up the glasses.

Alison nodded. "Yes, please. And then you can help me put the tablecloth and napkins on."

"In the dining room? Seems like a lot of trouble."

"It is," Alison replied cheerfully. "But it's worth it."

"I guess." Patsy turned on the water and squirted some dishwashing liquid into the pan.

Alison dried the glasses as Patsy washed them. "I didn't know you'd been asked to the dance. What kind of a dress do you want?"

Patsy kept her eyes on the glasses. "I dunno."

Alison touched her shoulder. "Don't you want to go? Don't you like Luke?"

Patsy's head jerked up. "Of course I like him! I just...just—" her shoulders lifted "—I don't know if we were still going to be here."

Alison set one glass carefully on the counter and picked up another. "Why wouldn't you be?" she asked gently.

In the living room, as if it were in another world, she could hear Sue chattering over the football announcer, heard Dottie give a little squeal and Jess say, "Oh, yeah. Look at him go!" Alison kept her eyes on Patsy.

The girl sighed, and flicked a strand of dark hair out of her face with soapy fingers. "Oh, well, you know. This won't last, us staying here."

Alison stopped drying the glass. "Why not?"

Patsy didn't look up. "It never does," she muttered.

Alison wanted to put her arms around the girl and hold her. She wanted to give Patsy all the security and stability she'd never had. She wanted to say, *Yes, it will. We'll do it. We'll be a family.*

She couldn't.

Not yet.

They would say it together, she and Jess. But first they had to settle things between themselves. They were making progress, yes, but their love was too new. Too fragile.

"You don't put your heaviest saddle on a fresh broke horse," her grandfather had often said.

You didn't ask a man, used to going it alone, to suddenly take on the responsibilities of the world. She had no doubt that Jess would do so in time.

But so far he hadn't even asked her.

And until he did . . .

"You'll be here for the Christmas dance," Alison said firmly after a moment. She could promise that much at least. "And for Christmas."

Patsy looked skeptical.

"I promise," Alison said. "I'll help you find a dress in town. Or if you can't find one special enough, we can get a pattern and some material."

Patsy just looked at her, eyes wide. "I've never made anything like that before. Not a real dress. A fancy one."

"You sew for Sue's dolls all the time."

"But those are just from scraps."

"They start out as scraps," Alison corrected. "They turn out to be beautiful clothes."

"But...what if I wreck it?" Patsy asked, concern evident in her deep brown eyes.

Alison smiled. "I don't think you know your own abilities. And, anyway, if you sew something wrong, you can always rip it out and try again. Everything I've ever made has seams like that," she admitted ruefully. "What do you say?"

There was a tiny smile on Patsy's face, almost the first one Alison had seen there since the girls had arrived. "Thanks," Patsy said softly. "I say, thanks, Alison."

THE POTATOES were cooked and Patsy was mashing them. The cranberry sauce had jelled and cooled and was in place on the table. The green beans and Dottie's fruit salad were waiting, all ready to go. The table was set, gleaming with old china and highly polished silver. At last Alison pronounced the turkey ready to carve.

She called Jess.

He limped into the kitchen and leaned on his crutches. "What's up?"

"You get to carve."

He looked at her, dismayed. "I don't know. I've never..." His voice trailed off and he looked away, as if casting about for a means to escape.

But she wasn't going to give him one. If he didn't have traditions of his own yet, ones worth keeping at least, they would start some here.

"Nathan always did," she said softly and held out the knife for him.

He hesitated, then nodded. He set the crutches aside and took the knife.

"I could read to you out of my *How to Carve a Turkey* book," Alison offered with a grin.

One dark brow lifted. "You have one?"

She gestured to the new bookshelves in the kitchen which he had helped her hang.

He shrugged. There was a hint of a smile around his mouth. "Read away," he said gruffly.

Alison read. The book even had pictures. She held them up at appropriate intervals just like the well-practiced librarian she was.

The girls came out to watch.

Jess grimaced. "Just what I need, an audience."

"You're doin' good, Uncle Jess," Dottie told him.

Sue's fingers snaked out and snitched a piece of meat from the plate. She popped it into her mouth. "Very good," she said through the mouthful.

Jess tapped her fingers with the fork. "No stealing," he told her with mock seriousness. "You get caught stealing, you have to do the dishes."

Sue's eyes widened. "Really?"

He nodded. "It's a tradition."

She looked at Alison for confirmation. "Is it?"

Alison smiled. "A tradition has to start somewhere. But I think, in this case, we can all do the dishes together. Finished?" she asked Jess, looking at the platter piled with meat.

"You tell me."

"It's fine," Alison told him. "Better than I could do. And you'll improve."

"We gonna have turkey every night until I get it right?"

"Often enough," she promised. "Another one at Christmas. And then next Thanksgiving. And the next." Her eyes met his. She smiled. "Right?" she asked softly.

Jess cleared his throat, pressed his lips together, then gave her a faint answering smile. He laid his hand on Sue's shoulder. "Come on, gang. Let's eat."

JESS HAD NEVER HAD a Norman Rockwell Thanksgiving before, the type you saw on television and hanging on the walls in doctors' waiting rooms. He'd never believed in them.

Now he did.

Or maybe he believed in Alison.

Certainly it was Alison who'd made it happen.

It had begun almost before dawn, with the sound of Alison tiptoeing through the hall, with the faint creak of the bedroom door, with the sight, through his lashes, of a tousled and beautiful Alison Richards standing in the doorway looking down at him.

He'd missed her when she'd left, had wanted to hold her back and make her stay.

He hadn't dared.

What they had shared had been wonderful, more wonderful than he ever could have imagined. Too wonderful to last?

He knew that was possible.

In any case, he couldn't hold her then. What if she regretted it? What if. . . ?

The worry made his gut twist.

Even if she'd enjoyed it every bit as much as he had, he still couldn't make her stay. There were the girls to be considered. He didn't want Alison embarrassed in front of them. If Dottie or Patsy or even Sue walked in on them, it would change everything.

Jess knew things were changing, anyway. But he didn't know which way and he didn't know how far. And he certainly didn't know, any longer, the limits of his own control.

When Nathan had left him half the ranch, he'd been pleased; who wouldn't have been? But he'd felt an unholy sense of panic all the same.

With the bequest had come responsibilities, potential, expectations. It was as if he'd been given the best wild horse in the world—a bronc that, well broke, would be the finest saddle horse imaginable.

All Jess had to do was break him.

And so he'd begun. He'd taken a deep breath, dug in his heels and hung on, doing his best.

And just when he'd felt as if he was beginning to get a sense of the horse's rhythm, fate had tossed him a beautiful crystal ornament, saying, "Here, catch. Hold on to this, too."

And "this" was Alison.

Alison. The most beautiful person ever to touch his life. The sweetest, the kindest, the strongest.

And he knew he could break her if he wasn't careful. What had happened between them last night was fragile and tentative. She'd told him that she loved him. But for Jess sex didn't necessarily mean love—except with Ali. He'd been almost afraid to hope.

Then she had peeked into the room, had stood looking down at him. And coward that he was, he hadn't admitted that he'd seen her.

But the look on her face had given him faith.

When she'd come back inside after feeding the cattle, he'd thought she might come upstairs. But Dottie had appeared instead, full of news about the cattle and more news about the holiday preparations going on in the kitchen. It hadn't taken him long to realize that Alison had plenty to do, that even if she wanted to, it would be unlikely that she would be able to come to him.

Finally he could resist no longer. He was drawn from his bedroom lair by the tempting smells and the soft sounds of shared laughter emanating from the kitchen. But mostly he was drawn by a need to see Alison again, to test her feelings. And his own.

Her eyes and her smile told him all he needed to know. And if they hadn't, the way she had touched her lips to the rim of his coffee cup and silently invited him to do the same would have.

It had been a promise. And he had spent the day basking in the sense of expectation, the warmth, the caring.

And as the day went on, she'd wrapped them in it—all of them, himself and the girls—drawing them into the spirit of sharing and thanksgiving that she had grown up knowing.

And now he sat at the table, set with white linen and damask napkins, laden with holiday fare made by Alison and each of the girls. He looked down the table, past the three bowed heads of his nieces, and met Alison's smiling eyes.

"Do you want to say grace, Jess?" she asked.

His throat felt tight, as if half the turkey were lodged there. He wanted to. He couldn't. "Will you?"

Alison bent her head. "Bless us, O Lord, and these thy gifts which we are about to receive through your bounty."

She lifted her eyes for a moment, letting them linger briefly on the girls before they connected once more with Jess's. "And thank you especially for giving us each other," she went on. "Help us keep on giving to each other. Please give us the courage to be what you would have us be. Amen."

THE GIRLS, after considerable urging, straggled upstairs to bed, first Sue, then Dottie and finally, half an hour ago, Patsy.

No one had wanted to leave the cozy living room, the warm fire, the casual sporadic conversation that they'd enjoyed all day. And Alison had been glad because it was what she wanted, after all, to make them a family.

But she also wanted something else: she wanted time with Jess. Alone.

She'd thought he wanted it, too. But as soon as Patsy went up, he'd got to his feet hastily, stretched and yawned, then said, "Think I'll turn in, too."

Alison had stared at him, nonplussed, as he moved to bank the fire. Then she'd swallowed her hurt, put the dog out one last time, shut off the lights and followed him up.

By the time she got there, he was in his room with the door shut. She stared at it, felt her throat tighten, felt a faint ache begin to grow somewhere deep inside, and turned to go into the bath.

She took her time, soaked in the tub, told herself it didn't matter, that of course he was tired, that it didn't mean he didn't care. And finally, when the water had grown cold and she was shivering, she pulled the plug and stood up, reaching for the towel.

She remembered the time she had come back and surprised him, had caught him naked and unaware. Last night she had seen him naked again, and he had been very aware indeed.

She bit down on her lower lip, blinked hard and dried off briskly, swallowing hard against the rising sound of his name in her throat. She wanted him so badly. Worse tonight than the night before.

But she wouldn't go to him again.

She tugged her nightgown over her head and ran a comb through her hair, looking at herself in the mirror. It had been eighteen hours since she'd stood here, smiling at herself in possession of a giddy wonderful secret.

What secret did she hold now?

She flicked off the light and opened the door. Everything was dark. Quiet.

Alison eased her way carefully along the hall, avoiding the even darker blob that was Kitten's sleeping bulk. She hesitated a moment outside the girls' door, then slipped in. They were sound asleep, Dottie with the current issue of *Western Horseman* sticking out from under her pillow, Sue with "Alison" and "Jess" tucked in neatly next to her. They were kissing, the way Sue had shown Jess that they could.

Alison shut her eyes, heard a sound, turned.

Jess stood in the doorway.

He didn't have his crutches and he was leaning against the doorjamb. He looked at her, his expression unreadable. Then slowly he limped in, came to stand beside her, looked down at the girls asleep in their beds.

She heard him swallow and felt hard, callused fingers touch hers. "Thank you," he whispered. "From all of us."

Alison heard the ragged edge to his voice and smiled. She turned to look up at him. "Anytime," she told him. "All the time."

His hands slid up her arms, pulling her close, drew her with him out of the room, into the hallway. And Alison went with him, unresisting.

"Please," he murmured against her hair. "Come to me."

And Alison framed his face in her hands, touched her mouth to his lips and breathed her deepest prayer of thanksgiving as she whispered, "Oh, yes."

Chapter Twelve

Their loving was silent yet passionate, hungry yet tender. The perfect ending to a perfect day.

And afterward, when Alison lay snuggled in Jess's arms, her head on his chest, one hand trailing, stroking across his thigh, she turned her head, kissed him lightly just above the breast bone and said so.

"I've had some wonderful Thanksgivings in my life," she told him. "But this one is the best by far."

She felt his hand caress her cheek, felt his breath tease her hair. "It's my best, too," he said after a moment. His voice sounded slightly hoarse.

"I love it every year. I love the sense of family, the sense of continuity, of wholeness," Alison went on. "I remember feeling that way when I was really small. No matter where we were—Mexico, Lebanon, Spain—my parents took the time to celebrate, to share. It was different every year. And yet—" she smiled "—somehow it was always the same."

"It was always the same for me, too," Jess muttered after a moment. He sounded tense, almost angry.

Alison lifted her head and looked into his eyes. "Tell me," she said softly.

He shook his head. "It doesn't matter now."

She rested her chin on his chest, reached up her hand and threaded it through his hair. "You matter, Jess."

He pressed his lips together, looked at her from beneath hooded lids. The lines of his face seemed harsh and cold in the moonlight. She could feel the tension in him, as if an internal battle was being waged.

Finally he sat up, lifting her away, pulling up his knees, wincing a bit, then wrapping his arms around them. "You want to know what Thanksgiving was like for me? Besides beans in a can since I've grown up?" he asked harshly.

Alison nodded. "Yes." The word was barely more than a breath.

"It was my mother savin' up everything she could out of the rent money, tryin' to get a little bit ahead, hoping like hell my old man might send a bit so she could put on a little extra. And then her cookin' whatever she could get. Sometimes a turkey or a chicken or, once, a piece of venison a neighbor gave us. An' then we'd wait, hopin' that my father would come. He'd always promise he'd be there." Jess swallowed and rubbed his hand across his face.

"I could hardly wait. I'd run down the road to see if I could see him comin'. And I used to stand there, watching, waiting. Expecting him, you know? Counting on him." His voice was ragged. "And then finally I'd have to go home alone. Ma and Lizzie'd be standing on the porch, waitin' too, lookin' hopeful, and then kind of sad, and my mother'd shake her head, but she wouldn't say anything. She never said anything."

The words seemed dragged out of him, his voice ragged, his fingers clenching into fists against his knees, then unclenching, hanging limply. He rested his head on his knees.

Alison touched Jess's calf, rubbed her hand against the hair-roughened skin, kneaded the tight muscles.

Slowly he lifted his head. He didn't look at her, but stared out across the room toward the moonlit window. But Alison knew he wasn't seeing the gently falling snow.

She pressed her head against his knee, slipped her arms around him, holding him, feeling the shudder that ran through him.

In her mind's eye she could see what Jess had seen, the hopeful faces, the dawning realization, the resignation.

"I don't ever want to do that to anyone," he said, his voice shaking with emotion.

"I know." Alison soothed him, stroked him, kissed him. "You won't. I have great faith in you, Jess. I love you."

His head came up and he looked at her. She reached out and touched his cheek. He caught her hand in his and held it against his face, pressed his lips into her palm.

"I love you," she whispered again and showed him what she meant.

For a moment he held back, resisting, fighting her and himself. And then his control broke.

"I need—" he muttered.

And Alison met those needs, loving him and relishing the love she received from him, the eager hunger of his kisses, the fine tremor of his fingers as they stroked her heated flesh, the hard thrust of his body as it melted into hers.

And in the still, silent aftermath of their loving, with Jess asleep in her arms, Alison said one final grateful prayer for the day—and for the man—and went to sleep with a smile on her face.

SHE AWOKE with a start, realizing where she still lay, at the same time she realized she was alone in the bed. She sat up, looking around in the darkness, picked out movement, heard the soft sounds of clothes rustling.

"Jess?"

"Shh. Go back to sleep."

"But it's—" she glanced at the luminous dial of the clock "—past five. Brian will be coming. And Dottie—"

"I'll do it."

"Your knee—"

"—is a lot better. I can't lie in bed forever. There's work needs to be done."

"But—"

"No buts, Alison. I'm not stayin' in bed."

He finished buttoning his shirt, shoved it into his jeans and crossed the room to drop a quick kiss on her forehead. "Much as I wish I could," he said with a wry grin, then turned toward the door.

Alison scrambled out of bed. "I'm coming with you."

"But—"

She smiled and shook her head. "No buts, Jess, just like you said."

It was the only way she could keep an eye on him. And it didn't take Alison long to realize that he really should have stayed in bed.

She watched him limping as he helped Brian load bales into the wagon and bit her tongue on what she would have liked to say to him. She knew better than to chastise him in front of Brian and Dottie. But, damn the man, that leg needed more rest.

She was happy to note that even Jess seemed to recognize the problem by the time they had finished with the cattle and were heading home. It wasn't nearly as difficult as she had imagined, to extract a promise from him that for the rest of the day, while she and Patsy went into town to shop for a dress, he would stay in the house.

"Off your leg," she added for good measure when he quite readily agreed. "You can read to Sue or play checkers with Dottie."

"Or we can read the horse book," Dottie said eagerly. Dottie had recently discovered Nathan's cache of stud books, and she spent hours poring over them, deciding which horses she most wished she owned and consulting Jess whenever she couldn't make up her mind.

Alison smiled. "You do that," she said. "And we'll see you by suppertime. We'll bring a pizza from town."

Patsy scarcely said a word all the way in to town. But her reticence didn't mean she wasn't interested, Alison was beginning to realize. A quiet demeanor and a careful lack of enthusiasm were Patsy's way of defending herself.

Alison didn't know, but she suspected that Patsy, like her uncle, had seen her fair share of disappointments. Alison wanted to teach them both to hope.

Bluff Springs had three dress shops, one in the old downtown area and two in a small strip mall west of town. They tried them all without finding anything that Patsy or Alison thought suited her.

"I think you should make one," Alison said and she whisked Patsy off to look at fabric and patterns.

Here they were luckier. They found a pattern with a fitted bodice and a high waist that would complement Patsy's developing figure, and a full skirt that would swirl through the dance. They also found a deep green velvet and a sparkling, iridescent matching taffeta.

"Yes," Alison said, holding the fabric up next to Patsy's face. "Oh, yes."

Patsy looked panic stricken. "I've never sewn velvet," she whispered. "Or taffeta."

"Don't you want to?"

Patsy hesitated, then bobbed her head, her dark brown eyes sparkling. "Yes. But—"

Alison smiled. "No buts. Your uncle and I agreed. It's a house rule."

"It—it's very expensive." Patsy made one last protest.

"And worth every penny," Alison told her as they carried both bolts to the cashier. "Out of the remnants you can make Sue's doll a Christmas dress."

Alison found a pattern for a girl's Western shirt in Dottie's size. "I hope Grandma's old treadle survives all this sewing."

Patsy nodded. "Me, too."

The saleslady measured out the velvet, then turned a smile and inquisitive eyes on Patsy.

"You're Jess Cooper's niece, aren't you? I'm Betty Wells. My daughter, Carrie, is going to the dance, too. Do you sew well?" she asked Alison.

"Patsy's the seamstress. I'm going to be moral support."

Betty Wells gave Patsy a smile. "Good for you." She put the fabric and sewing notions into a bag. "I don't suppose you'd be interested in being moral support at the dance, too, would you?" She looked hopefully at Alison.

Alison turned to Patsy. "What do you think?"

"Would you want to?" Patsy asked, and Alison heard that familiar studied indifference in her tone.

"Very much," she said firmly. She gave Betty Wells a smile. "We'll be there."

"A DANCE?" Jess stopped dead in the middle of the snow-covered pasture and looked at her, horrified. "You said we'd go to a high school dance? Cripes, I never went to a high school dance when I was in high school!"

"You don't have to dance," Alison said soothingly, laying a hand on his arm as they walked. They were headed toward a small stand of spruce to cut the perfect Christmas tree.

The trees here were all the right size and close enough to the road that they wouldn't have to carry their tree miles on foot.

Thank heavens, thought Alison, since Jess, even five days after Thanksgiving, was still limping.

"We've only got to chaperon. Stand on the sidelines and drink punch and smile," Alison said.

Jess made a doubtful snorting sound and trudged on.

"I suppose you'd rather stay home and play checkers with Dottie?"

"I'd rather stay home," he said, slanting her a grin. "But I can think of a few other things than checkers I'd rather be doing."

Alison tilted her head. "Oh? Polishing the silver maybe? Reading the stud books?"

"Keep trying," Jess said. "I reckon you'll come up with it." His fingers squeezed hers gently. Alison squeezed back.

The girls far outdistanced them, bouncing on ahead, nibbling candy bars Alison had brought and, between bites, pelting each other with snowballs. Even Patsy was showing enthusiasm today, as she had been, more and more, since they'd brought home the pattern and the fabric and begun work on her dress.

"I found one!" Dottie yelled at once, pointing at a spruce twice as tall as she was.

"Me, too!" Sue hollered, hugging a little lopsided one to her chest.

"Or maybe this?" Now Dottie had found another. Then Patsy did.

Jess leaned against a fence post and pulled Alison back into his arms, his breath lifting the strands of hair by her ear, making her quiver.

"Do you think they'll ever decide?" Alison asked.

He nibbled her ear. "I don't much care if they do or not."

Neither did Alison. She watched the girls bob and skitter among the trees with amused indulgence, content to snuggle in Jess's arms. To someone who had always bought her trees off lots on corners in New York or Paris or wherever, they all looked wonderful.

"Let Uncle Jess decide," Patsy said finally, and her sisters agreed.

"Me? What do I know?"

"You know best," Sue said simply.

And Jess just looked at her, taken aback.

"Come on, Uncle Jess," Dottie urged. "Pick one."

"It doesn't matter which we choose really," Sue said with cheerful matter-of-factness. "We can use the other one next year."

Next year.

It was so casual. So confident. And so welcome that Alison wanted to rush over and hug the little girl.

She didn't, because she knew that Sue wouldn't understand why her offhand acceptance meant so much.

Next year.

Alison looked at Jess. He was looking at her. There was something infinitely vulnerable in his gaze.

Then slowly he nodded, took the saw Patsy handed him and made the cut.

They all took turns towing the tree down the hill and across the pasture. First the girls, then Alison and Jess.

Dusk was falling as they went, turning the sky a purplish red in the west, fading almost to indigo in the east. Just above the horizon Alison saw the evening star. And below it the trees stood in dark ragged silhouettes against the pink snow. The girls' parkas, lime and neon orange and turquoise, were bright splashes of color as they hurried through the twilight. They were laughing, still pelting each other with snowballs, ducking each other in drifts.

Alison smiled, then smiled more broadly as Jess's free hand came and took hold of hers.

"Want some help?" she offered. He'd been pulling the tree for quite a ways.

He smiled. "A little sustenance would be nice. Some instant energy."

"I'm all out of candy bars."

"Then I guess I'll have to settle for a kiss, won't I?"

And Alison slipped her arms around his waist and lifted her mouth to meet his. "I guess you will."

IF THE STARLIT mountainside was a natural fairy-tale setting, the Bluff Springs High School gymnasium, decked out for the Snow Ball celebration, was a man-made one. Shimmering, glossy white and foil paper snowflakes hung from invisible threads, catching and reflecting the arcing strobe lights. An old-fashioned sleigh, heaped with gaily wrapped presents, stood at one end, and a lavishly decorated Christmas tree, lit with hundreds of twinkling colored lights, graced the other.

"I'm nervous," Patsy confided.

"Don't be," Alison said as they stood waiting while Luke deposited their coats in the foyer of the gym. "You're one of the loveliest ladies here."

She lifted Patsy's hair and spread it against her shoulders so that it lay in a glossy dark cloud against the deep green velvet.

"You really think it looks all right?" Patsy was still worried. "Not... homemade?"

"Only if Christian Dior whipped it up on his sewing machine."

Patsy giggled, then turned. "What do you think, Uncle Jess?"

"That if I could dance, I'd be in line to ask you," he said, his voice gruff.

Patsy looked astonished. Impulsively she put her arms around him and hugged him hard. "I love you, but you're nuts," she said.

Jess blinked, then rubbed a hand between his starched white collar and his neck, then grimaced. "Probably. Otherwise I'd be home and playing checkers tonight."

Luke appeared then, looking almost as uncomfortable as Jess, in his rented tux and pleated white shirt. He gave Patsy a shy smile. "Ready?"

Patsy flicked a quick glance at her uncle, then at Alison. Both of them smiled at her. She nodded and held out her hand to Luke. He took her into the dance.

Alison looked at Jess. He was watching Patsy, his face taut, his expression unreadable. She touched his sleeve. "Jess?"

"Hmm?" Then he gave his head a little shake, held out his arm and slipped her fingers through it. "Oh, yeah. Right."

At a small-town high school dance, if you didn't know everyone at the start of the evening, Alison discovered that you knew most of them by the end. Betty Wells introduced her to several teachers and parents. And those she didn't meet seemed to come by as she and Jess sipped punch and watched Patsy swirl in Luke's arms.

The first was a teacher of Dottie's, who was also the parent of one of the high school boys. She cornered Jess right after the first dance, squeezing his arm and smiling. "I'm Dottie's English teacher, Arletta Sprague. You've got a bright one in that girl, Mr. Cooper."

"Thank you," Jess said politely.

"I mean it. I thought from the first she was quick. Always raising her hand, always on top of things. But we just got her test scores back and, my goodness, they were incredible."

"She does like to read," Alison agreed.

"And she's lucky to have you to encourage her," Arletta Sprague went on. "But she'll need a lot more before long. She can go places, that girl."

"She's been places," Jess muttered into his punch.

Arletta looked momentarily blank, then seemed to catch his meaning.

"Well, yes," she said, then added brightly, "and that even makes it more amazing, what she's able to do. Dottie has amazing potential. I'm counting on you to encourage her." She gave Jess's arm another squeeze and hurried off to refill her punch glass.

Jess looked at Alison over the rim of his glass. "I thought all she read was stud books. Is she that good?"

Alison smiled. "She does have a lot of potential."

"Well, look who's here!" a voice boomed behind them.

Alison looked around to see Frank Kirby. She hadn't seen him since the day he'd read them the will. He beamed at them and cuffed Jess on the arm. "Fancy meeting you here."

"Yeah, how about that?"

Frank winked. "So Nathan was right after all. I thought about calling you the other day. Fellow rang me from Denver, looking for a ranch to buy. But from what I hear, you two aren't selling." He smiled, cocked his head and studied them both for a moment, then nodded approvingly. "Nathan would be pleased."

Jess lifted his brows. Alison smiled. "Yes," she said softly. "I think he would."

A sudden swell of music almost drowned out her words.

"Not dancing?" Frank asked.

"Not me." Jess nodded at his knee.

"Ah." Kirby nodded, then looked at Jess. "But would you object if I..." He smiled and held out his hand to Alison.

Alison looked at Jess. He shrugged. "Go ahead."

Frank Kirby was a good dancer. He didn't have to look at his feet and count his steps as he twirled Alison around the room. He could even talk while he did it. Alison talked, too, and smiled, but always she kept her eye on Jess.

One woman after another seemed to appear at his side, talk for a few moments, brush against him, lay a hand on his arm, smile, then move on.

Alison liked the part where they moved away.

She was glad when the dance was over, when Frank Kirby took her back to Jess's side. He was talking to a tall willowy vision in a shiny purple dress and matching turban. She had her hand on Jess's arm.

"This is Alison Richards, my ranching partner," Jess introduced them offhandedly. "Diana Lee, Patsy's home ec teacher."

"How nice," Alison smiled tightly, remembering all those canned "yummies" in the cellar. "Did you make your dress?"

It was pretty clear Christian Dior hadn't, she thought uncharitably, then felt immediately ashamed of herself when Diana smiled.

"Yes. But Jess says Patsy did, too, and it can't hold a candle to hers. She has such a wonderful sense of color and design, as well. I've been encouraging her to start thinking about fashion college after graduation. It's never too early to start planning, is it?"

"Never," Alison said.

"There are some excellent ones in New York. I had a friend who went to one. She worked in Paris for a while, and now she's in Milan." Diana shook her head. "I wish I'd had an opportunity like that. I'd love to travel, see the world."

"You should," Alison said. "You'd love it. Paris, Milan, New York. Go for it." *Go far. Fast. And get your hands off Jess.*

"I will," Diana said earnestly. "I don't want to be stuck in a backwater like this forever." She turned determined blue eyes on Jess. "And you make sure Patsy isn't, either."

The music began again and one of the science teachers appeared at Diana's elbow. "May I?" he asked her.

She smiled and held out her arms to him and they floated away.

Alison looked at Jess. His eyes were hooded, his expression brooding.

The music was slow, slightly bluesy, moodily romantic. The lights began to dim, casting the room in a soft silvery glow.

Alison lifted the punch glass from Jess's hands and set it on the table. Then she slipped into his arms, putting one hand in his and the other on his shoulder, then rested her cheek against his shoulder.

"I don't—"

"You don't have to dance," she promised him. "Just sway a little."

He swayed. His grip on her hand was hard and warm, so were the fingers splayed against the back of her red wool dress. He bent his head, and his forehead rested against the top of her head. She moved her head a little, felt the slide of his smooth-shaven jaw against her hair. Then she drew a breath and held it, savoring the faint hint of leather and pine, the indefinable essence that was Jess. She snuggled closer. Jess's grip tightened.

Yes, Alison thought, her body moving to the music. *Hold me. Love me. Now and for the rest of our lives—just like this.*

The music wrapped them in their own little world until suddenly she felt Jess jerk. He lifted his head, and Alison pulled back, too, looking around.

There was a man standing just behind Jess's left shoulder, a hopeful smile on his face.

"It's a cut-in dance," he apologized. "I'm Tom Quinn, Patsy's gym teacher. May I?"

Jess hesitated, then stepped back. His hands fell away. "Be my guest."

Before Alison could say a word, Tom Quinn stepped forward and took her in his arms and danced her away.

She did her best to smile at Tom Quinn, did her best to listen to him tell her how he'd just come to Bluff Springs, too, how he'd taught in Denver for five years and was looking for a temporary change. He was going back, he said. He wanted to travel, see more of the world.

Alison thought of asking him if he'd thought of dating Diana Lee. But by then he'd gone on to talk about what a good volleyball player Patsy was, how hard she tried even though she was rather short for the game.

"Short people have to try harder," he said, with a self-deprecating grin, and Alison realized for the first time that he wasn't quite as tall as she was.

"There's nothing wrong with being short," she told him. Gary had barely looked her in the eye, either.

Tom smiled. "I'm glad to hear you say that." Then, "Are you serious about Jess Cooper?"

Alison pulled back, blinking at the sudden question.

Tom shrugged. "Why beat around the bush? I'm attracted. I admit it. I want to know what my chances are."

Alison shook her head, then smiled to take the sting out of her words as she said quite frankly, "Not good."

THEY GOT HOME a little before midnight. Luke had taken Patsy out with some of the kids to get a pizza. He promised they'd be home within the hour.

"You'd better be," Jess had told him with such authority that Alison had giggled.

She'd snuggled against him in the truck all the way home, resting her head on his shoulder and slipping her shoes off to tuck her cold feet up under her coat. In her head she could still hear the music, could still feel Jess's arms around her.

They had "swayed" together once more, right at the end. She had taken his punch cup away again and pulled him onto the floor, determined that this time no one should come between them.

But this was a "no cuts" dance, and they had it all to themselves.

Jess had held her, lightly, carefully and yet securely. He hadn't said a word.

He scarcely spoke all the way home. He seemed withdrawn, distracted.

Alison knew how to reach him, though, and she would...later. For the moment she was happy just to be with him, to touch him, to smile at him.

She went upstairs to check on the girls as soon as she got home. Jess did a last check of the barn.

He was out there a long time. Luke brought Patsy home, came in for a few minutes and left again. Still Jess didn't come.

Patsy went to bed, smiling and humming snatches of dance tunes. Alison got undressed and put on her nightgown. Then, wrapping her robe around her, she padded softly into Jess's room and looked out the window toward the barn.

The night was clear and cold, a full moon spilling bright silver light across the snow-covered yard. The light went off in the barn at last. The door opened.

Jess came out. Stopped. Stood looking up at the house.

Alison waited, watching him. For the longest time he didn't move, just stood still looking up toward the house. Then he did, walking slowly, still with the trace of a limp.

She heard him come in, heard his footsteps on the stairs. She went out into the hall to meet him. She touched the fine wool of his suit jacket, felt the tension in his hard-muscled arm.

"I love you," she said, brushing a kiss along his jaw.

She felt a muscle twitch beneath her lips. Jess shut his eyes, bowed his head. She tugged his hand.

He loved her that night with something akin to desperation, as if he needed all that she could give . . . and more.

Alison sensed it from the start. She felt it in the tremor of his hands as he stripped off her nightgown, felt it in the harshness of his breath against her cheek, in the frantic need with which he joined his body to hers.

She cherished it—cherished him—and met him with an equal need of her own.

THE NEXT MORNING he was up and gone to load the wagon before Alison was even awake. She dressed hurriedly, woke the girls, then went after him.

"You don't want to overdo it," Alison told him. "What will Charley say?"

"He'll say I'm fine," Jess told her gruffly. "Stop worrying. It's startin' to snow. Go on back to the house."

Alison went. She walked slowly, taking her time, enjoying the gently falling snow, the delicate frosting of the house and trees, the beauty that she seldom took time to appreciate in the city.

Jess would say that snow was cursed hard to work in, that it mucked up the roads and hid the cattle's feed. But she knew he relished it, too.

She'd seen him often enough, sitting astride Dodger, just staring off at the mountains or tipping his head back and, when he thought no one was looking, catching snowflakes on his tongue.

Jess.

Tough. Tender. Strong. Gentle.

"Jess," she said softly as she climbed, the steps, "whom I love."

Dottie and Patsy appeared in the doorway in front of her. "Doesn't he want help?"

Alison shook her head. "He says not."

"We could all go," Sue said. She held Kitten in her arms and was still wearing her fuzzy cat pajamas.

Alison smiled, picked her up and gave her a hug. "How about if we make him a good breakfast instead?"

The girls all nodded. The tractor started up and rumbled out from behind the barn toward the lane. Alison, still holding Sue, turned and waved.

Jess looked at them, all clustered there on the porch, hesitated a moment, then waved back.

IT WAS STILL SNOWING late that evening. The Rocking R had become a winter wonderland. Of course work would be harder, of course they might be snowed in, of course there was a price to pay for the beauty of it. Alison was willing to ante up.

She curled in the corner of the couch, the afghan wrapped around her, Kitten and Scout both sprawled on the braid rug in front of the fire.

It was quiet now, though an hour ago the living room had rung with the shouts of Sue and Dottie who got overexcited whenever they played a game of Pit. Jess could quell their noise with a look, but Jess had been out at the barn. She and Patsy and the younger girls had been on their own since supper.

Now the girls were in bed, the fire was burning down, and the room was lit only by the light of the fire.

When she'd been little, Pops had called it "sparking time," and Alison hadn't known what he meant until Doug had explained.

"Courting," he'd told her. "You know—" he'd looked faintly embarrassed as only a twelve-year-old could "—mushy stuff between guys and girls."

Alison thought it was time for a bit of that tonight. Or even a little more than a bit.

"The *M* word, you mean," she said aloud to herself. "Marriage. Or the *P* word. A proposal."

It seemed possible. They loved each other. There was no question about that. And Jess had been looking a little nervous all day, skittish almost. He'd kept his distance most of the day, but she'd caught him looking at her with that hungry, desperate look in his eyes.

Alison smiled. She heard the door open. Heard it close. Heard Jess get a drink of water. Shut off the kitchen light.

And then he was standing in the doorway, looking down at her. She smiled again, opened her arms, beckoning him.

He flexed his shoulders, cleared his throat, ran his fingers through his hair. "Alison."

She sat up, let the afghan fall away. "Come here. You must be freezing. I'll warm you up." Her grin was impish.

He didn't smile.

She did.

It was going to be a proposal. She could feel it.

But it wouldn't be easy. Not for Jess.

She patted the couch. "Come and sit, Jess."

He came in. He didn't sit. He stuffed his hands into the pockets of his jeans, rocked back and forth on the soles of his feet. "We need to talk, Alison," he said finally.

She nodded, waiting, suppressing her eagerness to say it for him, to give him her answer: "Yes, oh, yes!"

"I think we ought to sell the ranch."

Chapter Thirteen

"Sell the ranch?"

"You heard what Frank said last night. He's got a guy who's interested. He wants what we've got..."

Jess was talking quickly, staring at the fire, not even looking at her. His forearms rested on his thighs, his fingers knotting together. He shot her a swift sideways glance. "It only makes sense."

Alison gaped at him. Her mind reeled.

Sell the ranch? What kind of a proposal was that?

She tried to marshal her thoughts, create some sort of coherence out of the chaos she'd just stumbled into.

"What if...*I* want what we've got?" she asked him at last.

She was proud of herself. Her voice didn't quaver, it didn't rise shrilly at the end of the sentence. She sounded composed, not frantic, which was how she felt.

"You don't," Jess said abruptly. He got to his feet, wincing as weight came down on his knee. He began pacing the room. "I mean, you might think you do, but it won't last." He looked at her as if beseeching her to agree with him, then began pacing again.

"What do you mean it won't last?" There was perhaps a hint of shrillness now.

"You're an intelligent woman, Alison. You've got a college education. A degree!"

"Two of them," Alison said quietly. She didn't know what difference that made.

"Yeah, *two* of them. You don't need a degree to feed a bunch of cattle, to mend a blinkin' fence! It might be fun for a while, but it's gonna get old fast. And startin' up some two-bit library isn't gonna make any difference. You'll be miserable. You'll hate it. Like you said to Diana last night."

"I said to Diana?" She stared at him.

"New York, Milan, Paris. All those places you've been! You'll miss 'em. You won't want to be stuck here." He stopped in front of the fireplace and turned to face her.

Alison took a careful breath. She strangled the afghan with agitated fingers and tried to articulate what she was hearing. "Let me get this straight. You want to sell the ranch to make me happy?"

"Yeah. Besides, you'll want to get married, have a family."

"Yes." She agreed with that. She looked at him with her heart in her eyes.

"Well, then—" He spread his hands.

"Well, then, what? I'm supposed to go to Paris and marry someone? Who? I love you! You know that, Jess."

He grimaced. "You could do a lot better, a hell of a lot better, than me. That guy you were dancin' with last night, the blond guy—?"

"Tom?" She couldn't even remember his last name.

"Yeah, Tom. Frank says he's just takin' a little break, then he's gonna head back to the bright lights. You could go, too, and—"

"Jess! I danced with the man. He didn't ask me to marry him!"

"You know what I mean," he said stubbornly.

She shook her head. "I don't. I don't want him. I don't want anyone but you. I think you're losing your mind."

"Finding it, more like," Jess muttered. He shoved his hand through his hair. "We've got to sell."

"I thought the ranch was your dream, Jess," she said after a moment.

"Dreams aren't that important."

Alison felt as if he'd punched her in the stomach. She stared at him, saw the fierceness in his face, then anguish in his eyes, and knew he didn't believe what he was saying. "Don't give me that!"

"It's true."

"It isn't! You don't want to try. You want to give up."

"I don't want to, damn it! I've got to!" He was glaring at her now. Cords stood out on his neck.

"Besides trying to do the best for me," Alison said with as much irony as she could muster, "why?"

"Because—because of the girls."

"They love it here!"

"Maybe. But they need better than growin' up out on some backwoods ranch! You heard what Dottie's teacher said last night. You heard Diana talkin' about Patsy's potential, about how she ought to go to New York. You reckon either of 'em are gonna realize any of that potential here? Hell, no, they're not! They need schools where they can learn what the rest of the world is like. They need chances, opportunities! We sell the ranch, and I can send 'em to boarding school."

"Boarding school?" Alison stared at him, aghast.

His jaw thrust out. "What's the matter with that? They'd get the education they need there. They'd have opportunities!"

"They wouldn't have a family!"

"Lucky them," Jess muttered in a voice so low she almost couldn't hear. His words made her cold.

She wrapped her arms against her chest as if doing so might warm her, but it didn't. The cold wasn't outside, but within.

"And for 'educational opportunities' you'd sell the Rocking R?"

"Why not? I don't need this place." He kicked at the rug beneath his toe. "I can go back and work for somebody else. It's all I ever expected, anyway." He bent his head, staring at the floor.

"But is it what you want?" she insisted.

His eyes came up to sear her. "Damn it, Alison, it doesn't matter what I want! It's what *they* need!"

She leapt to her feet and slammed her hands on her hips. "What they need, Jess, is an uncle who will stand by them, who will be there for them, who will love them!"

His jaw clenched, his face became a mask. He looked right past her.

"I want us to sell the ranch, Alison," he repeated. The words were flat and hard and cold.

"You won't discuss it? You won't try?"

"I won't let them get settled in, expecting things, counting on things..." His voice trailed off. "It wouldn't be fair."

"And this is fair?" Alison's voice shook.

"Life isn't fair!"

"No," she said quietly. "It's not. But that's no excuse for giving up. Let's be honest, Jess. You can rant about my supposed inability to adjust and the girls' need for educational opportunities, and you can rave on and on about how I need to be protected from myself and they need to be protected from the inadequacies of a rural education. But when it comes right down to it, Jess, it isn't us you're protecting at all, is it? It's you."

THE TRUTH HURT.

And there was no doubt about it: Alison had cut right to the heart of the truth. He shouldn't have been surprised.

He knew she wasn't going to buy his altruism argument. Not that there wasn't an element of truth to it.

But, damn it, he thought, as he carried the last of his gear back down to the bunkhouse, a little bit of hurt now, a little bit of anger, was better than years of disappointments and a lifetime of frustrated hope.

And he knew, if he didn't walk away now, that was what the future would bring.

He slung all his clothes in a heap on the table. He'd put them away in the morning. Tonight domesticity was beyond him. If it hadn't been snowing so hard he could barely see his hand in front of his face, he'd take Dodger out and ride.

He needed space. Wide open space. No walls. No fences. No commitments. No demands.

He'd felt the pressure building for weeks. He'd known what was happening, sensed himself being drawn into the web of family life that Alison and the girls represented. And after an initial instinctive resistance, he hadn't fought it.

Not the way he should have.

He should have known better. But he'd been lulled by smiles and encouragement, by wide blue eyes and a gentle touch. And so he'd ignored his better judgment. He'd let down his armor and had allowed himself to simply take it a day at a time. And damn it all, because it seemed to be working, he'd dared to begin to believe.

Until today.

It was funny the way the mind worked, how it stored up images a guy thought he'd forgotten—*hoped* he'd forgotten—and then, out of the blue—they'd come back to haunt him.

He'd driven the tractor around the corner of the barn, half thinking about how much work there was to be done and half thinking about how he was going to see that Dottie got challenged and Patsy eventually made it to New York, wondering whether Alison was as happy as she said she was, and he'd looked up to see them all standing there on the porch.

Only as he looked he hadn't seen Alison and his nieces smiling and waving anymore. Instead he saw his mother and Lizzie, standing and waiting, twin looks of hope and expectancy on their faces.

And then, when they saw him—and him alone—their expressions had changed.

Jess had never hated his father more than he had in those moments. He'd never felt so helpless.

Until now.

Now he could see a time when Alison and the girls would look at him with those same identical expressions. He could see the hope and eagerness in their eyes turn to disappointment, to disillusion—because he couldn't do it, couldn't give them what they had every right to.

For a few brief days Jess had thought it might work. He'd held slender hopes that he and Alison and the girls might really make a family.

Then, at the dance, his dream had begun to unravel. He'd begun to get an idea of what was expected, of what promises he might be asked for, of the dreams he might have to fulfill.

And the weight of being Les Cooper's son had begun to bear down on him. He'd fought it off, loving Alison last night with a desperation that he hoped would banish his fears. And afterward, lying in her arms, holding her in his, for the remainder of the night, he thought he'd succeeded.

But this morning as he'd come around the corner of the barn, he'd seen the truth, standing there on the porch, staring him in the face.

If he married her, if the girls stayed on, he would only have the chance to prove again what he'd proved as a child. He had no doubt that he'd fail them, too.

SHE WAS A FOOL.

A naive, blind, airy-fairy fool. Princesses in fairy stories had better sense than she did. Cows stuck in thickets had better sense than she did.

Alison sat on her bed in the darkness, wrapped her arms around her legs and pressed a hot tear-streaked face against her knees and felt so cold she thought she'd never be warm again.

She should, long ago, have heeded Jess's words.

"I'm not getting married. Ever." He'd told her that twelve years ago. He said it again on the way to Denver.

"I'm not having children ever." He'd been adamant about that, too.

But Alison had turned a deaf ear. She'd been arrogant enough to think she could change him, make him want what she wanted.

The more fool she.

But he had made love to her, she argued with herself. He had shown her a tenderness and a passion that proved how much he cared.

And yet he had turned away.

Why?

Because he was afraid. She'd flung the accusation at him more in anger than in certainty. She'd known it for weeks, had told herself over and over. And she'd thought she could talk him out of that fear.

Again and again she'd told him with words and actions that he didn't have to be afraid.

But she knew now that sometimes words and actions weren't enough—that sometimes even love wasn't enough. She had done everything she could. The choice wasn't hers.

"I HAVE two requests," Alison said to Jess's back.

He'd heard her come into the barn, had sneaked a glance to see who it was, and, finding out, had kept his back turned. He continued brushing down Dodger, getting snow clumps out of his mane. He waited until he heard her footsteps right behind him before he turned.

He hadn't seen her since last night when she'd rounded on him in a fury, nailing him with her fiery blue eyes, her chin out thrust, her cheeks an angry red. Now she looked pale, but composed, her hair pulled back, neat and anchored with a ribbon, her lips almost colorless.

Like a librarian, he thought. Proper and sedate.

She was wild when she had loved him, rosy and passionate. Who would ever believe—?

He shoved away the thought, clenching the brush with one hand, jamming the other into his pocket.

"What requests?" he asked warily.

"There's only a week left until Christmas. I want you not to do anything until after—not talk to Frank, not tell the girls."

"I—"

"You may think it's hypocritical," she went on without giving him a chance to speak. "I don't care. I'm not asking you to lie. Except," she added honestly, a faint grimace accompanying her words, "perhaps by omission. But if you say anything to Frank, he might say something to someone else. Word might get back to the girls. And if you tell them now, that will ruin it all. The girls are looking forward to Christmas. Planning on it. *Counting on it.*" She hit the words with obvious emphasis, echoing his own of the night before. "They've had a hard time this year, a sad time, Jess. They're happy right now, and I don't want it spoiled."

Her blue eyes were wide and guileless as she stared at him; her chin was determinedly stubborn.

"I don't want to hurt them, damn it. I don't want to spoil it for them, either," Jess said gruffly. "Making their lives miserable isn't the point."

Alison made a noise that sounded distinctly like a muffled snort.

Jess gritted his teeth. He yanked off his hat and shoved his fingers through his hair. "The new semester starts the end of January," he said harshly. "There'll be time enough to tell them after the holiday. All right?" He glared at her.

She met his glare. Her own expression wasn't angry, just sad. "Thank you." She turned on her heel and walked out of the barn.

HE THOUGHT he'd left in time, thought he'd got out by the skin of his teeth.

He'd believed that determination and distance would solve the problem, hoped that if he left the house, kept himself occupied with other things, he wouldn't miss them a bit. He'd had the girls less than two months, for heaven's sake, and Alison for less than three.

But he'd only had to spend a couple of nights alone in his bunk, staring around at the four bleak walls before his gaze would inevitably go to the window. And he would look up at the lights and warmth within the log house, knowing where he wanted to be.

He couldn't go, though.

Wouldn't.

It was more than his life was worth, trying to smile, to pretend that everything was fine.

So he stayed away. Heaven knew, he did have work.

The snow was thick on the ground now, making the feeding more difficult. He and Brian had tried using the tractor Monday and found it next to useless. They'd had to hitch up the old Belgians and use the sled.

Afternoons when Brian went home to help his father, Jess broke ice in the creeks and water holes so thirsty cattle could get a drink. In the evenings, he was bushed, but he had plenty to keep him busy, mucking out the barn, going over the books, mending harness.

And staring out the window up at the house.

Damn it! He shoved away from the window now and strode over to the table, forcing his gaze back to the broken hame strap in his hand. He lay it on the work table and punched the hole, did it carefully and deliberately, trying not to think about what Alison and the girls would be doing.

He'd hardly seen them in the last three days. Waved at them from the barn when they'd waved to him, talked to Dottie once after school when she'd come out to the pasture where he'd been breaking ice.

She'd looked at him curiously, and he'd wondered if she might ask him what was wrong, why he had moved out, but she didn't.

She'd told him about going down to see the horses with Davy Gonzales. She'd told him about a particularly pretty one, a sorrel with a white blaze and four white stockings that Davy's father, Mike, had let her ride.

Her eyes had shone when she'd talked.

He'd listened but he hadn't said much, and finally she'd stopped talking. He finished cutting the ice and he let her ride Dodger as they went together back toward the road. He let her take Dodger in and unsaddle him and brush him down, telling her he had work in the bunkhouse to do.

She'd smiled, but her smile hadn't reached her eyes, and when he turned to go, she'd called after him, "We miss you."

He missed them, too.

Right now the stereo would be playing, with Christmas music no doubt. He knew Alison had several tapes, and since Thanksgiving, they'd been on almost every night. And while they were listening to them, Alison would be baking or reading or making a Christmas gift. Patsy'd be sitting at the kitchen table doing her homework, chewing her pencil while she tried to puzzle out some algebraic equation. Dottie'd be sprawled on the floor, fists propping her chin as she pored over the stud books, dreaming.

And Sue?

Sue would be sitting on the rug in front of the fire, creating a world for her dolls—dreaming up adventures for "Alison and Jess."

Jess's mouth twisted at the thought. If Sue were running the world, she'd do a damn sight better than this.

He settled the rivet in the hole in the leather and let fly with the hammer—and hit his thumb.

"Geez!" He dropped the hammer, shook his hand, popped his thumb into his mouth.

There was a tiny tapping sound at the door.

He stopped dead, still sucking on his thumb, listening, not crediting what he'd heard.

Until it came again.

Tap. Tap, tap.

Alison. It had to be. But why? Jess took his thumb out of his mouth, gave it one more shake and went to answer the door.

"Uncle Jess?" It was Sue, looking up at him, her big brown eyes smiling at him.

He swallowed, pushed the door open wider, let her in. She wore jeans and her bright lime parka, and her dark brown hair was dusted with snow. She was lugging a small red trunk.

"What's this? Are you running away from home?"

"Course not." Sue dumped the trunk on the floor and proceeded to open it. "Alison" and "Jess" and the rest of their universe tumbled out on the floor. "We came to see you." She looked up at him with wide brown eyes. "We thought you might be lonely," she said. "You haven't been coming home."

"I—I've been busy."

"That's what Alison said." Sue sat down cross-legged and began sorting through the dolls and their accessories. "We've been busy, too," she told him, picking up the boy doll. "'Specially Jess."

"Oh, yeah? Feeding cattle, is he?" Jess asked. He should be bundling her up and sending her back to the house. He sat down on the bed and watched her.

"Oh, he always does that," Sue said casually. "He's busier now 'cause it's almost Christmas. He's makin' things special, you see."

Jess looked into her eyes. "Is that what Alison told you?" He'd kill her if she had.

Sue shook her head, the dark bob swinging back and forth. "She doesn't tell me 'bout Jess an' Alison. I know," she said with a child's faith, "because he is."

Jess digested that. "What's he making for Christmas?"

Sue smiled. "I can't tell you. It's a s'prise."

"What would you like him to make for Christmas?" He studied the dolls in her hands, tried to guess what they would need. "Doll furniture? A table? Chairs? A bed?" He supposed he could do that for her, and then she would have them, wherever she was, to remember him.

"I want a swing."

"What?" His head swiveled. He stared at her.

"Doll furniture's okay," Sue said. "But I got lots of nice cloth so they can have sleeping bags and picnics. I want a swing."

"For the dolls, you mean? For... Alison and Jess?"

"Nope. For me."

"But where would you put a swing?" How could she take a *swing*?

"In the yard, silly." And in case he had any doubt where she meant, she pointed back toward the house up the hill.

"A swing is awful big," Jess managed at last.

"Uh-huh. That's what I mean. I always get doll clothes from Patsy, an' Dottie always gives me a book. They give me things I can take when we move." She tilted her head and looked at him solemnly. "We've moved a lot, you see."

Jess saw—saw a child's hope, a child's faith. He shut his eyes.

"Alison said she moved a lot, too. But once, she had a swing. Not a real swing, but a board and two ropes that her grandfather put in an apple tree."

"I remember that tree," Jess said softly, the memory floating back unbidden. "It was a Greening."

"It was up behind the house," Sue went on. "An' once when she came in the spring, it had blossoms on it. An' she said it was the most beautiful thing she ever saw."

"It was," Jess murmured, remembering.

"But it's not there anymore."

"A few years back it got hit by lightning."

Sue nodded. "If I had a swing, she could swing on it. But it wouldn't have blossoms," she added sadly.

"Maybe you could... you could draw her some blossoms. Make her a picture. For Christmas."

Sue's face broke into a grin. "Will you help me?"

"Well, I—"

"An' will you help me write a letter to Santa?" She looked at him hopefully. "Mama always used to."

Another memory came winging back, smiting him, causing more pain than Sue could possible know.

Jess felt his throat tighten. He swallowed. "She used to help me, too," he said roughly. "Even when I told her it was stupid." His voice felt as raw as his emotions.

He shouldn't have said the words aloud, shouldn't have infected Sue with his own cynicism.

He needn't have worried.

She reached over and took his hand in hers. "It's not, Uncle Jess," she said in her clear child's voice. "Mama said it's never stupid to believe."

AND LIZZIE would know, Jess thought savagely hours later, pounding his fist on the bunk, glaring at the ceiling in the dark. Lizzie who'd had her life snuffed out on the brink of her dream.

"Damn you, Lizzie," he muttered raggedly, his throat aching, his eyes stinging. "Damn you for doing this to me."

For Sue's words had skewered him, stopped him right where he was, making him remember what he hadn't remembered in years.

He could see his sister now, as clearly as if she were right beside him, her impish ten-year-old face serious for once as she'd come to try to get him to write the letter to St. Nick.

"I don't want to," he'd told her, pushing her away, trying to brush her off.

But she'd just grabbed his arm and hauled him into the house. "Mama says you got to. She needs to know what you want."

"She knows what I want," Jess had said stubbornly, folding his arms across his chest.

Lizzie looked at him sympathetically. She knew what he meant: that he wanted his father to come home. He'd wanted it so desperately and for so long.

She'd put her arm around him. "She can't make him do it, Jess. And neither can you."

"But I want—I need—!" His voice had broken. He sniffled, swiping at shameful tears. It was worse at holidays, when hopes rose, when he told himself, "Maybe this time," and "Just this once."

He wiped his nose on his sleeve, straightened up, rubbed his eyes. "I could be a better dad than him, Lizzie," he'd said at last.

And Lizzie had looked at him with more than ten years' understanding in her deep brown eyes. She'd smiled then, a thin, sad smile. "I know."

Jess didn't remember what he'd written down on the letter to Santa. Lincoln Logs maybe. Or Matchbox cars. His mother had done her best. She always had.

Lizzie had written, "I want a Patsy Cline record and Dottie West's 'Here Comes My Baby.' And Johnny Cash's record 'Bitter Tears.'" Jess pressed his eyes with his fingers now, remembering how the words had looked in Lizzie's loopy, little-girl handwriting.

Then at the bottom she had written, "I want to be a country-western singer."

Her mother had smiled when she'd read it. She'd stood by the kitchen table and stroked a work-roughened hand down her daughter's long dark hair. "Santa can't bring you that, sweetheart," she'd said.

Lizzie had shrugged her irrepressible shrug. "That's okay," she'd said. "I believe in me." And then she'd looked across the table at Jess. "And I believe in you."

ALISON WAS DOING her best.

She was making cut-out cookies and marshmallow fudge, she was tying little red bows so the girls could hang them on the huge tree to fill in the empty spaces after all the ornaments and lights had been used. She was, when the girls were in school, making the Western shirt for Dottie and a funky shirt and jacket for Patsy. She was trying to be upbeat and cheerful and positive.

She was trying not to think about Jess.

She rarely saw him. The night he moved out of the house, he had, physically at least, moved out of her life. She might see him at a distance now and then. She might answer the phone and send one of the girls down to give him a message. But since the day she'd talked to him in the barn, she hadn't seen him face to face.

She'd thought she might when Sue had said she was going down to the bunkhouse. She'd half suspected that he might pick his niece up bodily and bring her home.

But Sue hadn't come right back. Jess hadn't dumped her on the doorstep and stalked away. He'd been perfectly pleasant and glad to see her, according to Sue.

Alison had been glad. But she'd noticed as well that the next day he virtually disappeared.

She'd seen him come back from feeding the cattle in the morning. But instead of retreating to the bunkhouse or heading back out to chop ice, he got in the truck and drove away.

He hadn't come home before she and the girls went to bed that night. Probably, Alison thought bitterly, to avoid a repeat of Sue's visit. The next day he'd done the same.

The day before Christmas, Sue had gone back down there in the afternoon. She'd come back an hour later.

"Was Jess there?" Alison asked casually.

Sue nodded. "He helped me write my letter to Santa."

Oh, dear. "I don't think— You know the North Pole is a very long way," Alison began, envisioning disappointment on Christmas morning. Damn Jess, anyway.

"He said he'd take care of it," Sue said confidently.

Alison hoped to heaven the little girl's confidence wasn't misplaced. But maybe Jess would be able to find in town whatever it was Sue had on her list. And maybe he'd bring it up so that Alison could slip it under the tree before Christmas morning.

Maybe, just for the memory, he could be persuaded to come.

But she wasn't going to ask the girls to invite him. If he didn't want to come, it would just hurt their feelings. And, she thought resignedly, if he refused her, she could always give the girls the excuse that she'd been giving them for the past week: a cowboy's work is never done.

She went down to the bunkhouse that evening after the girls were in bed. He wasn't home. She went back on Christmas Eve afternoon. He still wasn't there.

It occurred to her that he might have been invited out for the evening. It didn't seem likely. She couldn't imagine he'd do it. But she'd certainly been wrong before.

Clouds moved over, low and leaden as the afternoon waned. Inside Dottie built up the fire and turned on the lights. Alison and Patsy began supper preparations.

It started to snow.

HE SAW THE HOUSE like a beacon, the golden glow of its windows signaling to him the minute he came around the bend in the road. The truck slipped and skidded on the turn, and Jess urged it on as if it were some reluctant pony.

"Come on, come on. Don't die on me now."

The drive back from Durango had been murder. The snow had been falling there since early afternoon, and the storm came with him as he moved eastward again, getting heavier and thicker as the day wore on.

He could have stopped any of a dozen places. He had friends along the highway, acquaintances of Nathan's, plenty of people he knew.

But he kept going, driven as much as driving. He had to. He needed to.

At last he wrestled the truck into the yard, pulled up alongside the barn and got out. The snow whipped around him, blotting out the tire tracks, stinging his face. He yanked his hat down to shield it as best he could and moved to unload.

He worked as fast as he could, stowed everything. Then he ducked into the bunkhouse, washed his face and combed his hair, jammed his hat back on his head and made his way through the snow.

He could see them through the windows: Patsy moving across the kitchen with something in her hands, Dottie zipping past, then Sue. He moved closer, watching them. He saw the tree all lit and decorated for the first time. Saw the presents. Saw the stockings. Saw Alison.

And he stopped, couldn't go on.

He loved her so much he ached with it. Loved her so much that he was terrified of failing her.

"I believe in you," Lizzie had told him all those years ago. And she must have, for she'd left him the girls.

"I believe in you," Nathan had said and he'd left Jess half the ranch and a chance with his granddaughter.

"I love you," Alison had said to him time after time. And he'd been afraid.

Hell, he still was afraid.

He could turn around and walk away or he could open the door and go in.

Jess knew the choice was his.

ALISON DIDN'T HEAR him come in. She'd been hanging up a stocking that Kitten had knocked down, she'd heard Sue give a tiny shriek, she'd turned around.

And there he was.

Lean and rangy and every bit as beautiful as she remembered. And she was glad he came at the same time she felt the ache in her heart.

But in spite of her own pain, she was glad for the girls' sake that he'd bothered. It proved he had feelings. It meant that he cared.

He was holding his hat in his hands, crushing the brim, as he looked at her. His face was wind reddened. His hair was tousled. Snow melted on the hems of his jeans, dripping on his socks. He looked down, noticed, bent quickly and nervously to wipe it up.

"I'll do it," Patsy said, just as Alison said, "It doesn't matter," and Dottie said, "We were afraid you wouldn't come."

Jess straightened up, and the look he gave Alison was apologetic. "I didn't know if..." His voice trailed off.

She managed a smile. "We're glad you did."

"We get to open one present apiece tonight, Uncle Jess. But the rest have to wait until morning," Sue told him. "That's what Alison says."

Jess nodded. "Whatever Alison says." His voice sounded hoarse.

"Can we open 'em now, Alison?" Dottie asked her.

Alison looked at Jess. "We've already eaten. But if you're hungry, I can get you some dinner, and we can open them after."

"No. Let's do it now. Please." She heard an urgency in his tone that made her unaccountably angry. Did he want to get out of here that badly?

"Can I...can I give you mine tonight?" He looked from one girl to the next, his gaze finally resting on Alison.

She looked at him stonily. *So you don't have to come back tomorrow, you mean?* she asked him with her eyes. But she turned to the girls to get their response.

They nodded.

"Wait here," he commanded. He went back out on the porch, they heard him open the door again, heard movement, scraping sounds of chairs being moved, a quiet thud. The girls looked at Alison. She shrugged and shook her head.

Jess came back into the living room. "This is for Patsy," he said and he motioned them into the kitchen.

It was there under the bookcase where the rickety desk had been. It was walnut, with a desk-like look to it. Patsy stared. Then she walked slowly forward, her eyes going from the piece of furniture to her uncle and back again. Hesitantly she reached out and touched it, licked her lips, ran her fingers along the edge.

"Is it..." she ventured, then stopped. Her eyes went straight to Jess.

"Lift the edge," he prompted.

She did. The other girls gasped. Alison did, too.

"A sewing machine!" Patsy's eyes were huge and sparkling. She looked at Jess, gulped, then blinked hard and bit down on her lip. "Oh, Uncle Jess!" She crossed the room in a rush, wrapped her arms around him and hugged him.

And Jess hugged her back this time, pressed his face into her hair and whispered, "I love you."

He lifted his gaze and met Alison's. She felt her heart begin to beat more quickly, felt her pulses begin to pound. *What are you doing?* she asked him silently.

She got a faint smile in return.

"Put on your boots," he told them now. "We've got to go outside for the rest."

There was no grumbling about heading out into the blizzard. The girls wrapped up eagerly and followed him out. Jess held the door for them, then led them down to the barn.

"A new tractor?" Dottie guessed, grinning at her uncle.

"Only if you'd rather," Jess said. He led them into the barn, to the stall next to Dodger's. In it stood a sorrel horse with four white stockings and a white blaze.

Dottie's face went as white as the blaze. Her eyes filled with tears. "You don't mean—" She couldn't finish.

Jess handed her the bridle. "He's yours."

Alison just looked at him. "I hope this boarding school has a stable," Alison said to him as he led them from the barn.

"I think she'll be able to find a place for him," Jess said quietly. "I hope so, anyway."

He took them next to the shed behind the barn. He stopped them by the door, hunkered down so that his eyes were on a level with Sue's and said, "You're going to have to use your imagination for this, but I don't know anyone who's got a better one."

Inside there was a pile of lumber, chains, and a thick webbing of rope. He picked up a piece of paper off the top of the pile and handed it to her.

Sue didn't even look at it. She didn't need to. She just beamed up at him, her confidence justified. "My swing."

Her "swing" was going to be rather elaborate, Alison saw from the sketch Sue held in her hands. When it was built, it would have two swings, a climbing rope, a climbing web and, at one end, a ladder and a fireman's pole that would reach a second-story fort.

She looked at Jess. He was looking at Sue. "Santa asked me to take care of it for him," he told the little girl. "It was a lot of lumber to get in a sleigh."

Sue nodded her head.

Jess lifted his gaze and his eyes met Alison's.

"Quite a boarding school," she said. Her voice felt shaky. Her heart was racing. Her palms were damp.

Please, God, she prayed. *I'll try to understand if he only wants the girls. Really I will. But please, God, I love him so.*

Jess reached for her hand and drew her back to the house with him. "Your turn."

She hoped—she prayed—it might be a tiny velvet-covered box. She mounted the steps, feeling as if she were walking a plank and that when she reached the end, she would fall, and only then would she know if she'd reached heaven. Or hell.

She held her breath, willing him into the kitchen, willing him to reach into his pocket.

He stopped on the porch.

She looked around, saw some garden tools, a ball of twine, a gunny-sacked shape. She felt her chin begin to tremble. She clamped her teeth shut tight.

Jess crossed the porch, reached down and picked up the gunnysack. He turned and carried it back to her. It was a little more than half as high as he was.

She looked at the sack, looked at him.

"You're going to have to use your imagination, too," he said. He held it out, motioning for her to slip off the sack.

Her fingers were cold, that's why they fumbled, why they scratched ineffectually before they pulled the sack away.

It looked like a branch, brown and scrawny, poking up out of the soil. There was a small, white plastic tab stuck in the pot. With nervous fingers, Alison picked it up.

"*Malus pumila.*"

"It's an apple tree. A Greening," Jess said hoarsely. "I know it's not much, but it's—" His voice faltered. He stopped.

Her eyes blurred, her mind spun. Not much? It was everything.

It was a promise. It was a sign of hope in the future. A man didn't buy an apple tree or a horse or enough lumber to build a castle unless he was committing himself for years and years.

She looked into his eyes and saw the love she knew she hadn't imagined. She saw fear and worry and, most of all, hope that it would grow and strengthen and bear fruit like his gift to her.

"I love you, Ali," he whispered.

And Alison went into his arms, parka, scarf, apple tree and all.

Jess held her as if he would never let her go, kissed her as if his very life depended on her touch. And Alison felt, for the first time since he'd left, the ice melt around her heart.

"Thank you, Pops," she whispered. And she thought she heard Jess murmur, "Thank you, Nathan. And thank you, Lizzie."

And then they were kissing again.

There was an insistent tug on her jacket. Still holding on to Jess, still wrapped in his arms, she looked down to see Sue looking up.

"What about Uncle Jess's present? We all got one, but he hasn't."

"Yes, I have," Jess said, opening the circle of his arms to draw them all in. But his eyes stayed locked with Alison's as he whispered, "I've got the best present a guy could ever have. Right here."

IT WAS 3:45 in the morning when Jess remembered what he'd forgotten to ask her.

She was curled into the warmth of his body, snuggling against him, and if he lifted his head from the pillow he could see the curve of her lips, as though she smiled.

They hadn't got to bed until past two. There'd been a doll-sized ranch house to build for Sue after the girls had finally gone to bed. And then there'd been their time alone in front of the fire. He'd put it to good use, he remembered with a smile, loving Alison with a thoroughness and an abandon that had left them both limp.

It had been all they could do to climb the stairs with their arms around each other. And they'd fallen asleep at once, still embracing, in Nathan's big feather bed.

Now he sat up, looking down at her in the faint pinkish silver glow cast by the swirling snow outside. He was loath to wake her, knew how exhausted she was, yet knew as well that he couldn't wait.

He touched her cheek, drew a line along her jaw, watched her nose wrinkle, her brow furrow, her eyes open.

"Jess?" She looked at him, her smile fading to worried concern.

"It's all right," he said quickly. "I just . . . just forgot to ask you something."

She sat up, draping the blanket around both of them, huddling close, cocooning them in their own little world. "Oh? What?"

He hesitated, waited for the familiar shaft of fear, then looked right past it into her eyes. "Will you marry me?"

"Marry you? You *forgot* to ask me to marry you?" Alison stared at him wide-eyed.

He ducked his head, sheepish. "It's not like I go around askin'! I've never done it before!"

"And thank heavens for that." She was smiling at him.

"Well," he said, exasperated, after a moment. "Will you?"

She giggled. She started tickling his ribs beneath the covers, pummeling him until he fell back onto the mattress and dragged her on top of him, imprisoning her hands, locking them against his chest.

"What do you think?" she whispered against his lips.

"Um . . ." He considered it, considered the way her body moved against his, the way her eyes smiled at his, the way her heart beat in a steady rhythm with his. "Yes?" he ventured at last.

"Yes," Alison said. "Oh, yes."

They loved again, then. Slowly and sweetly. With a tenderness and a passion born of years of dreams and need and hope.

Then Alison snuggled in the crook of his arm and lay her head on his shoulder. She pressed a kiss against his chest, whispered, "I love you, Jess. Merry Christmas," and then she slept.

Christmas.

For years it had been a day like any other when he'd done his chores, checked his horses, fed the cattle. And he'd do all that again today, because those things were a part of his life.

But they were no longer all of his life.

Today when he finished, he would come out of the barn and look up toward the house where the warmth of light and love were waiting. And he would hurry.

He would admire the skirt and jacket Alison had made for Patsy, he would talk horses with Dottie, he would see "Alison" and "Jess" settled in their brand-new ranch. He might even be talked into helping them with a little kissing practice, if Sue would let him.

But he'd save the best of his practicing for Alison—for Alison who had made him a believer, who had taught him to love and to risk and to hope, for Alison who had brought him home.

One year later

ANOTHER COWBOY CAME HOME FOR CHRISTMAS

Jess and Alison Cooper
and Patsy, Dottie and Sue
are delighted to announce the birth of
NATHAN PETER

on

December 24

weight: 7 lbs. 9 oz. ***length: 21"***